I0642554

The TAHOE MYSTERIES

MYSTERIES

BE QUICK OR BE DEAD

A Miss Finch Novel

VIKKI KESTELL

Faith-Filled Fiction™

www.faith-filledfiction.com | www.vikkikestell.com

BE QUICK
OR
BE DEAD

THE TAHOE MYSTERIES | BOOK 2
Vikki Kestell
Also Available in eBook Format

BOOKS BY VIKKI KESTELL

THE TAHOE MYSTERIES

Book 1: *Number 1 with a Bullet*
Book 2: *Be Quick or be Dead*
Book 3: *Death on the Big Blue*, 2026
Murder by Accident, A Miss Finch Prequel, 2026

A PRAIRIE HERITAGE

Book 1: *A Rose Blooms Twice*
Book 2: *Wild Heart on the Prairie*
Book 3: Joy on This Mountain
Book 4: *The Captive Within*
Book 5: *Stolen*
Book 6: *Lost Are Found*
Book 7: *All God's Promises*
Book 8: *The Heart of Joy*
Book 9: *Rose of RiverBend*

GIRLS FROM THE MOUNTAIN

Book 1: *Tabitha*
Book 2: *Tory*
Book 3: *Sarah Redeemed*

LAYNIE PORTLAND

Book 1: *Laynie Portland, Spy Rising*
Book 2: *Laynie Portland, Retired Spy*
Book 3: *Laynie Portland, Renegade Spy*
Book 4: *Laynie Portland, Spy Resurrected*
Book 5: *Vyper, A Laynie Portland Sequel*

NANOSTEALTH

Book 1: *Stealthy Steps*
Book 2: *Stealth Power*
Book 3: *Stealth Retribution*
Book 4: *Deep State Stealth*
Book 5: *Stealth Insurgence*
Book 6: *Stealth Triumph*
Book 7: *Stealth Genesis*,
    A Nanostealth Prequel

STAND-ALONE BOOKS

I Can't Hear You
The Christian and the Vampire

BE QUICK or BE DEAD
Copyright ©2025 Vikki Kestell; All Rights Reserved.
ISBN-978-1-970120-42-4

BE QUICK
OR
BE DEAD

THE TAHOE MYSTERIES | BOOK 2
Vikki Kestell
Also Available in eBook Format

———————•————————

THREE YOUNG MEN have gone missing from different points around Lake Tahoe. When Miss Finch catches the scent of a killer, she enlists the help of her friend, Simon Fletcher.

Fletcher, however, is skeptical. "Tell me why you think it's murder."

"They found the first victim, also the first to disappear."

"Whereabouts?"

"A not particularly deep part of the lake."

"But wasn't that guy hiking forty-some miles north of the lake when he disappeared? How did he end up in the Big Blue?"

"Ah. It seems that a person or persons unknown gifted the young man with an ankle bracelet attached to three cinder blocks."

Simon stilled. "So it *is* murder."

When a second victim is found and a fourth individual disappears, the threat becomes clear to Simon and Miss Finch: *Lake Tahoe adventurers had best be quick . . . or end up dead.*

Prepare yourself for . . . **The Tahoe Mysteries**.

Book 1: *Number 1 with a Bullet*
Book 2: *Be Quick or Be Dead*
Book 3: *Death on the Big Blue*, 2026
Murder by Accident, A Miss Finch Prequel, 2026

ACKNOWLEDGEMENTS

As always,
to my esteemed teammates,
Cheryl Adkins and **Greg McCann,**
you are worth more than gold and rubies.
I cannot do this without you!

———•———

And in acknowledgement of
the basic idea behind Miss Finch's Gospel card trick:
https://www.youtube.com/watch?v=G5ZYubQQXY8

SCRIPTURE QUOTATIONS

The HOLY BIBLE,
NEW INTERNATIONAL VERSION®, NIV®
Copyright ©1973, 1978, 1984, 2011 by Biblica, Inc.®
Used by permission. All rights reserved worldwide.

COVER DESIGN

Vikki Kestell

CHAPTER 1

BRIGHT STAR SUMMER RV RESIDENCE, SOUTH END OF LAKE TAHOE

SIMON FLETCHER, BRIGHT Star's Facilities and Security Manager, blew out a cleansing breath and squeezed his eyes shut . . . not that shutting his eyes did much to relieve his stress. Behind his closed eyelids, the long Fourth of July weekend loomed large—the busiest, *craziest* three days of the entire summer season. *Wait.* The holiday weekend *loomed large?* No, it hurtled toward him like an incoming torpedo, locked on to its target, pinging away, and accelerating *hard*, the closer it got.

Starting tomorrow evening, the cusp of the big weekend, a crowd of somewhere between seventy-five and a hundred *thousand* "summer people" (highly reminiscent of Genghis Khan's Golden Horde pouring over the Mongolian Steppes) would encircle, take captive, and subjugate the people and property of the lake area. Masses of voracious tourists, like swarms of brightly colored locusts, would descend upon Lake Tahoe and invade its towns and communities until all available hotels, motels, condos, timeshares, campgrounds, RV parks, Vrbos, and Airbnbs were booked and more than likely overbooked.

Even the spare bedrooms of year-round Tahoe citizenry and the uninhabited RVs parked in their driveways or backyards were offered up for rent—at hyperinflated prices.

Yes, summer bookings of any and every kind around the lake, but especially over the Fourth of July weekend, were like hotcakes sizzling on a perfectly heated griddle: They flipped fast and were snapped up just as quickly.

Good grief. I could probably make a killing renting out street-corner cardboard boxes.

And yet the occupancy glut couldn't touch sustenance and recreation! Each and every restaurant, café, bar, grill, coffee shop, ice cream cart, and hotdog stand would shovel food and drink down the gullets of the hungry and thirsty horde day and night, while the rental of boats, jet skis, paddleboards, bikes, and snorkeling gear would be in fiercer demand than the most recent drop by the hottest pop icon out there.

For three days, Tahoe business owners would rake in the bucks, hand over fist, while about killing themselves and their employees in the process. Come Monday, those same establishments would be closed for Tahoe's version of R&R—resuscitation and recovery—from both physical and mental exhaustion.

Bright Star would have its share of tourists for the holiday weekend too, stretching the park's staff. The many residents of Bright Star's twenty-four RV sites had duly preregistered their expected guests and extended family for the Fourth, and those additions would more than double Bright Star's population. Accordingly, the upcoming weekend had *tripled* Holly Mitchell's expectations of Bright Star's preparedness and the "upholding of our reputation" through the long weekend.

Simon was acutely aware of Holly's expectations. They resided on the very long list tucked into his shirt pocket, a list that Holly added to and/or modified hour by hour. At this point, Simon felt like one of those poor martyrs in a Roman arena, each arm and leg strapped to a different horse: four rearing, chomping, stomping equines straining toward the four corners of the earth.

While Simon and his summer intern chewed doggedly away at their task list, Simon sucked down yet another deep breath. He blew it out slowly, the corners of his mouth turned down in a tetchy, irritable scowl.

We've posted the "No Fireworks of Any Kind" signs right next to the regular "No Smoking Anywhere on Bright Star Property" and "Fires in Designated Firepits Only" signs at the turnoff to the park, on both sides of Bright Star's entrance gate, several places inside the park, and at each site in the park itself.

Will it be enough?

It was July now and *very* dry. The air was dry, the ground was dry, and the park's forest of lush trees, bushes, and shrubs were drying out too. Bright Star could not afford even the most remote possibility of a conflagration on park property, let alone inside the park itself.

It wasn't the extra work of the long weekend that irked Simon. Well, not *exactly* the extra work. It was more that he had other concerns that superseded the ever-changing, never-ending list of tasks burning a hole in his shirt pocket.

A *heap* of other concerns.

Undoubtedly, Simon was a hard worker, and he was able to do most of his chores on autopilot. Regrettably, "autopilot" left his thoughts free to consider those "other concerns," those problems and issues creating in him an unaccustomed disquiet.

I'm a Marine.

Marines take care of business.

They don't . . . brood.

Simon disliked that word, *brood*; it tasted of defeat. And Simon *really* disliked the turmoil churning up his gut. He might admit that he carried a heavy internal load, but if he were being absolutely truthful with himself? That load was starting to wear a distinct traffic pattern in the generally smooth and serene carpet of his brainpan.

Simon had even ordered his ears to tune out his young intern's incessant natter so he could focus on his worries. His order had worked fine until the fourteen-year-old kid's "blather spigot," cranked wide open, began to gush outright complaint.

"Sweat and toil; toil and sweat! Like, it's *way* too hot for outside work today, Fletch. Even Napoleon thinks it's too hot—doncha boy?" Skipper Mitchell paused his scouring of one of the picnic tables in Bright Star's barbecue area to reach under the table and scratch the aging boxer's head.

"Sounds like an excuse to me, Skipper. And Napoleon is fine where he is. The table is all the shade he needs. Get back to work."

Two Saturdays past, quite early in the morning but still as dark as night, and with Bright Star evacuated in order to protect the park's residents, the police had arrested Marie Santini, the resident of Site 19 and Napoleon's previous owner.

Why?

Among other things, for hiring a hit man to take out Miss Finch.

Miss Finch.

Simon's lungs sort of seized up and left him short of breath.

Stop it. Turn your thoughts elsewhere.

He switched back to Napoleon. When the police had asked Santini what to do with her dog, she ordered him destroyed. Simon, astounded and appalled, refused to do so. Napoleon had done nothing to warrant such betrayal!

He sighed to himself. *So now we have a dog. Super.*

Unwilling to leave the slow, elderly boxer alone in his cabin all day, Simon and Skipper had since then taken Napoleon along with them while they worked, and the accommodation seemed to suit that good old boy. He was happy to be boosted into the back of Simon's small maintenance truck where he climbed onto a doggy bed, delighted to ride along and remain close to Simon and Skipper throughout the day. In a nutshell, Napoleon was no trouble at all, and unlike Simon's helper, he raised no complaints.

Take a page from Napoleon's book, Skipperdoodle!

But Skipper's griping seemed to have no "off" button. "See, the temperature out here is like a hundred and ten in the shade—and there ain't no shade where I'm working. I'm telling you, I'm not cut out for this kinda heat! Seems to me that working under these conditions is just plain, old child abuse. I'm telling you, Fletch, I'm gonna die out here. *Die* I say!"

Yanked again from his carpet-fraying worries, Simon rounded on the young man. "Stop exaggerating, Skipper Mitchell. Just *stop*. Yeah, it's warm, and we have a lot of outside work to do this afternoon, but the temperature is eighty-five degrees, not a hundred and ten."

Simon squinted. "Hey! Why aren't you wearing your hat?"

Skipper's hand flew to his bare head. He shrugged with sheepish indifference.

Simon scanned around for Skipper's floppy safari hat, the kind with a flap that hung down the back to shade the wearer's neck. He spied it, dropped and abandoned on the grass, grabbed it up, and slapped it across Skipper's chest.

"*Put. That. On.* And I'd better not see you working outside without it on again, Skipper Mitchell—*get me?*"

"Yessir. Sorry. My bad," Skipper muttered. He added softly, "Just seems hotter today, Fletch."

"Well, it's *not*, and all your cranky, irritating objections are like the annoying whine of a mosquito in my ears! Need I remind you that Friday is the Fourth of July, the first day of our busiest three-day weekend of the season? Or that, starting tomorrow, midday, every blessed Bright Star summer resident will be 'in' residence and that our forty-some-odd residents are expecting, in total, upwards of sixty guests this weekend?"

Skipper muttered under his breath. "Yeah, 'cause you've only reminded me like six times."

"Then suck it up, Buttercup—and keep scraping and scrubbing the bird poop off these picnic tables. The sooner we finish today's chores, the sooner you and your friends can hit the pool."

Skipper brightened. "Oh, yeah." Reminded that his friends Zane and Kevin would be coming to swim at Bright Star later that afternoon, he went back to work.

Simon breathed in and out several times to calm himself.

It didn't help much.

He walked out onto the grass to take both a visual and mental inventory of his domain, the beautiful, well designed RV park he was responsible for. Bright Star's order and tranquility usually spoke to Simon. Helped him put his problems into perspective and appreciate his many blessings.

I've grown to love this place, Lord, but lately . . .

Bright Star was not, by any stretch of the imagination, your ordinary, run-of-the-mill RV park, offering disorderly rows of cheek-by-jowl RVs with nary a tree nor spot of shade to be had. In fact, even calling Bright Star an RV "park," upscale or otherwise, might be construed by certain individuals as something of an insult. No, Bright Star, the brainchild of its owners, Joe and Holly Mitchell, was the only RV resort around Lake Tahoe to bill itself as a summer *residence*, a spacious retreat where every site provided its residents with peaceful seclusion under a canopy of trees.

Joe and Holly, largely with Simon's advice and assistance, had sketched the park's single road as a graceful, elongated loop within the Mitchells' thirty-acre property. Only twenty-four RV slots sprouted from the loop's outer perimeter. An ample distance between each site provided the privacy Bright Star residents prized.

The Mitchells had envisioned the swath of land left inside the loop's circumference as Bright Star's activity hub. To make that vision a reality, they had added to the swath's height and created a picturesque "island" central to the park. After much work, the tip of Bright Star's island, facing the entrance gates, boasted a rocky promontory topped by gorgeous and mesmerizing "dancing" fountains. Farther along the island, residents were free to enjoy a number of amenities: a splendid though modest-sized swimming complex that included a family pool, a kiddie spray-and-wade pool, and an adult-only lap pool; the large barbecue zone where Simon and Skipper were at work; a group firepit surrounded by log seating; a spacious grassy lawn with a volleyball *slash* badminton net; a fenced pickleball court; a large rec hall that included a kitchen and dining area, a small gym, and a game room; and, in a separate building, Bright Star's resident laundry facility. Today, Simon and Skipper were prepping the barbecue area on the island for the busy weekend ahead.

The sum of her features and conveniences made Bright Star completely unique and both exclusive and expensive. By design, one did not merely stay overnight at Bright Star or check in one week and check out the next. In *this* RV park, guests were *residents* who paid handsomely (in advance) to call Bright Star their home away from home for the entire Tahoe summer season, Memorial Day weekend through Labor Day.

Simon snorted to himself. *And yet we lost two residents the first month of the season—for which I cannot thank you enough, Lord.* He shuddered as the memories of the past month's calamities and near disasters flooded his mind and heart, close to swamping him.

Good thing Holly kept a wait list, just in case we lost a resident . . . or two.

He stared around him a last time before goading himself back to work. Taking these mini breaks usually appeased any normal stress.

But not today.

Things were "off." Had been "off" since Monday, less than forty-eight hours ago. But who's counting?

His thoughts were disordered, his usual self-motivation was missing, his self-discipline unruly. Furthermore, a sick, deep-down, achy sensation had taken up residence in his chest.

Why? Not because of anything I said, but because of a "look?" An unanticipated, unplanned, inadvertent facial expression?

The memory of her fingers tugging at an errant strand of curly hair tickling her cheek flashed through his mind. He recalled the moment she tucked it behind her ear . . . and how he'd thought it the dearest thing he'd ever seen.

She'd seen it then. That unpremeditated "look."

Had read its significance in his eyes? Apparently.

And she hasn't spoken to me since. Has avoided me at every turn.

Simon's hands returned to his hips of their own volition. He tried to distract himself by, yet again, running today's list of tasks and chores through his head—said list courtesy of Holly Mitchell because *obviously* Simon, Bright Star's Facility and Security Manager, wasn't actually capable of managing Bright Star's facility in her estimation.

Simon's hands left his hips and fisted at his sides. *Holly.* Holly and her determined slide into micromanagement, the "Holly aggravation factor" spooning fuel onto the already angry undercurrent smoldering in Simon's head. Without realizing it, his face resumed its twitchy, "scowly" frown.

"And here I thought you and I had this licked, Holly, but *nooo*," he growled.

"*And don't forget, Fletcher*," he muttered, mimicking Holly. "*The two new residents are checking in tomorrow morning.*"

"Why, thank you, Holly—I was totally unaware."

Grr.

"It's gonna be weird, don't you think, Fletch?"

Simon jumped, surprised to find Skipper at his elbow, Napoleon glued to his side. "Hey! Uh, you startled me."

Skipper shrugged. "Sorry. You look . . . you look kinda mad, Fletch."

Simon scrambled to change the subject. "What do you mean by 'it's gonna be weird'?"

When Skipper didn't answer right away, Simon realized his assistant was having trouble putting his feelings into words.

Finally Skipper cocked his head and said, "Well, see, we know everybody at Bright Star, right? And, that's cool because, I mean, they belong here, like we do. Together."

The park had opened the Thursday before Memorial Day Weekend, about six weeks back, but Simon figured he knew what Skipper meant.

"I get you, buddy. Although Bright Star hasn't been open all that long, we've grown friendly with the residents. Everybody knows everybody, we get along, and it feels right. But now two sets of strangers are moving in. Is that it?"

"Yeah, so it's gonna be . . . weird."

Not as weird as our two former residents were, Simon thought.

He said aloud, "Maybe it will feel strange or odd to begin with, but that feeling shouldn't last long. So, give the new folks a week or two to fit in and find their place, okay?" Then he added with a chuckle, "And face it: whatever the new people are like, they *have* to be an improvement over those last two residents, right?"

Skipper's uneasy silence told Simon his little attempt at humor had fallen flat.

Can't really fault the kid. It's been a rough couple of weeks.

The previous occupants of Sites 2 and 19, Terri Rickert and Marie Santini, respectively, were presently guests at one of the State of California's all-inclusive "resorts," awaiting trial on a variety of charges. Both stood accused of being in possession of illegal high-powered rifles. But the second of the two? She had personally attempted to shoot Skipper and Miss Finch, while they—oblivious to lurking danger—had been enjoying a bike ride near Olympic Village.

And that was before she hired a hit man to kill Miss Finch!

Simon shivered.

Fletcher, we've been ambushed.

That ache in Simon's chest pulsed, and his heart attempted to pole vault into his throat.

*I've faced riots of drunken, belligerent Marines and been pinned down by overwhelming enemy fire. **You**, my dear old heart, don't get to scare me. Just replant your sweet little bippy back down in my torso where you belong.*

He swallowed then, and prayed, *Lord, am I ever going to stop hearing her say those words in my head or get over what hearing them does to me? And when will I get this awful, squeezy achy pain out of my chest? Or be rid of this . . . this strange turmoil in my heart?*

———◆———

THREE HOURS LATER, Simon and Skipper had thoroughly scoured the half-dozen barbecue grills and had cleaned the picnic tables, both tops and undersides. They had removed gum wads, grease spots, bits of dried food, and deposits of bird poop, sanded away graffiti, and touched up the tables' paint where needed. Lastly, they scrubbed the patio itself until it was spotless.

"Hey, Fletch, buy me a Coke, please?" Skipper wheedled. "I already drank my water, and I'm parched!"

The kid could have easily refilled his water bottle from the several chilled water dispensers on the island, but Simon answered, "Sure. You've worked hard."

"Buy me two? It's awful hot. And a bag of peanuts?"

The kid was shameless. He was also a growing teen—aka, Skipper the Bottomless Pit.

Two Cokes and a bag of peanuts? Seriously, I need to ask Joe for a stipend to cover his nephew's snacks. That, or Joe needs to give Skipper an allowance. The kid is draining me dry. Keep going like this, and I should be able to claim him as a dependent on my taxes.

Instead, he answered, "Fine—but before we do, let's wash the rags and scrubbers, clean the paint brushes, and put everything away. And after our break, we can collect trash, last chore of the day."

"Cool! You got it, Fletch."

After a twenty-minute break, they climbed into Simon's maintenance truck and began the daily task of driving Bright Star's loop and collecting the residents' trash—a task that, over the busy weekend with all the extra people and the big holiday meals, they might need to perform several times daily.

At Site 1, Simon had barely slipped the truck into park before Skipper jumped from the passenger seat and jetted down the long double drive. Simon watched Skipper skid to a stop at the cozy little travel trailer angled across the drive's width.

As customary for this time of day, Site 1's diminutive resident was seated under the trailer's tiny awning in her kiddie-sized lawn chair, her tablet perched on her lap, preferred beverage in the chair's cupholder, her lithe Siamese cat, Pouncer, lounging across her shoulders, her Welsh Terrier, Hugo, sprawled at her feet. The trailing geranium hanging from the awning, its vining buds and blossoms spilling a cascade of soft pink colors, was the crowning touch on the perfect homey scene.

Simon refused to take it in or let a sudden sense of loss overwhelm him. Instead, he climbed from the truck, tied up Miss Finch's garbage sack, tossed it in the back of the truck, and lined her trash can with a new sack. He did so while studiously averting his eyes. Yet, at the same time, he found himself straining to catch Skipper's dialogue with the site's resident, while casting an occasional furtive gander down the drive.

"Hey, Miss Finch!" Skipper called.

"Good afternoon, Skipper."

At Skipper's greeting, Hugo jumped up and ran to the boy, expecting and receiving many pats and scratches about the head and ears. Pouncer, on the other hand, cracked open one eye and exerted herself just enough to hiss at him.

"Yeah, I love you too, Pouncer," Skipper laughed. "Fletch and I just came to get your trash, Miss Finch."

"For which I thank you, Skipper."

Skipper glanced from Miss Finch to the truck, having apparently expected Simon to follow him down. Simon caught the moment puzzlement bloomed on Skipper's face. He jerked his eyes away and spied an offending scrap of paper on the ground. He bent to grab it, then called, "Hustle up, Skip. Lots to do."

When Simon climbed behind the truck's wheel and glanced down the drive, Skipper was still staring at him, his puzzlement now confusion. In the next moment, the kid turned obediently back to Miss Finch to say goodbye. Except Miss Finch was looking anywhere but in Skipper's direction . . . which happened to also be in Simon's direction.

Simon exhaled on his pain and frustration. *Talk about awkward.*

Right then, his phone buzzed a text message, so he pulled his phone from his shirt pocket and glanced at the lock screen. The text was from Holly Mitchell, Bright Star's office manager and Simon's personal thorn in the flesh.

Wonderful. Another task. Lord, I've got one nerve left, and this woman is sitting on it.

He swiped to read the message.

> *Joe not yet able to park*
> *new resident rigs*
> *prefers Miss Finch do it*
> *make the arrangements*

He sighed over the many unarticulated layers embedded in Holly's text. To start, as a matter of liability, Bright Star's policy stated no resident was allowed to back their own high-end and costly rig into their site. Normally, the job of parking rigs fell to Joe, but his truck had been run off the highway near Las Vegas and his leg severely broken just before Bright Star opened for the season over the Memorial Day weekend. Simon figured it might be weeks before Joe's still-swollen and painful leg could handle the workout of backing up a big RV.

Simon was, as a matter of record, Joe's alternate. However, while Joe had been hospitalized in Las Vegas and Holly remained with him, Simon and Skipper had been forced to run Bright Star on their own. Miss Finch, the first resident to check in, had volunteered to help them. Completely astonishing Simon, Miss Finch had shown herself to be an *artiste* at backing big rigs. Simon, only moderately confident in his ability to do half as well, had gladly turned the job over to her.

Holly, however, had been against Miss Finch's presence in the park from the moment Miss Finch tried to check in. Why? Because Miss Finch's little travel trailer, while entirely renovated, from the metal frame up, did not—in any shape or form—rise to the level of Bright Star's exclusive standards. For those reasons alone, Holly had been neither thrilled with nor grateful for Miss Finch's assistance during Holly and Joe's forced absence while Joe mended in a Vegas rehab facility. Even when the Mitchells returned—after Miss Finch had helped Simon hold Bright Star together for many weeks— Holly continued to view Miss Finch with distaste.

You are a snobbish, ungrateful individual, Holly, Simon grumbled to himself, *which is the only reason you're trying to push "make the arrangements" onto me!*

Well, you know what? Nope. Not this time.

He keyed in a blunt response and sent it.

If you want Miss Finch
to park new resident rigs
pick up the phone
and hire her yourself

Caught up in his own thoughts, Simon was stunned to see Skipper sitting in the passenger seat, staring daggers at him.

"What?"

"That's what I'm wondering, Fletch."

Simon put the truck in gear. "Time's a-wasting."

"What's wrong with you and Miss Finch?"

"Nothing's wrong."

"Riiiight. You guys won't even look at each other." His voice softened conspiratorially. "Did you and Miss Finch have a fight or something?"

"No, we did not have a fight." *Not exactly.*

"Then what's wrong?"

Simon bypassed unoccupied Site 2 and stopped at Site 3, occupied by Sam and Mary Jean Redwine. "Why don't you mind your own business, Skipperoo?"

Simon's response came out harsher-sounding than what he'd intended. Hurt flashed across Skipper's freckled face.

The kid crossed his arms. "Fine, but I don't think you're telling the truth, Simon Fletcher, and aren't Christians supposed to be truthful?"

Simon felt like Gunny Barker had just socked him in the gut. "I . . ."

He had no excuse to offer.

Skipper jumped out and handled the Redwines' trash. When he climbed back into the truck, Simon didn't drive on. Instead, he gripped the steering wheel.

"Skipper."

"*What*."

"Miss Finch and I are . . . working through something."

"Working through what?"

"See, when I say it is none of your business, I'm not trying to be mean, Skipper. What I'm saying is that it actually *is* none of your business. People are allowed to have private business, and they are not required to share everything with everyone."

"Hmph."

Up went the crossed arms again—which only irritated Simon.

"Look, if you're so intent on being mad at *me*, why don't you ask your precious Miss Finch what the problem is, okay? Bet you get the same answer from *her*."

Another text buzzed in his shirt pocket. He plucked out his phone. Stared at the lockscreen. And saw red.

> *You work for me*
> *not the other way around*
> *make the arrangement*

"Nope, and you can't make me," he muttered. He copied his previous message to Holly, opened a new text, this one to both Holly and Joe, pasted the copied message, added Holly's name so Joe would be clear who the message was intended for, and sent it.

> *Holly:*
> *If you want Miss Finch*
> *to park new resident rigs*
> *pick up the phone*
> *and hire her yourself*

He threw the truck into gear and sped along the loop to Site 4. Skipper handled the trash in silence. They had arrived at Site 5 when Simon's phone warbled an incoming call.

Simon sighed. Joe was calling. He answered.

"Hey, Joe."

"Fletcher, what in the world is going on? I've never gotten a text like that from you."

"Honestly, Joe? It's Holly. She doesn't want to talk to Miss Finch, so she's trying to make *me* call her, and I'm not going to."

Silence. Then, "You don't want to call Miss Finch because . . ."

"Because it's not my job to hire contract workers."

"I see." Joe, obviously, did *not* see.

"Look, Joe, Skipper and I are up to our eyeballs in alligators getting the park shipshape for the Fourth. And since parking the rigs would normally be your job, why don't *you* call Miss Finch?"

Simon heard more astonishment in Joe's reply. "Well, I would have called her if I'd known Holly was going to tell you to do it."

"So, you'll take care of it right away?"

"Sure, Fletcher. I'll handle it."

"Thanks, Joe."

Simon hung up and drove on without looking Skipper's way. He didn't need to look to feel the kid's glare burning a hole through him.

CHAPTER 2

THURSDAY, JULY 3

SIMON AND SKIPPER were putting the final touches on the swimming complex's most recent cleaning—a cleaning they would repeat each morning through the three-day weekend—when Skipper's chin jerked up. Simon heard it too, the rumble of a powerful engine, possibly a large pickup truck rolling up to the park's entrance.

Not only would many Fourth of July weekend guests begin arriving this afternoon, but Bright Star's two new residents were also scheduled to check in. Of course, these new residents would be hauling or driving their pricey RVs and stopping at the park office to check in.

Skipper, in a dither to scope out the new residents, had been fretful and distracted all morning, making it difficult for Simon to get any real work out of him. As the sound of the arriving engine softened to an idle, the kid—mop in hand—took two steps toward the pool gate before he caught himself, whirled, and cast pleading eyes Simon's way.

"Can I go take a look? Just a peek? Please? Pretty please?"

Simon tamped down his disgust. *Lord, I despise begging and emotional manipulation, and you **know** how much I despise it, so why in the world did you tether me to this whiny, hormonal—*

"All right."

Simon scratched his head. *What just happened? Did I, like some brainless, doting, yuppy dad, give in to that kid's wheedling? I'm a Marine, for heaven's sake! What has happened to me?*

"Thanks!" Skipper dropped the mop he was using, ran to the pool area's gate, threw up the latch, and raced directly to the far edge of the island where he had a partial view of the front gate. He flew back directly. "Hey, Fletcher! Some of the new people are here! Looks like some dude and a lady and maybe three kids."

"That's nice. Anyone your age?"

"I think so. Maybe. Can't really tell . . . from here."

Simon saw a sudden reticence creep over Skipper and morph into firmness. He could scarcely believe his eyes and ears when he saw Skipper pick up his mop and heard him say, "It's okay, though. I have chores to finish. I'll meet the new people later."

What planet are you from, and where have you hidden Skipper's real *body?*

Then Simon was shocked at what came out of his own mouth. "Well, I suppose we're about done here . . . "

And I suppose you are well on your way to earning the trophy for 'Pushover of the Year,' Simon Fletcher!

He found himself adding, "How about you and I head over to the office? We can introduce ourselves to the newcomers and extend them a Facilities Team welcome. Besides, didn't you offer to install Miss Finch's pedal extenders for her?"

"Oh, right!"

"Huh. I wonder if Miss Finch knows new residents have arrived."

"Golly! Maybe I should run over to her site and tell her. Yeah, that way, I can carry her stuff to the office for her."

Simon nodded his approval. "Good thinking. I'll tidy up here then meet you at the office to greet the new folks."

"Super cool!"

Skipper took off like a rocket, the mop again abandoned on the deck, leaving Simon chuckling.

You, Simon Fletcher, have lost it.

Yeah? Well, I like it when the kid is happy.

And I like you better when you don't talk to yourself.

Really? 'Cause, it's only a problem when you answer me.

Five minutes later, Simon drove his maintenance truck through the front gate, passing by a shiny, late-model king cab pickup idling in front of the office, a long and equally shiny fifth wheel hitched to the truck's bed.

That there is a cool half mil on wheels, Simon told himself.

He passed the fifth wheel, flipped a U-turn, drove up alongside the other side of it, and pulled into the lot behind the office. Just as he sauntered from the back around to the front, Skipper and Miss Finch came through the gate, Skipper laden with Miss Finch's gear: a tool box in one hand, the case that contained Miss Finch's pedal extenders in the other, and a couple of collapsible traffic cones under his arm. Miss Finch clutched with one hand the handgrip of the thick cushion that boosted her high enough to see over a truck's steering wheel. Her other hand clasped the head of her cane.

Now that the bone shard causing her so much pain had worked its way near the surface of her ankle's skin—close enough for the doctor to cut into the infected area and pluck it out—her injury was nearly healed. She continued to use her cane, however, for the occasional moment of instability. Still, Simon marveled at how well she was getting around without that unwieldy orthopedic boot on her foot.

Simon nodded politely but distantly to her and did his best to ignore the stupid, dull ache in his chest. "I see Skipper arrived in time to help you."

She nodded back with the same level of frosty distance. "For which I am grateful."

Skipper snorted and rolled his eyes with dramatic flair. "Wow. What is *wrong* with you two lately? You're both like, all kinda—"

"*Were I you*, Mr. Mitchell, I would exercise great care at this juncture, lest those loose eyeballs of yours *somehow* carom right out of your skull," Miss Finch warned solemnly.

Skipper, his eyes about to commence another circuit, yanked himself up short. Out of pure habit, he opened his mouth to spout a sarcastic comeback, caught himself again, and snapped his jaws shut.

"My, my. Quite right. You chose wisely," Miss Finch murmured, "particularly since I understand that a *solid whack* to the back of one's cranium might send one's marbles flying into the open air, never to be recovered."

Skipper's jaw slackened in stunned disbelief, while Simon had to clamp down on the guffaw trying to jump from his mouth.

Yee-ouch! What tool has Miss Finch been using to sharpen that tongue of hers?

About then, the office's inner door opened and three kids barreled through the screen door onto the porch. The kids, two early teen boys and a much younger girl, skidded to a halt. They eyed Skipper collectively; he eyed them right back. The kids were followed, at a more sedate pace, by three adults: Holly and, presumably, the kids' parents.

Holly lifted her chin. "Oh. I see you are already here, Miss Finch."

Holly managed to make her greeting about as welcoming as an ice bath.

Miss Finch inclined her head. "I congratulate you on your powers of observation, Mrs. Mitchell."

Holly flushed and Simon turned aside to stifle another laugh threatening to burst from his chest. When he pivoted back, Holly had clasped her hands in front of her . . . almost as though her fingers had fastened around someone's neck.

Miss Finch, droll as ever—or would "*troll* as ever" be more apropos?—remarked, "Perhaps you might do the honors?"

Holly stiffened. "Yes. Why not?"

She indicated the hardy-looking middle-aged man with sandy hair and ruddy complexion and a tall, fit female of similar coloring. "Mr. and Mrs. Nadeau? May I introduce Miss Finch? Miss Finch, this is Mr. and Mrs. Nadeau and their children, Wyatt, Eli, and Sophie."

The two teen boys were carbon copies of their dad. The girl, on the other hand, was petite with dark curly hair and sparkling brown eyes. The boys shuffled their feet and tipped obligatory nods in Miss Finch's general direction. The girl added a solemn dip of her head, then glanced at Simon and offered him a shy smile.

Simon was instantly smitten and sent a grin in return. He was gratified when her eyes brightened and her smile widened.

Miss Finch tucked her seat cushion under her left arm and held out her right hand. "Good morning, Mr. and Mrs. Nadeau. Welcome to Bright Star. I hope you enjoy your stay here."

"Thank you," Mrs. Nadeau replied. "We were completely delighted when, out of the blue, our travel agent received email from Miss Holly informing her that, due to unexpected vacancies, Bright Star had two open berths for the remainder of the season. Why, this park is so perfectly lovely that we immediately asked our agent to book a site for us."

She smiled. "Oh, and please call me Eva. My husband is Lucas."

Simon was distracted—for a millisecond—by another twitch of Holly's hands, before Miss Finch smiled in return and answered, "Thank you, Eva."

Miss Finch did not reciprocate Mrs. Nadeau's invitation to familiarity, however. Instead, she added, "Quebec is beautiful. I have visited your province several times, but I particularly enjoyed one wonderful winter in my youth doing nothing but skiing Quebec's best slopes—Mont Tremblant, Mont Sainte-Anne, Le Massif de Charlevoix, Stoneham, Ski Bromont. Which part of Quebec do you hail from?"

Mrs. Nadeau's brows shot up. "But we did not say . . ."

Holly's eyes narrowed, her clasped fingers tightened, and Simon started to speculate if those clenched fingers might be hiding a makeshift voodoo doll.

He stepped in, offering his hand and his most friendly smile to the Nadeaus. "Good morning. Simon Fletcher, Bright Star's Facilities and Security Manager. You will soon find that Miss Finch is one of the most traveled individuals you are likely to meet. She also has a great ear for accents. I'll go out on a limb here and say that she homed in on your particular Canadian inflection." He turned and, without a word, dared her to contradict him.

She never batted an eye. "Of course, *Mr.* Fletcher is correct. Having spent some time in Quebec, I merely recognized in your accent the dulcet intonation of your native French. Now, has Mrs. Mitchell explained that I will be parking your rig?"

It was Mr. Nadeau who reacted. He regarded Miss Finch up and down—but mostly down—and shifted foot to foot, suddenly nervous.

"Indeed? But . . . but my goodness!" He swung subtly toward Holly. "Are you . . . certain, Madame Mitchell? My brand-new *rig*, as Miss Finch calls it, is quite long and, shall we also agree . . . costly?"

Before Holly could grind out a less-than-confidence-inspiring reply, Simon said, "You need not be concerned for your RV; Miss Finch is an expert rig wrangler. She parked every Bright Star resident's rig without incident and has, to speak candidly, amazed most of our residents with her artistry."

"I'll say!" Skipper added, beaming at Miss Finch. "She's a total whiz."

Skipper caught sight of Miss Finch's lifted brows and blushed. "Sorry. Forgot to introduce myself. I'm Skipper Mitchell, Mr. Fletcher's summer intern."

"And my assistant for the duration of this task," Miss Finch added. "Shall we commence?"

As she turned to move toward the Nadeaus' truck, Simon suggested to the reticent Lucas Nadeau, "How about I tag along with you when she's ready to move your rig . . . in case you have questions about the hookups. How's that sound?"

"Yes, please. I must, er, *insist*."

With Simon, Mr. and Mrs. Nadeau, and the Nadeau kids trailing behind, Miss Finch and Skipper made their way to the driver's side of the Nadeaus' truck. Skipper opened the tool box and the case of pedal extenders. Before an audience of three intent young Nadeaus, he went to work.

"What are you doing?" Wyatt, the older Nadeau boy, asked.

"I'm attaching pedal extenders to the truck's accelerator, clutch, and brake. So Miss Finch can reach the pedals."

Wyatt and Eli released a shared "Ahh," in the same breath.

Sophie, perhaps seven or eight years old, moved closer to Skipper and whispered, "She is very small, is she not?"

Skipper snort-laughed. "Don't let that fool you. Like I told you, she's a beast. Used to ride motocross. Now she has an electric bike and rides out in the woods with me and other Bright Star kids. Trust me: She's a *total* beast!"

Sufficiently awed, the three young Nadeaus were content to finish watching Skipper complete his task without comment.

While Skipper worked, Miss Finch asked, "And which site have you reserved, Mr. Nadeau?"

"Number 19. We studied the online photographs of the two available sites. If Site 19 is even half as nice as it appears in the pictures, we shall be quite pleased."

"Prepare to be pleased then. Bright Star is the most carefully considered and planned RV park it has been my pleasure to visit." She pointed through the front gate and to the left. "Site 19 is around the bend that way; however, as the loop is one-way, we'll drive most of it before we arrive there. Are we ready, Skipper?"

"Yes, Miss Finch."

"Very good!"

Miss Finch threw her cushion onto the driver's seat and began to pull herself up. "Mr. and Mrs. Nadeau, if you would care to ride along with me? Skipper, why don't you walk the children up the road the other direction and meet us at their site? And please have the cones set up when we arrive."

"Will do, Miss Finch!"

Mr. Nadeau opened his truck's rear passenger door for his wife. Before he took the front passenger seat beside Miss Finch, he looked pointedly at Simon and gave a small jerk of his head toward the truck's remaining seat, indicating Simon should join them.

"Oh. Right. Said I'd come along with you." Simon opened the rear door opposite Mrs. Nadeau and got in.

"Everyone ready?" Miss Finch asked.

"*Oui.* Er, *yes*, of course," Mr. Nadeau muttered with absolute absence of certainty.

Skipper, with Miss Finch's toolbox and pedal-extender case in hand, and Wyatt, carrying the collapsed cones, led the Nadeaus' three children onto the loop, turned left, and began to walk the wrong way around the island. Simon saw that Skipper was already playing tour director, using his chin to point to the dancing fountains as he talked, and then to the trailhead.

Just then, Miss Finch put the truck in gear and pulled smoothly through the gate and around the curve to the right. The first hurdle safely past, Mr. Nadeau began to breathe again. To keep him from fretting, Simon engaged in small talk.

"What do you do for a living, Mr. Nadeau?"

"Ah, me? I am but a humble program manager at Collège CDI in Laval. Eva, too, works in the college's early childhood program."

At that moment, they approached the hanging banner that marked Site 1. Mr. and Mrs. Nadeau both exclaimed when they peered far down the long driveway and spied Miss Finch's homey little trailer, its exterior a pleasing palette of blue, cream, and gray, and the trailer's matching awning and outdoor carpet. They exclaimed over the ivy geranium hanging from the corning of the awning trailing its pink blossoms and then the restored woody parked on the far right of the driveway, sporting the same expert paint job as the trailer.

"Why, how picturesque," Mrs. Nadeau exclaimed. "Like a fairy cottage in the woods."

"Thank you," Miss Finch murmured.

"But, this is *your* site, Miss Finch?"

"It is."

"Perfectly lovely!"

Mr. Nadeau, however, muttered, "But I thought . . ."

Simon knew exactly what he thought. "Miss Finch is an old friend of the Mitchells, and they made certain . . . accommodations for her. I especially like her panel wagon, don't you?"

"*Oui!* A classic! I should like to examine it up close sometime."

"You are very welcome to," Miss Finch murmured.

Mr. and Mrs. Nadeau continued to express their delight over their glimpses of the various sites connected to the loop by their lengthy driveways, like so many spokes poking out the wrong side of an irregularly shaped wheel.

"*C'est parfait!*" Mrs. Nadeau exclaimed. "I cannot wait to see our site."

"Coming right up," Miss Finch said. She motored slowly past the site previously occupied by Marie Santini, then stopped and put the truck in reverse.

"If you please," Mr. Nadeau said. "I wish to get out and watch as you . . . back our fifth wheel into our site."

Miss Finch braked obligingly, and her three passengers exited. Mrs. Nadeau went down the driveway and joined the children who were eager to show her everything the site offered.

Simon hurried around the front of the truck and over to Mr. Nadeau. When Mr. Nadeau remained rooted, staring at his truck and fifth wheel—while possible praying under his breath—Simon nudged him gently.

"Let's go down the driveway, shall we? Skipper will have the cones in place. You'll like this part." *Meaning you'll like it when it's over*, he added silently, recalling his near heart attack while watching Miss Finch back Ray and Irene Kinzer's sizable RV.

Reluctantly, Mr. Nadeau followed Simon down the double driveway. Simon stopped and pointed to the two cones lined up on the driveway, the farthest one a few feet from the cement parking block at the end of the driveway. Nadeau stared at the cones.

"She will park what you call our 'rig' along this line?"

Simon was proud of Miss Finch and perhaps a bit biased. "She absolutely will—she's that good, believe me."

Even if she's an absolute harridan otherwise.

Through gritted teeth, Mr. Nadeau replied, "What is that old saying? 'I believe; please help my unbelief'?"

"Mmm."

More of a heartfelt prayer, Simon thought.

The fifth wheel was easing slowly down the driveway, rear first, the angle not quite right. A moment later, Miss Finch had adjusted and aligned with the first cone. By then, Mrs. Nadeau, her children, and Skipper were watching from a few feet off the driveway.

Mr. Nadeau's breathing was coming in short, shallow gasps when Skipper asked, "Everybody see that cone down there?"

Six sets of eyes swiveled to the far cone.

"When Miss Finch stops, the rear corner of your RV will either be touching or right over that cone."

Mr. Nadeau swallowed and muttered an unconvincing, "*Merveilleux*."

Two minutes later, Skipper, standing a couple of feet from the cone, gave Miss Finch a thumbs up. She put the truck into park and clambered down from the driver's seat to check the RV's position for her own benefit.

Nodding to herself, she called out, "Mr. Nadeau?"

The poor man, panting now, relieved but near hyperventilation, answered with a shaky, "*Oui?*"

"Will this suit you, Mr. Nadeau?"

"Yes, very much. Th-thank you."

"And, I presume you would prefer to chock your rig, then unhitch and level it yourself?"

"If you please."

"Very good." Miss Finch nodded to Skipper, who immediately grabbed Miss Finch's toolbox and headed for the truck. He was followed by the oldest boy, Wyatt, perhaps Skipper's age, carrying the case for the extenders, while Eli, a year or so younger than his brother, ran and grabbed the two cones and brought them back to Wyatt who, under Skipper's tutelage, collapsed and stacked them.

Several minutes later, Miss Finch, carrying her cushion and trailed by the four kids and her equipment, headed down the road to her site.

"Wait till you meet Hugo and Pouncer," Simon heard Skipper tell the Nadeau kids.

Simon turned to Mr. and Mrs. Nadeau. "Any questions about your site or about the hookups?"

Nadeau shook his head. "No, everything is perfect, but Mr. Fletcher, you were wrong, I am afraid. Quite wrong."

Simon looked up, surprised and dismayed. "Pardon?"

"When you called Miss Finch a mere expert? *Bah!* You were in error. She is a genius! An artiste. *Une maîtresse*—a master!"

Simon laughed aloud and clapped Lucas on the back. "Master, huh? That I cannot disagree with. I will amend my description of her and, going forward, will title her a *master* rig wrangler."

———————— ⬥ ————————

SHORTLY AFTER 3 P.M. that same day, one of Bright Star's friendly residents, Chet Bigalow, drove Simon and Joe into town. Simon and Joe picked up two rented passenger vans and drove them back to Bright Star in preparation for Friday evening.

By the time they returned that afternoon, the whole of Bright Star's property was humming with activity and high spirits. Miss Finch's new neighbors, the Gillespies, were settling into Site 2, formerly occupied by Terri

Rickert, and many of the residents' weekend guests had already arrived. The barbecue zone was "a-cookin'," the scent of savory meat on the grill filled Simon's nostrils, happy voices percolated through the warm early evening air, and multiple families and youngsters, including the Nadeau kids and Skipper, were using the pool.

Simon's stomach rumbled a protest over his skipped lunch. "Oh yeah," he realized. "Haven't eaten since breakfast."

He parked near the swim complex, walked up to the pool, and signaled Skipper. Dripping and grinning, Skipper came toward him.

"What's up, Fletch?"

"Having a good time?"

"The best! I really like Wyatt and Eli."

Simon was gratified to hear Skipper's declaration, particularly since none of Skipper's other Bright Star friends—the Gormans' granddaughters, Becka and Melissa, or Bruce, the nephew of the Mullers in Site 7—would be visiting their relatives at Bright Star over the long weekend. However, it wasn't as though Skipper would have much time to hang out with his new friends except at the tail end of the long weekend. Rather, Simon and Skipper were in for three lengthy and grueling work days.

"That's great; I'm happy for you. And did you get all the fliers out?"

"Yup. Posted fliers at every site. Wyatt and Eli helped. Holly is handing them out when visitors check in too."

"Good job. Well, enjoy the rest of your afternoon. I'm headed home to fix dinner."

"Wyatt, Eli, and Sophie want me to eat with them and their folks."

"That's fine, but only if their folks actually invite you. And you know the drill afterward—"

"Yeah, be home before it gets dark."

"Yup. And before you leave the park and head home—"

"Turn on my bike's headlight even if it isn't dark yet."

"Right. Additional visitors coming in this evening means more vehicles on the gravel road from the turnoff to Bright Star's gate. Oh, and call me if you're heading back to the cabin and, by chance, have *not* had dinner. I'll rustle up something for you."

"I will. Thanks, Fletch—hey! Watch me dive off the high platform?"

"Sure."

Simon smiled. Yes, he liked when Skipper was happy and content.

CHAPTER 3

INDEPENDENCE DAY

ON FRIDAY, THE Fourth of July, the usually sedate Bright Star Summer RV Residence went nuts. Officially bonkers, crazy, deranged, and certifiable, all rolled into one.

Simon and Skipper started their chores early that morning, before most of the park's residents were up and about. After cleaning the swim complex and restocking towels, followed by cleaning and straightening up the rec hall, Simon and Skipper spent the next hours cruising the park in their maintenance truck, delivering firewood for the residents' firepits, picking up each site's trash, policing the park in general, and being flagged down by residents and guests to answer a myriad of questions.

Except today, most of residents and visitors asked the same questions . . . over and over and over.

"Say, can you tell us what time the fireworks show starts tonight?"

"Where's the best place to watch the fireworks this evening?"

"We heard the town of South Lake Tahoe has a Fourth of July parade each year. What time does it start and where should we park?"

Because a large part of his job was to cater to the wishes of the park's residents and their guests, Simon patiently repeated festivity options, which included delivering the bad news that the South Lake Tahoe parade had run on Thursday—as in *yesterday*.

"Look," he repeated for the third time in the past half hour, "the closest and biggest fireworks show on the lake is South Lake Tahoe's, but other parts of the lake area host spectaculars you can choose from: Kings Beach, Tahoe City, Truckee, and Incline Village, to name a few.

"But back to South Lake Tahoe's event. Officially, the fireworks start at 9:45. You'll be able to see them from most anywhere along the south shore, although the closer to Stateline, the better the view. All that said? I should warn you: Finding and claiming a space to watch the display will be only the second half of your problem. The first half? Should you choose to leave Bright Star's property today and turn north on the feeder road? Once you reach Emerald Bay Road, you would certainly encounter gridlock—everybody and their dog trying to get into town. Once there, thousands will be desperate for a place to park. You'll be lucky to find anywhere safe to leave your car within two miles of the shoreline.

"Knowing what we do about today's logistics, we've come up with what we think is the best option with the least amount of stress for Bright Star residents and their guests to see the fireworks. Management has rented two passenger vans. Starting at 5:00 this afternoon, Mr. Mitchell and I will begin ferrying people down to Emerald Bay Road. From there, you will get out, cross the road on foot, and walk down to one of the beaches.

"The beaches, too, will already be crowded, so you should expect to walk quite a ways to find and claim a decent viewpoint. For that reason, we recommend you keep the gear you take with you to a minimum: folding lawn chairs you can sling over your shoulders and backpacks with food and drink. We'll run the vans until 9:30, take a break until the fireworks are over, then return and begin ferrying folks back to Bright Star. Or . . ."

Simon paused to draw a breath. "Or you can stay right here and watch from the lawn around the barbecue area on the island. The island is the highest spot in the park. Watching from there won't give you the greatest view, of course, but since the fireworks are synchronized to music that is broadcast on the radio and for us to make the experience a bit more authentic, we'll set up a sound system and will pipe the music through it. That way, by staying here, you can avoid the hassle of the crowds altogether."

Many Bright Star senior residents were all for avoiding "the hassle of the crowds." The remainder of the residents and their guests, however, were determined to see the famous South Lake Tahoe show closer up. They peeled away from Simon and Skipper to make their plans, and Simon drove on—until flagged down by yet another resident or guest with questions.

The same questions.

"Good grief! It's not like we didn't print up a list of questions and answers and hand them out to *everybody* when they checked in!" Skipper grumbled. "Instead of stopping to answer any more of the guests' stupid questions, we should just throw fliers at them as we drive by."

Simon thought he heard Skipper snicker under his breath and add, "Yeah, throw fliers at the guests with *rocks* attached."

———— ⁕ ————

THAT WAS THE MORNING—mainly repetitious and annoying. But by noon, every late-arriving guest had checked in and the sheer volume of people out and about within the park had doubled and then some.

It wasn't until around two o'clock that everything that could go awry did so, on a scale and of a magnitude Simon could scarcely believe.

It began with a panicked call from Holly. "Fletcher! One of our residents just called—a pipe in the rec hall kitchen is spewing water!"

Simon and Skipper raced to the scene in their maintenance truck. A dozen residents and guests, standing around and pointing at the water flowing out the rec hall door, cheered when Simon and Skipper arrived. Simon sent Skipper straight to the laundry facility with a key to the linen closet and orders to bring back the mop and wringer bucket and all the towels he could carry, while Simon went in search of the source of the flood.

A pipe under the kitchen sink had, indeed, split wide open. Unfortunately, Simon had no means of replacing the split section, particularly on a holiday as packed as this one. He turned the water off to the rec hall kitchen instead, which, thankfully, did not also turn off water to the rec hall's two restrooms accessible from both inside and outside the cabin. Then he and Skipper got busy with the mop and towels, sopping up and wringing water into the bucket.

Twice, three guests in particular tried to tip-toe through an inch of water to reach the game room. Both times, Simon pointed them back out the rec hall's door.

"Sorry. No access until this has dried," he told the disappointed teens, possibly eighteen or nineteen years old. "The rec hall is closed until further notice."

That didn't deter them. "Well, the game room isn't wet. We looked through the windows. We could climb in that way," a young man suggested.

"You tell him, JJ!" laughed one of his pals. "We definitely know how to climb through windows, yeah?"

"Shut up, Marc," JJ growled.

"Uh, just so you know, if I were to catch a guest climbing through a Bright Star window, I would, regrettably, be forced to ban that guest from the rec hall for the remainder of the weekend," Simon said, in no fit mood to be trifled with.

"Yeah, well you'd have to catch us first, *old man*," Marc sneered.

Still grumbling, the three guys walked off—but only, apparently, to phone the office and lodge a complaint.

Minutes later, Holly pulled up to the rec hall in the other maintenance truck, and appeared in the doorway. "Fletcher, a word please. I received a complaint—" She stopped, aghast, as though she'd only then noticed the water sloshing across the floor. "The floor! It will be ruined!"

No duh, Simon thought.

"Very likely," he said through his teeth.

"Why, there must be an inch of standing water in here! Think of the damage to the subfloor, Fletch!"

"I am aware, Holly; after all, you *did* tell me a pipe had burst, didn't you? This is the result when an uncontrolled flow of water has nowhere to go but onto the floor. Well, I've shut off water to the split pipe, and we're—"

"Fletcher, I must insist you get this water mopped up immediately so our guests can use this facility. We have several young gentleman guests who wish to use the game room."

Simon stood slowly to his feet, struggling to rein in his temper. "Do you not see what we're doing here, Holly? Me, with the mop and Skipper on his hands and knees? We're sopping up the water as quickly as we can. However, even after we finish, the entire floor will need to dry, overnight at the least, perhaps even a second day and night, before we let anyone in—that is, if you want to save the floor. A lot of foot traffic over a soggy subfloor could warp it or even punch through. Of course, the possibility of an accident of that sort is a liability issue."

"But that is completely unacceptable! Our residents' guests expect—"

A long, frenzied burst of firecrackers intruded on what was shaping up to be yet another Holly Mitchell over-the-top rant.

Simon scooped up several wet towels. "Skipper! Throw some of your wet towels into that bucket and follow me!"

Holly's eyes jerked from Simon to the wet towels he clutched. "Those towels . . . those aren't our swim complex towels, are they? *Our **new** towels? Being used as rags?*"

Simon barreled out the door, elbowing Holly aside, scanning and listening to determine where the sounds had come from. Another round of firecrackers lit off with a prolonged series of *pop-pop-pop*. Simon homed in on the sound. He took off at a run, reached the truck, and backed it out, barely waiting for Skipper to jump into his seat. Around the loop they flew, Sites 12 through 16 flying by.

There. In the middle of the road opposite Site 17, Simon spied the same three older teens who had suggested they climb through a window to reach the game room. They were lighting off another string of firecrackers—out of a huge pile of firecrackers—and had perhaps twenty additional fireworks staged and ready to go, *including aerials*.

Simon braked sharply. "Follow me and do what I do," Simon ordered.

He jumped from the truck, grabbed his pile of wet towels, and stomped up to the makeshift fireworks display. He dropped the towels on the asphalt except for one that he spread hastily over the freshly lit firecrackers. Under the wet towel, the firecrackers popped and jumped, sizzled and died. Simon grabbed a second towel and wrung it out over the staged cones and aerials, then unfurled the towel over the dampened fireworks, and reached for a third.

"Dump the water in the bucket right here, Skip," Simon ordered, pointing to the staged cones and aerials.

One of the youths grabbed Simon's arm. "Hey, man, stop it! You're ruining everything!"

Simon shook off the kid's hand and kept going. Within moments of arriving, Simon and Skipper had used a dozen dripping-wet towels and a couple inches of water from the bucket to drown the impromptu fireworks display.

"Dude, those fireworks cost me a fortune, and you're going to pay me for them!" sputtered someone. It was JJ, the enterprising young adult who'd suggested climbing in the game room window.

"What's the problem here?"

Simon shifted his attention to the sole resident of Site 17, James Crowley, middle-aged, divorced, well-to-do. Simon gestured to the young men.

"Are these your guests, Mr. Crowley?"

"Yes, my son, JJ, and his friends, Marc and Dan."

By this time, a small crowd of residents and their guests, summoned by the unsanctioned firecrackers, had begun to gather. Simon noted Wes and Polly Trujillo, the Bhattacharya family, the Bigalows, and the three Misses Benowitz, Dina, Gracia, and Margola. Not one of them said a word, but if looks could speak, their narrowed eyes and the disdain leveled at the disrespectful young men spoke volumes.

Simon looked at his watch. "Mr. Crowley, I am evicting your guests. They have exactly thirty minutes to pack and leave. They will not be allowed to return to Bright Star."

Crowley gaped at Simon, dumbfounded. "What? Evicting them over a couple of harmless firecrackers?"

Simon pointed to where he knew the signs were posted under Crowley's site banner. His finger might as well have been the staff of Moses: The crowd parted like the waters of the Red Sea, leaving a clear sightline straight to the posted signs.

No Fireworks of Any Kind
No Smoking Anywhere on Bright Star Property
Fires in Designated Firepits Only

"No, I am evicting them over the reckless and prohibited use of fireworks on this property and for the strong likelihood of starting a forest fire." He stared hard at Crowley's son. "You now have twenty-nine minutes to vacate the property."

One of the young man's friends tugged on his shirt. "Come on, JJ. Told you it was a stupid idea."

When the crowd of bystanders began to applaud softly, the three visitors beat a hasty retreat to Mr. Crowley's RV.

Furious, James Crowley shouted, "We'll just see about this!" He spun on his heel and followed his guests.

Wes and Polly Trujillo approached Simon. Wes whispered, "Thank you, Mr. Fletcher. We appreciate your hard line on this sort of reckless behavior."

Polly nodded. "Agree."

Other residents murmured similar sentiments. Simon heard growls of, "Burn Bright Star down around us?" and "Privileged little twits!" before the crowd melted away.

Simon shook himself and took stock of the mess on the asphalt. "Right. Okay, Skipper, let's do this. Grab a broom and dustpan from the truck while I shake the debris from the towels into the bucket. You sweep up whatever debris is still in the road and dump it into the bucket. Step lively; we need to get back to the rec hall and finish mopping up."

Skipper glanced nervously down Mr. Crowley's driveway. "But those guys. Think they'll go? I mean . . . without doing something else?"

Simon experienced a sudden recollection of how Skipper had gotten himself assigned to a summer of supervised work at Bright Star, how Joe and Holly's nephew had engaged in vandalism at his school by hanging around with two older, and more "experienced" boys—bored teens with no respect for the property of others.

Boys not unlike Mr. Crowley's son and his friends.

"Good intuition, Skipper. Let's call Joe, finish here, and head over to where he's working."

Simon figured he needed to get to Joe before Holly heard what he'd done and unilaterally undid it.

"Joe? Where are you? Need to see you ASAP."

"I'm at the wood pile, using the splitter, Fletch. What's up?"

"Trouble and possibly more trouble. Be there shortly."

Joe was waiting for them when Simon drove through the gate and around back of the office.

"You said trouble, Fletch? What's going on?"

Simon explained, then added, "I have two concerns, Joe. First, that Crowley will call Holly and she will reverse my decision. Second, that these boys will engage in some sort of mischief on their way out."

"You're right about Holly—I'll call her and head that situation off. But . . ." here Joe paused. "But perhaps you should have talked to me or Holly before you evicted guests? I imagine Crowley will try to weasel out of his lease, and that will set Holly off but good."

Simon was astounded. "I should have talked to you? Joe, I'm Bright Star's Security Manager. If I don't have the authority to evict a dangerous element from the park *on the spot*, then why did you give me this title?"

Joe nodded slowly. "I'm sorry, Fletcher; you're absolutely right. It was your call, and I'll stand by it. I'll handle Holly, and Crowley too, if necessary. More immediately, what's your plan for getting these boys off the property without another incident?"

"I'll return to Site 17, escort the boys all the way out to the feeder road, and warn them that if they return, they will face trespassing charges. In fact, I'll follow them until they reach Emerald Bay Road."

"Good plan." Joe's phone rang just then, and he grimaced. "It's Holly. You'd better get moving."

"I'll see you later, then. Thanks, Joe."

Simon and Skipper drove up the loop, passing Miss Finch on her bicycle, Hugo and Pouncer in the front basket. Skipper waved and shouted; Miss Finch rang her cheery bell in response.

Simon, eyes straight ahead, nodded. Miss Finch, doing her best imitation of Miss Gulch, did the same. Skipper, checking them both, frowned.

Simon continued up the loop, headed for the rec hall. "I know it's not fair to ask this of you, Skipper, but I need you to do some things for me. First, finish mopping up the water on the floor until the floor is mostly dry. Second, keep people out of the rec hall until I can get a sign posted. In fact, just lock yourself in while you're working and while I make sure those boys leave without vandalizing anything. If you finish and want to leave, lock the door behind you. Can you do all that? I'll be making sure our uninvited guests leave without making any trouble."

Skipper scowled. "Stupid jerks! They could have caught Bright Star on fire! Yeah, I can mop up the water, but I'd rather watch you kick those guys out of the park."

Simon laughed. "I'll bet you would. Well, hopefully, I'll be back by the time you're done. Then we need to take the dirty towels to the laundry and try to salvage them."

"Salvage them?"

Simon shrugged. "Holly sets great store by the swim center's towels, Skipper. Before we used them to mop the floor, then put out firecrackers, they were a brilliant white. Think we'll be able to get all the dirt and firework residue out of them?"

Skipper looked into the bucket between his feet. "Well, *crud.*"

"Yup. Pretty much." Simon stopped at the rec hall. The maintenance truck Holly had driven from the office to the rec hall was gone. "Okay; you know what to do."

Me? I'll be making sure Holly doesn't countermand my eviction notice.

———— ◆ ————

AS SIMON APPROACHED Site 17, he spied the other maintenance truck pulled off to the side, Holly on her phone, still seated behind the wheel. Based on her body language and dramatic hand gestures, Simon supposed she and Joe were engaged in yet another battle of wills.

Simon pulled up alongside the road behind Holly. As he got out, Holly put her truck in gear and drove away, nose in the air.

"Guess that settles it," Simon murmured. He walked down the site driveway, and encountered Jim Crowley and his guests, JJ, Marc, and Dan.

"Haha! Joke's on you, dude!" JJ smirked.

"Nope. Joke's on you," Simon said evenly, shifting into his MP persona. "I'll give you exactly ten more minutes to load your stuff in your vehicle and head for the front gate."

"Now, see here," Crowley growled. "Mrs. Mitchell said the boys didn't need to leave, that you 'misspoke.'"

Simon retained his professional composure. "Actually, I just confirmed the eviction order for your guests with Mr. Mitchell, and I believe Mrs. Mitchell has heard his decision by now. If you take a look, you'll see she has left."

Simon looked at his watch again and set the timer on it. "Ten minutes, boys, starting now."

JJ stared a challenge at his dad and didn't move. Marc and Dan, however, hustled into Crowley's RV.

Crowley edged closer to Simon, encroaching on his personal space, and opened his mouth to speak. He wasn't expecting Simon to step forward, bringing them chest to chest. Simon's impressive bulk had intimidated many unruly Marines and didn't fail him now. His unanticipated move caused Crowley to stumble backwards.

"You . . . you . . ." he fumed.

Simon tsked. "Is this where you usually say something brutish and self-righteous like, 'I want your badge number and the name and number of your supervisor,' or 'I'll have your job for this,' something along those lines? To be blunt, your own blatant disrespect for authority is the likeliest reason your son, like you, has no respect for authority or for the personal boundaries or property of others—like father, like son."

"You can't talk to me this way!" Crowley shouted.

"And yet I just did. Furthermore, this situation can go *one and only one* of two ways, Mr. Crowley, and it is entirely your choice. Option A, you accept that your guests, by breaking Bright Star's posted 'no fireworks' policy, created a situation dangerous to the lives and property of every individual in this park, and thereby, your guests earned their eviction. By accepting their eviction, you may continue to reside at Bright Star until Labor Day. Or, Option B, you can, if you continue to resist your guests' eviction, receive your own eviction notice and leave Bright Star within the next twenty-four hours."

"Evict me? Oh, I'll leave all right! I'll sue this place and you personally, and I'll demand a full and complete refund—plus damages!"

"You may demand all you like; however, I refer you to the lease you signed, the binding agreement for your residency at Bright Star. You paid up front for your residency, which, during your first full week here, is refundable. However, after your first full week, your lease payment is neither refundable nor will it be pro-rated. It is nonrefundable should you choose to leave voluntarily, and it is nonrefundable should you be evicted for refusing to follow the safety and security rules of the park and the orders of its managers—in this case, the Facilities and Security Manager, which would be me. Have I made myself clear?"

"But she said you misspoke—"

"Actually, Mrs. Mitchell herself misspoke." He glanced at his watch. "Six minutes."

"Until what?" sneered JJ.

"Until I call the police to remove three trespassers. I have friends in the SLTPD, so trust me when I say that, as a town dependent upon tourism, our police force has little patience with those who abuse the hospitality of its citizens."

Simon looked again at his watch. "Five minutes."

Marc and Dan burst from Crowley's RV carrying their duffel bags. "C'mon, JJ! We gotta go! We can find some fun back in Sacramento."

JJ stared hard at Simon for a few seconds longer. "Yeah. Be right there."

Two minutes later, JJ's vehicle, with Marc and Dan onboard, backed out of Site 17.

As Simon moved toward his truck, he said over his shoulder, "Let me know what you decide, Mr. Crowley."

He dogged JJ's car to where Bright Star's road reached the feeder road, then turned left and followed them down to Emerald Bay Road. The kid stopped only once . . . at the turnoff to Joe and Holly's cabin.

Now, why would he be stopping here?

Simon didn't care for any of the possible reasons that came to mind. He pulled up directly behind the kid's vehicle and nudged his bumper.

Don't even think about it, you young idiot.

JJ apparently heeded his unspoken advice, because he drove away, turned left onto the feeder road leaving Bright Star property, and didn't slow again until he turned right and merged into the traffic already clogging Emerald Bay Road and slowly motored toward town and the junction where the road joined State Highway 50, the route leading toward Sacramento.

Simon breathed a prayer of gratitude as he turned around and drove back to Bright Star.

Whew. Glad that's over. And surely this will be the last crisis I need to deal with today. Right, Lord?

Oh, that it were.

———————•———————

SIMON STOPPED AT the office on the way into the park, grabbed a pre-printed sign that read "Closed for Maintenance," and headed for the rec hall. He was gratified to find Skipper nearly done mopping up.

"Hey, Fletch," the boy said, intent on finishing the last wet section, close to completing his task.

"Hey yourself, Skipper. Great job, by the way—your persistence is commendable. Knew I could count on you, Bud. Let me post this sign, then I'll grab a dry towel; while you're finishing up, I'll go over the floor one last time; try to catch any bit of moisture left behind. We'll lock up after."

Skipper grinned at Simon's praise. "So, did you kick those guys out, Fletch?"

"Yup. That I did. "

"Holly's sure mad about this floor."

"I'm not particularly pleased myself, but stuff happens, right? Part of our job is dealing with problems, especially the surprise kind."

"Well, she's *really* mad that we used the towels that are only for the swim complex."

Simon shrugged. "It was an emergency and couldn't be helped. Look, if any of them are ruined, we'll put them in a stack by themselves and make sure we use *them* as rags should we suffer another water leak." More to himself he added, "And I'll be ordering us a wet/dry vac."

Simon had just got on his knees with the dry towel when his phone rang. He looked at the lockscreen and sighed. "Holly. Again."

He stood and straightened out his attitude. "Hey, Holly." As he listened, his mouth opened and his jaw dropped. "*What!*" Then, "Be right there."

He was rushing for the door before he even hung up.

Skip caught the urgency of Simon's actions. "What's wrong, Fletch?"

Without slowing, Simon threw over his shoulder, "Holly says Mr. Trujillo is having a heart attack."

CHAPTER 4

SIMON BROKE THE posted speed limit to reach the Trujillos quickly. While he drove he prayed, mentally reviewed CPR protocol, and recalled that Bright Star's defibrillator was in the office.

While he was a Marine MP, Simon had received extensive first aid and CPR training. As Bright Star's Facility and Security Manager, he had insisted that both Joe and Holly be trained, certified, and proficient in CPR and the use of the defibrillator. He hoped they would have thought to bring the defibrillator to the Trujillos' site.

It also dawned on him, what with the choking traffic on Emerald Bay Road, headed primarily *into* town, that getting an ambulance to Bright Star would likely be faster than retracing their route and getting Mr. Trujillo to South Lake Tahoe's Barton Hospital's Emergency Department

Lord, we need your help here. Thank you.

The other maintenance truck was parked down the Trujillos' driveway. Simon pulled up behind it and ran down the drive.

Mrs. Trujillo, wringing her hands, spotted him first. "Mr. Fletcher! Please help us!"

An unconscious Mr. Trujillo was lying flat on his back on the patio; Joe was on his knees, performing chest compressions. Holly was in a dither, all thumbs while attempting to prep the defibrillator.

Obviously, Holly needs a refresher on her CPR training, Simon noted.

"Did Mr. Trujillo have a pulse when you started compressions, Joe?"

"No. Wasn't breathing either. That's why we're trying to get the defibrillator set up."

"Got it." Simon dropped to his knees next to Joe and felt for a pulse on Mr. Trujillo's neck. It was there, but weak. Simon leaned over and listened for breath sounds.

"Okay; good job on the compressions, Joe, but Mr. Trujillo has a pulse and is breathing on his own now, so you should stop for the time being. Anyone call for an ambulance?"

"I did," Mrs. Trujillo answered. "You say he is breathing again?"

"Yes, but we need to monitor both his pulse and breathing and be ready should his heart stop again."

"You do it, Fletch," Joe said. "I'm mighty shaky at the moment."

"It's the excess adrenaline in your system, Joe. It'll wear off in a few minutes. Holly, please keep the defibrillator out in case we need it."

Simon set a fifteen-second timer on his watch and began checking Mr. Trujillo's pulse and breath sounds each time the timer alarm went off. After the third check, Mr. Trujillo began to stir; he rocked his head side to side and tried to lift his hands.

"Mr. Trujillo, it's Simon Fletcher. Open your eyes, please."

The man's eyes fluttered open.

"Look at me, Mr. Trujillo."

Slowly, the man's eyes found Simon's face and fixed on it.

"You're experiencing a medical emergency, Mr. Trujillo. Please don't try to move; I need you to lie still and breathe as normally as you can—no, don't try to speak. Blink if you understand me."

The older man's eyes fluttered then opened again.

"Good. Just focus on your breathing: in and out, in and out."

A shadow fell on Simon, and he glanced up. Miss Finch stood above him, watching and appraising. And Simon's heart did that strange leap into his throat.

Stop it, he commanded . . . not that his command had any effect on his heart . . . or his eyes, for that matter, as they, of their own accord, drank her in.

Miss Finch's eyes, however, were carefully averted, fixed on Joe even as she said, "I was riding my bike around the park and passing by, when I saw both maintenance trucks here . . . and a number of residents gathered at the top of the drive. Can I be of assistance in any manner?"

Simon forced himself to reply, "I imagine you have some training?"

Joe huffed a small chuckle. "The woman's a nurse, Fletch, although a retired one, I would assume. Still, she's a nurse by profession. That's how I met her."

"Something of a short-lived profession," Miss Finch murmured, "although I do have, as you suggested, some measure of training."

Simon's response was a sardonic laugh. "Why am I not surprised? Did nursing not hold enough of a challenge for you, so you took up, what? Thoracic surgery instead? Or was it rocket science?"

"Financial planning, actually," was her soft answer.

"That's quite the leap—from nursing to stocks, bonds, CDs, and money market accounts."

She shrugged and a smile tugged at her mouth, despite her best efforts. "The leap came later . . . after I took up sky diving."

"Well, of course it did." Simon couldn't disguise his sarcasm or the laughter burbling under his words—laughter he squelched as soon as it bubbled up. "Still, you never mentioned nursing . . . before."

"I never mentioned it because I was a nurse only in Joe's estimation, Mr. Fletcher. When I met Joe all those years ago, I was on a six-month stint as a volunteer aide at Landstuhl Army Medical Center in Germany. It's where the military often airlifts and treats military personnel wounded in action before they ship them home. During his monthlong stay, I never once said I was a nurse. Quite frankly, I am a bit perplexed to hear that he believes I was one."

Joe blinked in amazement. "What?"

"In all fairness, you were grievously wounded, Joe, heavily medicated, and at times—not to put it too indelicately—quite out of your head. But whether you were lucid or in a fevered state, your attention was inflexibly fixed upon one and only one thing. I happened to be assigned to your ward and, as a volunteer, had the time to listen to your concerns."

Joe turned inward and frowned in concentration. "You're right about my injuries. I was a mess and in and out of consciousness for quite some time, even after they airlifted me back to the States. With the exception of a few semisolid memories, those weeks at Landstuhl remain swathed in haze."

He sighed. "And as for my state of mind? What I cared about was my buddy Rob. Best friend I ever had. We were in the same unit, deployed together to the Middle East to serve in the Gulf War. Only two months in, our forward unit came under attack. In the same action in which I was wounded, Rob was killed . . . saving my life. I owed and still owe him a great debt. At that time, I needed help and needed it urgently to . . . to take care of something for him. Something vital."

Joe stared at Miss Finch. "I was all of nineteen years old at that time, but my most persistent memory from Landstuhl was of you, standing or sitting by my bed. I recall you listening patiently to my ravings, and I *think* I remember you asking lots of questions and taking notes. I really don't know how you did it, but months later I found out that, somehow, you'd come through. I do know I can never repay the favor I owe you."

Miss Finch slowly nodded. "And yet, I must credit the Lord for his help in that situation, Joe. He is the one who made a way where there was, quite literally, *no* way. But we need not discuss this any further here and now since we have bigger fish to fry. I presume an ambulance is on its way?"

"Yes," Joe answered, "and someone needs to meet it at the gate when it arrives and direct it to this site."

"I shall do that," Miss Finch announced.

Without another word, she turned and walked away. Simon's eyes followed her up the driveway to where she had left her bike. She climbed on the miniature electric bike and pedaled away.

As he returned his attention to Mr. Trujillo, Holly muttered, "Why is it you've never said much about your recuperation after you were wounded,

Joe, or about this dear friend of yours who died? Why have I never even heard of him? And what was this so-called favor Miss Finch did for you?"

"Later, dear. Now is not the time."

As much as Simon wanted to hear the answers to Holly's questions, Joe adamantly refused Holly's several attempts to draw him out, while Simon regularly checked Mr. Trujillo's pulse and breathing. The man became more wakeful but, as Simon had asked, was managing to keep still. Mrs. Trujillo knelt at his other side and held his hand, her face close to his while whispering encouragements in his ear.

Simon canted his head. "I think I hear the ambulance."

The siren's warble grew more pronounced, the sound louder as the ambulance approached Bright Star.

"Joe? Holly? Would you walk up to the road and clear a path for the ambulance and paramedics, please?"

The couple went together to persuade the curious and concerned of Bright Star, gathered at the top of the Trujillos' driveway, to move out of the way.

Moments later, the paramedics arrived, rolling a gurney between them. After a quick assessment, they inserted a line in Mr. Trujillo's arm and got him onto the gurney and into the back of the ambulance. Mrs. Trujillo followed after them, intending to stay with her husband and ride the ambulance to the hospital.

Simon caught up to her. "Do you have our cell numbers, Mrs. Trujillo?"

"Yes, I have Bright Star's card in my purse."

"Call any of us as soon as you know something or if you need anything, okay?"

"I will. And will you please pray for Wes, Mr. Fletcher? You see, I know you pray. The Gorman's grandkids, Becka and Melissa, have told us."

Simon squeezed her hand. "You can count on my prayers, Mrs. Trujillo."

"Please call me Polly, Mr. Fletcher. And thank you."

As the ambulance pulled away, its siren howling, Simon glanced at his watch. It read 5:15 p.m.

"Joe? Holly? We're running late. Need to begin ferrying the residents and guests down to Emerald Bay Road."

Holly, finding her efficient self again, answered, "I will keep the office open while you two make the runs."

Simon and Joe made three "runs" each, ferrying about half of Bright Star's residents and guests down to Emerald Bay Road. As Simon had predicted, the lane heading east, into South Lake Tahoe, was bumper to bumper, the cars slowly inching ahead, while traffic in the lane heading west was only moderate.

As Bright Star passengers disembarked, Simon and Joe donned orange safety vests and walked out onto the road. Joe stepped between two eastbound cars, held up a hand to pause the next car, while Simon stepped into the westbound lane and did the same with oncoming traffic. Their passengers scooted across the road, lawn chairs and back packs slung across their shoulders.

By the time Simon and Joe had delivered all of their passengers, Simon's stomach was rumbling hard. At a particularly loud grumble, he remembered Skipper.

"Yikes!"

The boy answered his phone on the second ring. "Hey, Fletch."

"Rec hall locked up?"

"Yup. And I washed and dried all the towels. Um, some of them don't look so good."

"I figured as much. We'll deal with that tomorrow. Listen, I'm starved. Are you as hungry as I am?"

"Uh, no . . . I'm at Miss Finch's, and she fed me dinner—chili and cornbread and ice cream bars!"

Simon grumbled right along with his empty stomach, *Must be nice.*

"Well, be sure to thank her for feeding you. I'll be up on the island, prepping the sound system for the fireworks."

While hoping and praying some of the residents who are barbecuing this evening will take pity and offer to feed me.

"Do you need help with the sound system?"

Simon thought a moment. "No; I can handle the setup. Are you planning to watch from the island?"

"Yup. I'll be up after a while. Right now, Miss Finch is teaching me how to play cabbage."

"Play what?"

He heard a murmured voice in the background, then Skipper corrected himself.

"Sorry. It's called *cribbage*, not cabbage—and did you know Miss Finch is a mean card player? Like, every time I turn around she hollers 'nibs' or 'nobs' or whatever and claims a bunch of extra points just because I forgot one of the rules. *Sheesh!*"

Simon smiled. "You'd better learn those rules before she utterly trounces you. Don't forget that she used to deal cards in a casino." He changed the subject. "Uh, just so you know, as soon as I have the sound system up, I'll probably run home to grab myself some grub. See you on the island at 9:45 for the fireworks."

He was about to hang up, when he remembered to add, "Oh. And don't forget that Joe and I need to ferry all the residents and their guests back to Bright Star after the fireworks finish. That means you'll need to get yourself home after the fireworks show, and it will be pretty late by then. Also, it's going to be fairly dark tonight, what with the moon only about half full. So don't forget—"

"Yeah, I know. Don't forget to turn on my headlight while I ride home, and don't forget to be careful."

Simon smiled to himself. "You're a good kid, Skipper."

"Yeah, yeah. Whatever."

But Simon could tell Skipper was pleased.

———— ◆ ————

BY THE TIME Joe and Simon transported all the residents and guests safely back to Bright Star, it was past midnight and Simon was exhausted. Wrung out. He jumped into his Bright Star truck, glad to be heading back to his cabin, grateful the Fourth was officially over, and thankful he wasn't scheduled to show up for work until noon tomorrow.

Skipper won't be the only one sleeping in!

That pleasant reflection was interrupted when his phone rang: *Holly.*

Blowing out a breath, he picked up the call. "Yeah, Holly?"

"Fletcher. Glad I caught you before you turned in. My, what an eventful day! Joe and I are absolutely bushed."

"Yeah, me too. I—"

"Listen, Fletcher, I know you're not scheduled to come in until noon tomorrow, but with all the unexpected happenings today and the number of the visitors we have in the park, Joe needs to get a full night's sleep. He's is still recovering from his accident, you know, so I need you to be in early, no later than eight o'clock."

So much for sleeping in.

"But you'll be in to open the office at 9:00 a.m., right?" Simon asked.

"Well, no, that is part of my call. I think it best if I remain with Joe and make him a hot, nourishing breakfast. The two of us should be in around 10:00 or so. But since you'll be in early, I'd like you to clean the pools and restock the towels, then reopen the rec hall, before opening and staffing the office."

"I'm not sure the subfloor will be dry enough yet—"

"Possibly, but I feel it is important that our guests have access to all of Bright Star's amenities, particularly this weekend, don't you agree? You should be able to get all that done and still open the office on time and staff it until we take over, right? Thanks. We'll see you then."

Simon sighed. *Sounds more like I need to show up around seven tomorrow, but sure, Holly. Whatever you say.*

CHAPTER 5

SATURDAY, JULY 5

SIMON YAWNED AND poured himself another cup of coffee from the office pot. Saturday morning of this long weekend was actually starting out pretty tame—compared to yesterday.

He'd left Skipper back in their cabin, still asleep, face planted in his pillow, a leg and an arm hanging off the top bunk. In solitary quiet, Simon had spent the hour between 7:00 and 8:00 a.m. cleaning the swimming complex's three pools and gathering up the dirty towels from yesterday. Next, he drove around to the rec hall to unlock it as instructed, intending afterward to load up on towels for the drive back. But when he opened the rec hall door, the musty smell of moisture greeted him.

He got on his hands and knees to test the floor. It seemed mostly dry on the surface, but he found a spongy dampness in several places, which signaled that the dank smell came from subfloor beneath.

"The subfloor is still wet, more so in some spots than in others." He thought for a moment. "I'm not comfortable reopening the rec hall just yet, but perhaps airing out the cabin will speed the process."

He went around and opened all the windows in the main section of the cabin comprising the kitchen and dining area for large group meals. He locked the rec hall door behind him, leaving the "Closed for Maintenance" sign posted.

"I might be able to reopen the rec hall by noon—if the fresh air clears out the remaining moisture. We'll see."

His next stop was the locked linen closet in the laundry facility, intending to put the dirty towels in the wash and pick up a load of clean towels for the swim complex.

I should go through those towels Skipper washed and see how they fared. Maybe a second wash would help.

But as he feared, the towels used on the rec hall floor would never again be the pristine white Holly insisted upon for the swim complex. Instead of rewashing the towels—a fruitless endeavor—he folded them all neatly and put the stack on a higher shelf in the closet to be used for other purposes later, then grabbed a load of good towels for the swim complex.

Back in his truck, he headed down the road. Those few hardy residents who were up and about were starting their day quietly.

In general, peace reigned over Bright Star.

I imagine every resident and guest in the park is tuckered out and sleeping in. Everyone but me, that is.

Simon's brow wrinkled when he passed Site 17. He hadn't heard anything further from Mr. Crowley since Simon evicted his son and his son's friends yesterday—not that Crowley's silence told Simon all that much. He had too many experiences with guys like Crowley to let down his guard.

Keep your ear to the ground, Fletcher. That guy has a slow fuse, and you haven't heard the last from him.

As he passed by Site 15, the Trujillos' RV sat dark and shuttered, confirming Simon's thought that Mrs. Trujillo was spending the night at the hospital with her husband.

Wonder how Mr. Trujillo is doing.

He picked up his phone, brought up the Trujillos' contact info, and dialed. Mrs. Trujillo answered on the first ring.

"Hello?"

"Mrs. Trujillo, ah, Polly? Simon Fletcher here. I'm calling to ask how Mr. Trujillo is doing this morning."

"Wes is so much better!" she enthused. "The doctor seems to think Wes may need a stent or two. He will undergo some tests today to confirm—and do call him Wes. We are forever indebted to your knowledge and quick actions yesterday."

"You're most welcome, of course. Do you need anything? Can we do something for you or, er, Wes?"

"How kind of you to offer! We don't need anything at this moment . . . except, perhaps for you to keep praying? I told Wes you were praying for him. He was very grateful."

"I'd be happy to keep praying, Polly . . . . and, especially, I am praying for the Lord to strengthen and encourage you both."

Polly's voice, a bit watery, answered, "How perfect. Thank you, again, Mr. Fletcher."

After they hung up, Simon stopped alongside the swimming complex and delivered the towels. He reached the office, unlocked the door, and at 8:45 turned over the "Office Closed" sign to read, "Office Open."

He sat, sipping coffee for an hour, until his empty stomach began to beat out a demand. *Need food, need food, need food,* it pulsed and rumbled. As soon as Holly arrived to take over, Simon intended to jet into town and sit down to a big breakfast.

But ten o'clock passed without Holly. Noon arrived, and still no Holly. Instead, Skipper pedaled up to the office, dropped his bike against the porch, and ran inside. "Hey, Fletch! I'm not late, am I?"

"Nope. You're right on time. I can't leave the office, though, until Holly takes over. How about you tidy up the swim complex restrooms and police the complex's trash? I've already cleaned the pools and stocked towels."

"Okay." The boy shot out the door as fast as he'd flown in.

Simon's stomach growled again. His fingertips tapped a cadence on the office counter, waiting on Holly, getting more impatient and hungrier by the minute. Finally, he called her.

She picked up with, "Yes, yes, we're on our way, Fletcher. There's no need to call me."

"It's just that I haven't eaten since last night, Holly, and I was planning to drive into town for breakfast as soon as you took over . . . at ten o'clock, like you said . . . and now it's lunchtime."

"I said *around* 10:00 or so. We slept in, so we must have needed the rest, and we're just finishing our breakfast. It's only 12:15. Perhaps you should have eaten breakfast before you came to work."

Simon tamped down his irritation. "Actually, because you wanted several chores done *before* I opened the office at nine o'clock, I had to get here at seven this morning. I didn't have time to eat before I left my cabin."

"Good gracious! You should have gotten up earlier!"

"Holly, unlike you and Joe, I only got five hours of sleep last night. And yesterday, I worked harder than both of you."

She huffed. "It's not like you to complain over a simple request to come in early, Fletcher. And really? You worked harder than us? *Really?* Furthermore, I don't care for your tone. Did you clean the pools and restock the towels this morning?"

Yes, Mother. Grr.

"Yes, I did. As I said, I came in at 7:00 a.m. to get those tasks done."

"And did you open the rec hall like I told you?"

"No, in fact, I didn't. I could tell by the musty smell and by patches of sponginess that the subfloor was still too wet to walk on. Instead, I opened all the windows to speed the drying process. I was thinking things should be dry enough to open about noon. I can drive over there now and check on it if you like."

Holly went quiet, but he could hear her breathing, and Simon realized she wasn't buying his rationale.

Her voice cold, she said, "I asked you nicely to open the rec hall first thing this morning, Fletcher."

"Yes, you did. However, you and Joe hired me for my expertise. I checked the floor and made the determination that the subfloor still was too wet to walk on. You don't want our residents to punch holes in the floor, do you?"

"What I want, Fletcher, is for you to *do what I tell you when I tell you.*"

Simon was stunned. "My apologies," he ground out. "I will rectify my mistake immediately."

"See that you do."

Simon grabbed another sign that read "Back Shortly," put it up in place of "Office Open," got in his truck, and headed up the road. When he reached the rec hall cabin, a few residents and guests were milling about. He nodded to them, unlocked the door, removed the "Closed for Maintenance" sign, and began closing windows. He nodded again to those waiting, returned to his truck, and told himself not to dwell on the state of the rec hall floor.

"Not my problem," he muttered under his breath. "If the floor suffers further damage, the responsibility rests on Holly. Of course, she will likely want *me* to fix it, but the blame will be on Holly . . . and her many years of facility management experience."

He shook his head. "Yeah, right."

When he returned to the office, the sign on the door was back to reading "Office Open." He didn't bother to check in, just went in search of Skipper.

"Bathrooms done?" he asked when he spotted the boy.

"Yup."

"Great. Let's get after the trash then, shall we?"

When his stomach complained yet again, he added, "As soon as we've collected and disposed of all the residents' trash and emptied the trash cans on the island, I was thinking you and I should head into town and grab some lunch. We can restock residents' firewood when we get back. What do you think?"

"What do I think? *Whoo-hoo!* Can we get pancakes? And sausage, bacon, and eggs, too?"

"Huh. Pancakes for lunch—on a Saturday?" But a vision of a tall, steaming stack drenched in butter and syrup rose in Simon's mind, and his stomach voted an enthusiastic *yes.*

"You got it, kid."

"Cool! Let's get moving!"

He and Skipper worked with a will and finished trash pickup throughout the park inside of forty minutes, something of a record, given the many questions and requests they usually fielded while working but today studiously avoided.

As they drove away from Bright Star, Simon heaved a heavy sigh. *Lord, I'm sure glad tomorrow is Sunday. I am physically beat and spiritually weary. I'm glad because what I need a lot more than pancakes is some time in deep worship and a solid Bible message.*

———————●———————

SUNDAY, JULY 6

SIMON TOWELED OFF, dressed, and turned the bathroom over to Skipper. In another twenty minutes, they'd be out the door on their way to church.

"Is Miss Finch coming by to pick us up, like usual?"

"What?" Simon was caught off guard.

"Are we riding in Miss Finch's woody?"

"Don't think so. Haven't set it up or anything."

"But we always go to church with Miss Finch. She drives or you do."

Simon deflected. "Grab your shower, Skipper, or we'll be late."

He busied himself fixing a quick breakfast of cold cereal and milk for the two of them, knowing Skipper would expect another "breakfast for lunch" after church.

As for Miss Finch? At the thought of her, that dull ache clutched at his chest.

I don't know what to tell Skipper, Lord. How do I explain to a fourteen-year-old how things got awkward between Miss Finch and me, when I can't explain it to myself? And how do I rationalize the wall that in an instant grew up between her and me . . . that high, chilly, disinterested, wall? Truth be told, I hate it, Lord, absolutely hate it! And yet, she's erected a barrier so high and wide that I can't even see over it. It's like . . .

"It's like I don't exist anymore," he muttered aloud, "like we were never friends, like we never shared the running of this place together or fellowship in you . . . or even shared danger and lived to tell of it."

He sat and put his elbows on the table. "What do I do, Lord? Can you fix this somehow? Because I'm not sure how much more of this . . . being cut away I can take."

Over on his bed, his phone jangled an incoming call.

"Better not be Holly," he growled.

It was.

"Fletcher, something tremendously important has come up. Listen, I realize you like to go to church on Sunday mornings, and I apologize again for changing your schedule, but I need you to come in and open the office at 9:00 a.m.—but before that, I need the park absolutely spotless. Pristine. Not a thing out of place."

"What tremendously important thing has come up, Holly, so important that the park has to be absolutely spotless, pristine, with nothing out of place?"

And that I have to give up my Sunday morning?

"I suppose I can tell you—although, really, I shouldn't have to give you a reason. But since you asked, a reporter and photographer from one of the top RV living magazines in the country is coming to visit Bright Star today. Isn't it wonderful? It's an online magazine with thousands of subscribers, and they intend to do a full spread on Bright Star for their readers!"

"Uh-huh. Well, Skipper and I left things in pristine condition yesterday evening around 5:00 p.m., so the park should still be clean enough for the reporter and photographer from one of the top RV living magazines in the country to check out."

And this "spread" you're so fired up about is definitely not more im-portant than Skipper and me going to church this morning.

"Like I said, Skipper and I left it in good shape last evening. So, if you want things spruced up beyond that, you and Joe should be able to manage. I mean, how badly could things have changed between then and now?"

"Pretty badly," Holly spat. "Around 5:30 last night, someone in the park got the bright idea of an all-park group barbecue and game night. About sev-enty-five people cooked, ate, partied, and played games on the island until around ten o'clock. When I came in just now, I found the island *a total mess*—which is why, Fletcher, I need you to come in *now*."

As though hearing how shrill her voice was, Holly calmed herself. "Once you have the island shipshape, you may take the rest of the morning off. But, see, people are already stirring all over the park, and most of the weekend guests will begin leaving in a few hours, creating a chaotic environment. This is why we need to run the photographer through *soon*, that is, before the mass exodus begins. You have to know that this article is for the good of Bright Star, Fletcher, the *future* of this park, of which you are . . . a part."

Only a part? Gee, I remember when we were "The Three Amigos" and you and Joe said we were partners, Holly.

He gathered himself. "Fine. We'll be there inside of thirty minutes."

"Sooner, if you can, please."

"Right."

Skipper griped and complained the entire five minutes' drive to Bright Star, employing his usual dramatic hyperbole. "Haven't had a day off in a month; gonna miss church, won't see my friends, and what about Sunday brunch? Sunday *ain't right* without brunch!"

"I know; I get you, kid. You've been picking up trash since the day you were born, your shackles weigh a ton, and the world is coming to an end. Yada, yada, yada. But don't forget: The minute we've thoroughly policed the island, we're out of here for a couple of hours. We'll miss church, but should have plenty of time to hit Maggie's for brunch if we hustle. That's *if* we hustle."

Skipper's attitude jumped out of its hole like a rodeo clown pops out of a barrel after the mad bull runs in another direction. "Really? Cool! And will Miss Finch meet us at Maggie's after church?"

Simon shrugged. "Don't know, but even if she doesn't, you and I will order everything we set our eyes on—including pie. Just gotta clean the is-land first. So, are you prepared to hustle, young Jedi?"

"You better believe it! Call me The Hustler, I'ma the Hustlemaniac, the Jedi Master of Hustle, the—"

"Yeah, yeah. Enough. Less talk and more walk."

"You got it. Watch me hustle."

CLEANUP ON THE island that morning was arduous and took them a good three hours, but the remainder of the morning was glorious. As soon as Simon and Skipper finished their work, Simon pointed his truck out the front gate—right past the office where Holly and Joe were posing on the front porch before a cameraman.

Holly made an attempt to flag Simon down, but he kept his foot on the gas and his eyes pointed forward.

If I don't look, then I didn't see her," he told himself.

"Who was that with Holly and Joe?" Skipper asked, gesturing toward the woman with a microphone talking to Joe and Holly while a cameraman shot video.

"Must be the big RV magazine that's here to interview Joe and Holly and take pictures of Bright Star. They're why we had to come in this morning and clean up the island. As soon as they finish what they're doing, Joe and Holly will take them around the park for more pictures and video. Holly said it's an online magazine with lots of readers."

"Huh. Whatever."

Simon laughed, feeling a strange sort of glee that they had escaped from Bright Star. "Exactly."

They stopped at Simon's cabin to change out of their dirty work clothes and wash up, then headed into town to Maggie's where they splurged. Simon let Skipper order whatever he wanted, more food than he thought the boy could hold . . . then he did the same.

While they waited for their order to arrive, Simon scooped up a Sunday paper left on a recently vacated table. He pulled the comics from it and handed them to Skipper, snapped open the front page, and scanned it for anything of interest. Most of the news consisted of glowing reports on the several Independence Day celebrations—in reality, the lake community patting itself on the back for pulling off yet another arduous Fourth of July day of celebration. Simon was about to turn the page when, below the fold, his eyes latched onto a heading that read **Missing Child**. The article was short and to the point.

Authorities are looking for
12-year-old Allysson Sharma,
who went missing Friday evening
following the Incline Village
Fourth of July fireworks display.
The Washoe County Sheriff's Department
has issued a missing person's bulletin
and asks the public to call the
Incline Village Sheriff's Substation
to report sightings of the missing girl.

The article provided a photo and a detailed description of the child who, the report read, "is shy and does not talk to strangers," according to her parents. "It is completely unlike Alli not to stay close to her family," her mother told reporters. "She only stepped away from our group to use the public restrooms, but she never returned."

Simon whispered a prayer for the girl's safe return and set the paper aside as two servers delivered his and Skipper's orders.

"You boys think you can eat this spread?" the waitress asked, laughing as she placed the last plate on the table.

Simon grinned. "We're willing to die trying."

"Yeah. Die trying," Skipper echoed.

After blessing the food, they tucked in and were astounded when, after twenty minutes, they had polished off everything they ordered.

"Wow," Skipper moaned, sitting back and patting his belly. "Epic."

"You're not wrong, but I may regret stuffing myself when it all settles. C'mon. We need to head back and get after our regular Sunday afternoon chores."

"But you said pie!"

"So I did. Take one to go?"

"Yeah!"

———— ⬥ ————

SIMON DIDN'T LIKE the fact that he and Skipper regularly worked Sunday afternoons, but when running an RV park, especially one as exclusive as Bright Star, the work never quit—not, at least, until September when the summer season formally ended. Still, he was relieved that Sunday afternoon signaled the official close of the three-day weekend. The resulting park exodus meant an end to his and Skipper's extra work hours.

By the time they returned to Bright Star, the expected evacuation was in full swing. The park was alive with the sounds of parents barking orders to their children and of slamming car doors, idling engines, and vehicles backing out of driveways, that last coupled with loud goodbyes as a line of cars departed the park.

Within those few hours, Bright Star returned to its normal serenity, and Simon couldn't have been happier.

"*Ahhh*."

"Ahhh what?" Skipper asked.

"*Ahhh*, peace and quiet."

"Oh. That."

"Yup. That."

Simon and Skipper worked the afternoon away like a well-oiled machine and finished off their chores by four o'clock. Simon left Skipper lounging in the pool with the Nadeau kids while he drove back to their cabin to shower, consider what he might fix for dinner, and reflect with gratitude that the long Fourth of July weekend had been successfully navigated, and all its frenzy, long hours, and effort, were over and done.

He hadn't a clue what Monday had in store.

CHAPTER 6

FOLLOWING SUNDAY'S EXODUS, Bright Star's residents went about policing their own sites, tidying up after their guests. When Simon and Skipper arrived Monday morning just before 8:00 a.m., their first task was to, yet again, collect trash and debris, and afterward detail every element of the park, returning Bright Star to its glowing glory.

Simon was actually relishing the changes in his and Skipper's relationship, the boy now shouldering his share of the work without complaint and working with a will to complete each task. But midmorning, an hour after the office opened, Holly called.

"Mr. Fletcher, I need to see you."

The "Mr. Fletcher" part told Simon things were not A-OK in Holly-world.

"Uh, see me for anything in particular?"

"The particulars are best discussed in person, Mr. Fletcher. Now, please."

"Right. I'll be there shortly."

Skipper looked Simon's way as Simon thought for a moment and said, "I'm going to drop you at the rec hall while I go talk to Holly. I'd like you to straighten the game room—it's a mess. I should be back by the time you finish. Before I drop you, though, I want to examine the rec hall's floor for damage."

At the rec hall, Simon spent several minutes on his hands and knees, studying the floor, looking for and finding the highly polished wood plank flooring subtly (and not-so-subtly) warped. Knowing that the slight dipping would only worsen over time, he pulled out his phone, placed it on the floor on its edge, and took photos of the worst of the damage.

As he drove toward the office, he prayed. *Lord, I don't understand what's gotten into Holly, but things aren't right between us. We used to be much more than merely employer and employee. In fact, it was the camaraderie Joe, Holly, and I shared that made working at Bright Star special. More than a job, it was a mission.* He thought for a moment. *I know you can fix whatever is wrong, so I'm asking that you bring peace between us again. Thank you.*

The bell on the office door jingled as Simon entered.

Holly called to him, "I'm back here."

When Simon joined her in her private office, he started to sit in the chair opposite her desk.

"No, don't sit down, Mr. Fletcher."

Simon blinked. "You want me to stand."

"Yes. I have things to say to you, and I feel it would be better for you to stand."

Huh. Got it. A proper dressing down, like in the Corps.

"All right. Fire away."

She nodded and marshalled her thoughts. "I believe you have developed a skewed view of your employment and status at Bright Star, Mr. Fletcher. I also feel your approach to our relationship has become too familiar and too forward. You have presumed to have the authority to make unilateral decisions that are not yours to make—such as evicting Mr. Crowley's son and his friends. I need you to understand that, as the park's GM, I am your boss: You work for and report to me. Furthermore, all major decisions must have my approval. Most importantly? When I give you an order, I expect it to be carried out in a timely manner, not ignored or rationalized away."

Simon frowned. "You're Bright Star's general manager?" At the same time, he was wondering, *Where's Joe in all of this?*

"In essence, yes."

"When did that happen?"

"Not your concern, Mr. Fletcher."

He took a breath. "*Understood.* Well, as a reminder, when you hired me, you and Joe called me your third partner. Told me that you needed me to make Bright Star 'happen,' that you would lean upon the advice and skills I brought to the table. The two of you also agreed that facility and security management decisions were mine to make."

"I am altering the conditions of your employment."

"So after all our shared sweat and labor to bring Bright Star to birth and make it a success, you're relegating me to, what—the position of a mere paid lackey? I'm no longer to employ the expertise you hired me for? I shouldn't use my brain, just do as I'm told?"

Holly pursed her lips. A moment later she answered, "Yes."

Simon was blown away. He began slowly wagging his head back and forth. "I hear you, Holly, but if I'm being honest, I'm disappointed and don't much like this *alteration*, as you call it. You didn't hire me to be a mindless drone, and since we're both being forthright, if I had wanted such a job, I wouldn't have left the military—"

Holly started to interrupt, but Simon, politely yet firmly, said, "I would like to finish, if I may?"

When, mouth tight, she nodded, he pulled out his phone. "Take the issue of the rec hall. I shot photos of the rec hall's floor before I came to meet with you. The floor now shows dipping. Why? Because when I gave you my advice Saturday, you chose to disregard it. Sure enough, the weekend's foot traffic, before the underlayment was completely dry, bowed the subflooring in places. And when underlayment dries 'bowed' like that, its ability to support the flooring above it is ruined. That means that not only will the subfloor remain warped, it will actually worsen over time and so will the flooring above it. As it stands, wherever the floor is warped, both the flooring planks and its underlayment must be pulled up, discarded, and replaced."

Grudgingly, Holly replied, "Fine. Send me the photos, and I'll file an insurance claim. Bright Star's policy will pay for the damages, and you can replace whatever parts of the floor needs to be replaced."

"Hold on, there. I'm not a construction guy, Holly. I don't know that I could restore the rec hall's hardwood flooring to its former beauty. If you recall, I wasn't the one to lay that floor in the first place. You'll need to hire the job out, just like you hired out the construction of the cabin."

"And yet I am convinced you can handle the task."

"Oh? And you would pay me overtime to do so, right?"

Now Holly frowned. "Why, no. I expect you to do the work within your usual allotted hours."

Simon cocked his head. "Okay, let's recap. I want to be certain I'm hearing you right. You intend to file an insurance claim and expect to receive funds sufficient to pay for the damage to the floor. Those funds will, of course, include the cost of labor to repair the damage, yet you expect me to tear up and fix the rec hall floor during my normal work hours—which isn't possible, by the way, if I'm to keep up with my regular chores. In other words, you intend to make *a profit* on the insurance claim by denying me overtime for the labor. Do I have it right?"

Holly jumped to her feet. "*That* is what I am talking about! You are insubordinate, question my decisions, and disrespect my authority!"

Simon waited several slow breaths to reply. "I'm sorry, but I won't repair the rec hall floor. As I said, I'm not a construction professional. I can and will, of course, repair the rec hall's kitchen plumbing. That falls under normal facility maintenance work I can handle."

Her mouth tightened. "I expect you to do whatever work I assign you."

"I won't be repairing the rec hall floor."

"Then consider this conversation a formal warning, Mr. Fletcher. I will write it up and put it in your file."

He nodded. "Warning received." He turned to go.

Holly said, "I am not finished, Mr. Fletcher—"

Simon cocked his head. "But I am. Feel free to replace me with someone less . . . *familiar* and *forward*, someone willing to be a drone. That's your right, but it's not what I signed up for, and it sure wasn't in our original agreement—you should check my job description to refresh your memory. For my part, I will consider my options and get back to you . . . in a timely manner."

With that, Simon pivoted and left her office.

He climbed into his truck, and as he drove slowly up the road, he prayed, *Well that didn't go well, Lord. Is it okay to remind you that I asked you to bring peace between Holly and me? 'Cause, that certainly wasn't peace.*

At the rec hall, he honked to let Skipper know he was waiting for him. While he waited, he alternatively sighed, fumed, and prayed. *I don't want to go off half-cocked or do anything precipitous or in anger, Lord. As a follower of Christ, that's not how you want me to behave. At the same time, it doesn't make sense to me that Joe is letting Holly take over the reins at Bright Star. I guess I'm wondering if he even knows the extent to which Holly has expanded her reach and how changed she is toward me.*

Please grant me your wisdom, Lord God. And . . . if I'm to leave Bright Star, I ask that you help me do so in the most professional manner possible.

Skipper ran down the embankment to the truck and jumped in. "What's next?"

Simon pulled himself together. "Brush cleanup."

"Ugh. Sorry I asked. Guess it's okay, though, as long as we have gloves."

"And long-sleeved shirts. Remember how scratched up your arms got last time we cleared dead brush?"

"Yeah. I also don't want to rip up my Bright Star polo, Fletch."

Simon smiled; Skipper had come to wear his Bright Star shirt like a badge of honor.

"I keep a couple of ratty, button-up work shirts under my seat. I suggest you wear one over your polo. As for the rest of the necessary gear? Gloves, loppers, and rakes are in the truck bed."

"Cool. Oh! As long as we're done by three o'clock?"

"That's right. I forgot you have friends coming to swim then. Don't worry; I'll cut you loose when they get here. So, let's get to it. I'd like to start at the back of the park, between Sites 12 and 13 where the dead brush is densest. We'll work our way down to Site 1, return to Site 13 and work our way down to Site 24."

In the spring, when rains were plentiful, forest grasses, shrubs, and bushes put on a lot of growth. But as spring shifted to summer and the rains were much less, grasses and many bushes withered and died from lack of water and became fire hazards. Especially in the super dry weather of mid-summer, clearing out dead, dry growth in the park, particularly between sites, was essential, because even the smallest spark might spell disaster.

Simon's train of thought reminded him of Crowley's son and his friends setting off strings of firecrackers in the park, not to mention the other fireworks they had lined up, ready to light.

He shuddered. *Doesn't Holly get it? If Skipper and I hadn't doused those aerials, we could have lost Bright Star. She's so focused on keeping Bright Star's reputation intact and keeping her residents happy, that she's lost perspective.*

Simon parked across from Site 12. While he and Skipper cut down withered branches and raked out dry grass and deadfall, Simon couldn't stop gnawing on his conversation with Holly. He also couldn't stop thinking about Joe.

Lord? It dawns on me that while Skipper and I have been busting our buns over this long weekend, we haven't seen much of Joe. I know he can't do everything he wants to just yet, but is he okay? I suppose I could ask him, but Joe's a pretty private guy.

He thought, too, about the text he'd sent Holly last Wednesday as to whose job it was to hire Miss Finch to park the new residents' RVs. Including Joe in the text exchange had worked to engage Joe in the tug-of-war between Simon and Holly.

Perhaps a similar tack would work to clear the air again.

If I sent a text to Holly and copied Joe, it would either bring Joe into the conversation or get me fired . . . which hardly matters at this point, if the situation isn't resolved soon.

Simon realized he'd come to a decision: If Holly didn't revert to the understanding under which Simon had been hired, he'd be quitting. Moving on. Leaving Bright Star.

Leaving Miss Finch.

That ever-present ache in his chest zinged him like a toothache.

Can't be helped, he told it. *It's been an entire week, and she hasn't lowered her guard once. Blasted woman has a will of iron, and she refuses to let me in.*

She hadn't always been that closed off. He found himself smiling and recalling her short, breathy *heh-heh-heh.*

That silly laugh—so stinking cute. And those crinkles at the outside corners of her eyes.

Simon sighed and shook himself. *She knows how to reach me. If she decides to. If she ever wants to.*

Miss Finch.

Stubborn old woman!

As for the text message? *I won't send it until we finish the north side of the park and start on the south side.*

He waited until he and Skipper had dumped three loads of brush to be carefully disposed of in the sheltered burn pit behind the office. He waited until the two of them drove up to Site 13, ready to attack dry brush and dead-fall down the south side of Bright Star. "Let's take a quick break, shall we?"

"Sure, Fletch. Clearing brush makes me thirsty!"

Simon parked and handed Skipper his midday snack and water bottle. Simon cracked open his own water bottle, gulped down a third of it, then picked up his phone and started keying in the message he'd been mentally composing.

> *Holly,*
> *I've given thought to our*
> *conversation this morning.*
> *Since you are dissatisfied with*
> *my work and attitude, it's your*
> *prerogative to let me go.*
> *I will start looking for other*
> *employment this evening.*
> *If you like, I can give you two-weeks'*
> *notice, time to find my replacement.*
> *It has been a joy and a pleasure*
> *bringing your and Joe's dream*
> *of Bright Star into existence.*

Okay. Here goes.

Simon sent the text to both Holly and Joe, hoping and believing Joe would respond before Holly did.

Simon was not disappointed. His phone rang minutes after he sent the text. It was Joe.

"Fletcher? You and I need to talk. I have absolutely *no* desire to let you go! What conversation with Holly are you talking about? Tell me about it."

"First, Joe, where are you?"

"Me? I . . . well, I'm at home."

"Why are you home? Are you okay?"

"Oh, I'm middling, I suppose. Just, perhaps, finding it hard to hit my stride. Fit back in."

"Is that why you made Holly Bright Star's general manager?"

"I did what?"

"Holly told me she's the GM now."

"Bright Star doesn't have a GM. We have a management team consisting of you, me, and Holly." To himself, he muttered, "Has to be that blasted magazine interview. The journalist referred to her as the GM just because she staffs the office . . . and I . . . I didn't speak up."

Tactical error, bud, Simon thought.

"So you haven't changed the terms of my employment?"

"What in the world are you talking about?"

"Holly called me into the office to reprimand me. Said the original terms of my employment have changed, that in a nutshell, I no longer have authority over the facility or security of Bright Star. From now on, I'm to do whatever she tells me to do, even should it go against my better judgment."

Here Simon paused, then continued, "Sadly, things got tense between us. She issued me a formal warning, and I said I'd be looking for employment elsewhere."

"No! Nope. No way, Fletcher. I'll . . . I'll drive down to the office and talk to her."

"Great, but since we're on the subject of Holly, I'd feel better if you and Holly would, together, reread my job description. My duties and authority as Bright Star's Facilities and Security Manager are pretty clear as presently written, but the waters have become increasingly murky since the two of you returned from Vegas."

He took a breath. "What I mean is that, when we started out last year, working jointly to plan and build Bright Star, the two of you regularly referred to me as your partner in this endeavor. Oh, I'm not saying I have a financial stake in Bright Star, but the two of you leaned heavily on the expertise I brought to the table in both the facilities management and the security aspects of the park. That's what I mean."

"I agree, Fletcher," Joe assured him. "That's how we started and, by golly, it's how we should continue."

"Okay, I'm glad to hear it, but Joe, I need to tell you that, since you two returned from Las Vegas, I'm feeling, shall we say, considerably micromanaged. Holly's continual, as in *daily*, *hourly*, and *minute-by-minute* 'guidance' is not sitting well with me. As a professional in my field, I don't need her to tell me how to do my job."

Now Joe sighed. "I know we asked a lot of you while I was out of commission, Fletcher. You shouldered *all* of the management responsibilities here, and did so brilliantly. Truth is, without you, Skipper, and Miss Finch putting yourselves out there, we could very well have lost Bright Star before the park even got off the ground. And I also know Holly hasn't . . . properly expressed her gratitude to either you or Miss Finch. For that, I apologize and will—"

Simon's phone warbled another incoming call. He glanced at the screen.

"Excuse me, Joe. Holly's calling me on the other line now, probably to chew me out for copying you on my text. Like I said, our recent conversation ended on a contentious note."

"Don't return her call, Fletcher. I'll come in and talk to her as soon as we hang up. But first, I need to know what the issue was when she called you in."

Simon glanced at Skipper. Wide-eyed, he was taking in Simon's side of the conversation.

"The issue is about the rec hall specifically, but in reality, the situation has been ongoing since you and Holly returned. Over this past weekend, things came to a boil. After the rec hall kitchen sink sprang a leak on Friday, and Skipper and I sopped up the considerable water on the floor, I posted a 'Closed for Maintenance' sign on the rec hall door, and advised Holly that the subfloor would need more time to dry.

"The next morning, Saturday, even though I advised against it, she instructed me to reopen the hall. I went, checked the flooring, and felt sponginess in places. Exercising my prerogative as the facilities manager, I opened all the windows and kept the 'Closed for Maintenance' sign up. When Holly asked me if I'd reopened the rec hall, I explained that I hadn't and why. She then *ordered* me to open the rec hall."

"Oh, dear."

"Right. She did not take my response well. This morning, she called me into her office, made me stand in front of her desk like a recalcitrant schoolboy, and as Bright Star's "GM," told me things had changed. From now on, I was to obey her orders and report to her.

"Of course now, because Holly required me to open the rec hall against my better judgment, the subfloor is warped, and the wood floor above it is too. The ruined elements of the floor need to be replaced. She told me the insurance would pay to fix the floor, and she wanted me to do the work. However, because she didn't intend to pay me to fix the floor, and since I didn't build the cabin and lay the original flooring, I refused."

"That went over well, I'll bet."

"Yeah, we were pretty far down the road by then. We left it with me looking for work elsewhere, and her finding someone to take my place."

"Nope. Not going to happen, Fletcher. I'll . . . I'll handle this."

"Uh, Joe?"

"Yes?"

"May I make an observation?"

"Of course."

"You're struggling a bit, trying to find and hit your stride again."

Joe sighed. "Yeah. I admit it. I am . . . flailing about."

"May I add a comment, boss?"

"I think I know what you're going to say, but go ahead."

"Thanks, Joe; I appreciate your trust in me. It's that, well, you can't just check out because you're having a tough time, right? Nature abhors a vacuum, and your absence here in the park has left a significant hole, which Holly has quite willingly stepped in to fill."

"You're saying I need to get off my backside and at least show up?"

"It's easier to steer a moving vehicle and all that jazz. Alternatively, 'flailing about' at home isn't going to help you get going again."

Joe was silent for several moments. "I know you're right, Fletch. I'll do better. Get myself up and out of here, if only to set things right concerning Bright Star's management team."

"Then may I make yet another observation and offer a suggestion, Joe?"

"Of course, Fletcher."

"Thank you. My observation is that Holly lacks the self-restraint *not* to micromanage my work. My suggestion is that I report exclusively to you. I realize how this might strain your relationship with Holly for a while, but if I cannot garner the respect and autonomy that my job title and qualifications should entail, then it's possible Bright Star is no longer a good fit for me . . ."

He let his thought trail off, and Joe went quiet for a long moment. When he answered, he asked softly, "Are you saying you're still thinking of leaving, Fletcher?"

Simon blew out a breath of frustration. "It's not like I *want* to leave Bright Star, Joe."

He left the "but" unspoken.

"I see. I'll . . . get back to you."

"Okay, thanks, Joe."

He was halfway to their next cleanup point before he realized how quiet Skipper was. He turned and was shocked to see the boy's face turned to the window, his shoulders trembling.

Simon pulled off the road immediately. "Skipper? Skip?"

Skipper's shoulders heaved once, but he didn't respond; instead, Simon thought he heard the boy sob.

"Skipper? What is it?"

"Y-you're gonna leave? Without saying anything, just like that, you're gonna go?"

"No. At least, I hope not—"

"I thought you were different!"

Simon reached for the boy. "Now, hang on a sec, Skipper. This doesn't have anything to do with you—"

"No! Leave me alone!"

Skipper threw open the truck door and jumped out.

"Skipper. Wait. Let's talk . . ."

But the boy stumbled across the road, clambered up the embankment onto the island and disappeared, leaving Simon stunned and aggrieved.

After the intense labor of the long weekend had passed, Simon had not expected Monday to produce such a sharp break in his relationship with Holly. And after the many difficulties he and Skipper had surmounted to this point, he had certainly not planned to hurt Skipper in the process!

How deep was the breach between them? Could it be fixed?

Perhaps not.

Not if the frozen state of his friendship with Miss Finch were any indicator.

Lord? How did everything that was so good here at Bright Star suddenly turn into such a mess? I don't get it.

Please! Please help.

The TAHOE MYSTERIES

CHAPTER 7

FOR THE NEXT hour, Simon cleared brush by himself, chopping, hacking, raking, and filling the bed of his truck, all the while thinking, praying, and mentally kicking himself while he worked.

Way to go, Simon Fletcher, he growled internally. *You took a kid whose father has abandoned him, a kid just barely starting to feel loved and secure, and you let **your** frustrations out of the bag to run amok all over him. Yup. You gave Skipper exactly what he did **not** need to hear—that yet another adult in his life, one he had grown to trust, was going to abandon him. Yeah. Well done, **you bozo**.*

Lord, I admit it. You put this kid in my life to help him, and I blew it. Please show me how to make it right with him.

Every few minutes, he called Skipper's phone. Each time, it went immediately to voicemail. "Skipper, please call me," was the message he left.

He texted the same message, but received no response, so when he finished filling the truck bed, he began driving around, scanning for the boy. The first place he checked was the rear section of the rec hall. Skipper had spent many of his afternoons after work playing video games in the game room.

He wasn't there.

Simon drove around to the swim complex and checked there too.

No joy.

He sprinted back to his truck, just as the three Nadeau kids rode up to him on their bikes. Seeing them on their bikes, made him wonder if Skipper hadn't taken his bike when he left.

The eldest of the kids, Wyatt, asked, "Hi, Mr. Fletcher. We were hoping Skipper would take us riding in the woods. Is he around?"

"Uh, not at the moment. He works with me most days, you know, although he usually gets his chores done quickly so that he has more time in the afternoon to play video games or ride his bike. Next time you see him, ask if, some afternoon when he's off work, he can take you into the woods, okay?"

He broke off, got into his truck, drove through the front gate, and slowed down at the office to see if Skipper's bike was beside the porch. While Joe and Holly were gone, Simon had allowed Skipper to park his bike in the office; once Joe and Holly had returned from Vegas, Holly had required Skipper to keep his bike elsewhere. Simon bought Skipper a locking bike chain, and Skipper now kept his bike parked off the side of the office porch, chained to the porch railing, the key to its lock on a lanyard around Skipper's neck.

The bike was gone.

Simon left his truck and plodded to the gate. He stared beyond the island's promontory and dancing fountains, toward the trailhead, roughly equidistant from the office and Site 24.

Maybe he rode his bike into the woods?

Skipper and two of his friends, sisters Becka and Melissa, granddaughters of the Gormans in Site 21, and another boy, Bruce, who was spending much of the summer at Bright Star with his uncle and aunt, Frank and Gretchen Muller, often rode their bikes together on the forest trails. However, Becka and Melissa had spent the Fourth of July weekend with their other grandparents, and Bruce's parents, ER docs in Oregon, had wrangled the long weekend off from work and had taken Bruce snorkeling in Aruba. But Skipper had an aversion to exploring the forest when he was alone, so Simon doubted the kid would go riding the trails on his own.

Where else would he go?

One place, perhaps.

Simon went back to his truck and drove reluctantly toward Site 1. He stopped at the top of the driveway, got out, walked partway down the drive, and halted.

Miss Finch was seated outside under her little awning as usual, Pouncer and Hugo close to her, Skipper nowhere to be seen. Miss Finch eyed Simon with wary eyes, her greeting detached.

"Yes, Mr. Fletcher?"

That ache in Simon's chest made sure he knew it was still alive and kicking. Kicking hard.

"I'm looking for Skipper. Have you seen him recently?"

She blinked and the wariness gave way to concern. "Not since the two of you cleared away the brush and deadfall along the road nearby, but that was several hours ago. Why do you ask?"

Simon stared at the toes of his work boots. "He got upset with me and took off. Can't think of many places he might go, but his bike is gone."

"Could he have ridden into the woods?"

Simon shook his head. "I doubt it. Not by himself."

"Perhaps . . . perhaps he went back to your cabin?"

Simon thought for a moment and nodded. "Yeah. I suppose that's a possibility. Thanks."

With nothing more to say, he returned to his truck, flipped a U-turn, and drove the wrong way on the road the short distance to the front gate. Two cars were now parked in front of the office, most likely belonging to the guests of Bright Star residents, stopping to check in.

He ignored them and sped through the gate and down Bright Star's road. Two hundred yards later, he pulled off the road and into the Mitchells' yard. He looked but saw no sign of bicycle tire tracks in the loose gravel. He took a quick look around anyway, then pulled back onto the road.

He soon arrived at the cabin Skipper had shared with him since Joe's accident and went inside. The customary disorder of the cabin's single room was considerably less, in the main, Simon realized, because a lot of the things Skipper usually left lying around in disarray were gone. His duffle bag, pillow, and sleeping bag were gone too, as was the handful of bungee cords Simon kept hanging from a nail on the wall.

Looks like he loaded everything onto his bike . . . but went where?

He felt an urge to check for his small tent, usually stored under the bunk beds.

It, too, was gone.

Skipper is leery of riding too far into forest alone yet now he's what? Planning to camp out by himself somewhere deep in the woods? That makes no sense.

With worry drumming a call to quarters in his gut, Simon drove back up the road to the office.

He pulled over behind the two cars still parked there. A man and two teens standing by the rear car waved at him, and Simon recognized them as Skipper's friends from the church youth group, Zane and Kevin, and Kevin's dad, Tobias.

Crud. Skipper invited Zane and Kevin to swim today. Super. What in the world do I tell them?

He got out and plastered on a fake smile. "Hey guys. Tobias. How's it going?"

How's it going? Good one, Fletcher; real smooth.

Tobias offered his hand, and they shook. "Hey, Fletcher; just dropping off the boys. Do you know where Skipper is? We've been calling and texting, but haven't gotten a reply."

"I'm afraid he . . . may have forgotten they were coming to swim today." Squeezing those words through his teeth was like eking out the last dab of toothpaste from the very end of the tube.

Zane's eyes narrowed. "But we were texting with him about it until a couple of hours ago, Mr. Fletcher."

"Uh, and he hasn't texted you since then?"

Zane frowned. "Actually . . . no."

Kevin, picking up on Simon's ill-concealed concern, shifted from foot to foot and asked, "Is Skipper okay, Mr. Fletcher?"

Simon sighed. "Not sure. Truth be told, Skipper and I had a little . . . spat today."

"What's a spat?"

"It's a disagreement. Anyway, he took off, and I haven't seen him since. I'm sure he'll come around before long and he and I will get things ironed out, but since he's not here at the moment, I suppose we'll have to . . . postpone the swim thing to another day."

Zane and Kevin looked at each other with consternation; Tobias's brow creased in empathy. "Well, Skipper's a teen . . . and a relatively new Christian, isn't he?"

Simon cleared his throat. "Yes, only a couple of weeks old in the Lord. Lots of rough edges and . . . some hurt places."

Tobias briefly placed one hand on Simon's shoulder. A simple gesture of reassurance.

"God can fix this. We'll pray for you both—won't we, boys?"

"Yeah, we will," Zane said. Kevin nodded his agreement.

But the two teens looked as worried as Simon felt.

"Thanks. I really appreciate it. Uh, we still on for Thursday night?"

The promised star gazing event down on Baldwin Beach.

Kevin answered, "Yup. Pastor Kent has a guy lined up to talk to us. He knows all about stars and galaxies and stuff."

Zane added, "And some of the parents are supplying food so we can eat dinner before it gets dark. I heard they're bringing an already cooked barbecue dinner since we can't barbecue on the beach. 'Course, most everybody is coming to see Miss Finch do her card tricks."

Tobias added, "To be honest, Miss Finch's card tricks are all the youth group has talked about since Zane and Kevin told us about her. Barbecue and the Milky Way? They don't hold a candle to the tales these boys have spun around her."

"I'm sure she won't let you down."

Sure. She would never let you kids down. Me, on the other hand? Chopped liver.

Grr.

Simon watched as they got in their car, turned around at the gate, and drove off before he glanced up at the sky and took notice of a band of dark clouds edging in from the northwest. Tahoe was a mountain lake; afternoon and evening mountain showers were not uncommon.

Was Skipper really planning to camp out somewhere on Bright Star's thirty acres? He and Simon had camped in Miss Finch's site, behind her trailer not that long ago, but Simon doubted Skipper would recall how to set up the tent and the rain fly, let alone recall the wisdom of trenching the tent's perimeter against a heavy rainfall, and staking down the tent's corners and rain fly nice and taut in case the wind kicked up.

Lord, you have to help me! I haven't a clue what to do next.

While standing there muddling through his options, he realized a woman was sitting in the passenger seat of the first parked car. Rather, he noticed a woman's arm hanging out the open car window, a lit cigarette dangling from her fingers . . . its hot coal suspended carelessly over the dry grass between the road and the office porch.

At the same time, he heard the murmur of overlapping voices coming from the office, Holly and a man, presumably the driver of the car . . . going at it? Simon had received a text from Joe an hour ago saying he'd spoken to Holly and would catch Simon up later, but at the moment he needed to head into town to pick up the Trujillos and bring them home from the hospital.

Simon, who wasn't interested in another encounter with Holly today, hadn't paid much attention to her conversation with the driver of the parked car, nor did he want to involve himself in her business. Besides, Holly could usually hold her own. Simon rather pitied the man who ignorantly thought otherwise.

Simon was more focused on the dangling cigarette and the danger it posed.

His eyes followed the arm hanging out the window to the youngish woman who was, obviously, waiting for the car's driver. Simon moved to where he had a better angle to watch her through her lowered passenger window.

That's when he caught motion in the back seat, and a set of wide blue eyes peered out at him. A kid, perhaps three, belted into a booster seat.

Simon nodded to the child and returned his attention to the woman in the front passenger seat. She was blond, pretty, maybe in her late twenties . . . though based on the downturned corners of her mouth, quite bored. She took a drag on the cigarette and, out of habit, flicked away the ash without looking. A spark from the coal flew with the ash to the ground.

Simon's eyes followed the ash and watched it until he was convinced the spark was out.

Guests often skip over our signage and don't realize Bright Star is a non-smoking property. From the moment a vehicle turns onto Bright Star's road, no unauthorized fires or smoking of any kind are allowed—period.

Like we need additional fire hazards in the woods in July!

In any case, I'm not budging until the driver comes out and I have an opportunity to remind him and his passenger of our no smoking—

The conversation inside, rising in volume and anger, jerked Simon's attention away from the lit cigarette. He heard Holly struggling to be heard over the man's raised voice. She finally shouted, "And I am telling you *no*, you may *not*. We have a court order to that effect, and you have no standing here! Now, if you do not leave the premises immediately, I will call the police and have you arrested for trespassing!"

Simon changed his mind about keeping out of Holly's business. He charged up the porch and barreled through the office door.

Inside he found a stranger, a man of perhaps forty years or so, fairly fit, but whose hair was beginning to gray, and whose face was contorted and scarlet with rage. Worse, he was shaking his clenched fist very near Holly's mouth. Holly, as usual, appeared undeterred and wagged her finger under the man's nose.

"You will leave Bright Star right this minute!" she responded at the same volume.

If Simon hadn't known Holly as well as he did, he would have missed the faint note of desperation she was trying hard to hide.

"We'll just see about that," the man shouted back.

Simon, employing his best Marine MP voice, bellowed, "Hey!"

Both the stranger and Holly jerked, swiveled, and stepped apart, startled.

Holly recovered first. "Fletcher! Am I glad to see you! This man—"

The man, who looked suspiciously familiar, glared at Simon. "Who do you think you are?"

Still employing his authoritative voice, Simon answered, "Me? I'm Simon Fletcher, Bright Star's Security Manager, and regardless of your beef, I'm ordering you to *step away* from Mrs. Mitchell immediately and *calm down*. If you do not obey my order, I will remove you bodily from this building, escort you to your car, and see you off the premises—and believe me, I am well able to do so."

The man's eyes widened. Still shaking with anger, he appeared to be weighing Simon's threat, particularly the impressive breadth of Simon's shoulders and chest.

Simon added, "Sir, when you have yourself under control, we can see about handling your issue in a civil manner."

Simon's threat worked. The man took a step away from Holly and settled noticeably.

Tucking his thumbs into his belt, Simon then asked, "Holly, what seems to be the problem here?"

The man started to speak; Simon's hand shot out in the universal sign for "stop."

"Holly? Why don't you start by introducing me to this gentleman."

Holly took a breath. "Sure, Fletcher. This . . . man," she gestured to the stranger, "is Pete Mitchell, Joe's brother."

Pete Mitchell? At first Simon didn't get it.

Not until Holly added, "Fletcher, he's . . . Skipper's father."

Skipper's father. Those two words landed like a lead weight in Simon's heart. *No wonder this guy looks familiar; Skipper takes after him.*

*Skipper's dad? No, Skipper's **deadbeat** dad.*

Before he could help himself, Simon rounded on the man. "*You.*"

It was one word, one solitary word, but that single syllable held an invective wrapped in a snarl, charged with accusation, and infused with loathing and disgust. And the guy felt and understood every nuanced facet of Simon's intended meaning.

Pete Mitchell's mouth clamped shut. His blinking eyes dropped to the floor. In a small, defeated voice he muttered, "I know . . . I know. Look. I just . . . I just wanted to see my son."

Simon was ashamed of himself. He had heard what came out of his mouth exactly the same way Pete Mitchell heard it.

Dear God, what is wrong with me lately!

For a long, protracted moment, the office was quiet.

Finally, Holly whispered, "Fletcher?"

Simon sighed and looked up. She seemed as startled by his uncharacteristically unkind outburst as he was. He shook his head.

I'm a mess. I can't help you, Holly—can't you see that?

"Please, Fletcher?" Holly whispered. "Joe isn't here, and I don't . . . I can't . . ."

Simon finally nodded. "Mr. Mitchell? Pete?"

The man swallowed and looked up. "Yes?"

"Look, here's the situation. Before the school year ended, Skipper got himself into some trouble."

"What!"

There was that anger again, but Simon recognized it as anger hunting for a place to lay blame. He'd seen it regularly as an MP and an MP investigator. It was common in young men who refused to take responsibility for their own decisions and actions.

"What kind of trouble?" Mitchell demanded.

Simon's "stop" hand signal snapped up. "Watch your tone, or this conversation is over. As for the details, they aren't important at the moment. What is important is that Skipper got into the kind of trouble that gets you in front of a judge."

"A judge! *Wow*. Wouldn't you know it. I mean, I figured Kathy wasn't up to taking care of Skipper, but *this—*"

Simon's disdain for the guy rose to the surface again, but this time he managed to slap some semblance of a rein on it. "Listen up, Mitchell: Want to know why Skipper got into trouble? He got into trouble because *his dad*, the guy who was supposed to *raise him to manhood*, up and left him and his mom high and dry. Yeah, *you*. You abandoned your wife and son, and you left them with zero support, forcing your wife to work two jobs to keep from losing her and Skipper's home, which left *no one* around to give a crap about *your son* and his activities—so I'd better not hear you running down Skipper's mom. *She* didn't bug out on him. Do you get me?"

At the last second, Simon refrained from drilling a finger into Pete Mitchell's chest.

"Now, are you going to let me finish?"

Mitchell acquiesced with a meek, "Okay."

"The judge gave Skipper probation in the form of house arrest for the entire summer, but Kathy, who has to work twelve hours a day, knew that Skipper, left to his own devices, would likely get himself in trouble again, so she petitioned the judge to allow Skipper to serve his probation working at Bright Star over the summer under Joe and Holly's supervision. You tracking with me so far?"

"Yeah. I mean, yes sir."

"Good. What happened next, is that your brother Joe got into a very bad car accident near Vegas just before Memorial Day Weekend. His injuries kept him in the hospital and rehab for close to a month—oh, you didn't know about Joe's accident, huh? Well, you can ask him about it later, because this conversation is about Skipper. So, while Joe and Holly were stuck in Vegas, Skipper's supervision was transferred to me. He lives with me and works for me. He doesn't eat, drink, sleep, or breathe unless I tell him he can. Are you with me?"

Pete frowned. "I think so."

Simon was laying it on thick, and he'd jumped over the part where the "transfer" of Skipper's supervision had been an entirely off-the-cuff verbal understanding among Joe, Holly, and Simon, but he wasn't going to elaborate.

He'd had experience with other Pete Mitchells, guys who swung like a pendulum, one moment compliant, the next moment shifting recrimination onto someone else. Simon knew for a fact that Mitchell's attempts to absolve himself would crop up again if Simon gave him opportunity.

He continued, "A person under house arrest isn't allowed to leave their home. Same thing here. Skipper isn't allowed to leave Bright Star and anyone he sees or spends time with has to go through me. Pass my inspection. Any questions?"

No way was Simon going to allow a surprise visit from this chump to mess up the good progress Skipper was making at Bright Star! He sighed inside. *Cause I'm pretty much managing to mess that up myself.*

Pete Mitchell lifted his eyes to Simon. "Are you saying you won't let me see Skipper?"

Simon folded his arms across the wide expanse of his Bright Star polo shirt. "Tell me why you want to see Skipper. Convince me how it will be for his good."

Pete seemed surprised. "Well, he's my kid. Of course I want to see him."

"He's your kid, and *of course* you want to see him, yet the fact that he's your kid hasn't been enough reason to financially support him?"

Mitchell's face reddened. "That's none of your business."

Simon leaned into the man's personal space. "It's my business because it directly affects me. If you were paying your share of Skipper's upkeep, Kathy wouldn't have to work two jobs and could be home in the evenings and on weekends to supervise Skipper. And if she had been able to properly care for Skipper this past spring, he might not have gotten into trouble, thus I might not be *doing your job right now*. See how that works?"

Mitchell's anger drained, leaving him looking slightly ill. "That . . . that's . . ."

"That's the cold, hard truth, Pete, so let's start over. Tell me why you want to see Skipper. Convince me how it will be good for him."

Pete stared at the floor for a minute, thinking, trying to frame a response. "Well, I thought maybe I could say I was sorry . . . for leaving the way I did. Without saying goodbye or anything."

"That's a start. Is that all you'd planned to do with Skipper? Have what amounts to a five-minute conversation?"

"No! I thought we could take him out, you know, for lunch or something, maybe drive him around the lake."

"Who's 'we'? Who's the girl waiting in the car?"

"Uh, that would be Shelly."

"And Shelly is who, exactly?"

"My friend. Girlfriend. Fiancée, actually."

"Figures. And the kid?"

"Shelly's little girl."

Simon shook his head. "Well, isn't that all kinda awesome? So, while you're apologizing to Skipper for leaving him without saying goodbye and for breaking up his family, you'll just casually introduce him to your *new* family, is that it? Tell him 'sorry' on the one hand, but 'not sorry' on the other?"

The spark Simon had been expecting fired in Mitchell's eye. He studied Simon for a long moment, before his lips twisted into a sneer. "Oh, I get it now. You don't want me to see Skipper because you've styled yourself as Skipper's new and improved dad. Yeah, that's it, isn't it? You're *so* much better than me, but you don't want me horning in on your action, so you're looking for reasons to deny me access to Skipper. Well, guess again—he's my son, *not yours*, and you can't keep me from seeing him!"

Amazement washed over Simon, followed swiftly by comprehending anger. Yeah, he'd seen similar reactions in the military many times—the same narcissistic blame-shifting.

"You're wrong on that count, Mitchell. As honored as I'd be to have Skipper as my son, he *isn't*, thus I don't view him as such. Also? Changing the subject won't work because we're not talking about me, Mitchell, we're talking about *you*, how you ditched your kid more than a year ago and went all stealth mode on him. Not a word in more than a year, yet you show up, unannounced, and expect him, inside of an hour or an afternoon, to forgive your abrupt departure from his life? No, I think the real reason you're here is to show off your hot young 'fiancée, a woman closer to your son's age than to yours, and introduce Skipper to his new 'sister.'"

Mitchell's confidence visibly wobbled for a second, before his expression hardened. "My fiancée is none of your business. I came here to see my son. Now, where is he?"

Lord, this guy's a trainwreck married to a five-alarm fire, and if I'm being honest, I don't want Skipper anywhere near him. Please grant me your wisdom here. And by the way? Please show me where to find Skipper and how to mend our relationship?

A moment later he found himself saying aloud, "Skipper is fourteen and doesn't have to see you if he chooses not to. I will ask him to consider it—but I won't rush him into a decision."

Again Pete Mitchell sneered at Simon. "Oh, yeah—I can just hear you 'asking him to consider it.'"

Simon ignored the dig. "Can you stick around Tahoe a day or two?"

"I suppose I don't have a choice, do I?"

"It's not a matter of choice; it's a matter of how much importance you place on seeing your son. Give me your cell number. I'll get back to you once I talk it over with Skipper."

As soon as I find him, that is, Simon thought as he took Mitchell's number.

"And oh, and by the way? Bright Star is a no-smoking, zero-tolerance property. When I came in, your sweet young thing was hanging her lit cigarette out the window of your car like we're not parked in the middle of Smokey Bear country. If, after you've driven away, I find ashes or a cigarette butt on our grounds, your odds of seeing Skipper drop to nil. You feel me?"

"Whatever."

"I see where Skipper gets it."

Shooting Simon a scathing glare, Mitchell turned on his heel and marched out the door. Simon and Holly both waited for Mitchell's car to start and pull away before they breathed again.

"Oh my, Fletcher," Holly gasped, when the sound of Pete's car faded down the road. "I've never heard you sound so . . . blunt. So cold and hard, I guess."

"Yeah. Not my proudest moment. Sorry, Holly." He started to leave.

"No, wait! Fletcher, a moment, please? What I mean is . . . Joe spoke to me about his conversation with you, that you're . . . unhappy with things at Bright Star, and he said something similar. That you didn't . . . you don't sound like your usual self."

Simon had to be honest with her. "I'm not unhappy with 'things,' Holly. I'm unhappy with *you*."

She swallowed. Slowly nodded. "Joe told me, but it was hard to for me to hear. He said if things didn't change, you were serious about leaving Bright Star, and we, Joe and I, had a fight over it. Then Mrs. Trujillo called asking for a ride from the hospital, and Joe left, still mad, not even ten minutes before Pete got here."

She sighed. "When Pete walked in and demanded to see Skipper, he said he was going to take him away for the afternoon. I tried to tell him about the court order, that Skipper wasn't allowed to leave the premises, but Pete wouldn't listen. Then he started shouting at me, and I didn't know what to do. I thought he might actually hit me!"

She sighed. "I was so relieved when you showed up. Talk about perfect timing . . ."

She stared at her hands. "I think that's when I finally realized that I can't . . . I can't actually run this place and handle every situation on my own, that I need you and Joe . . . a lot more than I thought I did."

Tears glistening in her eyes, she pleaded with Simon. "Fletcher, please don't leave. Joe says you told him I treat you like a-a *kid* and that he agrees with you. He said that from now on you're going to report to him instead of me. Fletcher, I'm sorry. I've decided I'm okay with you reporting to Joe. Just please . . . please don't leave. We truly are partners in this place, and Bright Star wouldn't be the same without you."

Simon studied Holly. He'd never seen her quite as vulnerable as she was in this moment, not even after Joe's accident. A great weight shifted and began to roll from Simon's shoulders. Not everything, but a significant mass.

"You won't change your mind, Holly? Won't slip back into your old ways of trying to tell me how to do my job?"

"N-no. At least I don't think I will."

"Can we agree that if you do start trying to micromanage me again, it will be okay for me to call you on it?"

"Y-yes. It will be okay. Again, I'm sorry, Fletcher."

"I . . . I forgive you, Holly."

Holly's eyes shot up to his. "You do?"

"Yes. It's over now. Behind us. Water under the bridge."

She seemed uncertain. "Just like that?"

"Actually, just like Jesus forgives me, Holly. Just like that. I want to treat you the way he treats me."

Holly's lower lip sort of "popped" loose from the top one. Dropped an iota.

Holly wasn't the hugging type—not by a long shot—so Simon took a page from Kevin's dad, Tobias, and did what he'd done. Simon reached out his hand and gently touched Holly's shoulder.

A simple gesture of reassurance.

Jesus, would you cross over from me to Holly, and let her feel you through me? Just a bit? She really needs you.

Then he left the office, and strode to his truck. On the way, he checked where Pete Mitchell's car had been parked. There, where Pete's sweet young thing had been flicking her cigarette ashes, the dry grass was heavily scuffed. Not an ash or a butt to be found.

He took me at my word. Good.

Then Simon climbed into his truck, bowed his head, and prayed. "Lord, I'm sorry. This mess with Skipper is my fault. I allowed my disgruntled feelings for Holly to get into my head and my heart until they got the best of me. I didn't bring those concerns to you the way I should have; instead, I let my sense of being wronged fester . . . right up to the point where I threatened to quit Bright Star and leave Joe and Holly high and dry, all without a single thought of how my angry words would affect them . . . or Skipper. I blew it with him, Lord. Me and my big mouth. No wonder he ran off!"

He sighed and added, "Speaking of Skipper, Lord, I really do need your help, first to find him and second to walk with him through the sudden appearance of his dad and how it will affect him. Obviously, I'm not up to the task on my own, yet I have only one friend close by who might be up for the challenge. The trouble is, I don't know if she still considers me a friend."

He shook his head. "I know what I need to do next, Lord, but that doesn't mean I'm looking forward to it. And I'm sorry for asking so many times today, but would you help me, please? Help us?"

Sighing, he added, "Thank you."

Simon drove through the gate and headed down the road to face off with his personal boogeyman. It was time to clear the air and let the chips fall where they may.

CHAPTER 8

SIMON PARKED AT the top of Site 1 and strode down the long drive. Since Pouncer had not yet demonstrated friendly feelings toward Napoleon, and since Nappy was—*quite* understandably—terrified of Pouncer, Simon left the dog in the truck, whimpering after his departing back.

He didn't slow partway down the drive this time. Didn't stop until he'd reached Miss Finch's trailer. However, she was no longer sitting outside in her chair. A quick glance around told him she wasn't elsewhere in her site. Her trailer's door, however, was open and latched to the trailer's side, so he knocked on the trailer wall beside the screen door.

Hugo bounded to the door, wagging all over, happy to see him. She arrived soon after.

"Yes, Mr. Fletcher?"

"Enough with the 'Mr. Fletcher' baloney. We need to talk."

"Do we?"

"Oh, stuff a cork in it! We certainly do and you know it. Listen, Skipper's dad just popped up out of thin air and wants to see his kid. By the way, I still haven't found Skipper, and the dude who calls himself Skipper's dad is a piece of work. I told the guy he can only see Skipper if Skipper agrees to see him, so I need to find that kid ASAP. That said, I don't know where else to look for him, and it's going to be dark early in a few hours, because we have rain coming our way."

Silence. Followed by, "I will be out directly."

"*I will be out directly*," Simon snarked under his breath as he moved away from the door to wait.

A moment later, the screen door opened and Hugo scampered down the steps. He raced to Simon, ran around him three times, then stopped in front of him and sat, his tongue hanging out to one side.

For the first time in what had only been days but seemed like years, Simon grinned and some of the stress he was carrying bled off. He squatted and scratched Hugo's head exactly where the little guy liked it. "Hey, buddy. Have you missed me? I've sure missed you."

Miss Finch stepped down from her trailer. She did not sit in her usual chair or approach Simon. Instead, she stood several feet away, hands atop her cane, and cleared her throat. "You wished to speak?"

Simon kept petting Hugo. "Yup. You and I? We need to stop with the whole avoidance and silent treatment, because, frankly? It's killing me."

He sighed and looked up at her. "You. *You're* killing me with your cold shoulder business, BeeDee. It isn't right, not by any measure! I mean, what, *exactly*, did I do to warrant the loss of your trust and friendship?"

Hugo shifted under Simon's hand and turned about ninety degrees, fixing his blissful eyes on the woods across the driveway. Simon figured the terrier had heard the rustle of a bird or a squirrel. He kept absentmindedly scratching the dog on the top and back of his head.

Miss Finch didn't answer, so Simon pressed on. "Look, I admit to doing nothing wrong, but let's say I *may have* looked at you . . . 'cross-eyed' last week. So what? Does that mean we're now polite frenemies, or worse yet, complete strangers?"

Miss Finch lifted her chin. "You looked at me 'cross-eyed,' hmm? Is that what they're calling it these days?"

Simon snarled to himself. *Yeah, well what would you call it, my oh-so-proper and totally **terrified** Miss Finch? That I looked at you all googly-eyed? Smitten? Twitterpated? Whatever 'it' is, it surprised and scared the poop out of me every bit as much as it did you.*

"How about we agree to employ the term 'cross-eyed' as a nonspecific placeholder. Can we do that?"

Simon gave Hugo a final pat and stood to face Miss Finch while Hugo stared unblinking beyond the front of Miss Finch's trailer, fixated on something in the brush.

Simon added, "And suppose I promise never to do *it* again—*it* being 'that which must not be named.' Can we simply forget what may or may not have happened and agree to go back to where we were a week ago—friends in Christ and complementary co-investigators? Skipper and I miss spending time with you, and I'd like to help with that new case you're looking at, the three young men missing from around the lake area."

"Bright Star has its own missing young man, Mr. Fletcher! If you cannot locate a fourteen-year-old boy who also lives with and works for you, that hardly recommends you to act in a professional investigative role."

Simon raised his voice. "Oh, give me a freaking break!" He started to roll his eyes and stopped himself "mid-roll."

Crud! Can't believe I'm picking up Skipper's sulky teen behaviors. Been spending entirely too much time with that kid.

"Now, look here, *Finchy*—" And there it was again. Another "Skipperism."

"*Mr.* Fletcher! Do not presume—"

"Presume? As long as you continue with the *Mr.* Fletcher *crapola*, I do presume! I—"

But she interrupted with a stern, "You will mind your tongue around me, *Mr.* Fletcher."

Despite his recent prayers, Simon saw red. "Mind my tongue? Oh, sure; by all means, please, let me rephrase: As long as you continue with the *Mr.* Fletcher *rubbish*—or perhaps you prefer *baloney*, *balderdash*, *nonsense*, or *folderol?*"

He moved toward her while he talked. "Whichever term you 'prefer,' you don't get to act like you hold the high ground or pretend that you and I scarcely know each other. No, nope, *not*— as in you do *not* get to ignore the fact that we fought through some pretty rough stuff last month, and we fought through it *together*. Yet here you are, bold as brass, doing your best to fake like we've never met!"

Hands on his hips, he stood within two feet of her, staring down, his volume increasing with each word. "Well, I'm not going to put up with any-more *blarney* or *codswallop* from you, *Finchy*—do you hear me? You can call me Fletcher, Fletch, or Simon, but I don't *ever* want to hear you call me *Mr.* Fletcher again!"

She narrowed her eyes and pursed her lips. "Are you quite finished?"

He inched closer. "Nope. As far as my PI qualifications go? My investi-gative creds are undeniably longer, stronger, deeper, and *more professional* than yours. That said, my investigative experience encompasses issues con-cerning US Marines. Full-grown men and women. *Adults*. I have exactly six weeks experience with teens under my belt, so stop trying to guilt me about not knowing how to find Skipper. I don't know what makes young boys tick—and by the way? Neither do you."

"I suppose that is true . . . to a degree." It was a reluctant admission, but an admission, even so.

"It certainly *is* true! Nevertheless, regardless of what expertise either of us can boast of, I need to find Skipper . . . and I need wisdom in dealing with his dad."

She slowly nodded and asked in a calmer, quieter tone, "What caused you to place conditions on the gentleman seeing his son?"

"You mean why did I tell Skipper's dad that it was up to Skipper whether or not they saw each other? Maybe it was because the guy showed up with a "fiancée" on his arm. Not only is she too young for the guy, she also has her daughter with her, and the whole "meet my new family" scenario isn't going to go over well with Skipper. He's hurting enough as it is without dumping gasoline on the fire."

Miss Finch murmured, "Indeed." She slipped out from under Simon's looming nearness and subsided into her lawn chair. "You say you've searched all Skipper's usual haunts?"

"Of course I have, but I doubt he planned on holing up in any of those places. When I searched our cabin, I found that he'd taken my tent and his sleeping bag with him. Looks like he intends to camp out, probably some-where on Bright Star property."

"He cannot camp long without food," she observed.

"Huh. I didn't think to look in the cupboards. He probably took a few easy meals, ramen noodles, that sort of thing."

"One cannot live on dry ramen alone; one must also have water and fire, not to mention a camp pot."

"Essential facts Skipper may be discovering for himself, but let's get back to my qualifications to assist in your investigation of those missing men—"

Hugo, his body taut, every part fixed on the bushes across the driveway, growled low in his throat.

Simon frowned. "What's up with Hugo? You haven't had any bears trying to get into your trash or seen any bear scat around your site, have you?"

"No, I have not. However, I believe Hugo has just outperformed your investigative prowess, *Mr.* Fletcher."

"That tears it, *Finchy!* I—"

Miss Finch huffed, "Oh, do give it a rest, *Fletcher!*"

She lifted her voice, "And, Skipper? Come out and show yourself before I sic Hugo on you. Or, worse yet, Pouncer."

Fletcher jerked his gaze toward the woods. A moment later, low branches crackled and moved as Skipper pushed himself through and into Miss Finch's site. Hugo switched from foe to friend in an instant and yapped an enthusiastic welcome.

For a moment, all Simon could think was, *How much of my conversation with Miss Finch did Skipper hear?* Then he swung from angry to relieved, back to angry, and barked, "Skipper Mitchell! Where have you been?"

Skipper didn't answer. He even ignored Hugo as he brushed bits of dried leaves and bark from his hair and clothes.

"I asked you a question," Simon said quietly.

Skipper shrugged. "Been in the woods."

"Why haven't you answered my calls and texts?"

Skipper shrugged again. "Why should I?"

"Really? Do you want to blow your probation? Is that what you have in mind?"

"I don't care," he scowled.

Simon cut his eyes toward Miss Finch, silently begging for help.

After a long, charged minute of silence, she murmured, "Skipper, do you know that you had both of us worried?"

The boy's anger simmered beneath his reply. "You guys, worried about me? *Sure* you were."

"But I assure you, we were," she answered, "Fletcher has been searching everywhere for you."

"You mean he was looking to get his slave labor back!" Skipper shouted.

Miss Finch ignored the accusation and pressed on. "But you've been doing so well, Skipper. Please help us understand why you ran off in the first place."

Simon, who knew quite well what had set Skipper off, chimed in with, "Did you know you missed Zane and Kevin this afternoon? They came as planned to swim with you. When I told them I couldn't find you, they became worried about you. They are praying for you, just like Miss Finch and I have been praying for you."

Skipper's anger boiled over in an instant. "You're praying for me? *Yeah, right!* Always talking about what Christians are supposed to do and how Christians should act. Well, you guys make me sick! Acting like you're all mad at each other and stuff but telling me nothing's wrong. Not talking to each other and pretending you don't see each other. Bunch of phonies!"

Miss Finch had the good grace to blush under Skipper's accusations. For his part, Simon was way past embarrassment. It had taken the weight of conviction, atop the heavy ache in his heart, plus the unexpected appearance of Skipper's deadbeat dad, to push him to confront Miss Finch and their unspoken feud.

Skipper wasn't done venting. "And I heard you talking on the phone to Uncle Joe. Heard you tell him you're gonna leave Bright Star! Just up and leave!"

Miss Finch's head snapped in his direction, setting her salt-and-pepper curls trembling. Simon had to ignore her response. His only hope for restoring his relationship with Skipper lay in the assurance that conflict *done right*, while frequently messy, could also yield good results.

Lord, this is where I need your help. Please help me do this your way.

He moderated his voice. "How are you, Skip? Are you okay? Not hurt anywhere?"

Skipper frowned. "I'm okay. Mostly just hot . . . and tired."

"It's been a long, hard day for both of us." Simon took a breath. "Listen, I want to apologize to you, Skipper."

Skipper eyed him with suspicion and disdain.

"I'm sincere, Skipper. I'm sorry for my behavior earlier today. I'm sure you're aware that Holly and I have been squabbling a lot more than usual lately. It more or less came to a head today when I threatened to leave Bright Star." He tried to smile. "That said, I'm grateful to God that Holly and I actually had a good talk a while ago and have made up. Things will be different going forward, and I won't be leaving Bright Star. Not sure I really meant it, actually, when I threatened to go, but I'm sorry you had to hear it. Most of all, I'm sorry that I . . . hurt your feelings."

Skipper was too invested in his anger and pain to receive Simon's apology. "Yeah? Well what about you and Miss Finch? Have the two of you 'had a good talk' and 'made up' too? Huh? And what's that all about anyway?"

He stared from Simon to Miss Finch and back, daring them to answer him.

Miss Finch cleared her throat. "We were, in point of fact, engaged in such a conversation before we became aware of your presence, Skipper."

Simon perked up at her words, but Skipper wasn't satisfied.

"Talk, talk, talk! Did you finish talking? Did you guys make up? Are you friends again?"

Miss Finch glanced Simon's way; he arched one brow as if to ask, "Well? Did we? Are we?"

She sniffed and lifted her chin. "I think not. We hadn't quite finished our . . . discussion."

"Don't let me stop you," Skipper growled.

"Some conversations take time and thoughtful reflection, Skipper, and by the by, certain issues are of a private nature. Perhaps we could table this subject for a day or two while our . . . conversations continue?"

Skipper wagged his head. "Nope. Nuh-uh. Fletcher claims he's sorry he hurt my feelings, yet a couple hours ago he was about ready to up and leave Bright Star—and I'm pretty sure him leaving has more to do with you than with that ol' hen, Aunt Holly, 'cause for a week he's been acting like he has a bad stomach ache or-or-or the squirts."

Simon nearly choked. *The squirts?*

"And you guys? You yak all the time about Jesus and how we're supposed to live like him, act like him, talk like him, *breathe* like him. Well, I don't think the way you're ignoring each other is living or acting like Jesus, do you?"

Skipper's rhetorical question hit home with Simon. It may have resonated with Miss Finch also, except her patience with the boy was ebbing fast. "Living for Jesus and living like him is not instantaneous, Skipper," she said. "It takes work and persistence. Fletcher and I are . . . working on it."

Skipper stared at her, his mouth turned down. "Sounds like an excuse to me."

Simon gaped.

"And your impolite and boorish response tells me you've been spending entirely too much time with Mr. Fletcher."

"Well, *duh*. Kinda hard not to since I work for him *and* live with him."

"Tone, young man," Miss Finch warned.

But like a dog worrying a bone and unwilling to give it up, Skipper pressed harder. "What I want to know is, are you guys friends again? Cause that pretending not to know each other thing you guys have been doing makes me want to puke."

Simon had heard enough. "Skipper, I've told you, and Miss Finch has said the same thing: Our private business is nunya—none of your business. Instead, let's talk about you running off. Where have you been and why have you ignored my calls and texts?"

Skipper's mouth went flat. "If you're gonna leave Bright Star, I'm not staying here either."

"Well, I'm not leaving, so answer my questions."

Skipper kicked at the dirt with the toe of his shoe. "I heard you say something about my dad. Why were you talking about him?"

"That's not what I asked. And just how long were you listening in on our conversation?" Simon demanded.

"Long enough to hear you say my dad's name," Skipper sniffed. "Couldn't hear what you said about him, just mostly the stuff you guys were yelling at each other.

"Nice deflection, Skippy," Simon replied.

"My name is Skipper! Don't call me Skippy!"

"Then don't change the subject."

"And we were not yelling at each other, Skipper Mitchell!" Miss Finch objected. Loudly.

"Yeah, right."

"Why don't you take a look at the sky, *Skipperoo*," Simon suggested.

Puzzled, Skipper followed Simon's pointing finger . . . and gaped at the imposing wall of clouds building across the sky.

"You took my tent, Skipper. Were you planning to camp out in the woods? Alone?"

"Maybe," he muttered.

"Where? And don't change the subject."

Skipper jerked his chin toward the end of Miss Finch's trailer. "Back there, on the other side of the creek. Not far."

"You forded the creek to get to the other side?"

"Been awful dry. Ain't hardly any water in it."

"Huh. Well, I bet you that changes later on this afternoon or evening. There'll be plenty of water in the stream then, so much so that you wouldn't be able to ford it, and the only way back would mean riding a ways west of Bright Star, crossing the bridge, then riding south until you reach the trailhead."

Simon chuckled in a sly, mocking way. "But, hey, maybe I should let you follow through with your plans. I think the experience might be . . . educational."

Skipper's eyes jumped back to the encroaching clouds starting to blot out the afternoon sunlight. Obligingly and right on cue, lightning flashed within the bank of nearly black clouds.

"Well, I didn't know it was gonna rain."

"But now it kinda looks like it will, right?"

Skipper was suddenly energized. "Guess I'd better fetch my bike and stuff before it does."

"Hold on a second, kiddo. I apologized for hurting your feelings earlier today, for letting my anger over the disputes I've been having with Holly overcome my good sense. For saying I was leaving Bright Star . . . and leaving you. Are you going to accept my apology, or do you still intend to camp outdoors tonight?"

Skipper scowled. "Changed my mind about sleeping outside."

"That's not what I asked. I asked if you were going to accept my apology and forgive me."

"I guess."

"*I guess* isn't an answer. I would like to hear you say you forgive me."

"Sheesh!" Skipper looked around, then muttered, "I . . . forgive you."

"Thank you. Now, it's your turn."

"My turn for what?"

"Your turn to apologize."

"What do I need to apologize for?"

"Really? Shall we take inventory? How about apologizing for running off and abandoning your job, for ignoring my calls and texts, for taking my tent and bungee cords without permission, and for bailing on the friends you invited to swim with you this afternoon—although you'll need to apologize to them separately and in person. Right now, you need to apologize for worrying me half to death. Just like I hurt your feelings today, Skipper, you hurt mine."

"And mine," Miss Finch injected. "You worried me also, Skipper."

"Well, I ain't doing any of that—"

Simon clucked and glanced again at the threatening sky. "Too bad. Looks like we can expect heavy rain in the next hour or so. Hope you pitched that tent far enough from the stream bank. Sometimes these seasonal streams overflow. You and my tent could get pretty wet. And cold."

"Ain't pitched your ol' tent anywhere, yet."

"I see. So you plan to pitch it in the rain, do you? Miss Finch and I are still waiting for your apology."

Skipper huffed and stared at his shoes. "Whatever. I apologize . . . for all that stuff."

"Thank you; I forgive you."

"As do I," Miss Finch added.

Simon nodded. "Good. Shall we get moving toward home now? All the gear you brought from our cabin needs to be gathered up and brought inside before the rain starts."

"Wait. You and Miss Finch were talking about my dad. Why?"

Simon put his hands on his hips. "Heard that, did you? I suppose it's all right for me to talk to you about your dad. I was telling Miss Finch that he showed up at the office earlier today."

Skipper's face registered astonishment. "My dad? He came here? He's here now? What does he want?"

"He's not here at the moment; I sent him away and said I'd call him after I spoke to you. As for what he wants, he wants to see you."

Skipper frowned. "That's it? He wants to see me?"

Simon prayed silently, *Now comes the hard part, Lord. Help, please!*

"Yes, he wants to see you; however, you should know in advance that he didn't come here alone."

Skipper started to get excited. "Is my mom with him? Are they getting back together?"

Simon slowly shook his head. "No, sorry. Your dad brought a young woman, name of Shelly, with him. Said he wanted you to meet her and her daughter, a little girl maybe three or four years old."

Simon saw the moment Skipper put it together.

"Is he getting married to this lady?"

"He says he is."

Skipper went silent, but the anger building in him was evident.

Simon added, "I told your dad you were old enough to choose for yourself whether or not you wanted to see him. Said I'd call him and let him know what you've decided."

"He's getting married," Skipper repeated as though he hoped Simon would deny it.

"Maybe. Right now he and this woman are engaged. Your dad didn't say when they intend to get married. Could be next month or next year. Engagements these days don't come with an expiration date."

Even though they should. More people today use engagements to legitimize living together than they do proceeding to an actual wedding commitment.

"Well, I don't want to see him *or* them."

The kid added several angry, choice epitaphs that Simon chose to ignore for the time being.

"I understand your feelings, Skipper, but . . . but perhaps you'd like time to think about your decision before I call him."

"What's there to think about?" Skipper shouted, tears building in his eyes. "He doesn't care about me or Mom. Just himself and his-his-his stinking *girlfriend!*"

"Have to say I agree with you, Skipper. That said, I think you have things you'd like to say to your dad. And maybe, just maybe, he has things he'd like to say to you, things you might like to hear."

Simon added, "Besides, in my way of looking at life, it's better to meet the 'enemy' face to face in order to evaluate and better understand the situation. Better to know what you're up against than to have your imagination fill in the blanks—not," he hastened to explain, "not that your dad or his fiancée or her daughter are the enemy."

He added, thoughtfully, "I rather think that the little girl is as unhappy as you are and is possibly frightened by all the changes happening in her young life. You understand that, don't you? I'd like to suggest, if and when you meet her, that you be careful what you say in front of her, so you don't hurt her further. She's innocent of this chaos and is certainly not your enemy. And since you already know how painful rejection is, I can't believe you'd want to add to her pain."

Skipper, his anger cooling but not abating, shrugged. "Yeah, I suppose."

"I just unloaded a bunch of hooey on you. Why don't you sleep on this info? I can call your dad tomorrow and let him know your decision then?"

"Yeah. Whatever."

Miss Finch spoke up. "Skipper, I can appreciate how upset you are, but, rather than trying to figure this out on your own, why don't we pray with you about it? The Lord can and is willing to do great things when we call on him. He may have just the answers you need. The right answers."

Simon could see Skipper's sense of abandonment growing, and that the boy's anger was crumbling under its heavy weight.

"I like Miss Finch's suggestion, Skipper."

"Don't feel like praying," he mumbled, his voice clogged with suppressed tears.

"I get it. How about Miss Finch or I pray for you and over this situation? Would that be all right?"

"I suppose," Skipper sniffed.

"Good." He nodded to Miss Finch. "Want to take this one?"

"Yes, I would. Thank you." She bowed her head. "Lord, we come to you in Jesus' mighty and holy name, asking that you come into this situation with Skipper and his dad and with this lady and her daughter. You know Skipper's heart. You, in fact, know everyone's heart—including their intentions. Please speak to Skipper and show him whether or not he should agree to see his dad and, if he does meet with him, what he should say and how he should act. Lord, in every situation, you want us to act in gentleness and love. Please pour your love into Skipper so that he can obey you in these circumstances. Amen."

Skipper was sniffling and teary-eyed when she said amen. "Thanks, Miss Finch."

She walked to the young man who was already inches taller than her, put her short arms around his middle, and hugged him. "I know this life is often hard, Skipper, but I also know two people right here who love you very much."

She cracked an eye in Simon's direction. "Am I right . . . Fletcher?"

Simon perked up. He joined Miss Finch and placed an arm around Skipper's shoulder.

"You're right, Miss Finch. We both love our Skipperdoodle."

It was evident that Skipper wanted to get angry again, but he couldn't—not with the grins Miss Finch and Simon were sending his way.

"Yeah, well you'll never get me to say sissy words."

Simon lifted his brows. "Sissy words? You mean, like 'I love you'?"

"Yeah, that."

"It's okay, Skipper," Miss Finch laughed. "We'll keep saying them to you until you can say them to us."

Skipper wiped his eyes. "I still have one last question."

Simon scanned the sky overhead. "Uh, okay. I suppose we have time. Shoot."

Skipper looked from him to Miss Finch. "Are you guys done being mad at each other? Are you friends again?"

Simon pressed his lips together, but didn't look her way. He already knew how he felt; he needed to hear *her* response.

As the moment dragged on in silence, he finally chanced a glance at Miss Finch.

A faux sternness creased her brow, but at the same time, an undeniable twinkle glistened in her chocolate eyes. She murmured, "Actually? That's two questions, not one, Skipper."

Skipper scoffed. "Okay, then just answer this *one* question: What does Fletcher looking at you cross-eyed got to do with anything?"

Miss Finch whirled about and surrendered to a fit of coughing.

CHAPTER 9

SKIPPER WALKED HIS bike across the nearly dry stream and up the slope into Miss Finch's campsite behind her trailer. Simon followed carrying his tent and a duffle bag. He and Skipper loaded the bike and camping gear into the truck with Napoleon, and they drove off. Back at his cabin, Simon gently but firmly oversaw Skipper as he hauled inside everything he'd taken with him and put it away.

They finished just as the storm that had been moving their way broke. Lightning flashed, thunder boomed, and sheets of rain pelted the cabin's roof and windows. As the flashes and booms inched closer, Skipper's eyes widened. He sat cross legged on the floor while poor, terrified Napoleon cowered in his arms.

"It's nice to have someone who needs you as much as you need them," Simon observed. "I really hope your mom allows you to bring Napoleon home with you when you leave after Labor Day."

"Yeah, me too. I've never had a dog before."

"If, between now and then, you demonstrate how to take proper care of Napoleon without needing to be hounded into doing so, I'll do my best to help you persuade her."

Skipper turned shy. "Thanks, Fletch."

"You bet. That's what people do . . . when they love someone."

Skipper scrunched up his face. "Nice try! Ain't gonna say no sissy words."

"Well, you love Napoleon, don't you?"

That question startled Skipper. "Hadn't thought about it that way. Suppose I do."

"Aren't those sissy words?"

Skipper reluctantly muttered, "Guess so."

"Well, there you are. I hope Miss Finch and I rate at least as high as Napoleon."

After dinner, the rain eased and stopped. The sun even made a last appearance in the sky before setting over Mount Tallac.

"Will you be all right here by yourself for a while?"

"Sure. Nappy will keep me company—won't you, boy?" He looked up. "Where are you going?"

"Oh, to pay a call on Miss Finch."

Skipper nodded his approval. "That's good, cause you guys make me want to—"

"Yeah, I heard you before: We make you want to puke. Let's see if she and I can finish our 'nunya convo' and get things back on track."

"You'd better," Skipper warned him, "or there's gonna be a whole *lot* of puking and hacking up going on around here."

"Well, I'm not promising anything."

"Sounds like an excuse to me."

Simon left Skipper, tickled with his own witty repartee, rolling on the floor and alternately laughing like a hyena and cackling like a goose.

Simon snorted. *Teens.*

—————◆—————

SIMON DROVE BACK to Bright Star and parked in Miss Finch's driveway. As he expected, her lawn chairs were folded and leaned against her trailer, the trailing geranium removed to inside the trailer, and the awning lowered to a steep angle to allow the rain to drain off of it and keep the wind from ripping it up. Everything in her site dripped from the recent downpour; the little trailer, however, glowed with warm light from within.

Simon sighed. Would he be welcomed into that warmth or turned away with cool disregard?

No way to know unless I knock.

Determined, he walked up to her door, cracked his neck one way, then the other, rapped on her door, and stepped back.

Hugo immediately sent up an alarm.

Great watch dog you are, bud! Don't you know bad guys rarely knock?

A moment later, the door swung out and she stood in the doorway, framed by the lights behind her. She didn't seem surprised to see him.

"Ah, Fletcher. I've been expecting you. Do come in; the rain has left a chill in the air."

Simon hesitated. *You've been expecting me?*

"Well?" she demanded.

"Right. Thanks." *I think.*

He stepped inside and immediately sat down at her tiny table to be out of the way. Hugo sat beside his seat and uttered a soft *woof.*

Simon, of course, leaned toward him and rubbed his head. At the same time, he scouted the back of the trailer for Pouncer and found her brilliant blue eyes studying him from the back of the cushions on the left side of the sliding tabletop that served as Miss Finch's desk.

"Hey, Pouncer."

She hissed her usual friendly greeting.

"Back atcha, Brat."

The tea kettle atop Miss Finch's two-burner stove whistled, so she switched off the burner and poured the water into a waiting teapot.

"Tea?" she asked. "Decaf, of course, given the hour."

"Sure. Sounds good."

"And the purpose for your visit?"

Simon snorted. "You should know, seeing as you said you've been expecting me."

"Ah, but perhaps I wish to hear it from you."

Well, of course you do.

He came straight to the point. "I suppose I came to get answers to Skipper's last two questions. Are we done being mad at each other? And are we friends again?"

From the little stove, she side-eyed him. "Skipper asked a third question at the end of our little tête-à-tête, quoting a conversation we assumed was a private affair."

"Yeah, well I don't need to address that 'nonspecific placeholder,' and I have no desire to open said can of worms ever again. In my humble opinion, you and I discussed it to death and should now grant it a decent burial."

Surprising him, she said softly, "I agree."

"You agree to drop and never discuss you-know-what or does your agreement also cover Skipper's other questions?"

"The tea needs to steep several minutes." In complete silence, she busied herself arranging napkins and spoons on the table and setting out two pretty teacups near the stove, and took her time doing so. Eventually, she poured steaming tea into the teacups, added honey to both, and stirred, then brought both cups on their delicate saucers to the tiny table, set them down, and took her own seat.

Still, Simon waited for her answer.

She picked up her cup and sniffed of its fragrance. "I agree to all three."

The heavy, sick weight on Simon's heart sprouted wings and lifted away. He picked up his teacup to give his shaky, sweaty hands something to do and blew across the surface of the steaming brew.

When his voice was reliably steady, he answered, "Good."

"Yes."

They drank their tea without further conversation. When Simon finished his, he stood and nodded.

"Thanks for the tea."

"You are welcome."

He'd taken the single step necessary to reach the door before she added, "And if you are available tomorrow afternoon, perhaps I could bring you up to date on our case. Will four o'clock suit your schedule?"

"It will."

"I will see you then."

"Ditto—er, right."

He drove back to his cabin in a delighted daze, alternately praising God and moving his head back and forth in disbelief. Skipper, of course, was waiting and anxious when he stepped inside.

"Well?"

Simon kept his joy bottled up tight lest he lose even a drop of it, but he allowed himself to crack half a smile.

"We're back."

"Whoo-hoo!"

Back to square one, Simon thought, *but back, nonetheless.*

CHAPTER 10

TUESDAY, JULY 8

SIMON CHECKED HIS watch or phone with regularity during the following day's work, silently urging the time to pass quickly, impatient for his
appointment with Miss Finch to arrive—not meaning at all that he shirked
the day's duties. He ran early that morning, showered and read his Bible, got
Skipper up and ready for work, then sat with him over breakfast, and again
discussed Skipper's upcoming decision concerning his father.

"I prayed about it before I went to bed, like you suggested last evening,"
Skipper confessed to Simon over his cereal, "but I don't feel any different
about it. I mean, I'm glad he wants to see me and everything, but I sorta don't
trust him."

Avoiding Simon's gaze, the kid mumbled into his bowl, "Is it wrong that
I don't trust him?"

Skipper was hunched over in his seat, and the dejection enfolding him
clutched at Simon's heart. He thought for a moment. "No. No, I don't think
it's necessarily wrong that you don't trust him. You have reason to be . . .
leery of his motives."

"Leery? What's that mean, exactly?"

Simon knew he had to be careful of what he said so that he didn't exercise undue influence over Skipper's decision. "I guess it means to be cautious
or watchful of someone because of their past actions. As regards your dad, I
think it could also mean that you are anxious because you love him and don't
want him to . . . trick you. Most likely, you feel that way because when he
left you and your mom, he did so without any warning."

Skipper set down his spoon and thought about Simon's explanation.
"Yeah. That's kinda how I feel, like maybe he's not really here to see me . . .
just because he loves me."

Simon heard Skipper's words dry up in his throat and saw the sheen of
tears that gathered in his eyes.

He placed his hand on the boy's arm. "Can I tell you something about
love, Skipper?"

Skipper managed a single, jerky nod.

"Love always means taking a chance."

And boy, don't I know it, Simon reminded himself.

A small crease appeared between Skipper's eyes. "Taking a chance?"

"It's taking a chance on the other person's actions and behaviors. How they might treat you, whether good or bad. You love your dad, right?"

"Yeah. Sorta."

"I'll bet you wouldn't have said 'sorta' before he left."

Skipper sniffed and nodded.

"Loving someone means that person's choices can hurt you. Like when your dad left, he hurt you."

A large tear trickled down Skipper's cheek.

Napoleon, who'd been lying near the table, must have sensed Skipper's pain, because the old guy struggled to his feet and padded up to Skipper's chair. He stared up at Skipper with sad, rheumy eyes before laying his droopy, grizzled muzzle in Skipper's lap.

Skipper smiled and stroked Napoleon's head. "You're a good boy, Nappy."

Without looking up at Simon, Skipper replied, "Yeah. It hurt when Dad left, and I guess it still does."

"Sure it does. Nobody enjoys being hurt, so when someone causes us pain, we pull back, and it's hard to show love to that person again. Why? Because we don't want to run the risk of being hurt again."

Simon groaned inwardly. *Sheesh. Am I preaching to myself here?*

He added, "I think that's the real reason you are undecided about seeing your dad."

Skipper nodded his agreement and swiped away more tears. "Yeah. So what do I do? What's the right thing to do?"

"That's the right question, Skip. For starts, I'm grateful to Jesus for showing us how to love even when it hurts. Did you know Jesus' family hurt him? Practically turned against him at one point?"

Skipper eyed Simon. "I didn't even know he had a family."

"Sure. He had parents and siblings. Well, Joseph was his stepdad, of course, since God was Jesus' real father. But anyway, apparently Joseph died at some point before Jesus began his ministry, but when he did start to preach, he still had his mom, two or more sisters, and at least four younger brothers, James, Joseph, Simon and Judas—that's according to Matthew 13.

"One day while Jesus was teaching in a house, his mom and brothers came and tried to take him home. We don't know *why* they came for certain, but we can construe a couple of reasons.

"See, Jesus was raised by a carpenter and trained as a carpenter himself. He wasn't schooled to be a rabbi. The fact that he was crisscrossing the country, preaching repentance, healing the sick, casting out demons, and arguing with the teachers of the Law of Moses and other high-up religious leaders was, well, to put it bluntly, *totally crazy*.

"That's why some bible teachers think Jesus' family may have thought he'd lost his mind and why his family wanted to take him home. They probably wanted to get him out of the public eye before he brought down trouble on himself and, by extension, on his family. At that point, Jesus' own brothers didn't believe he was the Messiah, although later some of them did."

"That's wild!" Skipper exclaimed. "I mean, what kind of trouble could Jesus cause his family? And didn't they have freedom of speech back then?"

Simon laughed. "No, not exactly. In fact, saying the wrong things could get you in very hot water. What kind of trouble might Jesus' family have been worried about? Well, the Jewish rulers could have labeled Jesus a blasphemer and thrown both him and his family out of the local synagogue—that's a Jewish church. Worse, the Romans in charge of the town where Jesus was teaching could have arrested him and charged him with rebelling against Roman rule and stirring up a riot. That would have gotten him executed. Whatever their reasons, Jesus' family did not support his ministry, at least not in the beginning.

"Think about it a second: These were Jesus' younger brothers, his *little* brothers. After their dad died, Jesus would have had to take on the role of 'head of house,' responsible for supporting his mother and siblings. Can you imagine raising your younger brothers to adulthood, only to see them turn on you? That had to have hurt Jesus a lot."

Skipper nodded thoughtfully. "So what did Jesus do?"

Whoops. I may have painted myself into the very corner I'm trying to avoid, Simon realized, recalling how Pete Mitchell had accused him of wanting to supplant him as Skipper's father.

"Well, he told the people listening to him that his real mother and brothers were those who did what God wanted."

That furrow between Skipper's eyes deepened. "Sooo, you mean like you and Miss Finch?"

Danger close, Marine! Evasive action!

"Maybe don't mention either of us to your dad by name, Skipper. He might feel that Miss Finch and I were, um, trying to undercut him. However, if you decide to see him, what you *could* do is listen calmly to what he has to say, and when it's your turn to talk, be honest about your feelings—like how he hurt you and it's hard to trust him right now—but also say that you're open to seeing how he does going forward."

Skipper blinked several times. "Not sure I can remember all that."

"That's okay; the Holy Spirit is a good memory keeper, Skipper. You pray, ask the Lord to put good words in your mouth, and then trust the Holy Spirit to lead you and help you. The important thing is to make up your mind beforehand that you won't get mad and stomp off in anger. Remember when Miss Finch taught you how to run the office, how to answer the phone or greet Bright Star residents?"

"What, like with a big cheesy smile?"

Simon laughed. "Not that part, Skippernoodle. I mean how she taught you to act in a professional manner or, loosely translated, how to be courteous and helpful."

Simon was surprised when Skipper grinned at the nickname instead of getting annoyed. "So I should be courteous and helpful to my dad?"

Simon nodded. "That's a good start, Skipper. Courteous includes being kind and patient, so while you're being kind and patient, it will give the Lord a chance to tell you what to say. Also? Remember that words are cheap; what matters are people's actions. Do yourself a favor and reserve judgment until you actually see if your dad is trying to live up to his words or not."

"I think I can do that."

"Then do you want me to tell him you will meet with him?"

"Yeah, but . . ."

"But?"

"Can you be there too?"

"Uh, how about if I stick around nearby so it doesn't look like I'm interfering?"

"Well . . . okay."

"Great. Let's get ready for work; I'll call him when it's not quite so early."

———— ● ————

WITH NAPOLEON FED, walked, and boosted into the back of the truck, Simon and Skipper headed to Bright Star. Simon was grateful that the day's tasks and chores were about as vanilla as they could be. All except the big bright spot far ahead in his day, his 4:00 p.m. meeting with Miss Finch.

Lord, please help us start on good footing today and get back to our shared investigations . . . and budding friendship.

Simon set Skipper to work skimming the pools while he called Pete Mitchell.

"Good morning, Mr. Mitchell. Simon Fletcher here. Skipper is available to meet with you today. Would around noon work? After talking for a bit, and if he's up for it, you might ask him to go out for lunch with you."

"Great!" Mitchell answered. "We'll be at Bright Star's office at noon."

Simon refrained from offering Mitchell advice on how to introduce Sherry and her daughter. *You're on your own there, bud. The less I inject myself into your business, the better.*

He hung up and told Skipper, "You'll meet your dad at the office, noon. After you've talked a few minutes and if things go well, he'd like to take you out to lunch."

Skipper hesitated before saying, "That's good, right? I mean, you'll take me to the office?"

"Sure. We should go back to the cabin first so you can clean up and change clothes. Then I can drop you at the office."

"Yeah, okay, only . . . I kinda meant you'll stay . . . for a minute?"

Skipper's really nervous about seeing his dad.

"How about I hang out in the truck? Be your backup guy."

Relief washed over Skipper's face. "Yeah. That. Thanks."

———————— ● ————————

WHEN NOON ARRIVED, Simon pulled up to the office and Skipper got out. From Simon's view from the truck's driver's seat where he watched Skipper and his dad on the office porch, their initial encounter must have gone well. After several minutes, Skipper waved to Simon, and climbed into Mitchell's back seat.

Simon was gratified. *Looks promising, Lord.*

———————— ● ————————

AN HOUR AND a half later, Simon was behind the office, tossing firewood into the back of the truck, but taking his time, watching for Pete Mitchell's car. Eventually, it came down the road and stopped in front of the office.

A few minutes later, a calm and settled Skipper walked around the back of the office. He climbed into the truck bed, rubbed Napoleon's head and ears, and began stacking the loose firewood.

"How'd it go?" Simon asked.

"Okay, I guess. Met Shelly and her daughter, Demi. For a little kid, Demi's cool."

He blushed. "She kinda likes me. Wanted to sit by me in the restaurant and stuff."

"And conversation with your dad?"

Skipper shrugged. "He said all the right stuff, and Sherri was nice, except she smokes—*gah!* When Dad dropped me off afterward, he told me he'd call me at least once a week and promised to come back to see me by himself before summer's over."

He shrugged again. "Like you always say, words are cheap. Guess I'll wait and see."

"Glad it went well, Skipper."

"Yeah. Me too."

With the weight of the world off his shoulders, Skipper worked with a will and finished the last of his tasks by three o'clock. Simon rewarded Skipper's hard work by letting him off for the remainder of the day. The boy grabbed his bike and pedaled off to Site 19 to meet up with the Nadeau kids and keep his promise to take them riding in the woods.

Minutes later, Simon also started to relax and realized why. *Man, dealing with and worrying over teenage issues most of the day is flat-out exhausting.*

CHAPTER 11

THE LAST HOUR of his work day dragged for Simon, and when four o'clock arrived, he was more than ready for a change of pace. He drove toward Miss Finch's site with equal measures of anticipation and trepidation jumping around in his chest. Above all, he was hoping his friendship with Miss Finch would truly be back on an even keel.

He found her as he so often had, seated in her little lawn chair under the awning, her tablet on her lap, a can of Zero Sugar Cherry Dr. Pepper in her chair's beverage holder, Hugo at her feet, and Pouncer draped across her shoulders. Hugo greeted Simon with enthusiasm; Pouncer yawned, stretched, and couldn't be bothered to hiss.

To Simon's amazed delight, Miss Finch herself behaved as though the eight-day interval between today and Monday a week ago had never occurred, including their several uncomfortable exchanges during that interval. She acted as though that disastrous day had never happened, the day when Simon's feelings for Miss Finch had surfaced and revealed themselves to her in a single unguarded look.

"Ah, Simon. Good. Take a seat. We have work to attend to."

Whoa! Is this déjà vu or is this honest-to-goodness freaky-deaky? Simon wondered.

He added to himself, *I'll take freaky-deaky for a hundred, Ken.*

He shrugged and wondered, *So, that's it? Sheesh, lady. You sure can turn it off and on like a spigot.*

Well, I'll take it. Gladly.

He didn't immediately mention the article he'd read concerning the disappearance of twelve-year-old Allysson Sharma from the Incline Village Fourth of July celebration. That could wait.

Instead, he ventured, "We left off with the disappearances of three young men, Haoyu Xú, Caesar Morales, and Donald Whatley and that the body of the first man to go missing, Xú, was found sunk in the lake. Who found him, by the way?"

"A scuba club, doing advanced rebreather training at the Rubicon Wall. It was luck, really. If you believe in luck."

"And you said the medical examiner ruled the guy's death a homicide. Have you learned cause of death since then?"

Miss Finch's chocolate brown eyes gleamed as she tapped her tablet. "My source inside the coroner's office sent me only the autopsy's bare bones. Although she was initially more than willing to share details about Xú, she has since turned skittish and has not responded to any of my follow-on inquiries. Of course, the reason behind her reticence is patently obvious."

Simon began to ask the obvious, "What reason—" only to be cut off.

"What reason might that be, you ask?"

Yup. We're back.

"Yes, that's what I'm asking."

"You see, based on what she *did* send me, my sense is that this case is going to blow up shortly and come under a great deal of public scrutiny . . . and my source prefers not to be skewered with shrapnel from the explosion."

"How soon is shortly?"

"The very minute the media catches wind of the body's condition at autopsy."

"Which was . . ."

Miss Finch's slanted lids descended to half-staff, and her voice dropped to a confidential whisper. "Two words, Fletcher: *organ harvest*. Every major organ in Mr. Xú's body had been surgically removed: heart, lungs, liver, kidneys, pancreas, and corneas. And when I say, 'surgically removed,' I mean harvested by individuals who know how to do so properly."

Simon was thunderstruck. "Holy spumoni."

"I much prefer cherry chocolate chunk over spumoni, but I agree with your sentiments."

She was quiet, so Simon asked, "Individuals who know how to do so properly, you say? You're saying medical professionals?"

"From what I've found through my research, *an entire team* of highly trained medical professionals would be required to complete all six organ removals in a manner that retains their transplant viability. Organs harvested incorrectly are unusable. Moreover, in such situations, *time* is of the essence. For example, hearts and lungs are only viable outside the donor body for four to six hours and the liver twelve to fifteen hours. Apparently, kidneys are hardier and can survive thirty-six to forty-eight hours."

She sipped on her can of soda. "You see, one does not harvest an organ for transplant where a matched recipient has not already been selected and notified to report to a transplant-ready medical facility in which a transplant surgical team is assembled and ready to go."

"A matched recipient. You mean tested for a compatible blood type?"

"Actually, three tests are necessary to determine if a donor's organs will be suitable for a waiting recipient: a blood-type test to determine the donor's blood type, then a crossmatch blood-type test between the donor and recipient to ensure that the donor-to-recipient blood types are compatible. Lastly, a Human Leukocyte Antigen or HLA matching test to match tissue types.

"However, as I said, time is also of the essence, so other factors come into play, including the distance between the organ donor and the hospital where the transplant will take place so that the harvested organs are still viable and the recipient prepped for the surgery when they arrive at the transplant facility."

"But Tahoe isn't the most accessible of locations. Sure, we have a couple small airports, but why intentionally choose an involuntary donor from such a remote area?"

"An excellent question, Fletcher, and one to which I have also given much thought. My answer? I suggest that Tahoe's location and the vast wilderness surrounding the lake area may provide the desirable layer of privacy and concealment necessary for this scheme to work."

Simon sucked in a breath and exhaled slowly before he muttered, "Scheme, huh? But what about the transplant-ready medical facility you said was needed, not to mention a transplant surgical team?"

Her dark eyes gleamed from under her thickly fringed lashes. "Seeing as how such a venture would require significant capital outlay, is it a leap to posit that the person or persons behind this scheme already own private property in the lake area? And would it not follow that this person hired or partnered with those who have the appropriate skills to design, build, and oversee a facility on that property and employ staff necessary to perform the transplants?"

"What you've described would cost a *ton* of money."

"Oh, yes. Financing for such an undertaking would be a massive expenditure." With a sarcastic chuckle, she added, "And as you are most certainly aware, the lake area can hardly boast of even *ten* such ultra-wealthy property owners—am I right?"

Simon snarked, "Sure, pal! You and I both know that the affluent and super-rich who flock to Lake Tahoe are like a cockroach infestation—*they're everywhere*."

She held up one tiny finger. "Everywhere *and* continuously developing or remodeling their extravagant residences or vacation homes—am I correct?"

Simon knew she was. "Absolutely. Can't go anywhere around the lake without encountering construction crews. I mean, if the owners of cheek-by-jowl properties can't build *out*, they build *up*. Some neighborhoods along the lakeshore are literally lined, wall-to-wall, with narrow, three-and-four-story homes. Those people are up for anything that gives them their coveted view of the water."

"But are the actual über-rich relegated to such close quarters, Fletcher? Could not any number of them own estates on sizable parcels of land removed from the lakeshore?"

"Yes, of course. Those who can afford to buy larger dwellings or home-sites do so . . . and, yes, those places are usually some distance removed from the lakeshore itself."

"Which makes the entirety of the lake area the ideal location to construct a privately owned and staffed medical facility . . . hidden in plain sight."

"Huh! Sounds kind of crazy when you say it aloud. Still, it's also feasible." Simon thought a moment. "And you say the police have released nothing at all regarding Xú's cause of death?"

"They have issued no statement *to date*. That said, by digging into Mr. Xú's family ties, I find he has none with the exception of an elderly grandmother with dementia living in a Chinese care facility. Such absence of family ties means no one is pushing for the COD to be made public."

She frowned. "I have been sitting on this information for days now, patiently waiting for South Lake Tahoe PD to release Xú's COD to the public before pressing my source in the ME's office for more details. However, at this point, I have arrived at the settled conclusion that local *politics* have played and will continue to play a significant role in the delay of the release . . . although that delay may be at an end shortly."

"You're talking about the Fourth of July being over," Simon mused, "the biggest-earning three-day weekend of the lake's summer tourist economy. The gruesome announcement of a body with its organs surgically harvested found in the lake just prior to the holiday might have put a dent in the weekend's revenues . . . and in the survival of Tahoe's many small businesses."

He shook his head. "Such an announcement could still have a negative impact on the lake area's fragile economy."

She pressed her lips together and slowly nodded, the movement setting her wayward curls into a gentle rocking motion.

Making them shimmy and sway.

Mesmerizing Simon until he shook himself and pointed his eyes elsewhere.

Unaware of his fascination, she went on, "We agree on the need to protect Tahoe's business communities, and thus we understand the politics protecting them. Scary news has the ability to torch tourist fervor. Truthfully, I cannot see how such hideous news, even now, after the Fourth, could fail to damage Tahoe's economy to some degree. When the news does break, a media feeding frenzy will undoubtedly ensue—and I speak not of merely local media. This is a story that could detonate on the national and even international stage."

Simon felt a frisson of concern for Bright Star's future jitter down his back. He ran a hand across his chin, then added, "I can't disagree. I mean, what could possibly appeal more to the shallow and lascivious appetites of network news and social media than an epic tale of body snatchers and organ harvesters? Ghastly and indecent, but media gold."

He uttered a wry laugh. "At least journalists and media talking heads have expense accounts. If and when they descend on Tahoe, they will need rooms to sleep in and food to fuel their interagency rivalries—all to be the first to acquire the juiciest bits of news."

She stared at him, her eyes fully open and searching. "There is no 'if' about this, Fletcher. We're sitting on a bomb with a lit fuse, an explosive device that has the potential to devastate the lake area for years. Far more than that, it is a moral crisis, a travesty! You and I must act."

"Act? Who, us? What in the world could the two of us do? Just Friday, a child twelve years old, one Allysson Sharma, vanished from Incline Village's Fourth of July fireworks show. There's no possible way anyone could have foreseen and prevented such a crime—if it is a crime and not a childish prank. But, see, if *kids* start disappearing from around the lake? The lid blows straight off this thing."

"I am aware, Fletcher, which is why I believe our first step should be to consider the child who escaped."

Astounded, he blurted, "Someone escaped? Who?"

"Little Cameron Easton."

"Who is little Cameron Easton, and how did you hear about him or her? I've been keeping an eagle eye on the news and never once saw nor heard that name."

She picked up her soda can, jiggled it, and swallowed down its dregs. "I have told you about my tech friends and the search program they built to my specifications, have I not? I input the location and type of news I am seeking, and the program gathers such news from all available online news sources around my desired location, using the key words I input to assemble the result I desire."

She crumpled the can and dropped it to the ground. Hugo immediately jumped up, picked it up in his teeth, and delivered it to a small trashcan by the catio.

"Nice trick."

"And, as it happens," she murmured, "my teammates, too, have a few nice tricks up their sleeves. You see, I placed my friends on high alert a week back, and they moved quickly. In response, they assembled and released a number of data-gathering bots into the interwebs of certain organizations within a fifty-mile radius of Lake Tahoe. The bots' objectives? To seek out and scour pertinent databanks."

"Databanks?"

"Cloud-based institutional data repositories."

"Whose repositories?"

"Hugo. Fetch, please."

Hugo jumped up again, ran to a tiny refrigerator up against the trailer. He nosed the door open and pawed a fresh can of soda onto the outdoor carpet. He rolled it over to Miss Finch, returned to the fridge, nosed the door closed, then ran around her chair and sat in front of her, grinning.

"Who's a good boy, Hugo? You are, my darling! Good boy!" She tossed a small biscuit into the air. He caught it and retired to his spot under her chair.

Simon fought to keep the sounds of Hugo's small teeth crunching the biscuit to pieces from distracting him.

"I asked whose repositories, Miss Finch."

"Oh, that."

"Don't 'oh, that' me. Whose cloud repositories?"

She glared. "I have misremembered the annoying quality of your persistence, *Mr.* Fletcher."

He glared back. "And *I* haven't forgotten your penchant for dissimulation, *Miss Finch*. Let me refresh your dissembling recall, shall I? *Whose* cloud-based data institutional repositories did your people hack?"

"As I said, only certain institutions of a . . . peacekeeping nature."

Simon snapped to her meaning and gaped. "Wait—hold up there! You're not saying you asked your 'techy friends' to hack *local law enforcement databases*, are you?"

She pursed her lips and looked aside. "Perhaps."

"Perhaps, my left foot! And why, *exactly* did you feel the need to hack local law enforcement databases?" The imprudence, the audacity, the sheer chutzpah of her actions were clanging like alarms in his brain.

She was unfazed. "Why, to search out, locate, and collate essential and relevant data that we were not as yet privy to. Information, such as the Washoe County Sheriff's Substation interview of young Cameron, who was visiting her aunt and uncle who live in Crystal Bay when a man and a woman attempted to abduct her."

Good grief! This is far worse than I imagined it could be. Way worse.

He was only thinking of the hacking which had altogether chased the attempted abduction from his mind. He was further astounded and more than a little annoyed when, under her breath, she giggled a soft "heh-heh-heh."

He scowled. "You think a cybercrime of this magnitude is funny?"

She grinned at his outrage. "I suppose it is possible I might be accused of a cybercrime—although, technically, *I* never breached their databanks myself. But funny? No. Mostly, I am just tickled to have you back."

"I . . . don't get you."

"Oh dear—and here I was extending you a compliment, Fletcher. Why? Because, for the most part, I am not compelled to spell things out for you."

"*Hardy har har.* Commence with the spelling out, please."

Her hand flew to her heart. "You cut me to the quick!"

"Riiight."

"Hmph! Quite frankly, Fletcher, you have an amazing capacity to make connections and arrive directly at the logical conclusion . . . in the main. Just not at this moment, apparently."

He frowned at her jab. "And you have the amazing capacity to disregard the law?"

She inclined her head. "*Touché.* As poor an excuse as my rationalizations may provide, my intention, *my objective*, is to save lives."

Her expression turned sober. "You do intuit the terminal point of our little mystery, do you not—'terminal' being, undoubtedly, a poor word choice. But I digress. Have you reached the correct conclusion at last?"

When Simon only frowned, she muttered, "For goodness sake, can you not see that the lake area has a serial killer at large?"

When Simon gawked, she huffed her disgust. "No? I cannot believe I thought I would *not* have to spell it out for you! Moreover, must I help you realize that the various and *quite* disconnected law enforcement agencies all around the lake have not, as yet, grasped this horrifying fact?"

Simon started to speak, but she shushed him. "*Tush!* Let me finish. I do not speak, Fletcher, of a commonplace, mundane, plodding, pedantic serial killer. No, this one is sophisticated and purposeful, organized, extraordinarily well-funded, astonishingly bold, and . . . growing bolder."

"A serial killer? His purpose being . . ."

"Unproven, yet decidedly *inferred.*"

"Bold and growing bolder?"

"But of course. Why, how can one read the mounting intensity of his behaviors and not understand? To abduct three victims while they are each alone in remote parts of the forest is a relatively simple matter, but to snatch a young girl from a crowded public event or attempt to take a child from a well-used bike trail? Those heinous undertakings require considerably more planning, coordination, and logistical support—not to mention cunning and audacity."

"So you already knew about Allysson Sharma disappearing from Incline Village's Fourth of July spectacular? She's the 'crowded public event' disappearance you're referring to?"

"I am gratified to hear you spotted *her* disappearance on your own."

"And I suppose I'm gratified to hear she's not yet *another* disappearance I totally missed. So, tell me about the attempted abduction of a child from a well-used bike trail. I'm not familiar with that case."

"Then I must introduce you to young Cameron Easton, whom I mentioned earlier."

"Yeah, yeah. Get on with it already."

"Patience, Fletcher."

She popped the top on her fresh can of soda, sipped the foam that spilled from it, then took several long, slow swallows, using the time to marshal her thoughts.

"Where was I? Oh, yes. Cameron Easton. Eleven years old. Riding her bike with her older sister Nina the morning of July 2, on the Tahoe East Shore Trail, which originates near Incline Village."

"Near Incline Village, July 2. That was the Wednesday before the Fourth, just two days before Allysson Sharma disappeared. Suggests Allysson was your serial killer's second choice."

She swirled the contents of her can in a leisurely manner, as if checking how much of the beverage remained.

"Yes, to last Wednesday, yes to your astute observation, but no to him being *my* serial killer. I claim no part in his evil deeds. Think on it! While we were busy welcoming the Gillespie and Nadeau families to Bright Star and situating their RVs, this serial killer made an attempt on Cameron, one that, praise be to God, *failed*, yet the attempt on Allysson Sharma did not."

To Simon's amazement, Miss Finch upended her soda, and drained the can's contents dry.

Holy cow—where does she keep all that? I'd be oozing from every pore by now.

It was then he realized she was deeply disturbed and operating on nervous energy. She didn't even seem to realize she was squeezing the empty can until it protested with a sharp *crunch*, one that called Hugo out from under her chair. Without conscious thought, she dropped the can for him to dispose of it.

She whispered, "I was not entirely certain, of course, that the disappearance of Allysson Sharma was related to the attempt on Cameron, although I felt its strong possibility. I am, however, now convinced. You see, Allysson and Cameron's blood types are the same, O negative."

"What! How on God's green earth do you know their blood types?"

When she said nothing but crooked a one-sided smile at him, he muttered, "Again, your programmer teammates are efficient hackers."

"Indubitably, unquestionably, irrefutably, and indispensably so."

Simon snorted. "Whatever. Back to Cameron Easton. When they, whomever *they* are, tried to take Cameron while she was riding with her sister on the Tahoe East Shore Trail, how far south of Incline Village were they when the attempt occurred? And how did the kid escape?"

Her levity dropped away. "It was, I believe, a true God thing, Fletcher. The Easton family is devoted to the Lord, and he was merciful to them in this situation. As to where on the Tahoe East Shore Trail the attempt occurred? The trail terminates as it reaches the parking lot belonging to Sand Harbor State Park and its boat launch. A park restroom lies straight ahead, conveniently located for cyclists or hikers. Cameron and Nina, who were riding quite early that morning to avoid the heat of the day, said they chose to use the restroom before retracing their route back up the trail.

"They both said the parking lot was sparsely filled. None of the parked cars' occupants appeared to be around as they were likely already out on the water—all except for a van stopped alongside the restroom. The girls didn't pay much attention to it, figuring the driver was using the men's side. They parked their bikes, and Cameron went around to the girl's side of the facility."

Her tale continued, "Nina Easton told the sheriff's deputy interviewing her that while Cameron was inside the restroom and while she, Nina, watched their bikes, a man jumped out of the van's side door and grabbed her. She let loose a shriek but told the deputy that the man almost immediately pressed a rag over her mouth and nose, a rag I surmise was doused with chloroform or some similar tranquilizing drug easily poured onto cloth. Nina did not recall anything else until she woke sometime later.

"When Cameron, still in the restroom, heard her sister's curtailed cry of protest, she unlocked the restroom door, went out, and peered around the edge of the building. That's when she saw a man lowering Nina to the ground. The man saw Cameron and shouted to someone else. Cameron, understandably, ran back into the restroom. Just as she was pulling the door closed again, a woman grabbed the door's edge and tried to yank it open. That little girl, using the good sense God gave her, braced her foot on the door jamb and used all her strength to jerk the heavy door toward her, pinching the woman's fingers in the process. When the woman swore and yanked back her hand, Cameron quickly closed and relocked the door, stymying the female abductor.

"Cameron then heard a great deal of furious whispering and, I quote, 'a lot of bad words too.' Later, Cameron heard the van drive off, but she was too frightened to come out of the restroom, lest the kidnappers had returned to the restroom on the sly and were waiting for her.

"After several minutes, Cameron heard her sister groaning and called out to her. When Nina finally answered back and said the van was gone and no one was around, Cameron unlocked the restroom door and came out. Nina, who had a cell phone on her, immediately called their parents, who rushed to their location. When Mr. and Mrs. Easton heard the girls' story, they notified the park rangers. The rangers, in turn, called the Washoe County Sheriff's main dispatch number at their Incline Village substation."

"Hmm. I gather your hackers obtained all these details from the sheriff's cloud repository?"

She inclined her head. "You gather correctly."

"*Outstanding*," Simon growled.

CHAPTER 12

WHEN IT DIDN'T look like Miss Finch had picked up on the sarcasm in his remark, Simon began to think aloud. "You say Cameron Easton and Allysson Sharma both have O negative blood type. If my grasp of the facts doesn't elude me, only something like six or seven percent of the world's population is O negative. That's opposed to O positive being, narrowly, the most common type at thirty-seven percent, give or take a percentage point."

"So far, so good, Fletcher."

"Your approval is noted, Miss WhyNotHackTheWorld. And while O neg is not the rarest of blood types, it is considered a near-universal donor, with much higher usage than O positive, since *most*, but not quite all blood types, whether Rh positive or negative, can receive O negative transfusions, whereas O positive, much more readily available, can be given only to all Rh positive blood types."

He mused aloud, "Yet, on the flip side, an individual with O negative blood can receive transfusions *only* from other O negatives. This sharply reduces the number of potential transfusion donors for O negative individuals and, I presume, means that the supply of organ donations available to an O neg patient would also be limited."

"Statistically nil, in fact. You are catching up, Fletcher."

"Gee, thanks. So, if the purpose of these abductions is to supply immediately needy individuals with black market organs, can we then assume Cameron's sister, Nina, isn't O negative?"

"Correct again. She is O positive. Deductions?"

"Hmm. Two abduction attempts of O negative blood types less than seventy-two hours apart and the fact that a second successful attempt was made soon after the first attempt failed tells us one thing: Our individual in need of a transplant is on a clock—in desperate need."

Miss Finch didn't look up, but fiddled with her tablet. "Certainly . . . *someone* is."

The way she said "someone is" gave Simon pause, and he mentally reran the facts. "Hang on. What about the first three abductions—Haoyu Xú, Caesar Morales, and Donald Whatley? What were their blood types?"

She stopped working on her pad and turned her attention to him. "Two B positive and one B negative. Care to reexamine your hypothesis?"

Simon sat back. "Well, all three could take an O negative donation."

"Indeed, but we are not looking at them as recipients, are we?"

"Oh. Right. They would be . . . donors."

"Yes, and to bring us to a more perfect understanding of the situation, let us consider the three men, Xú, Morales, and Whatley, and their blood types, B positive, B positive, and B negative, respectively. The little mental exercise at hand is to identify with which *recipient* blood types would *all three* of the involuntary donors be compatible."

She turned her tablet to Simon. "This chart may help."

He stared at the image on the screen.

"Go through the chart, Fletcher, and note which *recipient* groups can receive both B positive and B negative donor transfusions," she murmured, "since those are the two donor types the three young men represent."

Blood Type Compatibility Chart	
Recipient Type	Compatible Donor Types
O+	O+, O–
O–	O–
A+	A+, A–, O+, O–
A–	A–, O–
B+	B+, B–, O+, O–
B–	B–, O–
AB+	AB+, AB–, A+, A–, B+, B–, O+, O–
AB–	AB–, A–, B–, O–

Simon scrutinized the chart, reviewing each recipient group in turn, O, A, then B. He kept the B positive group but was forced to discard the B negative group since they could not receive transfusions from a positive blood type. He did the same for the AB group. He kept the AB positive group, but threw out the AB negative group.

"Two recipient types can receive blood from all three of our abducted young men: B positive and AB positive—"

"Ah, but AB positive has a large donor base," Miss Finch interjected, "Those with AB positive blood can receive transfusions from *every* blood type, which also means that an AB positive patient awaiting a transplant would have the greatest chance of receiving an organ, all other factors disregarded. Knowing this, I would discard the AB group as the recipient type in need of a black market organ. That leaves us with a B positive recipient, someone whose donor base is limited to B and O and either positive or negative."

"But why three abductions in a row, a few weeks apart, if any of the three kidnapped victims could have, theoretically, supplied the required organ transplant?" Simon felt callous and ill just saying those words aloud.

"Theoretically is the key word, Fletcher. Is blood type the only qualifying element for transplant?"

Simon frowned. "No. After the donor and recipient blood samples are cross typed and matched, the tissue compatibility test, the HLA, must be a good match too."

"Yes, a good match of all three tests is necessary for the best outcome. In addition, the donor candidate has to be healthy, free of bloodborne diseases such as HIV, hepatitis, and so on. Cancer is also a disqualifying condition."

"So, you're suggesting that Morales and Whatley, for whatever reason, didn't work out."

"No, I am suggesting, *first* of all, that not only was it necessary to find the best possible match for the recipient in question, it was also necessary to do so *quickly*. If the recipient's health had taken a downturn, it would explain why multiple 'donor candidates' were taken in rapid succession." She tapped a finger on her chin. "All of that said, it is possible that you are partially right. For example, Morales may have been a better match than Xú, but unfortunately, he was being treated with interferon."

"And you know this how?"

Miss Finch lifted long-suffering eyes toward heaven.

Simon sniffed. "Fine. Another gold star for your hackers. Was the interferon for hep B or C?"

"Hepatitis B."

"So Xú drew the short straw."

"I rather think all three of these young men 'drew the short straw,' Fletcher, since I do not foresee the police ever finding Morales or Whatley alive, do you? Furthermore . . ."

She lapsed into silence until Simon could take it no longer.

"Furthermore, what?"

"Oh, just more theorizing."

"Tell me."

"Very well. I can tell you that while our enterprising serial killer may have been hired to obtain a specific organ compatible with the transplant needs of a difficult-to-match recipient, he would soon have realized he would have viable organs left over and all the other components of a successful transplant—surgical suite, equipment, pharmaceuticals, and medical staff— already at his fingertips. What then?"

"Are you saying he went trolling for buyers? Other transplant patients?"

"I am. Either he convinced his client to defray expenses by finding other patients, or our doctor acted on his own volition, identified other likely recipients, and lined them up to receive their transplants just as quickly as the staff could run them through."

She sighed. "And what of the two 'extra' unwilling yet viable donors left on his hands? If our doctor is acting on his own while his initial client heals, the organs of two healthy donors represent a figurative gold mine."

"I thought you said Morales had hep B."

"Ah, but hepatitis B is generally a short-term virus infection of about six months, although Morales' condition must have been chronic enough to warrant being treated with interferon. However, if, after treatment, he were to fully recover without damage to his liver, he could be passed off as a viable donor too."

"So, why the recent O negative abductions?"

Her response was cool and detached. "Why, indeed . . . and why children?"

Simon mulled over her response. "O neg blood is fairly rare, so transplant organs would also be rare."

He stilled. "Whoa. You're saying that now . . . now the killer is taking 'orders' for hard-to-find organs? And to fill those orders, is seeking out, then disappearing 'donors' likely to match the patient's need?"

"I posit that patients in need of a transplant, but who are so far down the transplant list as to despair of receiving a matched organ before their time runs out? *Those* patients present a high-end niche market, and our killer is attempting to cash in on that market. Why? Because an individual who can afford to pay an outrageous price for what may save their life will certainly do so—no questions asked."

Simon stood, paced to Miss Finch's firepit, and stared up at the sky, noting the scudding clouds overhead, before plunging headfirst down the horrible, yawning abyss before him. "Tell me: How much money are we talking here for custom-procured, black-market organs?"

"Potentially? Whatever a needy individual or individual's family can bear. Easily several hundred thousand dollars per organ. Millions, at the top end, I should think. Consider this: If you had unlimited funds, how much would you be willing to pay to save, say, your spouse or your child's life?"

Simon didn't have to think long before images of Miss Finch and Skipper rose before him. He swallowed hard. "Whatever it took . . . but only if the transplant were legit."

"Ah, but if you strike the moral clause entirely, you will soon begin to understand what we may be up against. Desperate people do desperate things."

She twiddled with her pad, and went on as though Simon had asked additional questions.

"Usually, when a donor is declared brain dead, their body is kept 'alive' through machines. At that point, the organ procurement team will test each organ to determine whether or not the deceased person's organs are viable for transplant."

She again glanced up. "If Morales and Whatley were not good matches for the transplant need that kicked off this string of abductions, but if they are otherwise healthy—or, as in Morales' case, will be healthy in time—they might still be alive, waiting to be matched with paying recipients. Of course, our killer would want to maximize his profits, so I surmise that he would wait until he has garnered recipient candidates for as many organs as possible. Then they would schedule and perform all the transplants in quick succession, heart and lungs first, followed by liver, then kidneys, pancreas, and corneas."

"What if . . . what if an otherwise matching donor has a disease?"

"As I alluded, a donor with cancer or a dangerous virus would be unacceptable in most instances, but even organs from an HIV-infected donor have their uses. An HIV-positive recipient can receive an organ from an HIV-positive donor. A real moneymaker, that one."

Nausea boiled in Simon's gut. "You're saying these guys, Morales and Whatley, are still alive, being kept against their will, being fed and cared for like cash cows? In other words, fattened for slaughter?"

"Yes, if our emerging hypothesis is correct."

"Then Allysson Sharma could be alive too."

"Sound thinking; appalling likelihood."

"The police need to know all this! I mean, some law enforcement agency has to be aware of Xú's COD, but beyond that, they need to understand that they have an active organ harvesting ring right here in the lake area!"

"I may be going out on a limb here, Fletcher, but I suggest they already 'get' it. It is, after all," she murmured, "only a matter of distilling the facts down to the reasonable conclusions you and I have reached in less than half an hour of discussion, *if* . . . if they are paying attention to other news throughout the lake area."

"You said we should do something about this. Well, I want to understand how our mastermind finds his victims. Like, before he kidnaps them, how does he know a victim's blood type?"

She slowly nodded. "Yes, I will assign that task to my tech team. We have a total of five abductions or attempted abductions at the moment. My team will scour the victims' lives until their commonalities surface . . . if commonalities exist."

"Oh? How will they go about it this time? Hack the Pentagon?"

She scoffed softly. "Really, Fletcher! The Pentagon was hacked so many times in the past, the effort became passé. The truth is, the victims might not share *any* commonalities other than that their blood types are in one or more large databases along with thousands of others of the same desired blood type."

"And yet our victims just happened to visit Tahoe. How do you research that phenomenon?"

"Bots," Miss Finch murmured. "Automated AI-driven bots . . . not unlike what my team uses."

"Uh, I'm not up on all that cyber lingo. Care to explain?"

She sniffed in that supercilious manner he'd grown accustomed to, and he grinned to himself.

Grown accustomed to it? Or is it that I've grown fond of it?

"I am told that automated bot traffic now accounts for a hair more than fifty percent of all web activity today, meaning bot web traffic is greater than human-produced traffic. Programmers use artificial intelligence or AI to generate more sophisticated Application Programming Interfaces—APIs—then build those APIs into the bots. Result? A bot's ability to snoop through the internet and seek out its mission parameters expands exponentially.

"Foreign entities have used AI-powered bots to spy on us—and they're still one of the biggest threats to our nation and military. These bots, however, don't merely spy on us. They steal important ideas, break into our defense systems, learn how we operate, and look for ways to defeat us.

"But a simple sniffer bot? One whose API enables it to shake hands with, say, various regional blood banks, hospitals, and medical labs, and that simply returns info on individuals with the sought-after blood types? Those bots, because of their seemingly less harmful objectives, are not considered as dangerous as malicious spy bots. And sniffer bots are so simple as to be practically invisible, not scraping massive amounts of personally identifiable information, in fact, leaving no noticeable trace or damage behind, and copying only tiny bits of the data being sought—the names, date of birth, and social security numbers of individuals whose blood types are compatible with the most difficult-to-procure organ types.

"Why? As I said before, patients who are unlikely to procure a matching donor through legal and ethical channels, are desperate. And as we have previously discussed, a *wealthy* desperate individual will pay whatever is demanded—hang the ethics."

"So, our killer is—pardon me—a 'killer' programmer too?"

"Good catch. The answer is 'doubtful.' He may have his own team, based in Ukraine or Pakistan, writing the custom code for him at quite reasonable rates."

"But how does our killer know when unsuspecting victims will visit—or ever visit—Tahoe?"

"I assume that when potential donors choose to visit Lake Tahoe, they will do so, at least in part, as the result of a cyber psyop."

"A cyber psyop? What the devil is *that?*"

"Have you not experienced shopping online for a particular item only to have twenty ads for that item or its competition's item jump out at you from every site you visit?"

"Uh, I don't actually spend much time online."

"Well, for those potential donors who do spend time online, the bots can be programmed to put Lake Tahoe vacation ads and deals right in front of their faces."

"But kids? They don't make vacation decisions, do they?"

She shrugged "Easy enough to program AI bots to influence the prospect's parents. Our killer might even resort to such enticements as dirt-cheap packaged holidays to Tahoe, hotel and airfare included, or how about a 'you've won a free vacation' lure?"

"This is making me sick."

"And that is only the donor side of this scam. Our killer must also attract the recipient side."

"But how would he do that? Aren't private organ donations illegal?"

Miss Finch's glare reached out and scorched him where he sat. "They are most certainly illegal when the 'donor' *dies* to provide said 'donations.' I believe they still call it *murder*, Simon Fletcher."

He held up his hands to shield himself from her death ray. "Settle down, Finchy! I only asked in order to understand how one 'markets' an illegally obtained organ."

She leaned toward him, eyes narrowed to slits. "*Do not call me Finchy, Mr. Fletcher.*"

He leaned right back, invading her personal space, and matched her slitted eyes with his own. "I will abstain from calling you Finchy, *BeeDee*, when you stop trying to fry me with that scowl of yours."

She sniffed again. Sat back. Eventually nodded.

"Fair enough."

Simon tried to hide his amazement with his own cool sniff. "Good. Now get on with how our killer markets his stolen organs."

"Well, I doubt that somewhere on the web, our killer posts a great big 'Human Organs For Sale' sign."

Simon caught on. "Sure. Can't sell black market human organs out in the open on the world wide web. But if law enforcement can't find a site on the dark web, how does anyone seeking a less than up-and-up organ donation find one?"

"I highly doubt that *our* killer's endeavor is anything new or unique. Many individuals or groups may be engaged in illegal organ transplant commerce. Illegal organ procurement may even be a profitable segment of organized crime syndicates."

She sighed deeply. "If the industry is as extensive as I believe it to be, it will also be highly structured, systematized, and anonymized to protect each part and person of the system from exposure. I imagine that the industry engages with a network of freelance brokers who identify needy recipients, vet them, and when satisfied with their bank accounts—and after extracting their fee—provide the recipients with an introduction to an organ provider. The providers themselves may then employ single-use payment pages on the *dark* web to conduct their business."

Simon was trying to absorb the glut of information about this ugly industry when Miss Finch sighed.

"What? What is it?"

"I am supposed to be working on my second book, you know, *Forensics of a Suicide*."

"Not *that* bone of contention again! Because your first book wasn't problem enough?"

"I already told you that the first edition of my book contains three case studies unrelated to my grandfather, Don Massimo, or the Lucchese Family. It is a straight-forward teaching tome. It is, aside from final edits, ready to go to press in January. It is the *second* edition that requires additional work."

"The second edition that adds three case studies to your initial three, one of which is your grandfather's supposed suicide and that will prove that all three of the new case studies can be tied to Don Mossimo and his syndicate? Like you don't already have a target on your back?"

"It is the threat of publication that keeps Don Massimo at bay. Meanwhile, the feds are using my data to build their own case against the Don and his 'family.' That said, I am concerned that the scope of *this* case may delay the release of my second edition."

"I'm in favor of you pulling your proposed second edition altogether. You could inform Don Massimo that you will *not* publish it in exchange for him leaving you strictly alone. The old 'mutually assured destruction' routine."

She pursed her lips as though she might be considering his words.

Just then Skipper and the two Nadeau boys stopped at the top of Miss Finch's driveway. The three kids were hot, sweaty, and thoroughly dirty from the dust gathered while riding the paths out in the heavily treed property belonging to Bright Star.

"We'll talk more later, Fletcher."

"Right."

"Hey, Fletch!" Skipper shouted.

"Hey, Skipper. Did you have a good time?

"Sure did."

Simon looked them over and asked, "What happened to Sophie?"

Wyatt answered, "She's only eight, and she got tired, so we took her to our mom and dad, then we went back into the woods and had all kinds of races over the trails and bumps and stuff. It's a lot of fun!"

"Yeah, but we're headed back to their site right now," Skipper added. "They gotta be back by 5:30 for dinner every evening."

"Sounds like we should be headed home too."

"Okay, but I was telling Wyatt and Eli about the bike trail along Emerald Bay Road. If it's okay with their dad and mom, could you take us with you in the morning when you go running? You know, before it gets too hot?"

"How about I drive over and talk to their folks before I commit to anything?"

"That would be awesome, Fletch."

"Yeah, really cool, Mr. Fletcher!" Eli agreed.

"It's just Fletch or Fletcher," Skipper told him.

Eli slid his eyes to Simon; Simon nodded.

Eli nodded back. "Uh, okay. Thanks, Fletcher."

THE BOYS LEFT, and Simon said goodnight to Miss Finch. When Simon drove around to Site 19, the Nadeaus were happy to see him.

"Our boys are having such fun," Mr. Nadeau enthused. "The trails in the woods are great exercise for them."

"It's a bit much for Sophie, who is not as aggressive as her older brothers," Mrs. Nadeau added, "but the boys are talking about a paved bike trail through the woods along Emerald Bay Road?"

"They mean the Pope-Baldwin Bike Path," Simon answered. "It's just short of four miles long, all of it paved."

"And is this trail safe? Will the children need supervision?"

"Oh, it's quite safe," Simon answered. "I run the path each morning, and Miss Finch rides her bike on it regularly. The only thing I would caution is that they need to be watchful of the many pedestrians who walk the same paved path. The kids should be polite and considerate of pedestrians as they ride by. What I've found, however, is that the earlier you go, the fewer people you'll encounter on the path. If you approve, I suggest we get up extra early tomorrow to avoid the crowds *and* the heat."

Sophie spoke up, "Well, I want to go too!" She scowled at her brothers. "You went too fast out in the woods, and I couldn't keep up!"

"She was a trifle overwhelmed," Mrs. Nadeau supplied. "Our children are not used to such liberty. We live in Laval, a city that adjoins Montreal, you see, and we do not allow them to roam about freely in our neighborhood—too many cars and not many safe places to ride, not to mention how many strangers they might encounter. It is a real treat for them to spend so much unfettered time outdoors, and it is a pleasure for us to watch them enjoy themselves."

"I'm willing to take them and their bikes down to the trail tomorrow, but I'll be running while they ride, so I can't say I'll have eyes on them the whole time," Simon said, "but as long as they stay on the paved path and stick together, they should be fine."

"If you say the path is safe and you will take the boys down and back, we will agree," Mr. Nadeau said.

"I want to go tomorrow too!" Sophie declared.

Mr. and Mrs. Nadeau looked to Simon.

He grinned at the little pixie. She ducked her head, but her shy, dimpled smile appeared again. Simon looked at Skipper. "Will you make sure to keep Sophie with your troop? What I mean is, don't leave her behind?"

"Sure. We'll keep her with us," Skipper promised.

"Does that mean you'll take us tomorrow?" Eli asked, eager for Simon's answer.

Simon smiled. "If it's all right with your folks, I will take you."

Skipper bounced on his toes. "Fletch! Fletch! Just had an idea: Do you think Miss Finch would like to go with us?"

"Hey," Wyatt whispered—loud enough for all to hear. "Are you talking about that short old lady? The one who backed our RV? Won't she slow us down?"

Skipper guffawed. "Slow us down? Dude, she's got an eBike. We'll be lucky if we can keep up with *her*."

Simon tapped his chin. "Hmm. Her going with us would solve the logistical problem of where everyone sits. I can get all the bikes in the back of my truck, but can't seat six people at one time—just three, tops."

Skipper grinned. "Cool! I'll go ask her right now."

His feet were already moving in the direction of Miss Finch's site, then he skidded to a stop and turned to Simon.

"Hey, Fletch, Pastor Kent called to remind me that youth group is meeting down on Baldwin Beach Thursday evening to do that stargazing thing. He's calling Miss Finch to remind her to bring her deck of cards and asked me to remind you that you volunteered to be a chaperone."

"Right. Zane and Kevin reminded me the other day."

"Cool!" Skipper was halfway up the Nadeaus' driveway.

"What's youth group?" Wyatt asked, sprinting to catch up.

Eli was right behind him. "Yeah, what's this stargazing thing?"

Simon heard Skipper filling them in as they jogged down the road in the direction of Miss Finch's site.

———— ● ————

THAT NIGHT, AFTER Skipper went to bed, Simon stayed up, doing additional research about blood types on his laptop. Everything he read validated Miss Finch's tutorial, but as he kept digging, he learned more.

For one thing, he read how scientists had discovered that human blood had more than one Rh antigen, forty-nine, to be exact. The antigen they called Rh D became the most significant of the forty-nine antigens, because it was the missing piece when certain blood types were labeled Rh negative.

He even stumbled upon another type, "Rh null," a rare blood type identified in 1961 in an Indigenous Australian woman. This new type possessed *none* of the forty-nine Rh antigens, thus the "null" in its name.

Interesting, Simon thought.

He read until he grew too sleepy to keep going.

CHAPTER 13

THE MORNING WAS hot, the harbinger of midsummer heat to come. When Simon rolled Skipper out of bed, even before the sun rose, the air outside was still warm from the afternoon and evening before. Skipper was truculent and resisted Simon's efforts to get him up until Simon reminded him why they were getting up early. At that, Skipper shucked off his reluctance and got moving.

"This is gonna be epic," he enthused, trying hard to wake up by widening his eyes as much as he could several times.

"Yup. Why don't you take Napoleon out to do his business while I fix breakfast? When you get back, maybe you can tell me more about your visit with your dad."

"Sure. Hey, Nappy! Come on."

When Skipper returned, the two of them sat down at the table.

"Say, have you asked Wyatt and Eli to come to the youth group stargazing event tomorrow evening?" Simon asked while he poured out two bowls of raisin bran, coffee for himself, and hot chocolate for Skipper.

"Oh, man—and I even told them about it! No, I haven't, but I'll do it today. Thanks for the reminder. It's gonna be really cool."

"I think so too." Simon changed the subject. "So, Skipper, are you still happy about your meeting with your dad?"

Skipper slurped his cocoa and came up with a chocolate mustache. "Mostly. It was hard to say some things to him at first 'cause I didn't know how he'd react. But because you reminded me that Jesus didn't get mad at his brothers for not believing in him, I was able to not get mad at Dad. And because I didn't get mad, it made it easier to tell him what I was feeling."

Skipper picked up his spoon. "I think . . . I think he was kinda surprised."

"Oh?"

"Yeah, I told him how I felt about him up and leaving me and Mom without a word, how hard it is on Mom having to work so much. I even told him that if he's sincere about being sorry, he should start helping Mom by paying child support and that other thing."

"Do you mean spousal support?"

"Mom called it something else."

"Alimony?"

"Yeah, that."

"I believe spousal support and alimony are the same thing, although California doesn't call it alimony anymore." Simon thought a moment. "I'm surprised the court isn't garnishing your dad's wages to compel him to pay support. That's pretty common these days."

"Yeah, well I don't think they're officially divorced yet. Mom got a lawyer and all, but because she didn't know where Dad had gone, she wasn't able to finish the divorce."

"The lawyer should have hired someone to find out where your dad is living and working. Then he could have arranged to have the divorce papers served to him."

Skipper shrugged his shoulders and stared into his cereal bowl. "Lawyers cost a lot of money, Fletch, and Mom couldn't afford to keep paying him."

Simon realized the boy was conflicted. "Have you been hoping your folks would get back together, Skip?"

Skipper nodded. "Yeah, but I don't know if they will, now that I've met Sherri and Demi. Dad says he and Sherri want to get married."

Can't get married without getting divorced first, Simon thought.

"What kind of work does your dad do?"

"He's a software developer. Had a great job where we live, but Mom says he quit that job when he left. She said he probably took one outside of California."

If he's working, I know someone with a team of brilliant tech guys—and gals—in her employ. Bet they can find out where Pete Mitchell is working, Simon told himself.

"What did your dad say when you shared your feelings?"

"Well, he said he understood how I felt, and then he said he was sorry, especially for leaving without saying anything. Thing is, I'm not really sure he actually *is* sorry, but at least he said he was. And then I found myself telling him about Jesus, how he came into my heart and is changing me on the inside. That's when he got surprised."

Simon's lips parted. "Wow. I'm really impressed, Skipper—or maybe I should call you Skipporama?"

The kid's forehead scrunched up. "Why? What's the 'orama' part mean?"

"It means a wide or big view, I think, like a panorama photo is wide. I wasn't teasing you, by the way. It was meant as a compliment. I added 'orama' to your name because I think you acted wisely. You took the bigger, wider view, that leading your dad to Jesus could be your dad's first step toward getting his life right, maybe even reconciling with your mom. Because when you get truly reconciled to God, it often spills over into all your other relationships."

Skipper looked up with hope in his eyes. "Really? That's way cool."

"Yup, so when you pray for your dad, take the long, wide view and pray mostly for him to give his life to Jesus, okay? It doesn't guarantee he and your mom will get back together, but surrendering to Jesus is the first step anyone can take to get their messed-up lives fixed."

Skipper dug into his cereal. "Then that's what I'll pray." He glanced at Simon and, through a full mouth, grinned and said, "Skipporama, huh?"

"Yup. Sooo much better than Skipperdoomandgloom, don't you think?

Skipper cracked up. "Skipperdoomandgloom, huh? Ha ha! Good one!"

TWENTY MINUTES LATER, after Skipper had fed Napoleon, walked him again and put him back in his kennel, they headed for Bright Star to meet up with the Nadeau kids at Miss Finch's site. Another twenty minutes after that, they were on the road, all the bikes except Miss Finch's eBike in the back of Simon's maintenance truck. Wyatt shared the truck's cab with Simon and Skipper; Eli and Sophie rode in Miss Finch's woody with Hugo and Pouncer, her eBike in the back.

Around 5:15, amid sleepy-eyed yawns, they parked in the small but empty parking lot of Tallac Trail Bikes. Jasper's bike shop wouldn't open for several hours, and they would be back at Bright Star by then, so their vehicles wouldn't be taking up precious parking needed by Jasper's customers.

Simon and the boys unloaded the four bikes from the truck, then Simon lifted out Miss Finch's eBike from her woody and set it on the parking lot while she removed the harnesses Hugo and Pouncer wore while traveling in the rear seat of her woody.

"That's a strange bike," Eli said to Skipper.

Sophie, her curly hair done up in two pigtails touched Miss Finch's eBike reverently. "It's really pretty. I like the basket a lot."

Eli pressed his point. "But the wheels are awful . . . tiny."

"Well, it's the perfect size for Miss Finch," Skipper replied. "Besides, that thing can really go. Why, you should see her hit the bumps and moguls out in the woods. She catches considerable air, let me tell you."

"Really?" The Nadeau boys eyed Miss Finch with uncertain respect.

"No catching air today, though," Miss Finch said as she placed Pouncer in her front basket beside Hugo. "Now sit still, both of you," she ordered. Hugo grinned, his tongue hanging out one side. Pouncer yawned like bored royalty.

Sophie came alongside Miss Finch and carefully petted Hugo on his head. She smiled when he leaned into her hand and closed his eyes in bliss. Sophie thought to get acquainted with Pouncer too, but one look at Her Majesty's chilly blue glower was enough to convince Sophie to leave Pouncer quite alone.

"Even if the Pope-Baldwin Bike Path here had 'bumps,'" Miss Finch continued, twining a short bungee cord around her cane and her bike's handlebars, "we need to remember that we share this path with pedestrians, including older folk, and must be careful not to startle or endanger them."

She glanced up with a mischievous gleam in her eyes. "Besides, who would want to crash out on pavement? Not I! I'll save my crashes for the soft dirt trails in the woods, thank you very much."

"Speaking of 'crashing out,'" Simon interjected, "as a Marine, I would be remiss not to deliver a proper safety briefing before we head out."

Wyatt and Eli gaped.

Wyatt asked in awe, "You're a Marine, Mr. Fletcher? A real one? Like . . . the soldier kind of Marine?"

Eli added, "Why don't you wear a uniform?"

"I retired from the military," Simon told him.

"Oh," both boys breathed in unison, clearly disappointed.

"Yeah, but once a Marine, always a Marine, guys," Skipper intoned. "He really is a Marine—trust me."

Again in unison and recovering their awe, the boys said, "Really?"

Simon laughed aloud; Miss Finch cupped a hand over her mouth.

"Thanks, Skip," Simon said, still chuckling.

Then, entirely for the Nadeau boys' benefit, he stepped back, straightened, clasped his hands behind him, and turned his face to iron. Employing his gravest, most gravelly Marine MP voice, he rumbled, "Listen up, you sorry excuses for recruits! I served *twenty years* in the United States Marine Corps before I retired honorably. I was a Marine *then*, I am a Marine *now*, I will be a Marine when I *die*, and I will be a Marine while I molder in my grave—and don't you forget it. *Do! You! Get! Me!*"

Sophie's eyes went as wide and round as hubcaps, and she sidestepped to disappear behind Miss Finch. Wyatt and Eli paled, and immediately stuttered, "Y-yes, sir!"

Simon strode forward, leaned into the boys' faces, and barked, "Chest out! Straighten those shoulders! What did you say, *recruits?* I couldn't hear you!"

"Yes, sir!" Wyatt and Eli threw back their shoulders and shouted in unison.

Simon grinned and stepped back. "Well done, boys."

Relieved, Wyatt and Eli managed to smile in return, although a trifle nervously. As for Skipper and Miss Finch? They'd both turned away, shaking with shared laughter.

But Sophie? Eyes still wide, she slowly crept up to Simon and shyly asked, "You aren't really a mean man, are you, Mr. Fletcher?" She swallowed and whispered, "At least . . . I don't *think* you are."

The courage she demonstrated in overcoming her natural timidity made Simon's eyes sting. "No, little pumpkin," he whispered back, throat tight. "I am not a mean man. Jesus has made me a kind man."

She nodded once. "I thought so." Finally smiling, she added, "I like you, Mr. Fletcher, even if you do roar louder than a bear!"

Simon's heart squeezed until it hurt. "I like you too, Miss Sophie. I like you a lot."

He found himself wondering, *Did the Nadeaus pluck this child out from under a cabbage leaf? Such interesting eyes and such a sweet, gentle soul— not at all like her brothers.*

Stuffing all his feelings back into their usual places, and with considerably more than his normal volume, he announced, "Okay, everyone gather around for the day's safety briefing. Ready? Right.

"First? *Gear.* No one rides without proper headgear, said headgear worn right. Everyone put on their helmet and make certain it is positioned correctly, dialed in nice and snug, and with the straps reasonably cinched."

Five riders donned their helmets and made the necessary adjustments. Miss Finch helped Sophie get her straps straightened and snapped.

"Outstanding! Second? *Etiquette.* Ride on the right side of the path, just like cars drive on the right side of the road. When passing walkers, be courteous. Ring your bell, if you have one, or call out, 'On your left' or 'Passing left' to alert them before you get to them. And when you approach pedestrians walking on the right or those who are walking toward you, always slow your speed.

"Third, and most important ? *Ride with safety in mind at all times.* I'll be jogging the path, so I imagine all of you will soon be far ahead of me. Miss Finch and Sophie will ride together. Boys? I expect you to stick together, too. Under no circumstances will any of you go off on your own— am I right?"

Five voices answered, "Right!"

"Last of all? *Keep track of the time.* We'll meet back here at 6:30 sharp. Any questions?"

"Yeah, can we go now?" Skipper groaned, raising a laugh from Wyatt and Eli.

Simon smiled. "Sure. Turn right and ride down the alley between Jasper's bike store and the next building over; you'll see the bike path where it crosses the alley. Turn left onto the path and have fun."

He muttered under his breath, "I'll just wait until you kids leave so you don't run me down—in spite of my safety briefing."

Moments later, with much whooping and shouting, the boys disappeared, followed at a more sedate speed by Sophie, Miss Finch, Hugo, and Pouncer. Simon hung back until they were smartly away before starting his run.

He set a slow pace initially, giving his legs time to warm up, then moved up smoothly to a moderate speed.

Man, staying in shape is getting harder every year.

Down the familiar path he jogged, breathing deeply of the pine trees towering above him, reveling in the fresh breeze, the morning quiet, and the peace in his heart. As his legs warmed, he stretched out and lengthened his stride.

Lord, this is good. A great day to be here. Skipper is doing well, things with Joe and Holly are getting better, my friendship with Miss Finch is restored, and we're working on another case. We're even chaperoning the youth group together tomorrow evening.

Basically, all things are right in Simon Fletcher's world this morning, Lord, and I thank you.

The area where he was running was blissfully still and quiet this early in the morning. He nodded to the usual early-morning walkers, noted the area just past Camp Richardson with the downed log on which he'd found Miss Finch last month, nursing her knee after taking a fall on the path. When the trail curved sharply west, he gazed to his left, catching glimpses through the trees of Mount Tallac in the distance. The lake was on his right, not far, but unseen from the bike path.

Then Simon heard the boys' approach long before he saw them heading his way. They had already hit the end of the trail and turned around, while Miss Finch and Sophie were ahead of Simon but likely hadn't reached Emerald Bay Road yet, where the trail ended.

The raucous, unrestrained joy of three teen boys reached out and slapped him across the face as they blew by him shouting, screaming, and ringing their bike bells. Simon couldn't find it in him to fault their rowdy behavior. Hardly anyone else was on the path at the moment, so they were enjoying themselves to the full.

He smiled and picked up his pace. Yes, all things were right in Simon Fletcher's world.

CHAPTER 14

THURSDAY DAWNED BRIGHT and clear, an auspicious start to the church youth group's big stargazing event later that evening. Simon and Skipper were driving the loop, doing their usual morning trash collection at each site, when the Nadeau boys, on their bikes, passed them.

"Say, did you remember to invite Wyatt and Eli to youth group tonight?" Simon asked. "I need to get their permission slips signed if they are to come."

"Oh, wow—I completely forgot. Can I go ask them now?"

"Sure, but make it quick, okay?"

"You got it, Fletch."

Simon honked the maintenance truck's horn once to get Wyatt and Eli's attention. When the boys turned around and rode back to them, Skipper jumped from the truck and quickly explained about the event. "I was telling you about it yesterday. You guys should totally come with us tonight."

Wyatt didn't seem too hopeful. "It sounds great and all, but our folks don't let us go anywhere unless they know the adults in charge."

"We can fix that. I mean, they already know Fletcher and Miss Finch, and they will be some of the chaperones tonight," Skipper answered.

"Do you think you can get them to come talk to our mom and dad about it?" Eli asked.

"Pretty sure Fletch will do that. Maybe Miss Finch too."

Skipper glanced at Simon, and he nodded. "Sure. I'll talk to Wyatt and Eli's folks."

"What about Miss Finch?"

Simon thought a moment. "Boys, why don't you head back to your site and tell your folks about the outing. Let them know that I'll be by in a few minutes to fill in the details. In the meantime, Skipper, you and I can drive back to Miss Finch's site and ask if she would come with us to talk to the Nadeaus. We can hustle and finish the trash run afterward."

Wyatt and Eli immediately rode off to tell their parents about the outing, while Simon and Skipper drove the remainder of the one-way loop in order to return to Miss Finch's site.

Simon found himself smiling at the prospect. *Any excuse will do.*

They stopped at the top of her site and walked down together.

"Hey, Miss Finch!" Skipper called.

She was, as usual, ensconced in her chair with her tablet in her lap. "Good morning, Skipper. Good morning, Fletcher. To what do I owe the honor of your presence on this fine morning?"

Simon explained, then asked, "Skipper has invited Wyatt and Eli to come tonight. Want to ride with us to the Nadeaus' site to vouch for the youth group's leadership?"

"Certainly. Let me just put Hugo and Pouncer in the catio."

Simon helped Miss Finch clamber into the truck's passenger seat while Skipper climbed into the truck's bed and sat beside Napoleon. The ride to Site 19 took only minutes. Simon had no sooner helped Miss Finch down from the truck than Sophie edged her way between them and slipped her hand into his.

Simon looked down and grinned. "Hey, little pumpkin."

Sophie grinned back. "I'm not a pumpkin!" she protested, although her eyes were dancing. "Not *truly.*"

Simon sighed. "Well, goodness gracious. My eyes must be playing tricks on me."

Sophie sobered and crooked a finger at him. When Simon leaned down, she said quite sincerely, "It's okay if you call me a little pumpkin, Mr. Fletcher. I know old people sometimes have trouble with their eyes."

Miss Finch snorted a giggle. A *giggle!* But she squelched it so fast and hard, it turned into a hiccup.

Simon swallowed an inexplicable lump in his throat. "That's very considerate of you, Sophie. Perhaps you could fetch Miss Finch a glass of water," he angled a glare in her direction, "before she hurts herself?"

As Sophie scampered off, Simon grumbled, "Yeah, well, if *I'm* old, what does that make *you?*"

Miss Finch snickered. "What does that make me? Entertained, Fletcher. Quite entertained."

"Oh, shush and drink your water."

Sophie returned as Simon spoke and offered a glass to Miss Finch that Simon was certain had lost the majority of its contents during Sophie's race to fetch it.

"Thank you, sweet Sophie," Miss Finch whispered.

"Skipper says it's going to be really cool, with real American barbecue food," Simon heard Wyatt tell his parents, "Then, when it gets dark, someone will point out which stars and planets we can see just by looking up at the sky. A guy is bringing a telescope too, and we'll get to take turns looking at the stars through it. Miss Finch is even going to do card tricks!"

"Yeah, and Mr. Fletcher and Miss Finch already said we could ride with them down to the beach," Eli added.

"Calm down and let us speak with Mr. Fletcher before we decide," Mr. Nadeau told them, turning to Simon. "Mr. Fletcher, as we are only summer visitors and not members of your church, are you certain the boys can attend this outing?"

Simon nodded. "Yes, I'm sure. I spoke to Pastor Kent, the youth group leader, a couple of days ago. He said Wyatt and Eli are most welcome to come. We're meeting for dinner down on Baldwin Beach around seven o'clock. That means dinner will be pretty late, but the reasoning behind the late start is that the sky won't be dark enough to truly see the stars until at least half-past nine. And as Miss Finch and I are chaperones this evening, we'd be happy to transport the boys to and from the event."

"Can I go too?" Sophie begged. She leaned against Simon's leg and stared up at him, her deeply brown eyes pleading with him and somehow reminding him of Miss Finch.

Mr. and Mrs. Nadeau looked to Simon for the answer.

He shook his head in regret. "I'm sorry, Sophie, but Pastor Kent says that kids need to be twelve or older to participate in youth group activities."

"I'll be thirteen in September!" Eli announced.

"And I'll be fifteen in December," Wyatt added.

Simon looked down on Sophie's curly head. "How old are you, little pumpkin?"

She stretched as high as she could—barely as tall the bottom of his rib-cage. "I'm not a *very* little pumpkin, Mr. Fletcher . . . even though I'm just eight."

Mr. Nadeau grinned. "I've never seen Sophie take to someone like she's taken to you, Mr. Fletcher. She's generally shy around strangers, and it takes her a while to warm up to them." He added, "She must feel extremely safe with you."

Simon smiled back. "I feel honored."

He looked down to Sophie again. "If it were up to me, you could come, but unfortunately, I didn't make the rules. Can you be a good recruit and choose to have a great attitude, even though you're disappointed?"

She slowly nodded, then straightened her shoulders. "Yes, sir!"

He saluted. "You'll make a fine Marine someday, Sophie."

With a beaming Sophie again holding his hand, Simon pulled a folded sheet of paper from his shirt pocket and handed it to Mrs. Nadeau. "Pastor Kent emailed me a consent form for Wyatt and Eli. I printed it out in the office yesterday afternoon. The form lays out the scope of youth group ac-tivities and its rules and expected behaviors. Your signature gives the boys permission to attend—and by the way, *parents* are invited to tonight's shindig . . . which, if you choose to attend, also means Sophie can accompany you." He winked at her, having saved that nugget until last.

"Really?" Sophie squealed.

"Really," Simon answered, "but only if your folks bring you."

Mrs. Nadeau was delighted. "How very thoughtful!" She glanced at her husband, then back. "We'll fill this out right away. The boys may ride with you, and we'll bring Sophie with us tonight."

"Cool!" Wyatt whooped.

———— ◆ ————

THE BALDWIN BEACH parking lot was teeming with youth group kids and their families when Miss Finch, with Simon in the passenger seat of the woody and three boys spread across the back seat, pulled into the lot. Zane and Kevin, Skipper's friends, were excitedly waiting for them. What became quicky apparent, though, was that although Skipper's friends were happy to see him, they were actually waiting for Miss Finch.

"You came!" Kevin exclaimed. "We've been telling everyone about your card tricks."

"Yeah," Zane interjected, "and we have more kids at tonight's youth group than we've ever had before. They can't wait to see you do your stuff!"

Miss Finch leaned on her cane as she settled her legs into balance, then shook her head and muttered, a trifle ruefully, "Oh, dear. Goodness me! I may have completely forgotten that I was supposed to provide an exhibition this evening. Why, I cannot even be certain I remembered to bring a deck of cards."

Simon caught sight of the horror blooming across Kevin and Zane's faces and busted out laughing. While Miss Finch looked on with a bland expression, Simon chuckled heartily. As for the kids gathered around them? They found nothing humorous about the situation.

Not a single thing.

Until Skipper scoffed and shouted, "Hey, guys? I think she's playin' us."

"What! You messing with us, Miss Finch?" Kevin eyed Miss Finch with the degree of disdain he'd level on a stink bug crossing the road.

"*I,* mess with you young gentlemen? Would I do such a thing? *Moi?*" Her left hand shot out of her pocket and a font of cards riffled through the air. Almost immediately, she released her cane, received the flying cards in her right hand, and secured the cane with her left hand before it toppled to the ground.

"Why, look here! I believe I have located my deck of cards," she murmured. "How providential."

The kids cheered and led the way to the picnic area.

———— ◆ ————

UNDER PASTOR KENT'S often repeated and longsuffering direction, the youth unloaded, unfolded, and lined up tables and chairs from the church for the food and adult seating, while other kids spread blankets on the sand for the teens. By the time the food was laid out and ready to serve, around fifteen adults, a handful of younger kids there with their parents, and thirty chattering teens were queued up with empty plates in hand.

Pastor Kent raised a hand and the commotion died down. "Lord, we thank you for this food we are about to receive. Please bless it and the hands that prepared it, we ask in Jesus' name. Amen."

"Amen!" the answering refrain roared.

Simon noticed that Zane—with unmistakable stars in his eyes—had introduced a new girl to the youth group, Eldora Devons. She wrinkled her nose as if she'd caught the scent of something unpleasant.

"Do you always pray over food?" she demanded.

"Well, yeah," Zane answered. "Don't you?"

"Not at all. I don't owe thanks to some mythical god for the food my aunt paid for and cooked."

Zane frowned. "Huh."

Simon studied the girl. She was remarkably observant and self-confident. *So we have a skeptic in our midst—and that's good. Lord, I ask you to empower Miss Finch to preach your good news as she does her card tricks this evening. I wouldn't want this young woman to leave our event this evening without hearing how much you love her.*

The line surged forward. Each plate received generous portions of the promised barbecue dinner: tender slices of brisket and chunks of seared sausage drizzled with sauce, dinner rolls, baked beans, and steaming corn on the cob. For a change, not one of the teens offered the oft-heard complaints of "I'm not hungry" or "I don't think I like that." No, by 7:15, even the pickiest eater was hungry and salivating over the food plopped onto his or her plate. And as the teens settled cross-legged onto blankets, the most overheard comment was "Yum!"

"My, this is certainly delicious," Mrs. Nadeau raved from the tables where the adults and small children were seated.

Mr. Nadeau was busy using a dinner roll to sop up the last traces of sauce from his plate. "Thanks for inviting us, Mr. Fletcher," he murmured, stuffing the last bite into his mouth. "Best barbecue I've ever tasted."

A dad from the youth group parents who'd provided the dinner called out, "Who wants watermelon?"

Like a swarm of locusts lifting from a ravaged crop, thirty or so teens jumped to their feet and beat a path to the food table to grab slices of melon from a deep tub. Even after feasting on the barbecue dinner, they gobbled down the juicy fruit.

Simon, who'd spent half his Marine career correcting the cutups of new recruits, wasn't the least bit surprised when a burping contest broke out. Watermelon, eaten quickly, had that effect. In fact . . .

He strode to where seven male teens were competing. "Stand aside, boys and let a pro show you how it's done."

Simon pounded his chest and sucked in a breath . . . and let it out. His thunderous and protracted belch was a soundwave of shock and awe. It left the parents dazed. It even silenced the teens.

Momentarily.

As their awe wore off, they broke into whoops, shouts, and whistles of praise.

That got Pastor Kent up from his seat at a table. "Well, well. Along with the *parents* who are here this evening, I'd like to *thank* Mr. Fletcher for his powerful, er, demonstration. Youth, please take note: Mr. Fletcher has *pre-emptively* surmounted every belching challenge from now into the next century . . . leaving further such competitions redundant and superfluous—that is, unnecessary."

Zane spoke up. "I have no idea what you just said, Pastor Kent. Can you translate, please?"

Pretty much everyone laughed and seconded Zane's question.

Pastor Kent looked around. "It means . . . that Mr. Fletcher has already won every belching contest for the next hundred years—so I'd better not *see* or *hear* of another such contest until after Jesus returns."

At this, the parents clapped and cheered, Simon took a bow, and the boys sat down in disgust.

"Well done, *Mr.* Fletcher," Miss Finch said dryly. "I knew you were a man of many talents, but this does beat all."

"Er, yes," Mrs. Nadeau agreed, "but if it puts an end to our boys constantly trying to outdo each other in that regard, I thank you."

Mr. Nadeau, though, put out his hand. "Splendid job, Fletcher. Couldn't have done better myself."

Just then, Pastor Kent called for silence. "Next up, we will invite Miss Finch to entertain us with her card skills—but first, we need to clean up." He added before the groans began, "Miss Finch will not begin until all the trash is cleared away."

That got the youth up and moving. Simon, still watching the new girl, saw that she merely sneered as others hurried to comply. Zane, who had gotten up, turned back when he realized she wasn't with him. He walked back and offered to take her plate to the trash.

Okay, Lord, we obviously have our work cut out with this one. Holy Spirit, please move in power this evening. And please protect Zane's heart. Let him influence her toward you and not the other way around.

Soon it was time for Miss Finch's part of the program. Pastor Kent moved a card table to the spot on the sand she indicated, where her back was to the water. The youth spread out on blankets in front of her and crowded in close. Parents quickly scooted their chairs in for a better view.

Miss Finch took her place behind the card table and produced a brand-new deck of cards. Her audience dropped into an anticipatory hush.

"To begin, I will demonstrate a series of card shuffling methods."

Skipper, Zane, and Kevin had seen Miss Finch's flair with cards once before, but they were just as anxious as their friends to see her in action again.

She broke the seal on the box and slid the cards out, flexed the deck several times, then began, calling out the shuffling method as she performed each one several times.

"Overhand shuffle. Two-handed riffle-shuffle. Bridge."

Soon she was doing all three, one after the other, again and again, settling into a cadence. Simon knew she was about to shift into a higher gear.

"Faro shuffle, ending in a bridge. Waterfall . . . Cascade . . ."

Cards streamed from her left hand to her right, flowed up and down, as though entirely disconnected from her hands, her speed increasing until the cards mesmerized her audience. Lastly, they flowed onto the table into a tidy little stack.

"Ready for our lesson?"

Resounding applause and cheers answered in the affirmative.

"I want to use my deck of cards to tell you a true story, the story of God's love for us—the Gospel in a nutshell."

She looked up and said, "First, I need a voluntold. Wyatt, would you come up here and help me with my story?"

"But I didn't volunteer!"

"That's why it's called a 'voluntold,' she deadpanned.

Everyone laughed, cheered, and applauded. Wyatt, put on the spot, got slowly to his feet and joined her at the front.

"This deck of cards," she said, fanning the entire deck in one hand and holding it so that the teens and children watching her closely could see the faces of the cards in her hand, "represents God's creation."

She lifted the fanned deck and held it high so her entire audience could see the cards too. "Like this deck, when God created the world, it was brand-new: good, clean, and beautiful."

She turned over her hand and showed the back of the fanned cards, then used one finger to bring the cards together into a deck, tapped the top card with her finger, and flipped it over onto the deck.

It was the king of hearts.

"This card, the king of hearts, represents God and all of his love for us. In his love, he created us in his image and likeness and gave us this beautiful world to live in. She laid the king on the table and left it there, face up.

"But then man sinned, and the world became a very dark place . . ." Still holding the deck in one hand, she suddenly, using only her thumb, flipped up the next card and held up the deck to show the seven of spades. "This card represents us, all people, and our sin. What is sin? It is the bad things in our hearts and the bad things we do that grieve God who made us."

All eyes were on the seven of spades as Miss Finch used her thumb to flip it back over so it was again facing down, still the top card in the deck.

She looked up. "Wyatt, please hold out your hand."

A very nervous Wyatt held out his hand. With the index finger of her other hand, Miss Finch slid the top card off the deck into Wyatt's outstretched palm. "There. In your hand you hold the seven of spades, representative of your sin, my sin, the world's sin. Put your other hand on top of that card so it remains right where I put it."

Wyatt obediently brought up his other hand and covered the card with it.

Miss Finch again shuffled the deck, and again, one-handed, turned over the top card, keeping it atop the deck. The new card was the jack of hearts. She held up the deck and tapped the jack once. "This card, the jack of hearts, represents Jesus, the Son of God. Because Jesus loves us, he came to die for us and take away our sin."

She turned over the jack of hearts so it was again face down on the deck. "In fact, Jesus, *took* our sins, all of our sins, away from us, and put them on himself."

At that very moment, she, once more, turned over the top card and revealed *not* the jack of hearts, but *the seven of spades*. A gasp of astonishment rippled through her audience.

When her rapt audience quieted, she said, "In fact, when Jesus died on the cross, he took our sins with him to the grave so that when God looks at us, he no longer sees our sin, but sees Jesus."

She looked at Wyatt. "Show us the card in your hand, Wyatt."

Wyatt lifted his right hand off the card and flipped it over. It was the jack of hearts.

Wyatt stood stock still, astounded and . . . literally, the crowd went wild.

"Do you see?" Miss Finch asked. "Do you understand? Jesus will take *your* sin upon himself. As the Bible says, "God made Jesus, who had no sin, to be sin *for us*, so that in Jesus, we might become the righteousness of God."

"Nice trick, but I don't believe that Jesus did that," a young voice piped up. It was Eldora.

Miss Finch glanced up and met the defiant gaze of Zane's guest. "I believe Zane introduced you earlier. You are Miss Devons, if I recall correctly?"

She tossed her head. "I see no need for you to preface my surname with an outdated honorific. My aunt says such titles were designed to convey possession or availability—as though women were cattle to be raised then sold."

Thirty or so teens and their siblings blinked stupidly, unable to follow the girl's statements.

"Do you wish me to call you Devons? Or do you prefer Eldora?"

She shrugged. "Either will do."

"Well, Eldora, I understand your disbelief. I didn't believe at first either. However, now many years later, I know for certain that God loves me, that Jesus died for me, and that, once I surrendered my life to him, he forgave me. I know all these things from years of my own experience."

"You tell a pretty story; however, neither God nor Jesus exist."

"You are entitled to your opinion, of course, but I know from personal experience that they do."

"We really cannot know anything categorically," Eldora said with a shrug, "seeing as how absolutes do not exist."

The youth group began to fidget, and Miss Finch heard a low grumble emanate from the parents of the youth group. She held up her hand to forestall more vocal complaints.

"May I ask you a question, Miss Devons?"

"I cannot guarantee I can answer—or that you would agree with me should I give an answer."

"It is a simple ask," Miss Finch murmured. "You said absolutes do not exist, did I hear you correctly?"

"Yes. Absolutes do not exist."

"And are you *absolutely* certain?"

Eldora opened her mouth, then shut it. Her eyes narrowed. "I see what you're doing."

A few of the crowd's more observant parents tittered.

"What I am doing? I asked a question. Can you answer it?"

"I refuse to play your game," Eldora sniffed.

"But if absolutes in any form do not exist, how can you be certain of anything? Are you even standing here? How can you be certain, if certainties do not exist?"

Eldora glared at her. "You're just saying that to make fun of me."

"Dear girl, I do not wish to make fun of you, but neither do I wish you to be deceived. Truth exists everywhere in this universe. For example, it is true that the stars above us are farther away than we can imagine. It is also true that a mind far superior to ours designed this universe. But if you close your heart to truth, it will not, then, simply vanish or even ignore you. No, truth will, all your life, continue to tap you on the shoulder and prove itself to you."

Eldora fumed and no one else spoke or made a sound. The titters and whispers stopped.

Something holy was happening.

Miss Finch added, "Eldora, I would like you to take one thing, one precious, vital thing home with you this evening: God loves you. That is the greatest truth in the universe. The Bible tells it this way:

> *"For God so loved the world*
> *that he gave his one and only Son,*
> *that whoever believes in him*
> *shall not perish but have eternal life."*

"Well, I do not believe in him."

"That is your right; however, I will pray for you that God will open your heart to hear the Good News."

"Nothing about a fake god is good, let alone 'good news.' And I don't care if Jesus died. That was a long, long time ago."

"You would care if you knew he died *for you*, Eldora. Jesus himself said,

> *"There is no greater love*
> *than to lay down one's life*
> *for one's friends.*

"He loves you so much that he laid down his life for you, Eldora."

"Baloney."

"All right," Pastor Kent said. "Eldora and Miss Finch's discussion is good and can continue on the side, because God truly does want to answer our questions. Now, however, let's welcome Dr. Flemming, a retired astronomer, who will guide us in our stargazing expedition this evening. As you can see, he set up his telescope and, when he has finished his lecture, you can take turns looking through the telescope."

Dr. Flemming, an elderly gentleman, came forward. "Thank you, Pastor Kent. Since we're going to be looking up into the darkening sky quite a lot during the next thirty minutes, I recommend that all of you gather in a circle around me. If you are sitting in a lawn chair, you may lean your head back and look straight up. If you are seated on a towel or blanket on the ground in the center of the circle, you may wish to find space to lie back so you can stare straight up. In any event, do arrange yourselves in the next few minutes so we can begin."

Simon listened with half a mind as he watched Miss Finch and Eldora walk to a picnic table some distance away and sit down together.

He was surprised when Dr. Flemming's thirty minutes had passed by quickly and the kids eagerly put questions to him. He saw Miss Finch give Eldora a gentle squeeze on her shoulder before the girl brushed her hand away and walked off.

Miss Finch rejoined him as the kids were taking turns looking at Venus through Dr. Flemming's telescope.

"Any progress?" he asked.

"None to shout about; however, God's word is *alive*. I count on it continuing to speak into Eldora's heart and mind even should we never see her again."

Soon Pastor Kent said, "As we get ready to dismiss, let's do this, shall we? Our chairs and blankets are already in a circle. Let's join hands, all the way around, and pray that the God who designed and created everything we see, including the planets, galaxies, and stars shining in our night sky, and who loves us so much that he sent his Son to die for us, would reveal himself to every individual who gathered with us here this evening."

Amen, Lord, Simon prayed. *Please speak to this lost child, Eldora.*

CHAPTER 15

ANOTHER SIX DAYS passed—close to a week of blessed normalcy. No broken pipes, no flooded rec hall, no pyromaniac visitors, no heart attacks, and no out-and-out loggerheads with Holly. But also no word from Pete Mitchell, Skipper's dad, who had promised to call Skipper weekly.

It had been a week, to the day, since Skipper went to lunch with his dad, his girlfriend Shelly, and her daughter Demi. Skipper didn't say a word, but he worked at his tasks with lips thinned and tightly closed.

"Lord, if that guy breaks Skipper's heart, I'll gladly tune him up for you," Simon volunteered.

Your anger cannot produce my righteousness, Simon Fletcher.

"Uh, right. Sorry about that."

Tomorrow was Wednesday, also a week since Simon and Skipper had arranged for Miss Finch and the Nadeau kids to ride the Pope-Baldwin Bike Trail. That afternoon, Simon and Skipper again went about making arrangements for another early morning ride down on the bike trail with Miss Finch and the Nadeau children.

"We so appreciate you taking our children down to the trail," Mrs. Nadeau told him that afternoon. "They have had such lovely times in the woods with Skipper and with you and Miss Finch on the bike trail. We count ourselves quite blessed to have been given two months at Bright Star!"

For a second, Simon flashed back to the day the Nadeaus checked into Bright Star, just over two weeks ago. What she said just now, and something about Holly's hands that day nagged at him. A moment later, though, his half-formed thought whisked away as he became engrossed in nailing down the details of their ride in the morning.

At the end of the workday, Skipper and the Nadeau kids met up at the pool. Simon, of course, went straight to Site 1.

"Been thinking a lot about what you shared with me. The theories you've distilled and our conclusions."

"As have I," she cut in, "But first . . . unwelcome news."

Simon knew immediately. "Another body?"

She nodded. "Donald Whatley. I have no information on his cause of death, but I believe we may safely venture upon his body's condition."

"Yeah. Have to agree."

"Fletcher . . . what if we are somewhat 'off' in our suppositions concerning this serial killer, the person behind these abductions? Because three young men disappeared within a six-week period and someone harvested the majority of Xú's transplantable organs—and Whatley's also, we presume—we arrived at certain conclusions, *chiefly*, that our killer had a client for whom he or she had contracted to procure a specific organ."

"You have arrived at a different theory now?"

"More of an alternate but related theory. We assumed the motive for the abductions was the fee the client would pay our killer for a successful transplant. But what if, *initially*, money was not our killer's motivation? What if the abductions were to fill a personal transplant need?"

Simon slowly nodded. "You're saying that the killer may have needed one of Xú's organs for himself? Hmm. I'm not sure that works. If you are the patient in need of a transplant, would you to have the physical strength to oversee the work that goes into a transplant?"

Miss Finch sat still several moments, thinking. "Not for himself, then, but still personal."

"Someone close to our killer, then? A wife or child in need of a transplant?"

"It is a better fit. The best fit, actually."

"I have to agree. If so, let's try this scenario on for size: Say our killer, while well off, has financial 'limitations,' and let's suggest that of his three prisoners, he found Xú to be the best match for his loved one. *But* before the transplant could take place, the expenses began to overrun him. He may have needed additional funds immediately and realized Xú's other organs presented a golden opportunity to address his financial insolvency."

She shuddered. "I suppose the quickest way to find potential buyers would be the national transplant list, but access to that list is closely held and protected, usually limited to the staff at transplant hospitals."

"Right, but just how hard would it be for someone with the skills to custom build AI bots, to program an entirely different contingency of bots, send them to invade these transplant hospitals, and gain access to the transplant list?"

"Likely not all that hard. And once he had that list, he would know who was as far down on the list as his wife or child had been and, just as vital, *why* they were that far down. Some transplant recipients rank low on the list because of advanced age or disease or because of negative lifestyle issues. A patient too old, whose overall health is too far gone, who smokes, uses illegal drugs, or is morbidly obese? Those conditions make the odds of a successful transplant too low on which to waste a perfectly good organ—particularly when someone younger and healthier could make better and longer use of the available organ."

"But for our killer, it's the perfect setup, isn't it?" Simon asked. "Think about it: If your spouse or child were denied a legal transplant but someone reached out and offered you a black market organ, would you take it, no questions asked?"

Miss Finch sighed. "I would hope not, but I can certainly empathize with the temptation." She looked at Simon. "And really, regardless of which profile proves to be most accurate, it makes no difference to the innocent lives he has taken."

Simon thought of young Allysson Sharma. "If our killer has turned his actions into a purely money-making operation, it is possible for some of his involuntary 'donors' to still be alive."

"Yes, I agree," Miss Finch mused. "Our killer would keep his captive donors in good health until he has reached what he has determined to be his optimal sales quota."

"Gross."

"Indeed."

Lord, Simon prayed silently, *it is impossible not to hate what we have stumbled onto, and yet we cannot pretend we don't know about it. Please show us whatever we can do to end this . . . madness.*

———◆———

WEDNESDAY, JULY 16

EVEN THOUGH THEY again set out early the next day for the Pope-Baldwin Bike Path, Simon knew the morning would start out warm. Temps had only gone down to 73 degrees overnight, and the forecast called for a high in the mid-90s before the sun set. As it was, the thermometer was climbing toward 80 degrees when they reached the trail. They intended to ride quickly and return to Bright Star's sheltering trees by 7:30 a.m.—before the sun began to scorch everything in its path.

The boys had sensed the impending heat, and headed down the trail at a good clip to generate their own "air conditioning." Miss Finch had wiped her face as she and Sophie followed them at a more sedate speed.

Simon picked up his pace, moving reluctantly from a jog into a run. He was already sticky and sluggish.

Shake that off, Marine, he chided himself, pushing himself farther along the trail, passing his usual markers: Camp Richardson on his right, then the downed log on which he'd found Miss Finch nursing her knee, the trail curving sharply west, glimpses of Mount Tallac in the distance, his turnaround point not too far ahead.

The boys flew by him on their first return from the end of the trail. He smiled and waved; they jingled their bike bells.

He plodded on, goading himself, even though the day felt suddenly . . . different. Less sunny? Slightly chilly, even?

Strange . . . the sky was cloudless, the sun a blazing orb rising behind him, no cooling breeze touching his skin.

He didn't understand . . . and then he did.

The weather hadn't shifted at all. The change was inside him.

A foreboding. Growing. Prodding. Urging. Now hammering him.

A driving urgency, laden with sinister undertones.

Simon, aware at last, nerves tingling with concern, tore down the trail. He no longer needed to motivate himself to go faster. Fear was doing the job for him.

At that moment, the paved path began to bend north, away from Emerald Bay Road, putting more distance between him and the road, between him and . . .

Miss Finch. Sophie. They should be near the end of the trail . . . where it bumps up against the road.

I'll never get there in time!

Without missing a step, he spun to his left and sprinted through the trees and brush, leaping rocks and downed branches, making for Emerald Bay Road in great haste. He stumbled down the bank into a shallow runoff channel and back up the other side onto the shoulder of Emerald Bay Road. He ran, full out, his goal the point where the trail and the road intersected.

He could see all the way up the road to where it curved slightly to the right. Ahead of him, where the road bent away from view, the rising sun at his back reflected off a set of taillights, then silhouetted the rear end of a van.

A black van.

The van seemed to slow, not braking, more like someone had taken their foot off the gas. The van decelerated until it was barely rolling along, much slower than the posted speed limit or the usual flow of traffic, cautiously winding around the curve ahead.

The bike path ended at the road, just beyond that curve.

Lord, help!

He forced himself to go faster, and raged at himself for leaving his sidearm in the lockbox under his bed.

I should never have left my gun at home!

The van rounded the curve and was nearly out of Simon's sight. His last glimpse of the van was the glow of its brake lights when they came on . . . where Simon knew the bike path ended, butted up against the road.

But he was still too far away!

Too far from Miss Finch and Sophie.

Too far to save them.

CHAPTER 16

SIMON RAN HARDER than he'd run in his entire life. He pushed himself without mercy to close the gap between himself and the van ahead of him, and yet he acknowledged he would be too late to stop what he sensed was about to happen.

Faster! he demanded of his legs. *More!* he commanded his body, until his heart hammered violently in his throat and his labored breathing jangled in his chest with the deafening rattle of an elevated train lurching along its tracks. He pressed on, permitting himself no pity, no sympathy, no concessions.

Ahead, he heard the van brake hard and its doors slam. Seconds later, his ears caught shouted protests from Miss Finch . . . followed by a young girl's screams.

Sophie. Lord Jesus, please help me get there in time!

Holding nothing back, he goaded his body beyond its limits.

Miss Finch's bike was down on its side a few yards from where the path ended. Sophie's bike lay on the pavement farther back from the path's end.

An attacker wearing a ski mask was attempting to fend off Miss Finch —and Hugo? *Sweet little Hugo?* The snarling terrier had his teeth buried in the man's lower left leg and was tugging, shaking, and worrying the guy's calf for all he was worth.

Miss Finch's opponent kicked out and tried to dislodge Hugo, but at the same time Miss Finch kept attacking the man with her cane, doing those wondrous things she'd done to Craig Dinesh—those *whirling*, *whizzing*, *whacking* things—moving in to strike a knee here and a hand there—then quickly stepping back before attacking yet again.

Pouncer, on the outskirts of the fray, skulked back and forth in distress, her fur and tail standing straight up, distraught yowls emanating from her throat.

Miss Finch moved in and managed to land a blow on her adversary's jaw.

"*Yeow!*" the man screamed.

Simon's assessment of Miss Finch's situation took only a second. Of more dire importance was Sophie's safety!

A second attacker, an extremely large man also wearing a black ski mask, had one massive arm wrapped around the child, pinning her arms to her chest. He'd clamped his other hand over Sophie's mouth to muffle her screams, and he was running, carrying her while she kicked and struggled, straight toward the van's open side door, several yards from Simon.

Miss Finch struck her opponent another whack and shouted, "Fletcher! Save Sophie!"

Sophie's assailant hauled her to the open van door where he grabbed up a cloth of some kind and held it forcibly over Sophie's mouth and nose even as she twisted her head this way and that to stymy him.

As Simon pushed off the tree and moved toward Sophie, he recalled Miss Finch's recitation of Nina Easton's experience: "*She told the police that the man almost immediately pressed a rag over her mouth and nose, a rag I surmise was doused with chloroform or some similar tranquilizing drug easily poured onto cloth.*"

Sophie's struggles were waning when her assailant spotted Simon's approach.

The man shouted, "Keep back, dude, or I'll hurt her. I mean it!"

Simon slowed, but did not stop. He could not stop! Yes, Sophie's abductor was huge, easily one of the largest men Simon had ever seen up close, even in the Corps, and direct assault on the man holding Sophie seemed pointless. Yet the very idea of what might be intended for Sophie filled Simon's stomach with churning bile and added to the adrenaline already racing through his system. Inside of a few precious moments, he took stock of his opponent and evaluated his options.

I probably couldn't fight my way out of a wet paper bag at the moment, let alone take on this mountain on legs the size of railroad ties. At the same time, I must be exceedingly careful how I proceed. I don't dare give that thug a reason to hurt Sophie.

And yet, despite the odds against him, the only hope little Sophie had . . . was him.

I can't save her going up against that guy directly, Lord, but there has to be something I can do to prevent them from taking her. Something, Lord! Anything to keep them from driving away!

That "something" hit him like a brick.

Simon stumbled around to the driver's side of the idling van and yanked open the front door. There, in a cup holder, was the van's key fob. He found the engine's ignition button, pressed it to turn off the engine, then grabbed up the fob and hurled it with what strength he could muster, straight across Emerald Bay Road and into the brush on the other side.

The man on the passenger side of the van pulled open his door just as Simon threw the fob. A growl of rage issued from him. "I'm gonna kill you for that, you—" he cursed Simon viciously "—and then I'll have my way with that little girl!"

Sophie's timid brown eyes rose before Simon. "*I like you, Mr. Fletcher, even if you do roar louder than a bear!*"

"*I like you too, Miss Sophie. I like you a lot.*"

The sweetness of that exchange still sang along Simon's heartstrings—so much so that Mountain Man's vile threats filled Simon with a cold, righteous fury, a rage such as he'd never known.

"Lord, I'm going to need your help to take out that creep," he muttered, "because that's exactly what I plan to do."

He was recovering from his winded state, and strength was slowly returning to his limbs, yet it hardly mattered: Sophie's kidnapper was in a weight class far above Simon's. Despite his own muscled arms and the impressive breadth of his chest, Simon knew he was outmatched. The thug was built like an NFL linebacker: He was younger and taller, had longer arms, and carried more overall mass than Simon did. Nor had his opponent just run flat out to the point of collapse.

Whatever the odds, I have to do this. Must do this! I don't care about myself, Lord; just please grant me the grace to rescue Sophie from these monsters.

He ran around the back of the van with the words, " . . . *even if you do roar louder than a bear!*" rolling around inside him. He was flooded with determination, resolved to give *all* of whatever he had to stop those men from taking Sophie.

"GARRR!" he roared. "*GARRR!*"

His opponent looked startled, then he laughed.

Oh yeah?

Simon's sent his left fist toward his opponent's mouth, but the guy's arm shot through Simon's reach and served up a right to Simon's jaw before Simon could connect. He stumbled backward, stunned and bleeding.

As soon as he regained his feet, he stalked forward, shouting, "Come on! Is that all you've got?"

He came at his adversary, both powerful arms swinging like twin jackhammers, not unlike how he used to wade into a brawl of drunken Marines . . . except in this fight he was without the help of a baton, an aid he sorely wished he now had. He and his opponent clashed again, and exchanged multiple blows. For one short moment, Simon knew he'd stunned the guy. He even felt he might possibly win.

Then the other man's youth, longer reach, and superior physiology began to pay off. Simon endured hit after hit after hit—to his gut, to his jaws, cheeks, eyes, and alongside his head.

"I'm gonna pound your brain into mush," Mountain Man ground out. "You'll be a vegetable when I finish."

"You can try, you *coward*," Simon shouted back.

Mountain Man laughed and proceeded to pummel Simon, taking aim at his head, striking Simon's face over and over, landing headshot after headshot.

No matter what Simon tried, he couldn't keep the guy off him, nor could his fists get inside his opponent's reach to return the blows that kept coming and coming and coming. He danced back, then attacked, again and again, each time enduring far more than what he gave.

His resilience began to falter.

Lord, please forgive me! I'm too short and too old to take this guy. Help, please! Oh God! Please save Sophie!

Simon rushed the man once more, endured a pounding in order to duck under the guy's fists, came up in just the right place, and used what power remained in his legs to headbutt Mountain Man's chin. Simon felt his scalp split the same instant his opponent's jaws snapped shut and the man howled in pain and fury. That was Simon's opportunity. He threw his arms about the guy and tried to take the giant to the ground.

It didn't happen.

Instead, they became locked in a deadly clinch, with Simon's opponent using his left fist to land blow after blow to Simon's lower back, targeting Simon's right kidney. Mountain Man hit Simon until he couldn't take it anymore, couldn't bear the pain. His consciousness began to fade.

One thought emerged from the haze overtaking him. *If I can't beat him, I must at least snag a look at his face.*

He loosened his right hand's hold just enough to grab the neck of the guy's ski mask. He yanked on it until the fabric split and slid off his head. The man bellowed his displeasure.

But if I'm going to get a decent look, I need to put some space between us.

Simon didn't know how he'd manage that. He was nearly finished. He'd again locked his hands around the guy, and they would stay locked until his opponent knocked him clean out.

Simon was teetering on the edge of shadows when he felt the thump of something land on his adversary's back. Seconds later, the man screamed and released Simon.

Simon staggered backward, determined to get a look at the man's features. Sadly, his own face was bloodied, his eyes swollen, his strength gone. He could only really make out the thug's blond hair, cut quite short, while the man continued to shriek and struggle to dislodge whatever was glued to his back.

What? *Pouncer?*

Pouncer yowled, scratched, scrabbled, and clawed the kidnapper's neck, head, and shoulders. She sank her teeth into skin and muscle, and tore at the man's ears.

Simon's thinking was becoming increasingly disjointed, but his primary mandate, his most important task, found its way to the surface: *Use Pouncer's attack to grab Sophie out of the van and carry her away.*

He was moving before the idea crystallized. He grabbed Sophie up, careful to cradle her lolling head. At the same time, he was amazed at how very heavy she felt in his arms.

She's not heavy; I'm weak. Spent.

He called out, "Mish Finsh! Mish Finsh! Have Shophie!"

The man trying to defend himself—with little success—against Hugo's needle-like teeth and Miss Finch's whirling cane, jerked his attention to his co-conspirator now writhing on the ground, then to Simon and Sophie.

It was all the opening Miss Finch needed. Her cane came down at a slashing angle to the side of her opponent's neck. The man dropped like a sack of potatoes tossed from a truck bed.

"Simon, go!" Miss Finch pointed up the path, after which she ran for her bike, shouting, "Hugo! Pouncer!"

Simon started up the bike path, slow and sluggish, moving as best he could. A moment later, he made the mistake of glancing back to check on Miss Finch. That error cost him his balance. He lurched to a full stop just to avoid falling or dropping Sophie while he kept his blurry eyes fixed on Miss Finch. He watched her fuzzy figure pick up her bike, point it up the path, and slam the kickstand down.

"Hugo, now!" she shouted, squatting slightly.

Hugo scampered up her bent knees into her arms. She had scarcely deposited him in the basket before Pouncer climbed Miss Finch like a very short telephone pole and used Miss Finch's shoulder as a launch pad to leap to Hugo's side.

"Ouch! Pouncer!"

Simon regained his shaky equilibrium and forced himself to move forward again. He heard Miss Finch pedaling furiously behind him, coming alongside quickly.

"Can you not go faster? *Try*, Fletcher, *try!*"

What in the bloody blue blazes do you think I'm doing? But he could spare neither the air nor the energy to reply. He tucked his chin to his chest and attempted to quicken his steps. His breath was ragged; his heart thundered in his ears.

Miss Finch pulled ahead of him, looked back, and braked precipitously.

"Simon. Simon, stop!"

Who? Simon? Oh, right; that's me. She used my name, but . . .

Simon ground to a halt. He could move not another step. Every inch of his body screamed in agony and streams of blood flowed freely from his face and head.

"Wha . . ."

"Look."

He revolved sluggishly. The black van was pulling away.

"How . . ."

"How what?"

"Keysh. Shrew fob . . .'crosshh road."

"Quick thinking, yet one of the assailants must have had a second fob. Perhaps we can recover the tossed fob and use it to identify the vehicle—but no matter! You saved Sophie, Fletcher!"

Simon didn't respond. He heard or *felt* something tear, like a thick sheet of paper ripped from top to bottom. His mind stuttered and disconnected from his appendages. He swayed.

Miss Finch stared at him with concern. She dismounted. "Simon? Simon, are you all right?"

She called me Simon? Again?

Then . . . *Things fall apart. The center does not hold.*

His legs gave way.

Simon dropped onto the paved trail. Like a cake taken too soon from the oven, he simply fell in on himself with Sophie's unconscious body cradled in his lap. He would die before he let her go, but even hunched over Sophie, he struggled to remain upright.

He heard the boys coming back their way before they appeared. They came speeding around the curve, bells ringing, laughing and cutting up, only to fall silent when they spotted Simon sitting in the middle of the path, huddled over Sophie's unconscious form.

"Sophie!" Wyatt and Eli jumped from their bikes, letting them drop where they dismounted, and raced to their sister. Skipper approached more cautiously.

"What happened?" Wyatt demanded.

"Is Sophie all right?" Eli asked. "And what about you, Mr. Fletcher?"

Simon couldn't answer.

Miss Finch took charge. "Sophie will be fine, but Wyatt? Do take her from Mr. Fletcher; he's . . . exhausted. Eli? Please retrieve Sophie's bike. See it? It's just there by the end of the path. Go fetch it. Quickly now!"

Wyatt appealed to Miss Finch. "Mr. Fletcher won't let go of Sophie! What should I do?"

"I imagine he is locked in protective mode. I suppose we must leave them be for the time being."

Skipper asked in a subdued voice, "But . . . is Fletcher okay?"

Simon tried to answer Skipper, tried to say, "I'm okay!"

Not a thing came out of his mouth.

Miss Finch turned to Skipper. "I won't sugarcoat this, Skipper. He has been beaten badly and needs immediate medical attention. Do you have your phone? Good. I think I dropped mine back by the end of the trail. Listen, I need you to call 911. Report an attempted kidnapping. Ask them to send the police, Jonas Phillips in particular. That's Officer Phillips—do you remember him?"

Skipper nodded. "Well, yeah. Isn't he that cop whose SWAT team surrounded us in your campsite and then put Fletcher in handcuffs? The same guy who showed up when you and I were shot at while riding our bikes up near Olympic Village? Oh, and he's the guy who ran things when the police came to Bright Star and arrested Miss Santini, right?"

Wyatt stared at Skipper like he'd sprouted a second head.

From his armpit.

"Yes, the very one. Swat Team Lead Phillips. Be firm with the dispatcher, Skipper. We need Officer Phillips here, no ifs, ands, or buts about it. Oh, and ask for an ambulance to come at once. Do not forget that. No, better make it two ambulances. One for Simon, one for Sophie."

"But didn't you say Sophie wasn't hurt?" Wyatt demanded, his voice high pitched with worry.

"She has been drugged, Wyatt, but I believe she is relatively unharmed and will wake up when the drug wears off. My assessment aside, we most definitely want her checked out, just in case. Our need for an ambulance is, primarily, for Fletcher."

"No neee . . ." but Simon couldn't push the last words of his thought from his brain to his mouth. Shoot, he couldn't get the words straight in his *head* let alone dispatch them to his mouth. Even then, it dawned on him that something was quite wrong with his mouth. It felt . . . thick and uncooperative.

Miss Finch leaned over him. "Fletcher, you are, at the very least, concussed." She shook her head. "You took a horrid beating, and . . ." she tsked softly, "I foresee stitches. Many, many stitches."

"Yeah? Outshtanding."

Simon's eyesight was nearly obscured by the swelling of his eyes plus dried and dripping blood, and his head wobbled drunkenly upon his neck. Under all that, a reel showing Miss Finch attacking the smaller of the two kidnappers played nonstop. He needed to know if she had been injured.

"Finshy . . .'kay?"

She blew out a long breath. "I confess that I have not had a workout of such degree or significance in quite some time, and I thank you for your concern. That said, do *not* call me Finchy, *Mr.* Fletcher! I categorically forbid it."

"Riiii . . ." Simon wanted to marvel over his inability to sound out a simple "t," but he was too blotto even for that.

Miss Finch moved in closer to assess the damage to his face. She pursed her lips. "As stiff and sore as I expect to find myself tomorrow, my situation bears no comparison to the world of hurt I predict *you* will be in, Simon Fletcher. I, at least, have no bleeding wounds—barring," she muttered, "those inflicted by my *precious* little darling as she clawed her way up my front side."

"I am," she grumbled, "exceedingly perforated."

Simon imagined Pouncer, ensconced in Miss Finch's bike basket beside Hugo, altogether too busy grooming herself to express regret. He wanted to smile. He could not.

"Pounsher a braaa . . ."

That stubborn old "t" refused to punctuate the end of his sentence!

"You will hear no argument from me on that count."

Pouncer.

Pouncer attacked the man I was fighting . . . and losing to.

"Buuu Pounsher . . . thaa guy . . . ."

That guy would have killed me if not for Pouncer. Again, Simon's brain-to-mouth connection failed him.

The urge to laugh came over him and petered out just as quickly. He was far too exhausted to laugh. Or move. Or talk. Or think. Or breathe, for that matter.

What we've got here is failure to . . . failure to . . . what was that word?

Miss Finch leaned in and whispered softly, "I did tell you that you are one of Pouncer's favorite people, Simon. She could not bear to see that man hurt you. And by the by? *Well done.* I do not know how you managed to reach us in the nick of time, but you did, and it was your timely intervention that kept them from taking Sophie. Now, wait here and *please* do not even *attempt* to move."

Yeah, like I . . . but Simon couldn't track down the closing words of that thought either.

A moment later, he felt a cool, wet cloth cover his eyes. He sighed with gratitude, until the moisture penetrated the split skin beneath the cloth. The open cuts stung like fiery needles, and when the stinging became unbearable, he moaned and tried to rip off the cloth. Miss Finch's small hand captured his and returned it to Sophie's shoulder.

"Leave it, dear Fletcher, if you please," she murmured. "Allow it to soften the dried blood."

Okay.

Yes. To please her, he would suffer the burning pain, but it was hard and getting harder. Every inch of his body was now screaming so loudly he longed to jump from his own skin and escape. It took all his self-discipline to remain as still as possible lest he awaken another as-yet unreported but tormented body part.

To distract himself, Simon focused on Miss Finch's admonition, "Leave it, dear Fletcher."

Leave it dear Fletcher? *Dear* Fletcher?

It was minutes later, while she was gently sponging dried blood from his eyes, that they heard the wail of sirens coming their way.

CHAPTER 17

MULTIPLE POLICE CARS and ambulances arrived to the accompaniment of strident sirens, but a resolve deep within Simon made him keep his arms locked about Sophie's unconscious form. Then, before the warbling wails wound down and went silent, a man's shadow crossed over Simon and aroused a measure of angst in him.

When the shadow did not pause but moved on, Simon's suspicions began to calm—but only marginally.

Who was that guy? Need to get a look at him.

Not an easy thing to accomplish. Miss Finch had sponged the blood from Simon's face, but both eyes were swollen nearly shut leaving only a narrow tunnel of blurry vision. And although Simon tried hard to bring the man into focus, his efforts did little and required entirely too much effort.

Without warning, the objects around him multiplied, and two of everything jumbled his contracted field of sight.

Great. Now even the world has gone bonkers.

The man suddenly laughed aloud, and Simon thought he addressed himself to Miss Finch when he said, "*You* again? Hasn't it been less than a month since the last time I found you embroiled in trouble?"

After hunting around for a name to match the voice, Simon hit on it: *Oh, yeah. That guy. Jonas Phillips. SWAT team leader for . . . for . . .* but the words he reached for refused to appear.

Miss Finch's acidic response, as usual, was delivered with perfection. "My, my. In trouble? *Moi?* But a month? If I might correct your assertion, Officer Phillips, it has not been even three weeks since last we met—yet can you blame us for missing you? It was *you*, after all, who initiated our acquaintance . . . when you swatted Bright Star's own facilities and security manager in a dawn raid on *my campsite*. Imagine our surprise! Our chagrin! Why, we had no idea we posed such danger to ourselves and the public at large."

The guy blustered a wry chuckle. "Not going to let that go, are you?"

"Not likely. It is an endless source of amusement."

Phillips snorted. "Figures. Well, seems to me that the entanglements I find you in usually involve your aforementioned Bright Star facilities guy.

Where is your partner in 'grime,' by the way? Thought the two of you were joined at the hip."

"Oh, dear! Your powers of observation seem to have suffered significant slippage, Officer Phillips," Miss Finch murmured. "Perchance we asked amiss when we requested your presence in particular."

Simon heard Phillip's shoes rasp on the pavement as he swiveled one way, then the other. "Really? Fletcher's here? I didn't see him." Then the man expostulated, "What? Holy cow! I didn't even recognize . . ."

A laugh threatened to burst from Simon's throat, but he immediately quashed the urge. The pain ricocheting throughout his body was already approaching the limit of what he could endure.

*Listen, Marine: Do nothing to extubate your pain. Wait. Extubate? That's not it. Do nothing to exorcise the pain? Nope and double nope; not dealing with demons here. Exegete the pain? Hardly. This isn't Bible study, dufus. Do nothing to exterminate the pain? How I wish! Exacerbate? Yes! That's it! Do nothing to **exacerbate** the pain, Marine. For heaven's sake, don't make it worse than it already is.*

Phillips swung back to Miss Finch. "What the devil happened here?"

"Short version? Attempted kidnapping of the child in Fletcher's arms. Details to follow, film at eleven, and so on. At this moment, and most *urgently*, as you can see for yourself, Mr. Fletcher needs help."

The next while swirled by in agonizing fits and starts for Simon, blinks of clarity mixed with momentary lapses in his pain—and how he longed to glom onto and retain those lapses!

Disembodied hands pried Sophie from his clenched arms, and more hands lifted him onto a soft gurney. The EMTs poked, prodded, and questioned him, although Miss Finch always seemed close by to answer in his stead.

He groaned without meaning to and heard Skipper sob softly in the background.

"Shkip. Shkip! Mkay."

"No you aren't!" Skipper's watery voice protested. "I got eyes, don't I?"

"He will be all right in time, Skipper," Miss Finch murmured. "Trust God and take a moment to ask him to help Fletcher. Please."

"Y-yeah. Okay."

Simon heard Phillips' voice again. "Miss Finch? I've talked to those boys—the girl's brothers? I've asked them to call their parents and meet us at South Lake Tahoe PD. I need you to follow us there too. Given Mr. Fletcher's condition, you're the only available eye witness to this event, the only one who can give us an idea of actually happened here."

"I do apologize, Officer Phillips, but for now a brief description of the vehicle is what I can supply: black late-model van, no side windows, never saw the plates."

"And the attackers themselves?"

"Again, I apologize, but they were both wearing ski masks. I would be happy to add to my account; however, I am otherwise engaged for the next several hours as I will be accompanying Mr. Fletcher to the Emergency Department and seeing to his needs."

"But . . ." Phillips' mouth drew down. "Frankly, Miss Finch, we cannot do a blessed thing about this attempted kidnapping until you've briefed us. All three of these boys say they were not here when it went down and little Sophie is still unconscious. You are our only available witness."

"And Mr. Fletcher—"

"Sure. You and what's left of Fletcher here."

Hey! Simon protested. In his head.

Miss Finch, steel in her voice, replied, "What I meant to say before you interrupted, *Officer* Phillips, is that, *in my book*, Mr. Fletcher's *well-being* takes precedence over your investigation. And, for clarity's sake, should you mistake my meaning, 'in my book' in this instance, is what counts."

Now under the care of two EMTs, Simon alternately hoped, wished, and prayed they might give him something for the pain. To his consternation, in view of his concussion symptoms, the EMTs refused to give him even a small dose of morphine to take the edge off. They had, at least, tucked ice packs around his bruised ribs and back, and placed a few cold compresses on the worst of his facial and head cuts. He wanted desperately to sleep and escape the pain, but the unrelenting agony was keeping him awake, although only halfway lucid.

Seemed to him that Phillips wasn't letting up on his "request" for Miss Finch's cooperation, but neither was Miss Finch giving in. After Phillip's latest insistence, her tone hardened.

"I am fully cognizant of your position, *Officer* Phillips, and I sympathize with you, I truly do. Nonetheless, my availability is a matter of priorities. *My priorities.* Your interview must wait until I am convinced Mr. Fletcher is out of the woods. I assume I can apprise you of my availability in several hours."

"Several hours!"

"Yes, although . . ." She paused as she considered something that came to mind, then added, "although, in hindsight, I must counsel you to keep little Sophie under close police watch. She was the target—*is* the target—of this kidnapping attempt, and I continue to fear for her. Her abductors may try to take her again."

Phillips' frustration grew. "But why? Why is she 'the target'? Why would 'they' make another attempt to take her? And just who are 'they'? I don't get any of it!"

He lowered his voice. Tried to sound conciliatory. Failed spectacularly. "Listen, Miss Finch. You told Skipper over there to ask for me in particular. The station commander, to accommodate your request, assigned me as lead for this case. But you're not helping as much as you could." He ended on a pleading note, "For heaven's sake, I need something—anything—to go on!"

"Black Chevy van, late model, no side windows. Two men, one the size of Nebraska, possibly injured during his skirmish with Mr. Fletcher; definitely mauled by my kitty. The other man, normal sized, should show multiple bruises from my cane and distinct bite marks on his left calf."

"You *bit* him?"

"My *dog* bit him."

Miss Finch wouldn't budge further. "Now, for the time being, Officer Phillips, you must take my word for it that Sophie needs police protection and act accordingly. I will provide my rationale at a later time."

Phillips, hands on his hips, stalked away several steps, muttered to himself, then strode back. "What about this? What if I follow you to the hospital and join you there. While they are treating Mr. Fletcher, you can fill me in—in short intervals and only when you are not needed."

"Really, I must put you off, Officer. I want my focus solely on—"

"Yesh," Simon rasped.

Miss Finch's blurry face wavered overhead, peering down at him. "Given your wounds, I had hoped you were unconscious."

You and me both, lady.

He started to shake his head and thought better of it. "Lishening."

"Listening? You heard Officer Phillips' suggestion and agree with him?"

"Yesh."

She exhaled slowly. "Very well." Her face disappeared, and Simon heard her say, "I will see you at the hospital and speak to you as soon I am available, Officer Phillips."

"What about me, Miss Finch?"

Simon would know that voice anywhere: Skipper.

"And what about Wyatt and Eli? And what about Sophie?"

"Oh, goodness." A pause. "Skipper, for Sophie's sake, we must choose to err on the side of caution. I wish her taken to the hospital to be checked out. As for you, Wyatt, and Eli . . . Officer Phillips, can you coordinate getting these boys and our bicycles home to Bright Star?"

"Well, I had the boys call their parents a second time and reroute them to meet us at the hospital, but apparently the Nadeaus refused my request." Phillips muttered aside, "Seems to be a trend."

He added, "Anyway, they are on their way *here* and should arrive shortly. That said, if Sophie is being transported to the hospital, I foresee them wanting to stick close to her."

Skipper interjected, "Wyatt and Eli can take care of themselves if they can get a ride back to Bright Star." He said more firmly, "but I want to go to the hospital with Miss Finch and stay close to Fletch. I live with him, you know. He's kinda like my guardian for the summer."

Phillips ran a hand over his chin. "This is getting too complicated."

"I think not," Miss Finch said. "The Nadeaus have only their king-cab truck for transportation, thus they will be driving it when they get here. I suggest you prevail upon them to put all the bikes in the bed of their truck and take them and the three boys home, after which Mr. and Mrs. Nadeau can join us at the hospital and listen in as you and I talk."

"Yesh," Simon whispered for a third time.

"But I want to go to the hospital with you, Fletch!" Skipper protested.

"Not at this time, I am afraid," Miss Finch answered. "I need you to take Hugo and Pouncer home too. You are the only one Pouncer would possibly go with, Skipper! And once you have put them in the catio, please stay with Wyatt and Eli in their site. I would prefer *not* to call Joe and Holly and have them take you in hand."

"Yeah, no thanks," Skipper growled.

"Then you will take care of my darlings and stay with the Nadeau boys? Oh, and feed and walk Napoleon?"

"Whatever."

"Good." She turned to Phillips. "Complexities ironed out."

Phillips grunted his reluctant approval. "Fine. I'll make the arrangements with the Nadeaus, then follow you to the hospital."

———— ❖ ————

THE NADEAUS ARRIVED minutes later, understandably confused and upset. Mrs. Nadeau wept over Sophie's unconscious figure while Mr. Nadeau declared, "We don't understand! Why would anyone try to take Sophie?"

"She is a lovely child, and the world is full of unscrupulous people," Phillips murmured, hinting at a possible motive.

The Nadeaus sucked in their alarmed breath simultaneously, and Mrs. Nadeau wept anew.

"However, thanks to Miss Finch and Mr. Fletcher here, no one succeeded in taking Sophie. She is here and unharmed, sedated, however, I'm told. And I promise that we will do our very best to catch these individuals." He requested that the Nadeaus have the boys gather all the bikes and put them in the Nadeaus' truck, take the boys and bikes back to Bright Star, then meet him at the hospital after. With reluctance, Mr. Nadeau agreed to the task while Mrs. Nadeau insisted on riding to the hospital with Sophie.

The EMTs were almost ready to load Simon's gurney into the ambulance. Before they did, Miss Finch, who'd stuck staunchly to his side, placed gentle fingers on the nearest of Simon's battered hands.

She murmured, "Fletcher, I fear your mouth is quite cut up inside, and I really do not like for you to pain yourself further by trying to speak. Could you, instead, twitch a finger once for yes? Do nothing, however, if your answer is no."

Without waiting for his response, she whispered, "Officer Phillips is giving the Nadeaus the impression that Sophie's attempted abduction was for sex trafficking purposes."

She shivered. "But surely he must be familiar with the ME's report on Xú's missing organs, no? Either he is hiding what he knows about Xú's autopsy, or South Lake Tahoe PD has made none of the connections between Xú's death and the other disappearances over the last several weeks, including Allysson Sharma's disappearance and the kidnapping attempt on Cameron Easton. And if South Lake Tahoe PD is as clueless as you and I fear they are, Phillips may not have connected the attempted abduction of Sophie with Xú or the other cases."

She thought a moment. "I do not have the sense that he is prevaricating. I am not picking up on that 'vibe.' Do you agree? Twitch your finger once for yes; nothing for no."

Simon twitched his index finger once.

Ow. Good grief!

As much as he appreciated the sensation of Miss Finch's soft hand on his, even the slight weight of her tiny fingers added to his discomfort.

"I will know more after he interviews me," Miss Finch mused to herself. "Fletcher, this next question is important: Are you of the opinion we should tell Phillips what we have uncovered to date and what we have theorized?"

Reluctantly, Simon twitched his finger.

Gah!

"Yes, I suppose we must . . . although it is a very tall and bitter drink to swallow in one go. Despite the wealth of information we have collected and correlated, Officer Phillips may dispute our theories simply because we are long on conjecture and short on actual evidence."

Simon wanted to respond, but as she hadn't asked a question, he kept his aching hand still.

About then, the EMTs edged in and loaded Simon's gurney into the ambulance. Simon heard one of them offer his hand to Miss Finch to help her climb up and inside.

Moments later, the ambulance pulled away from the curb.

CHAPTER 18

TRUE TO HER word, when the ambulance arrived at South Lake Tahoe's Emergency Department and the EMTs rolled Simon into the ED, Miss Finch stuck like a burr to Simon's side except when she was detained by a nurse with a laptop and prevailed upon to answer the questions required to check Simon in. He was grateful that she would remain with him throughout his examination and save him the discomfort of answering the dozens of questions sure to be put to him during triage.

The nurses directed the EMTs to take him back to the treatment area, a large room with curtained beds down its two long sides. Most of the beds held patients, many of whom, if their curtains were retracted, regarded Simon with curiosity.

Great. The other animals eyeing the zoo's most recent acquisition, Simon thought.

Within seconds, the EMTs had transferred Simon to a bed and rolled their gurney away. Two nurses took over and pulled the curtain around his bed. Simon glimpsed Miss Finch as she withdrew to the other side of the curtain while the nurses cut his clothes from him.

Hey, I like this shirt! And those are my favorite running shorts!

Snip. Snip. Snip.

Gone.

Grrr!

On cue, a doctor appeared. He entered the curtained area followed closely by Miss Finch. The doctor, of East Indian extraction, dictated to the nurse in a singsong British accent as his fingers pressed and prodded Simon's bruises, studied his damaged face and battered hands, and queried him, obtaining responses to his questions from Miss Finch.

"Straight off to x-ray, if you please," he ordered, "full skeletal survey. No telling how many broken bones he has or where we might find them."

As they rolled Simon's bed out of his curtained slot, Miss Finch went along. She stayed close by until they returned him forty minutes later to his curtained slot in the treatment room.

Sometime after that, the doctor attending to Simon's care stared down his long nose at Simon and wagged his head in consternation. In his high-brow accent, he said, "I really must say, I have rarely seen anyone as damaged and bloodied as you are, Mr. Fletcher, as the result of fisticuffs alone. I would have thought many of your injuries to have come from a weapon of some type."

A weapon? Every inch of that guy was a weapon.

The doctor had asked no further questions, however, and the pain in Simon's mouth knew better than to answer back even if he had.

I'll be keeping my mouth closed for the foreseeable future, thank you very much, he pledged silently.

A young resident had already stitched up splits in both his upper and lower lips. Despite the numbing injections before she stitched him up and the salves a nurse applied afterward, his lips and the inside of his mouth hurt like the devil had skewered him with his pitchfork a thousand times. He'd bitten his tongue at some point too, and he was certain that a closeup of the inside of his cheeks would have mimicked so much ground round. In addition, several of his teeth had been knocked loose, leaving his bite temporarily askew.

The young doctor who had stitched Simon's mouth also stitched the split on Simon's scalp where he had headbutted Mountain Man, plus eight other cuts: two on his left cheek, one on his right, one above his right eye, another on his left jaw, two at his hairline, close to his left ear, and one over his collar bone. She had applied butterfly bandages to a number of lesser cuts.

When done, she offered Simon a glimpse of her handiwork.

"Not bad work, if I do say so myself," she laughed, holding the mirror to Simon's face. "If nothing else, you have certainly provided me with lots of practice."

Simon hadn't laughed. His features, although mostly numbed, were swollen and discolored beyond belief—not that he was able to focus on his reflection, *singular*. His face in the mirror, through the bit of tunnel vision his swollen eyes provided, continued to be multiplied by two.

Both were hideous.

Miss Finch hadn't laughed with the young doctor. "What *are* you thinking? Take that away *this instant!*" she demanded, adding, "Whatever do they teach you young people these days? Imagine: a doctor without the sense of a gnat!"

The doctor blushed, whispered, "Yes'm," and quit the room.

Don't mess with the Finchster, Simon's scrambled thoughts called to the resident on her way out.

Finally, the doctor reappeared, now ready to report on the entirety of Simon's injuries. He consulted Simon's chart, hemmed and hawed, and began with, "Suppose we start with a list of the damage? Chest and abdominal x-rays show multiple cracked ribs and extensive bruising of the chest wall, bilaterally. Five definite cracks on the left; four on the right. Severe bruising also on your lower back, right side."

He frowned. "Odd. I cannot construe how you received those bruises unless you were lying on the ground, your attacker kicking you."

Simon was insulted. *Me? On the ground?* Then he sighed to himself. *No, we were in a clinch: I wouldn't let him go, and he wouldn't stop pounding me.*

"As your questions are too difficult for Mr. Fletcher to answer at this time," Miss Finch replied, "perhaps you might continue without feedback?"

"But of course. The x-rays of Mr. Fletcher's hands show two fractured fingers on the left." He addressed Simon again, "Hopefully, you gave as well as you got?"

"He did," Miss Finch replied, growing testy, "although the beast he was up against had him by five inches and forty pounds."

Six inches! Simon protested. *Guy was at least six foot three.*

"Really! I suppose that goes a long way toward explaining the extensive damage." The doctor peered down his nose at Simon once more. "We already know you show signs of a concussion; however, we were quite delighted to see that your cranial x-rays indicate no bleeds. You must be blessed with an incredibly hard head, Mr. Fletcher."

Simon wasn't certain, but he thought he'd caught a muttered, "That he is," from Miss Finch.

You traitor. I'll get you back for that one, he pledged. *Just you wait and see! Well, maybe in a month . . . or two.*

In truth, he was struggling with more than physical discomfort and sluggishness. His mind felt like gelatinous sludge, his thoughts like shod feet mucking their way through said sludge, often bogging down entirely.

Gotta tell you, Lord: This whole situation stinks. Just being honest here.

The doctor continued. "Moving on to treatment. Doctor Beckman stitched you up nicely. We'd like you to keep an antibiotic ointment on all cuts until they heal, and I will prescribe an oral antibiotic prophylactically. We'll also strap your chest nice and snug to keep your ribs cushioned and where they belong. Having them strapped won't be an initially pleasant experience, but afterward you will appreciate being able to breathe without as much discomfort. Then we'll invite an orthopedic fellow to take a look at your fingers. Lastly, we will admit you today as an in-patient and keep you under strict observation for a period of not less than seventy-two hours—longer, if your vision doesn't resolve itself by then."

He looked up from the chart and offered a wry smile. "I should think it likely that you will pee blood for a week, given the pummeling your right kidney took, but your overall prognosis is good. Of course, your lower back and chest wall will grieve you until your ribs and all the soft tissue damage heals. Several weeks, I should think. You are also likely to carry around a cast on your left hand for as long as the orthopedic specialist decides. Lastly, but *most* importantly . . ."

The doctor's features drew down, and he made sure he had Simon's attention, even though, from Simon's perspective, the doctor, for the most part, was a white blob with fuzzy edges, whose twin mimed his every move.

"You, Mr. Fletcher, will abstain from absolutely *all* physical exertion above a sedate walk for a period of six weeks, depending upon how you do. And by 'a sedate walk,' I mean from your chair or bed to your lavatory and back. You may walk a bit farther—not faster—after your first week home, slowly adding distance as you feel up to it, but you will engage in *no* lifting, digging, pulling, heaving, running, jogging, or *anything* with the potential to raise your BP even an iota. *Not a single physical activity* other than moderate walking until your brain has fully recuperated and is less likely to spring a leak. Furthermore? *No stress* of any kind. Do I make myself clear?"

Simon, irritated by the doctor's strictures, couldn't resist sneering, "Shorry. Can' tell whish of you ish talking."

The doc didn't bat an eye. "*Precisely* my point, Mr. Fletcher. Six weeks, no activity in excess of moderate walking, and *no* stress. See me in my office following that span of time and I shall reevaluate your condition."

Simon struggled to speak. "Job . . ."

"Absolutely no return to work until I clear you." He glanced at Miss Finch. "If you provide the appropriate contact information, I will draft my orders for the HR department of Mr. Fletcher's workplace." Then he paused and frowned in thought. "Hmm. Any chance your injuries are workplace related?"

Simon blinked twice. Couldn't get his head around the question. Miss Finch, though, snapped to the correct conclusion immediately.

"Possibly. We were, after all, escorting Bright Star summer residents when I and a child were attacked and Mr. Fletcher came to the child's rescue," she murmured.

"And Mr. Fletcher is a Bright Star employee?"

"He is."

"Just so. You may be able to make a compelling case that Mr. Fletcher's injuries fall under Workers' Compensation, which should then cover his medical expenses and serve to preserve his job through his convalescence. You have, I believe, five days in which to report the incident or his claim will be denied with no further petitions allowed."

He snapped Simon's chart closed and again turned to Miss Finch. "I admit that I do not entirely trust Mr. Fletcher to mind the rules I have set—do you?"

"Not in the slightest."

"Ah. I thought as much. Seeing as you already appear to function in the role, I hereby appoint you 'watcher of the patient.' I repeat: We need that concussion resolved. I have no wish to see Mr. Fletcher in here exhibiting symptoms of stroke or aneurysm."

She nodded solemnly. "I have the watch."

He smiled at last. "I am relieved?"

"You are relieved, Doctor."

The physician saluted and moved on to his next patient.

Miss Finch stood looking after the doctor. Remained there, unmoving, for several moments before she, without a sound, collapsed into the chair beside Simon's bed. Her hand flew to the bridge of her nose. She rubbed it and sniffled, took a tissue from her pocket, wiped her eyes, and dabbed at her nose.

With his eyesight worthless, Simon's ears were already learning to function to a higher degree. He realized she was distressed, and he may have seen her distressed before, but he had rarely seen her in tears.

"Finschy?"

She didn't answer. More sniffles and the soft sounds of tissue wiping.

"BeeDee?" His tongue was thick but more articulate than the last time he tried to speak. His mouth was also numb enough from the injections that at least he did not flinch.

She sat up and sniffed back her tears. "Did you need something, Fletcher?"

Simon's mouth was suddenly dry. Parched. Desperate. His concern for her flew out the window. "Ice water?" Ice came out as "Eyshhh."

"One moment."

Soon what could have been a straw appeared in his narrow band of sight, and cool, refreshing water ran down his throat. She let him drink until he was on the verge of brain freeze.

"Enough?"

"Thanksh." Then he recalled her anguish. "Finschy, you 'kay?"

"I-I think so . . . although the unanticipated events of this lovely morning certainly threw us into a blender and—"

A whisper came through the curtains of his makeshift room. "Fletch? Miss Finch?"

Miss Finch sighed. "Come in, Skipper."

Skipper popped through the curtain. He fidgeted from foot to foot and his eyes took in all the medical equipment before they landed on Miss Finch. "Sorry. Couldn't hang out anymore with Wyatt and Eli. I just . . . I just needed to be here."

"And, pray tell, how did you get here, Skipper?"

"Rode my bike. Used the map app on my phone to find this place."

Simon heard rustling on his right side as Skipper came close. He turned his head a fraction. "Shkipper?"

Skipper sniveled. "Hey, Fletch. Told Joe and Holly about you."

"It hurts his mouth dreadfully to talk, Skipper," Miss Finch reminded him softly.

Skipper's voice broke. "But you'll be okay, won't you, Fletcher?"

Simon raised his good hand and found Skipper's. "Yesh. Time."

Another voice, this one querulous and out of patience, spoke from outside the curtain. "Miss Finch? Jonas Phillips here. I have been waiting for quite some time—hours at this point. If you and Mr. Fletcher now have time for visitors, you surely have time for our interview."

Simon would have bet money that Miss Finch snarled in her throat before answering sweetly, "I shall be out directly, Officer Phillips."

She exhaled. "Well. Since you are here, Skipper, I will leave Fletcher in your care while I find a quiet place to debrief Officer Phillips and return afterward. Oh, and if they come to move Fletcher to his room, please text me his room number so I know where to find the both of you. And do not ask Fletcher questions. He should really try to sleep instead. Can you remember all that?"

"Sure. You can count on me."

"I know I can, dear boy."

Just then, a nurse entered the curtained area, a glass of water in one hand and a miniature paper cup in her other. "Mr. Fletcher? The doctor has prescribed an antibiotic and some pain medication for you. Do you feel like raising your head a bit?"

Raise my head for pain medication? And more! Simon wanted to kiss, sight unseen, the woman offering him blessed relief. Of course, his ambition was all in his head.

"May I be of assistance?" Miss Finch offered.

"If you could lift his head?"

"Of course."

Simon felt her small hands, stronger than they looked, lift and support his head while the nurse tipped two tablets into his mouth followed by the smooth edge of the glass upon his lips. He swallowed and drank down most of the water, then Miss Finch let his head down.

"I will leave you now, Fletcher. I must meet with Officer Phillips." She looked at Simon. "It is also high time I call Holly and Joe and apprise them of your . . . situation. Back in a bit."

Simon was "out" before the curtains settled behind her departing figure.

———◆———

WHEN SIMON WAKENED later, he was disoriented, in a room he did not recognize. He turned his head to see more of the room but shuddered at the pain that small movement produced.

Apparently, Skipper had been sitting in a chair near Simon's bed. He stood and came closer to Simon's bed.

"Hey, Fletch."

Simon's mouth was as dry as dust, his tongue hugely swollen on one side. He tried to respond anyway. "Hey."

"The nurse said I should give you ice chips to suck on. She said it will help with swelling and stuff in your mouth."

"Pleash."

For the next fifteen minutes, Simon took every spoonful of crushed ice Skipper offered him. He held the cold in his mouth until the bits melted, then sucked down the moisture.

"Thatsh all, Shkip."

"Does your mouth feel better?"

It did, actually. Simon felt his mouth and tongue loosen up some. "Yeah. How . . . long?"

"How long were you asleep?"

"Yeah."

"About four hours. They moved you into this room about three hours ago."

"Huh. Time?"

Skipper lifted his eyes to the clock hanging on the wall across from Simon. "'Bout one o'clock." He pointed. "There's a clock on the wall. Can't you see it?"

Simon's eyes, reluctantly and in jerky fashion, followed Skipper's double fingers. Dual darkish blobs appeared in the distance. "Not really. Concussion, doc said, from getting my head pounded."

"Concussion. That's in the brain, right? Will it get better? Go away?"

"Yup. If I rest and don't overdo it."

But if I'm not up and around soon, my job will likely go away. I already know Joe and Holly can't manage Bright Star without me . . . or whomever they hire to replace me.

CHAPTER 19

MISS FINCH APPEARED again in his room, standing at the end of his bed. "I apologize for being gone so long, Fletcher. Officer Phillips was quite insistent upon nailing down every last detail of our ordeal. Of course, then I had to impart our suppositions to him and how we arrived at them."

Simon nodded. Grimaced as he adjusted his position in the bed. "Tell me everything?"

She side-eyed Skipper. "Perhaps not in present company."

Simon turned his attention back to his intern and croaked, "Skipper, I need your help."

"Anything, Fletcher!"

"Thanks, buddy." He tried to take in a cleansing breath; it was both painful and nearly impossible to do so.

Stupid cracked ribs.

He grabbed what air he could and said, "Well, first off, while I'm in the hospital, I would ask you to stay with Miss Finch like you did when I took Holly to Vegas after Joe's accident." He glanced at Miss Finch. "Is that all right with you?"

"Certainly. We do not want Skipper alone at night in your cabin." She thought a moment. "And please bring Napoleon with you. At night I will put Pouncer in her carrier. Napoleon can sleep under the little bed my table makes into. During the day, I can swap Pouncer and Napoleon in and out of the catio and their carriers . . . lest Pouncer's tyranny completely demoralize your old gent."

Skipper seemed relieved. "Thank you, Miss Finch. I *was* kinda wondering about tonight. What else, Fletcher?"

Simon drew another ragged, painful breath. "Good man, Skip. Secondly, you know how important our work at Bright Star is, how quickly our beautiful park can fall into disarray. Fact is, if either of us is going to have a job after I'm healed up, I'll need you to pair up with Joe to keep Bright Star up to our high standards. Physically, Joe's doing much better at this point, but I'm thinking you will need to kick in a lot of extra effort to cover my absence."

Skipper nodded vigorously. "You can count on me, Fletch. I won't let you down."

Simon felt affection for this young man wash over him, and he smiled. Well, he *tried* to smile. The pull of his stitches and the cracks in his lips prevailed upon him to reconsider.

"Come here, kid."

Skipper wrinkled his nose. "You're not going to hug me or anything, are you? You're awful bruised and bloody."

"Naw. Just give me your hand, but be gentle. I've lost some skin off my knuckles."

"Yeah, looks gross." Reluctantly, Skipper placed his hand in Simon's.

Simon squeezed Skipper's hand a bit. Held on to it. "I want you to know something, Skipper, and it's this: You're doing well. I see you growing every day, growing in Jesus and growing as a young man. I'm very proud of you."

Skipper hung his head and swallowed hard. After a moment, he whispered, "Thanks, Fletcher."

"Welcome. Now, scoot on out of here and report to Joe. He's probably feeling overwhelmed and will be grateful to see you."

Skipper sniffled, nodded again, and shuffled from Simon's room.

"Hard to believe he is the same spoiled boy who arrived here less than two months ago," Miss Finch observed. "You are doing a fine job with him."

Simon again thought better of smiling, although he was smiling on the inside. "Thanks. Now, spill."

For the next half hour, Miss Finch related her interview with Phillips. She ended with, "Officer Phillips is sharp, but he is not asking the right questions. I came away convinced he did not know of the several disappearances around the lake or, if he did know, had not, as yet, comprehended their implications."

"But you filled him in, right?"

"Twice and quite thoroughly, although he remained skeptical."

Simon closed his eyes and thought a moment. "I've had a lot of wild thoughts running around in my head ever since our run-in with Sophie's attackers. It's like, even while I've been foggy, disoriented, or asleep, my brain just kept working."

She leaned over him, her expression grave. "You are not having hallucinations, are you?"

"Don't think so . . . unless you aren't actually here." His right hand being the less painful of the two, Simon lifted it and touched her cheek with the tips of his swollen fingers.

"Nope. You feel real to me."

She smiled a genuine open smile then, gently pressed his fingers into her cheek, and as quickly, released his hand. "Tell me more about your brainstorm?"

"Yeah, I've come to the realization that an important part of our investigation has gelled or clarified. On the one hand, I'm afraid I might 'lose' it to my brain fog; on the other hand, it won't leave me alone."

He blinked several times. "Listen, it might sound crazy, but if what I've been mulling over is even partly true, it will certainly be essential to our case. At the same time, it may wipe away some of Phillips' doubts. I just need to test my theory. See if it's real or a product of my concussed imagination."

"Tell me what you have in mind."

"Are the Nadeaus still here at the hospital?"

"No, I believe Sophie was released and they have taken her home. Why?"

"I need Phillips and the Nadeaus here. Together."

Her dark, glittering eyes regarded him through narrowed slits. "I am intrigued, Fletcher. Care to share with me first?"

"Won't work. I need to ask the Nadeaus questions to confirm my theory. And, frankly, if I tell you what I'm thinking, I'm afraid you'll balk and convince me *not* to test my theory. Conversely, if my wild speculations are true, I will enjoy basking in your total amazement."

Chuckling, she asked, "Will you, indeed?"

"Indeed, I will." He winced as his body's overall ache woke up with the temperament of a cranky toddler. "Ow."

Miss Finch eyed him with concern. "Let me see what I can do to arrange your interview. In the meantime, I will let the nurse know you are awake and in pain."

"Please and thank you."

Miss Finch departed; five minutes later a nurse arrived with her little paper cup of relief. After he'd swallowed his pills and before she left though, Simon had her dial a number on his room's phone and hand him the receiver.

"Holly? It's Fletcher . . ." He waited until her excited babble tapered off. "Yes, doctor says I'll be in here couple days . . . ordered me not to exert myself for few weeks."

More babbling on her end.

"Look, I know this is going to be hard on Joe. I've sent Skipper back to Bright Star. If he isn't there yet, should be soon. Kid promised to be big help to Joe. Believe he will be."

He listened and sighed. "You know I want the same for Bright Star that you and Joe want, Holly. Do what's best for Bright Star. I'll . . . understand, whatever you decide."

He waited until he had the opportunity to interject the question he'd called to ask. He listened as Holly answered.

"Are you certain?"

Old Holly was instantly back: "Of course I'm certain, Fletcher! I take these matters seriously, and I haven't lost my memory."

"Okay. Just . . . verifying. Thanks, Holly."

He was too tired and in too much misery to turn onto his side and replace the receiver. Instead, he drifted into sleep with the receiver in his hand.

SIMON WOKE WITH a gasp, startled out of his sound sleep. His sharp intake was enough to awaken Miss Finch, scrunched into the chair beside his bed, a sweater draped across her shoulders.

"Sorry," Simon murmured. "I was dreaming. One of those nasty ones. Lots of running from monsters without getting away."

"Terrible, such nightmares. Who did you talk to while I was gone?"

Simon was slow to realize Miss Finch had to have hung up his phone. "Oh. Just checking in with Holly. What about Phillips and the Nadeaus? Are they coming?"

"Yes, they have agreed to meet with us, but I insisted they let you finish sleeping first. And now that you're awake, you need sustenance."

A ravening appetite rumbled through Simon's belly. "Food?"

"Given the condition of your mouth, the doctor thought to start you on milkshakes supplemented with protein. Chocolate or vanilla?"

"Uh, both? I'm starving."

"Well, while you were sleeping, I picked up some protein powder then made a run to that ice cream place people are always raving over. The nursing station's refrigerator has four ready-made shakes waiting for you."

"Don't just talk about it, woman! Bring it on!" Simon growled.

Miss Finch left the room, muttering that "heh-heh-heh" thing under her breath, and Simon wanted to grin in the worst way. He knew better.

Lord, thank you. I'm grateful beyond belief that Miss Finch and I are friends again.

Only minutes later, she returned with two modest-sized paper cups. "I've poured parts of two shakes into these cups and zapped them in the floor's microwave to cut the chill just a hair." She brought one cup near and poked a straw into it. "I realize you are hungry, but I would rather you not suffer brain freeze into the bargain."

"Thanks!" Simon's good hand scrabbled against his blanket as his swollen, painful lips worked to grasp and pull on the straw. He groaned when a liquid gush of sweet, cool ice cream hit his tongue and the back of his throat. Its pleasant chill soothed his mouth without freezing it, and the taste was sublime. He found himself gulping it down. The shake tasted so good that, before he knew it, he'd drained both cups.

"Better?"

"Much. Thank you." He was grateful to Miss Finch for her kindness and forethought.

With a start, he realized his hand wasn't grasping his blanket. His fingers were wrapped . . . around hers. His blurry vision drifted up to her face, but her features were indistinct. The confusing thing was, she hadn't tried to extricate her little hand from his rather large one.

"What you did to save Sophie," she murmured, "I know what it cost you."

She hesitated. "It wasn't that long ago that I was the one trapped in a bed as you are now. Helpless. In horrible pain."

Simon didn't speak. He did not even want to breathe. Something deep and precious was happening in this moment, and he feared to interrupt it.

"That man, that steroid-fueled freak of nature who grabbed Sophie and was putting her in that van? When you . . . when you went up against him, again and again, even though you were blatantly outmatched . . . when you took that beating to save Sophie, it was the bravest thing I have ever seen."

And then, there it was.

"I never said I didn't care, Simon."

Simon blinked. Wanted in the worst way to see her clearly, wanted to read what her eyes would tell him, but he could not bring them into focus.

She was quiet; he had to respond.

Lord! I need to say something. Please don't let me mess it up.

"And I care for you, BeeDee. You must know that."

He watched her blurry head slowly nod.

"I know." She looked away. "It is hard."

She carefully withdrew her hand and the moment passed. "I should put these cups in the trash."

Simon didn't want her to "step away." He floundered for some question that would keep her near him.

"Phillips and the Nadeaus?"

She glanced at the blur on the wall. "They should arrive in about twenty minutes. I shall go down, stretch my legs, and show them up when they arrive."

Drat.

———— ◆ ————

WHILE MISS FINCH was gone, the nurse came to medicate him again. He declined the pill.

"I am expecting visitors, and I need to be awake and alert while they are here," he explained. "Those pills you're pushing knock me out. Can you come back after my visitors leave?"

Miss Finch's absence also allowed Simon time to muster his thoughts. He was feeling better for drinking the shakes she'd brought, but he was distracted too.

It is hard?

What is hard, BeeDee? Tell me!

No, I can't think on that right now.

He'd just organized the questions he would ask the Nadeaus when Miss Finch reentered his room. Jonas Phillips and Mr. and Mrs. Nadeau followed behind her.

Phillips, having already seen the damage Mountain Man had done to Simon's face, merely shook his head. The Nadeaus were a different story.

Mrs. Nadeau took one look, burst into tears, and buried her face in her husband's shoulder.

"You cannot believe how sorry we are for your injuries," Mr. Nadeau explained, unable himself to keep his eyes on Simon, "yet how very grateful we are to you and Miss Finch for saving our Sophie from those . . . men."

Simon said softly, "Fact is, Mr. Nadeau, I would die for that child. I'm only sorry I was unable to keep those brutes from getting away."

Mr. Nadeau nodded, sniffled, and stared at his feet.

Without Simon asking, Miss Finch arranged three chairs at the end of Simon's bed.

"Please sit here," she murmured. "As you can see, Mr. Fletcher's eyes are swollen, which has narrowed his line of sight. Also, turning his head to one side is painful. It will be easier on him if you sit directly in front of him."

The three visitors sat, and she took another chair closer to Simon, ready with a glass of ice water and a straw should he need them.

Phillips said, "All right, Fletcher, we're here. What can you add to Miss Finch's account of the, er, incident?"

Simon started slow in order to ease his mouth and tongue into what would likely be a long session. "Actually, I'm not going to talk much about the attempted abduction. I believe, however, that I can provide some insights into the motives of the abductors."

Phillips huffed. "If your insights run along the lines of Miss Finch's wild ideas, I rather think the Nadeaus do not need to hear them."

"Oh, but they do, Phillips, because Sophie is still in danger."

"Really, Fletcher!" Phillips objected. "Haven't they been through enough without you adding to their paranoia?"

But the Nadeaus sat up straight, and Mr. Nadeau demanded, "Whatever do you mean?"

"I intend to tell you. I believe, though, that we must start our conversation with Sophie's adoption."

Four astonished faces stared back at Simon. Out of the corner of his eye, he could tell Miss Finch's astonishment was passing quickly and was already moving into deep deliberation as she tried to ascertain where Simon was going with such a provocative statement.

Yeah, I will indeed gloat over your amazement, BeeDee Finch, he promised silently.

To his credit, Phillips clamped his mouth shut. The Nadeaus, on the other hand, shifted from shock to indignation.

"That information is strictly private and legally protected," Mr. Nadeau ground out. "How did you come by it?"

"I did not 'come by it,' Mr. Nadeau, and certainly not by any illegal means. Sophie doesn't resemble either of you or her two brothers. In fact, between the four of you, I doubt you could come up with a single dominant gene, yet Sophie has dark hair and eyes . . . and interesting eyes, at that."

He watched as Mrs. Nadeau gnawed her lower lip.

Yup, I'm on the right track.

"From my perspective, it is the only thing that makes sense, but will you confirm that Sophie is, indeed, your adopted daughter?"

The Nadeaus looked at each other. When Mrs. Nadeau slowly nodded, Mr. Nadeau said softly, "Yes. Sophie is adopted. It was a private adoption and closed. We haven't told Sophie. She is . . . has always been somewhat fragile."

"Do your boys know?"

"No; they were four and two when we knew we were going to get her, so we told them ahead of time that Eva was pregnant with a baby girl. They were too young not to realize that she never really looked pregnant, although Eva wore maternity clothes and a small, fake baby bump toward the end of her 'term.'"

"Keep going," Simon urged him.

"Well, Sophie was born in a private birthing clinic, attended by a mid-wife and a doula. Eva was also present for the birth and stayed with Sophie's birth mother for several hours afterward. Of course, I told the boys their mother was there giving birth. When it was time for Sophie to come home, the boys and I went to the clinic and fetched Eva and Sophie home together."

"And you've told no one that Sophie is adopted? Not even other family members?"

The Nadeaus were increasingly uneasy. "Only the mother, the midwife, and the doula know. Our parents live at a distance and believe the same things we told the boys."

Simon took a sip from the straw Miss Finch offered and gently pressed them. "But why hide Sophie's adoption? Why the elaborate subterfuge?"

When the Nadeaus didn't answer, Simon said, "I can think of two reasons for hiding Sophie's adoption. Two reasons—am I right?"

"Our family is not your concern and not your business! It has nothing to do with what just happened," Lucas Nadeau insisted.

Simon saw that Phillips was intrigued, willing to let Simon's questioning play out. Miss Finch, too, was quietly watchful.

Simon said softly, "You told us Sophie is fragile. In what way?"

"She has a fragile immune system and sometimes has trouble keeping up with our busy lives. Although her health is well managed, we are, in the main, careful with her."

"To speak so confidently about Sophie's fragility, I imagine you would have had to involve a doctor, would you not? And, surely, her doctor, at some point, took blood samples to study and determine her system's state?"

"Again, that is not your business and is not pertinent!"

Simon cut to the chase. "What is Sophie's blood type, Mr. Nadeau?"

The man flinched. Mrs. Nadeau, whose expression had grown steadily worried under Simon's questioning, now appeared terrified.

"Please . . . please don't."

It was the confirmation Simon had been waiting for. "Sophie's blood type. It's Rh null, isn't it? Rh null, what is sometimes called 'golden blood?'"

Miss Finch's breath hissed out from between her teeth. Simon carefully turned his face toward her. "Are you tracking with me now?"

She blinked a few times. "I believe so."

"Well, I'm not," Phillips muttered. "What gives, Fletcher?"

"All in good time," Simon replied. "Mrs. Nadeau, when you and your family checked into Bright Star a few weeks back, you told us how glad you were to have received an email from your travel agent letting you know that two sites at Bright Star had just opened up. Can you reconfirm that you received such an email?"

The woman seemed mystified by Simon's switch of topics. "Why, yes, of course we did. How else would we have known?"

"Ah, and yet Mrs. Mitchell assures me that only days after she began to advertise the two newly available sites, she received an email from *you*, inquiring after a berth at Bright Star."

Four voices answered, "What?" in unison.

Simon couldn't resist. He shifted so he could see Miss Finch's reaction. "Consider me basking in your total amazement, BeeDee."

She chuckled. "I concede your point, Simon. Indeed, I do. Pray continue? I am all ears."

"But we never sent an email to Miss Holly," Eva said slowly. "Our agent handled all the details of our reservation."

"Merciful heavens!" Miss Finch exclaimed, while Phillips muttered something inaudible under his breath.

"I don't understand," Mrs. Nadeau moaned. "What is happening?"

"I hope to clear up the confusion soon. Just a few more questions first," Simon said. "Mr. Nadeau, when Miss Finch was getting ready to back your fifth wheel into your site, did you not mention that your rig was new?"

Mr. Nadeau cleared his throat. "It is."

"You might understand that, working at Bright Star, I've gained a measure of familiarity with RVs since joining the Mitchells. So forgive me, please, if I suggest that this year's model of your fifth wheel seems like it might have been priced . . . out of the range of a humble college program manager."

Mr. Nadeau pressed his lips together and looked aside.

"Hmm. Next question, then. How long *before* you received the email from your travel agent, did you receive an entirely different email, one that contained the news that you had won a brand new fifth wheel RV?"

"Not an email . . ." Mr. Nadeau finally whispered. "It was a phone call."

Beside him, Miss Finch twitched with suppressed excitement.

"A phone call?" Simon asked. "Did you take the call on a cell phone or on a land line?"

Lucas Nadeau tugged his cell phone from his shirt pocket. "On this phone."

"When?"

"Maybe during the third week of June?"

"Did you delete the call data?"

"No."

Miss Finch walked to Mr. Nadeau and held out her hand. "May I?" When Mr. Nadeau reluctantly gave over his phone, she moved to the other side of the room, pulling out her own phone at the same time.

Simon knew she would be contacting her tech team, texting them Lucas's phone info. They, in turn, would crack his cell phone records like one might crack a hard-cooked egg. If the "contest" caller's data were findable, they would find it.

Phillips spoke up. "I'm catching a glimpse of the big picture now, Fletcher, but not the meaning. Are you saying the abductors wanted Sophie—" he swallowed hard—"for that *thing* Miss Finch told me of?"

"Not precisely, but along those lines, I believe. I want to try to dig out a few more details before we explore that possibility. For example, Mr. Nadeau, did the win of your fifth wheel also include an all-expenses-paid stay at a Tahoe RV resort, and that your assigned 'travel agent' would provide you with all the details?"

Lucas Nadeau slowly nodded his head.

Simon's ire began to heat. "Not one but *two* unsolicited, out-of-the-blue 'wins,' and neither of them seemed the least bit contrived?"

Mr. Nadeau whispered, "W-we . . . we were just so happy about our good luck and grateful to be able to take our children on this amazing vacation. Our programs recess between terms, you see, so we can take leave during the summer. That said, since we can rarely afford to go anywhere special, we often work instead . . . and bank the time off for later."

"And you gave no thought to Sophie's safety?"

"Her safety? But why would we?" Mrs. Nadeau interjected. "Sophie's blood type was hidden, unknown! We had no idea anyone would go to such lengths to-to-to—" She couldn't finish her sentence, so ended with, "How could we?"

Simon stared at the Nadeaus, anger at the situation competing with frustration and an overall sense of impotence. It was when their fuzzy double images began to shimmer and spark that he recognized the symptoms . . . and his grave error.

Crud. I'm "overdoing it," just what the doctor warned me not to do.

He closed his eyes and kept them closed. Swallowed down a wave of nausea.

"A moment, please."

A minute later, with eyes still closed, he moved ahead. "Mr. and Mrs. Nadeau, I'm not completely clear on your reasoning for hiding Sophie's adoption. What can you tell us about Sophie's birth mother and father?"

Neither of Sophie's parents spoke, so Simon added, "It really does no harm to tell us. First of all, we have no reason to tell anyone of her true parentage. Secondly, I already surmise she has Asian blood, most likely Chinese. In fact, she rather makes me think of Miss Finch as she may have looked as a child."

Miss Finch, who'd returned to her seat, huffed. "Me? A child? Not in this century. Why, to quote George Burns, I am so old, I remember when the Dead Sea was merely sick."

Phillips chuckled, but the Nadeaus didn't even react; they were entirely too overwhelmed.

"Nice try," Simon murmured.

"Tough room," she whispered back.

"Mr. Nadeau, please," Simon said.

Lucas Nadeau sighed. "Sophie's birth mother was a young Chinese woman on a student visa to Collège CDI where Eva and I both work. Eva came to know this girl when she enrolled in the early childhood program in which Eva is an administrative assistant. They became good friends. When this student fell pregnant by another student, a young white man, she was terrified. Her parents were only middling officials of the CCP, but any such disgrace on their daughter's part could have spelled disaster for the entire family. The girl had decided to have an abortion, but Eva and I . . . we could not stand the thought, so we offered to take her baby. We kept the adoption private and pretended that Eva had given birth to Sophie to protect her birth mother's secret. An underground pro-life group helped us overcome the legalities by filing a falsified birth certificate for Sophie."

"But that isn't the only reason you kept Sophie's adoption a secret, is it?" Simon asked, keeping his head on his pillow, but pressing the button to raise his bed's head so he could better look them both in the eye. "Wasn't it also because you knew about the possibility of Sophie having golden blood?"

Mr. Nadeau caved. "All right! Yes, we knew it was a possibility, and we wanted to protect Sophie. You see, when Sophie's birth mother confided that she was Rh null, she painted an awful picture of what it was like. She said that, back home, from the time her blood type became known, she had been considered property of the state—subjected to regular exams and experiments and forced to 'donate' blood on a regular, ongoing schedule whether she wanted to or not.

"She won her long-held desire to attend university in Canada only by promising to give blood on schedule while at school. The Chinese government arranged for a doctor with CCP affiliation to take her blood, properly freeze it, and send it back to China. You can understand that Sophie's mother did not want her baby to have the restrictive life she had, a life of involuntary servitude."

He sighed. "She had a devil of a time concealing her pregnancy from the doctor who was paid by the CCP to collect and send her blood every eight weeks. In the end, she did so by bribing the nurse who drew her blood not to tell the doctor she was pregnant."

"What became of Sophie's birth mother?" Miss Finch asked.

"She finished her education and returned to China. We have had no personal contact with her, but she occasionally texts a fellow graduate who passes on greetings to Eva. She has not married or had children, and as far as we can tell, no one knows that she had a child while she was at school in Canada."

"I can understand how the mother's situation affected your decision to keep the details around Sophie's true birth a secret," Miss Finch said, "but when did you learn or confirm that Sophie actually did have golden blood?"

"We knew it was a possibility from the start, but it was such a slim possibility, that we honestly believed the mutation would skip over Sophie. When she was born, she was healthy and strong, and we felt we'd lucked out.

"Then, when Sophie was around age three, she seemed to bruise and become fatigued far too easily. Of course, we took her to our doctor, a family friend. When he said he needed to draw Sophie's blood, we panicked. Eventually, we confided in him.

"You see, if Sophie *did* have Rh null blood and it became known, we were afraid the Chinese government would hear of it and make the connection between Sophie and her birth mother. We feared they might deem Sophie's adoption illegal and demand that the Canadian government nullify her adoption, remove her from us, and send her to live in China!"

Mr. Nadeau paused to wipe his eyes. "Our doctor said he understood our fears, so he agreed to help us. He ran the blood himself and gave us the unwelcome verdict: Sophie *was* Rh null. She also suffers from a mild form of hemolytic anemia, a disease that afflicts many Rh null individuals. Fortunately, we have been able to manage Sophie's anemia with oral medication. But should her anemia become worse? We have, over time, banked several units of her own blood in a private repository, and will continue to do so. But should she ever need that blood, use it all up, and need more?"

Sophie's father shook his head and did not finish his thought.

"Wait," Phillips interrupted. "Would someone please explain this Rh null and 'golden blood' business and why the fuss over it?"

"It's like this," Simon answered. "Scientists have identified between fifty and sixty different proteins known as Rhesus factors or Rh antigens in human red blood cells. Most people have the expected antigens, but those individuals with Rh negative blood are missing what is called the Rh D antigen.

"What this means is that an individual with Rh negative blood can only receive a transfusion from another individual with both a compatible blood *type* and, of that type, from an individual also missing the Rh D antigen or, in other words, whose blood is both compatible and Rh negative. For example, a person with A negative blood can receive transfusions of both A and O blood, but only if the donors are A negative and O negative."

"Are you saying Rh negative and Rh null are the same thing?"

"Not at all. I was just providing enough background to explain Rh null. Rh negative is missing one Rh antigen, specifically Rh D. Rh null blood is missing *all* of the Rh factors. This means that Rh null blood is the *true* universal blood type. Sadly—and this is the rub—it also means that Rh null individuals can only receive transfusions from other Rh null donors."

"Well, I can't see how that poses a problem," Phillips argued.

"The problem, as you put it, is that only about fifty individuals possess Rh null blood."

"What, like fifty in the US?"

"No. Fewer than fifty confirmed cases exist *in the entire world.* The specific identities and locations of these patients are not widely published in order to protect their privacy and their exploitation."

Phillips appeared stunned. "So you're saying Sophie's blood is . . ."

"Extremely rare? Only one known type is rarer, blood with the SARA antigen, which exists only in two family lines across the earth. But for Sophie? Should she use up the blood Mr. and Mrs. Nadeau have wisely stored for her, yet needs further transfusions, it is unlikely she would receive them."

No one said anything for a long, tense moment, and Simon could see the officer struggling to process the information. Finally, Phillips lifted his head and looked at Miss Finch.

"You said the men who attempted to abduct Sophie weren't necessarily after her for . . . you know."

Sophie's father exploded. "For 'you know' *what?* Quit beating about the bush! What are you not telling us?"

CHAPTER 20

MISS FINCH STOOD and pushed her chair closer to the Nadeaus. She sat and took Mrs. Nadeau's hand in hers. "What I reveal shortly will be hard to hear, dear woman. So, before I speak, I want to say I am sorry if my words grieve and frighten you . . . for they surely will. However, I also want you to realize and acknowledge that you have friends here, and that 'forewarned is forearmed.' Now that we know Sophie is a target, we will protect her."

She lifted her chin to Phillips, daring him to disagree. "Will we not?"

He slowly nodded. "Sure. We will protect Sophie . . . somehow."

Phillips had to be thinking what Simon was thinking, that obtaining official protection for Sophie would be next to impossible without revealing the reasons she needed such protection, which would only endanger her further.

Lord, we must remove the danger to Sophie without exposing her secrets—not merely shield her from danger. Please show us how!

"What is it? Tell us!" Mrs. Nadeau begged of Miss Finch.

"Very well, this is what we know: Since around the middle of May, a small number of individuals around the lake district have disappeared. Three young, outwardly healthy men were abducted first, each about two weeks apart. The first was a Chinese national, in the US on a student visa, backpacking north of the lake. The second, an American, disappeared while mountain biking south of Olympic Valley. The third, also an American, disappeared while on a hike up Tahoe Mountain . . . not that far from here. To date, two of them have been found."

"Found alive, I presume?" Mr. Nadeau interjected, daring Miss Finch to say otherwise.

"I wish it were so, Mr. Nadeau, but it is not. The Chinese student's body was found in the lake. At his autopsy, the medical examiner found that all his major organs had been surgically removed."

Mrs. Nadeau swayed in her chair, but Mr. Nadeau swallowed and persisted in his questions.

"What does it mean that all his organs were surgically removed?"

"It means, we believe, that his organs were harvested to be implanted in persons in need of transplants."

"But . . ."

"It bears saying that all three of these young men had similar blood types: B positive and B negative."

Nadeau cursed under his breath and demanded, "What has that to do with Sophie!"

Miss Finch patiently pushed ahead. "On July 2, two men attempted to kidnap an eleven-year-old girl out riding her bicycle on the northeast shore. They failed—just as they failed to take Sophie. However, two days later, during Incline Village's Fourth of July celebration, another young girl, age twelve, disappeared without a trace. Both girls had O negative blood."

Mr. Nadeau was near tears. "Again! What has that to do with Sophie?"

Miss Finch persisted. "We have two working theories extrapolated from the facts we have gleaned and verified. The first theory is that someone local to the lake area, in dire need of an organ transplant, hired an individual with, shall we say, specialized medical knowledge and skills. We believe this 'employer' is independently wealthy, but could not obtain the organ he sought through normal transplant channels, most likely because his blood type was rare—not Rh null rare, but still difficult to obtain. Either that, or he had certain health conditions that pushed him far down on the transplant list.

"Our other theory, somewhat similar, is that the individual with the knowledge and skills necessary to put a transplant suite and team together was motivated by a personal need: a spouse or child needing a transplant."

"Was? *Was* motivated? What are you saying?" Nadeau begged.

"In either theory, we believe the evidence indicates that the individual in need of a transplant received the organ he or she needed . . . from the involuntary donor whose body was found in the lake."

Mrs. Nadeau pressed her hands against her bloodless lips.

Mr. Nadeau, thinking hard on Miss Finch's revelations, shook his head. "*The* organ he needed, as in only one? But you said—"

"I know what I said, Mr. Nadeau: *Six* organs were harvested from the young man: heart, lungs, liver, kidneys, pancreas, and corneas. It is unlikely that all six organs were needed by the recipient. And since all six organs were removed with the care and precision required for transplant, we must assume that five other needy patients received the surplus organs."

The Nadeaus were silent now, their eyes wide, as Miss Finch paused for a breath.

"We can also assume that each patient receiving one of those organs paid a hefty price for his or her transplant. After all, I cannot see our murderer, wealthy or no, wasting or merely giving away such lucrative 'gifts' of life. No, he would have charged each recipient a pretty penny and had them prepped and ready to receive their transplants immediately before or after he received his. After all, the price tag for the facility, staff, equipment, and pharmaceuticals necessary for such a surgery would be not be covered by insurance. No, it would require a cash payment, said payment astronomically high.

"You're saying this-this *murderer* sold the other organs?" Nadeau whispered.

"As I said, regardless of which of our working theories is most accurate, both are bolstered by the foiled kidnapping of the young cyclist followed immediately by the successful abduction of the girl at the Incline Village Fourth of July celebration."

"Because they share the same blood type?"

Miss Finch tipped her chin to her chest. "Yes, O negative. You see, while O positive is the most common blood type, O negative is relatively rare. Less than seven percent of the human population has O negative blood. And while it is true that individuals with O negative blood can donate their blood to most anyone, the inverse is also true: An O neg patient needing a blood transfusion can receive only O negative blood, which can be hard to come by. So, you see, a person with O negative blood needing an *organ transplant* would experience even greater difficulty obtaining a donor match."

She moistened her lips. "Hence, two young individuals targeted for abduction within days of each other, both with O negative blood? This strongly suggests our murderer has a young O negative patient as his most recent 'customer.' He is, we believe, determined to recoup the astronomical costs of his transplant facility and even, perhaps, turn a hefty profit."

In her shock, Mrs. Nadeau had turned inward.

Her husband, though, stared into Miss Finch's eyes. "You believe the killer wanted Sophie for her organs?"

Miss Finch shook her head. "No. That would be tantamount to killing the goose that laid golden eggs—pardon my crude metaphor."

"Then what? What would they want Sophie for?" Mr. Nadeau demanded, not quite convincingly.

Miss Finch exhaled. "I believe you know or suspect what they want of Sophie, Mr. Nadeau. I should think they want her to serve as a perpetual blood bank. One that could provide saving blood to anyone with both the need and the money—particularly someone with an acute need, whether Rh null or a less rare but still difficult to obtain type, such as O negative."

Mrs. Nadeau whispered, "They . . . they would keep our little girl alive just to . . ."

"A fate only marginally better than needing her for the *other* nefarious purpose."

Phillips, his brow creased in deep contemplation, asked, "But didn't you say only about fifty people in the world have this blood type? And doesn't that mean that the need for Sophie's blood is actually small and so specific as to be negligible?"

Simon watched Miss Finch bow her head to her chest. Even from several feet away, he could feel her praying, preparing herself to speak, asking for the right words in an answer to a question that had no good response. Then she raised her head.

"Mr. and Mrs. Nadeau, I have considered what you've told us about Sophie's birth mother, how she lived her life feeling she was property of the state—property of the Chinese Communist government—and how she was compelled to give blood regularly. That requirement for her to 'donate' blood on a schedule gave rise to another supposition, a rather unpleasant one."

She glanced at Phillips. "Officer Phillips has raised an essential point, and he is right in this regard: The pool of individuals needing Sophie's blood *is* small—although, as I said a moment ago, her blood could also be used for patients with other, less rare blood types, such as O neg. Still, however small that number may be, it is only negligible if those in acute need have no money."

Her attention returned to the Nadeaus. "You said Sophie is prone to anemia. Do you recall my saying that people with Rh null blood often have blood-related diseases? Now please consider and ask yourself, to what lengths would a wealthy, perhaps powerful, Rh null individual with a life-threatening blood disease go? What would such a person do to ensure regular Rh null transfusions? Would they not stoop to practice slavery of this sort?"

Simon felt nausea rise in his chest. He pictured Sophie's little hand in his as they prayed together—juxtaposed against an image of her strapped to a bed, unable to run or play. Unable to escape.

His gorge began rise.

"BeeDee. I-I-I need . . ."

The panic in his voice caused her to rush back to him. She lifted the cup of ice water and its straw to his lips.

"There, there. Please calm yourself. You heard what the doctor said: Nothing stressful."

"Can't bear it," he muttered. "I love that child."

Tears gathered in her eyes. "I know you do, Simon. I apprised Officer Phillips of the ongoing need to provide a guard for her. We will keep her safe."

"How?"

"We will find a way."

"Yes, but *how?*" Mr. Nadeau echoed Simon. "How can we keep Sophie safe? And how did this monster even discover that she has Rh null blood? Only our doctor knows, and his are the only records that exist!"

"AI bots," Simon muttered, staring at Miss Finch. "AI bots. Just as you said."

"If the doctor stores his records in the cloud, then yes."

"Back up the boat!" Phillips, agitated, stood and addressed Miss Finch. "Before we even tackle your bizarre and improbable idea that some wealthy but unknown individual in need of Sophie's 'golden blood' might be behind her attempted abduction, are you some kind of hacker savant? Are you telling me, Miss Finch, that's how you get your information? Is that why you're so far ahead of us peons in law enforcement when it comes to recognizing the moves of this serial killer?"

His voice dropped to a softer, more hostile tone. "Because if you are, there are laws . . ."

A frigid expression dropped onto Miss Finch. "I will not be responding to your interrogatives, Officer Phillips, and I pray you *think* before you dare make the official fuss you are contemplating. Yours would be an entirely *despicable* act, instantly able to snatch from our hands what opportunity remains to rescue these two missing individuals before their time runs out."

Phillips frowned. "You actually think the last young man, Morales, and that girl, Allysson Sharma, could still be alive?"

"Put bluntly, human organs have a *very* short shelf life. Most cannot be frozen and reconstituted like blood can be. In order to maximize his profit, our killer must first attract his customers and coordinate their surgeries, one right after the other, as quickly as is feasible, meaning he must keep his victims *alive* and at optimum health until that very day."

Phillips opened his mouth . . . then clamped it shut and dropped into an angry silence.

"But how . . . how would one go about 'marketing' such ghastly products? How would someone conduct such a horrific business?" Mr. Nadeau asked.

Miss Finch nodded, her cheeks still flushed with tightly held ire. "Quite carefully and cautiously, of course. That said, the idea of prospective buyers stumbling upon a website touting the perfect organ offer is unfeasible. No, our killer himself must actively *seek out* his 'customers.' He would need to hack the national transplant list and identify those patients whose names are far down the list, patients whose chances of an organ match are low, often patients with hard to match blood types. He would then hunt down 'donors' to meet their need. Do you follow me?"

Phillips and the Nadeaus nodded their understanding in concert.

"I imagine our killer then examines the finances of these prospective buyers, and selects only those patients or families that have the financial wherewithal our killer requires. Unfortunately, the ways in which Tahoe's serial killer might approach his selected customers? Too numerous and too varied to ever catch 'in the moment.'"

"I am less concerned with catching this monster than I am in keeping Sophie safe!" Nadeau snarled. "We must leave Bright Star immediately and disappear!"

Miss Finch rounded on him. "Do you think, given the level of financial gain this creature of Satan hopes to profit off of your precious daughter, that he will *ever* give up looking for her? No matter where you hide her, he will seek her out and find her!"

Nadeau, intimidated by Miss Finch's fierce response, shrank back.

She walked close to him and stared into his face. "If—*if*—you cherish hope for Sophie's future, you must be willing to put this monster where he belongs . . . in the ground, if necessary. It is the only way to be assured of Sophie's safety."

Jerked out of his silence, Phillips spoke up. "I'm going to pretend I didn't hear you say that, Miss Finch."

"Oh, posh! Do not tell me that you, in any way, shape, or form, do not agree with my sentiments," she growled.

"It's not about sentiments, it's about the law—"

Simon called out, interrupting them. "BeeDee! Phone! Need my phone!"

Miss Finch wagged a finger under Phillip's nose. "We are not finished here." She quick-stepped to Simon's side. "Your things must be in this room . . . somewhere."

She opened the nightstand drawer. It was empty. Opened the closet across the room. Also empty.

"Under bed?" Simon queried. He suddenly realized the tender inside of his mouth, particularly the damaged side of his tongue, was hurting again. About the same time, the rest of his punched and pummeled body telegraphed the same message, each adding an aching throb, a shouted exclamation point, to his mouth's cry for relief.

Miss Finch ducked down under Simon's bed and came up with a plastic sack. She pulled it open and yanked out the shreds of Simon's clothes. "What! They cut your shirt and shorts off you?"

"Phone," he muttered through his raw lips and around his swollen tongue. "Shophie at Bright Star. Only boysh to protect her."

"Merciful heavens!" She whirled toward Phillips. "Sophie is essentially unprotected at Bright Star? Did you not follow my *explicit* instructions?"

Phillips deflected her jab and muttered, "On it." He pulled his phone and punched numbers with the same ferocity Simon knew he'd apply to the man bent on owning little Sophie Nadeau.

"Phone!" Simon rumbled again through gritted teeth.

"Hold your horses, cowboy."

"Yesh, ma'am," Simon scowled.

Miss Finch pawed through the sack and came up with it. "Here it is."

He hit one of his saved Favorites entries, then speaker phone, and tried not to mumble or slur through the growing pain as he spoke.

"Joe? Lishen, have urgent security shituation. Closh gates. Nobody through. *Nobody!*"

All of them listened to Joe reply, "Sure. You got it, Fletcher."

"Thanksh. Now, where Shkipper and Nadeau kidsh?"

"They are all riding their bikes in the woods, Fletcher."

He felt the blood drain from his face. "No!"

Miss Finch grabbed his phone out of his hand. "Joe? Miss Finch. I'm on my way, and the police are too. Drive your truck out to the feeder road and park across it just before the turnoff to Bright Star. Yes, *across the road*. Do not let *anyone* through who might drive farther up the road bordering the woods where the children are riding. Oh—and make certain you are carrying."

She shook her head vehemently. "Do not ask or argue, Joe Mitchell. Just do as I say. I will be there in fifteen. Ten if I can swing it."

She hung up and tossed the phone onto Simon's chest. Turned to Phillips. "Police escort?"

"Why? Where are the kids?"

"They are riding their bikes in the woods around Bright Star. Anyone can get into those woods where it borders the feeder road."

He jerked his head toward the door. "Let's go."

Miss Finch and the Nadeaus rushed to follow Phillips out the door, and Simon found himself both alone and gritting his teeth against the pain.

Don't care. Until I know Sophie is safe, I'm not taking any medication that will zonk me out.

———————— • ————————

THE NURSE RETURNED several minutes after Simon's visitors tore out of his room. With great reluctance, Simon declined the pain pill she bore. Eyeballing the miniscule cup with longing, he told her, "I'll take the antibiotic now and the pain pill later."

"Are you certain? You are now hours behind your pain medication schedule. We like our patients to stay ahead of their pain."

"Well, I need to stay awake," Simon muttered.

"Okay. Your choice."

"Maybe I could have another cup of milkshake?"

"That, Mr. Fletcher, is a brilliant idea. I'll be right back."

An hour passed before Miss Finch called. "Is Sophie safe?" he demanded, the pain in his mouth calmer for the cold shake the nurse had fed him.

"Yes, she is. We found no evidence that anyone who normally shouldn't be close to Bright Star is or has been. Skipper and I even took our bikes into the woods and checked along the fence line. The dirt in the woods is pretty dry and dusty. If someone crossed the fence into the woods, we would have seen scuffs and footprints."

"What about official police protection?"

"I deduce that Phillips is suffering something of a quandary regarding a protection detail for Sophie, Fletcher. He can provide to his captain no reasons for ongoing protection without spilling the beans. Our beans, to be explicit. Our organ harvesting theories.”

“I confess to thinking the same.”

“Right. For the present. However, Officer Phillips has agreed to personally watch over the Nadeaus himself and has called on several officers of his acquaintance who will provide armed security during their off-shift hours . . . for a fee, of course.”

She exhaled hard. “I am considering a private solution of my own in the short-term. I know a couple of gentlemen who would fit the bill.”

“Oh? And do they owe you favors?”

She chuckled. “Actually, I owe them for their worthy care of me.”

“I imagine your gentlemen will charge an exorbitant fee. I’ll cover it.”

“I have it handled.”

“You? Just last month you needed your paycheck from Bright Star and needed it in cash.”

“The cash part was the essential element. I am not poor, *Mr.* Fletcher.”

“*Right.* I’m covering this expense. The entire nut.”

She sighed and sounded weary to Simon’s ears. “This is not the time to argue, Fletcher. If and when I can get them here, they are still only a temporary fix. We must hit upon a means of drawing out our adversary in order to end his threat to Sophie.”

“We’re not using Sophie as bait, BeeDee, and that’s final.”

She huffed. “I am gratified to find we agree on *that* matter. However, since when have I given you leave to address me in familiar fashion?”

“You lost our bet—remember?”

“You refer to your silly riddle? I have not yet conceded, nor would my losing the ‘bet,’ as you call it, result in permission for you to use my first name.”

“The whole point of our competition was that I don’t *know* your first name, lady. You agreed to tell me what your initials mean when you lost.”

“*If* I lost,” she insisted, and Simon could envision her nose in the air, her mouth pursed just so, utterly confident in her position.

Confident? Stubborn, you mean. Well, I can be stubborn too.

“You’ve had weeks to solve my riddle.”

“And you erred in not setting a time period for the contest.”

“Oh, yeah? Well, how’s this? You solve the riddle within the next forty-eight hours, or I start making calls. Maybe I’ll start with UCLA and the department you taught in. Perhaps I’ll speak directly to your department head.”

He could see her hooded eyes narrow as clearly as if he were sitting across from her in her trailer.

“You would not dare,” she hissed.

Simon snickered to himself and replied, “You have forty-eight hours.”

She hung up on him.

Arms hugging his chest, filled with ridiculous glee but trying his best not to laugh aloud, he managed to ring for a nurse. He was vainly holding his ribs, still struggling to hold in his burbling laughter, when the nurse appeared, the ubiquitous paper cup in her palm.

"You look happy," she commented, her name tag reading Woodrow. "And I assume you rang for your pain pill?"

"You got that right."

She tipped the cup into his mouth and held a straw to his lips. "There. Rest easy now, okay?"

He stared at her back as she left his room.

Rest easy now? I'll rest; just don't know about the easy part. Let's see . . . Phillips is watching over the Nadeaus tonight, he's rustled up some off-duty officers for tomorrow, and Miss Finch says she will recruit a couple private security guys.

*Will it be enough? If **they**, whomever it is hunting Sophie, want her badly enough, I doubt it will be.*

He began to feel the effects of the pill, a dulling of the sharp edges of his pain, then drowsiness as it continued to steal over him.

Lord? I need to get out of here, so please help me heal quickly. Nobody is going to protect Sophie the way she needs to be protected.

Like I need her to be protected.

CHAPTER 21

SIMON'S PHONE ROUSED him. He was again mildly disoriented but mostly sticky and stupid with sleep. He felt around until he found his phone tangled in his blanket. He punched the speaker button without glancing at the phone's screen.

"Hello?" he croaked.

"Fletcher, Miss Finch here. It is half past six in the morning. Were you sleeping?"

Sleeping? He tried to shake the fuzziness from his brain.

"Huh. Guess I was. Last thing I remember is the nurse giving me a pain pill after all of you tore out of here yesterday. No, wait—it was after you called . . ."

The details flooded back. "Oh yeah, it was after you called, pitched your little fit, and hung up on me."

"*Hmph.*"

Simon smiled to himself. *My dear Miss Finch, if Pouncer is a brat, she certainly caught it from you.*

He added, "In any event, I must have slept through the night."

"Do you mean to tell me they aren't feeding you?"

Change the subject much, Finchy? Why, you even managed to infuse your question with a touch of feigned outrage for me.

For me?

He kinda liked it.

"Did you not have dinner last night?" she demanded. "What about breakfast this morning?"

"I think I have to call the hospital kitchen when I want to eat." His stomach lurched the moment he thought the word "eat."

"Please tell me you will call and order a hearty breakfast as soon as we hang up."

"Yeah, okay. Thanks for waking me up. I sure didn't expect to sleep this long. Good grief, I'm foggy."

"If you slept that long, undisturbed, I suppose they must have checked on you throughout the night and felt that leaving you asleep was what you needed most."

Simon wiped his face with his uninjured hand. "I guess. Hopefully, they let me out of here today."

"Highly unlikely. The doctor in the ED said seventy-two hours of observation . . . plus, you will be having your broken fingers set tomorrow, will you not?"

"Crud!" Simon tugged on the vague memory of a new doctor visiting him yesterday at some point. Was it yesterday? So much seemed muddled together. He forced himself to refocus on what Miss Finch was saying.

"Good news. I have obtained private security for Sophie, security with whom I have personal experience and whom I trust. I will bring the two lead gentlemen by and introduce them to you as soon as they arrive, since you insisted on paying for them."

Simon saw dollar signs flashing by at an alarming speed. "I did?"

"You did. 'The entire nut,' I believe was the phrase you employed."

He sighed. "When do they arrive and how soon can they be on the job?"

"They left LA an hour ago. I expect to see them sometime this afternoon."

"And the Nadeaus know they are coming?"

"Yes, although they remain considerably reluctant—more 'squirrelly' than reluctant—about staying on at Bright Star. They continue to think they can hide Sophie from her pursuers. Twice, and rather bluntly, I am afraid, I have had to walk Mr. and Mrs. Nadeau through the facts that Sophie's pursuers not only hacked the records of Sophie's doctor—and likely thousands of other physicians and hospitals in their quest to identify the infinitesimally small number of people with Rh null blood—but, having once identified Sophie, they also lured the Nadeaus to Tahoe through their 'win' of a top-of-the-line RV and by pointing them to an available berth at Bright Star, even ponying up the money to pay for it."

She huffed. "Really! I cannot believe I had to convince Mr. and Mrs. Nadeau that if these people could locate Sophie out of all blood banks or medical records in Canada, or perhaps all of North America, how much less difficult would it be for them to find Sophie wherever the Nadeaus chose to hide her?"

"That doesn't relieve my concerns any. Do you think the Nadeaus might try to book it in the middle of the night?"

"I have apprised Phillips of the possibility. He has assured me that the officers on duty tonight will, gently, scotch such a plan. It is far better for Sophie that we know where she is and properly safeguard her than try to conceal her elsewhere and be too far away to help when her pursuers come for her."

"Better? The only thing better is removing the threat altogether."

"Agreed, although the most satisfactory means of removing the threat altogether is out of our discretion. Listen, Fletcher. I will be up to see you later this afternoon. I should have Sophie's protection detail with me so you can meet them. We must, soon, and as a group, plan how to make this all work."

Simon thought of something. "Would you do me a favor?"

"More protein-enhanced milkshakes?"

He laughed a little. "Gotta admit they are helping me a lot, so *yes*, but actually I'd like you to bring me my sidearm. I think you should be carrying at all times too."

"It's not legal to carry—open or concealed, licensed or not—in a California hospital, Fletcher. Hospitals are restricted areas. And even if it were legal, I doubt the hospital administration would permit you to have a weapon while you are a patient, particularly a patient not quite right in the head."

"What the hospital administration doesn't know won't hurt *them*, but lying here defenseless could sure hurt *me*. What am I expected to do if Mountain Man and his pal show up here? Use harsh language?"

"Silence."

Finally, she sighed. "The things I do . . ."

"Great! My cabin door is unlocked. My gun safe is screwed to the floor under the bottom bunk." He gave her the combination. "How are Joe and Skipper doing? Are they able to keep up with the work? Is Skipper helping enough?"

"Skipper is a treasure and is doing his very best to help Joe. And besides that, something quite wonderful has happened."

"I could use some 'quite wonderful' news."

He could tell from her voice that she was smiling. "As you might imagine, word of the attempted kidnapping has circumnavigated Bright Star. So has Skipper's version of our run-in with the would-be kidnappers. Likewise, the Nadeau boys have filled every willing ear with tales of your bravery and heroism, and Skipper, having seen your injuries, has recounted them many times in vivid, lurid detail."

Air hissed between Simon's teeth. "Oh, brother."

"Precisely. Quite the theatrical stir! And since Joe and Holly were being inundated with questions and concerns, they called an all-hands meeting last evening around the big fire pit to explain what happened on the bike path. After calling upon me to answer a multitude of questions, Joe also apologized in advance if service around the park wasn't one hundred percent up to Bright Star standards while they figured out how to, temporarily, fill your sizeable shoes."

"I knew it!" Simon sputtered. "Holly's pushing for a new hire, isn't she? Probably won't need me when I'm recovered, so what's wonderful about that?"

"What is wonderful is that it seems you have garnered a loyal following at Bright Star, Fletcher. Right there, in the middle of that all-hands meeting,

Ray and Irene Kinzer stood up and said, and I quote: 'This place, and Fletcher in particular, has treated us like family. What do you do when family is in need? You get busy, that's what!' Then he announced that he and Irene were taking over pool maintenance."

"What!"

"Oh, I am not finished, my dear boy, not by a long shot. The Redwines immediately laid claim to the barbecue area as their domain to manage, Chet and Justine Bigalow assumed daily trash pickup, the Benowitz sisters pledged to handle the laundry area, and Mr. and Mrs. Gorman, at their granddaughters' urging, declared they will keep the rec cabin tidy. Others said they would step in wherever they could help Joe and Skipper in your absence."

Simon was stunned. No, he was poleaxed. "Bright Star residents are pitching in to help Joe and Skipper? No way!"

"Oh, very much 'way,' Fletcher."

"And you say Becka and Melissa Gorman are back?"

"Yes, indeed—and Bruce has returned to his aunt and uncle's site. Skipper lost no time introducing Becka, Melissa, and Bruce to Wyatt, Eli, and Sophie. He also lost no time solemnly deputizing each of the older children, making them promise to keep Sophie under their watchful eyes at all times."

"I don't know what to say."

"Neither did Holly or Joe; Holly was in tears. I finally had to stand and thank the volunteers. We ended our little all-hands meeting in a very heartfelt round of applause. Oh. And I was commandeered to pass on to you Bright Star's best wishes for a full recovery."

"Wow."

"My reaction was, 'praise God!'"

"As usual, Miss Finch, you're right."

LATE THAT AFTERNOON, a knock sounded on Simon's hospital door. "Come in," he rasped.

The door opened and Miss Finch entered, followed by two men. Simon observed immediately that both were fit, with five to ten years on him, and carried themselves with military bearing.

Then it hit him. *Hey! My eyes! I can focus!*

Miss Finch smiled, and he grinned back.

"Your sight has improved, has it not?" she asked.

"I just realized it has."

"Keep it down, would ya? I'm trying to sleep over here." The complaint came from behind a curtain shielding the second bed in the room and a newly installed patient.

Miss Finch addressed the curtain. "We apologize . . . in advance," she answered.

"You what?"

"We have important business to discuss with your roommate. We promise to keep our discussion brief and our voices low, but only when we have finished shall we leave. Thus, I apologize for disturbing you *in advance*."

"Hey! This ain't no office—and I'm a sick man. You've got a lotta nerve, lady!"

"So I have been told."

She moved to Simon's bedside and showed her small, even teeth in a wide smile. "I have been praying for you. You are no longer seeing double?"

"I'm seeing single and clearly! No blurry images or fuzzy outlines."

And no shimmers or sparks. Thank you, Jesus!

"Introduce me to your friends?"

"Ah. Fletcher, please meet Grayson and Alberto from Gibson Security Services of Los Angeles. Gentlemen, this is Simon Fletcher, Bright Star's Facility and Security Manager. Call him Fletch or Fletcher."

Grayson nodded. "Pleased to meet you, Fletcher. Jarhead, I presume?"

"*Oorah*; Grunt?"

"Yup, and proud of it. Alberto here, however, was a squid."

"Can't win them all, right?"

Alberto frowned. "Hey, I'm not the one lying in that bed, half beat to a pulp."

Simon and Grayson laughed together easily, although Simon flinched and held his ribs with his right hand and arm.

Simon replied, "I apologize, Alberto. Denigrating the other branches is hard baked into the Corps. On the other hand, you didn't see the monstrosity I tangled with."

"Speaking of which," Miss Finch pulled up an image on her phone and turned it toward Simon. "Look familiar?"

Although Simon hadn't gotten a clear look at the face of the man he'd fought, the mugshot made the hair on his neck and arms stand up. "Pretty sure that's him, the mountain of a man who about took me out."

"We're pretty sure too. Mountain Man's name is Jürgen Münster, German immigrant, at present a less-than-exemplary American citizen. He has a long record and did time for involuntary manslaughter—with his bare hands."

"Not surprised about that," Simon muttered, "but really? His last name is *Monster?*"

"No, *Münster*, as in the cheese, although *Monster* might have been prophetic on his parents' part, would you not agree?"

"Ha ha. Very funny. Your geeks find Münster's ID for you?"

"They did."

"We have a location?"

"No. Current address and employer are unknown. We'll have more as soon as they track him down."

"More, as in where he sleeps at night?"

She grinned outright. "Hopefully, where his employer does also."

"Outstanding. So, who's watching Sophie right now?"

Alberto answered, "We brought additional personnel with us so we can cover all hours and needs. We've relieved the off-duty PD officers. Our people, Addie and Dorian, have the ball at present."

Simon glanced at Miss Finch and mouthed softly, "Everyone carrying?"

She nodded and pulled a small bundle from her bag and whispered, "Where will you keep this while you're here?"

"Where I can reach it," he muttered, taking and unwrapping his small semiauto, checking that the safety was on, and sliding it under the blanket against his thigh. "Does me precious little good if Monster Cheese comes through that door and I can't instantly reach it."

"But where will you stash it when they take you to cast your hand tomorrow?"

"Are you saying you won't be here?" Simon hadn't meant to sound pathetic; the question just came that way.

"If you wish it, of course I will be here." She added in a whisper, "I can return your gun to my purse while you are out of your room."

"Thanks." He wanted to say more, just not in front of the two guys who were, without a shred of subtlety, sizing him up.

She nodded. "We should let your roommate sleep now."

"Yes, you should," Simon's roommate called from behind his curtained bed. "And what's all this talk about monsters, you crazy woman?"

Simon snickered. "He said you were nutso."

She snickered with him. "Only because he doesn't know *you*, Simon Fletcher! Besides," she raised her voice a hair, "I think your roommate is a little nutso himself."

"I heard that!" the disembodied voice protested.

"See you tomorrow," she said softly.

They had scarcely turned toward the door when Simon heard Grayson drawl, "Cute, aren't they, 'Berto?"

"You mean how they're all sweet on each other, Gray?"

Grayson laughed. "Never thought I'd live to see Miss Finch blush—*ow!* Miss Finch!"

Simon lay back in his bed, grinning.

CHAPTER 22

FRIDAY, JULY 18

THE NEXT DAY began in fits and starts: Simon woke early, ordered some breakfast, and ate what barely passed for what he'd ordered. At least his mental fuzziness wasn't as bad and seemed to be easing. Bored and in need of coffee actually hot and brewed strong, he ventured to slide his legs over the side of his bed, put his bare feet on the floor, and stand.

It wasn't the best decision he'd ever made. The room whirled around him, and nausea hit him with a vengeance, flooding his gut. He somehow got himself back into the bed, breathing hard, swallowing convulsively.

Won't be doing that again real soon.

When the spinning of the room lessened, he was able to call the nursing station and ask if they had a pot of *real* coffee there. A congenial nurse, whose name tag Simon could actually see, brought him a cup that he sipped until his stomach settled.

Miss Finch arrived around 7:45 and took possession of Simon's handgun. Minutes later, an orderly pushing a wheelchair entered Simon's room, helped him into the chair, and sped Simon out the door and toward the elevator.

"Stop!" Simon shouted as best he could.

The orderly stopped. "What's up?"

"My breakfast if you don't slow down. I have a concussion, haven't been out of that bed in two days, and can barely keep the world right side up. Please, dude. Take it easy on me."

"Sorry, man. I'll slow down."

He was back in his room an hour later, his breakfast, such as it was, still in his stomach. The orderly and Nurse Woodrow, according to her nametag, changed his linens, helped him back into bed, and departed. Right away, he asked Miss Finch about his roommate, who was gone.

"He get discharged?"

"No; he requested the change." She moved to the side of Simon's bed and pulled his handgun from her purse. He quickly slid it under the covers.

"How does your hand feel?"

Simon lifted his left hand and displayed the cast, its outer cover a bright orange. The plaster encased his wrist, palm, and middle, ring, and pinky fingers.

"Doctor included my little finger to help stabilize the breaks in my middle and ring fingers."

"May I have the honor of being the first to sign?"

"Be my guest—but only if you spell out your first name."

"Of course. It is spelled BD."

"Nope. Those are initials. We had a deal, and I gave you forty-eight hours to put up or shut up, remember? Time to come clean."

"Ah, yes. Your little riddle."

Something about her response sounded too chipper for Simon's suspicious mind. "Well?"

Her hand slid something from her purse: a folded piece of paper. She pulled Simon's rolling table over his bed, unfolded the paper, and placed it before him on the table.

Simon recognized the writing on the paper. It was his.

M R **s M R
M No **s!
O S A R!
C D E D B D iis?

"Sooo, you're ready to solve this?" he asked—hoping against hope she would fail.

"I am."

Nuts!

"Go ahead, then. Read it aloud."

"Certainly." She cleared her throat, and read,

"'Em are spiders, 'em are.
'Em no spiders!
Oh, yes they are!
See de itty-bitty eyes?"

Without missing a beat, she added, "Ready for me to sign your cast?"

"Brat! The world needs to know where Pouncer gets her brattiness. You have a pen?"

"Better. An indelible marker with a nice fat tip."

"Well, of course you do."

With a flourish, in overlarge letters and flowing purple ink, she signed his orange cast, "BD Finch."

"You know," Simon mused, "you're going to have to tell me your authentic first name sooner or later."

"Oh? And how do you figure that?"

"For starters, your signature looks like you've marked your territory. Tell me: Am I your territory? Hmm? Am I?"

The startled expression that bloomed from her neck into her hairline was priceless . . . and egged Simon to throw caution to the wind.

"For another reason, because I told you I like you, and my feelings are only going to grow stronger, you know. But even before that? Because I looked at you *cross eyed*. So, *BeeDee Finch*, where do you and I go from here?"

She spun and blew out of his room so fast the resulting whirlwind may have warranted an EF rating.

———— ◆ ————

AROUND NOON SIMON ordered lunch and ate his fill, grateful that the nausea he'd experienced on and off since his bout with Jürgen Münster seemed to have passed. Afterward, though, he fought against an insidious boredom and a creeping anxiety for Sophie's safety.

He was relieved when the doctor with the British accent who'd treated him in the Emergency Department appeared in his doorway. He was accompanied by a nurse Simon didn't recognize.

"Mr. Fletcher?"

"Come in, come in!" Simon begged. "Please say you've come to spring me from this place."

"I did say seventy-two hours. However, let's take a look and see how you are faring."

Simon passed the doctor's vision questions, reading the wall clock with ease.

"Any dizziness, nausea, or vomiting today?

"Uh, I may have tried to get out of bed early this morning and was dizzy then, but I ate a good lunch and had no nausea."

The doctor eyed him. "I see. Why don't you get out of bed now and show us how you fare."

The nurse moved to pull Simon's blankets back. He grabbed her hand.

"If you don't mind, would the two of you turn around while I adjust this haute couture gown I'm wearing?"

The nurse huffed and turned; the doctor merely nodded and did the same.

Simon slipped his semiauto under his pillow, then tossed back the covers, swung his legs over the side of the bed, and tugged the short gown over his knees.

"Ready."

"Put your feet on the floor," the nurse said.

He scooted forward and put his bare feet on the cold linoleum.

So far, so good.

The nurse said, "Because of your bruised and cracked ribs, I won't be using a gait belt to support you. If you become dizzy or faint, tell me immediately. I have a wheelchair handy and will position it behind you."

"Got it."

She hitched her elbow under his shoulder. "Stand, please."

He did and tottered a moment, found his balance, then realized his lunch was whispering rebellious little nothings to him.

Nope. Not today! he whispered back.

"Any nausea?" the doctor asked.

"Maybe some."

"Let's see you walk."

Simon secured the gown's closure with his right hand and took several steps. The room slowly rotated. He halted, closed his eyes, and breathed through his mouth.

"Dizzy?"

"I guess."

"Can you keep going?"

Simon took five more steps, then stopped, breathing hard.

"That's enough for now. I'm going to order a nurse to walk you around your room three times this afternoon and evening. If you manage yourself well, I'll discharge you in the morning."

Crud.

Then, all he wanted was to get back into his bed.

"Okay."

"Bear in mind what I've said about your level of activity, Mr. Fletcher," the doctor reminded him. "Only the minimum of walking for a week, basically to and from the restroom."

"Got it."

After they left, Simon managed to retrieve his gun and again slide it alongside his thigh. He immediately thought better of it.

If they're going to get me up three more times this afternoon, it's safer tucked behind my pillow.

Such are the mistakes we look back upon . . . and shake our heads.

———— ◦ ————

AROUND 2:00 P.M., Nurse Woodrow walked him around his room several times. The dizziness was much less, but the effort still cost him. He felt depleted. Exhausted.

Once back in his bed, he slept for a while. When he woke, the wall clock read half past three. He yawned, remembered the one remaining milkshake in the nurses' refrigerator, and imagined its cool sweetness flowing up the straw, flooding his mouth.

He called the nursing station and asked if someone might bring the shake to him. He had only hung up when the door of his room swung slowly inward.

The hair on Simon's neck prickled and lifted even before Jürgen Münster's massive form filled the doorway.

187

CHAPTER 23

MÜNSTER BRANDISHED A firearm that seemed more like a toy in his meaty fist than a real weapon, yet Simon knew better: The man held death equipped with a silencer in that hand. Münster scanned the room, moved farther inside, and nudged the door nearly closed behind him. Then he grinned at Simon and showed a row of teeth entirely commensurate with the size of his body.

"I see we're alone. Good."

Oddly enough, Münster's voice was not in line with the rest of his impressive dimensions. His voice was high-pitched and held a breathy quality, almost like that of a high-school student.

Simon slipped his hand under the covers and toward his thigh, then froze in consternation.

You idiot.

"Get up," Münster ordered. He nodded toward Simon's bathroom. "In there."

Simon blinked stupidly before he fumbled with the covers and sluggishly swung his legs over the side of the bed. He scrunched his eyes closed, swayed on the bed's edge, and put out his right hand to steady himself.

"Concussion . . ." he murmured. "Dizzy."

Play it for all its worth, Fletcher.

Münster chuckled to himself. "And here I thought I'd surely made soup out of your brain when we fought. I must be getting soft! Either that or you have a very hard head."

I know someone who would not disagree, one segment of Simon's mind thought, while another part wondered if he'd seen her for the last time.

"Managed to break your hand, though, didn't I?" Münster added.

"And you thought *I* had a hard head?"

The man laughed aloud. "Hurry it up. I don't have all day . . . and neither do you."

Will I die without you ever sharing your name with me, BeeDee? Without you hearing me tell you what you mean to me?

As Simon put his weight on the floor, one tentative, lethargic foot at a time, the hand holding him steady slid ever closer to his pillow.

The room's door opened.

"Mr. Fletcher, I have your milkshake—"

Nurse Woodrow stood in the doorway. She glanced from Münster to Simon and back. Münster himself was momentarily distracted.

Long enough for Simon to pull his gun from behind his pillow.

In the same moment, the nurse spotted the weapon in Münster's hand and stepped back. But before she could flee or call for help, a huge paw reached out, wrapped itself around her neck, and pulled her into the room. With ease, Münster lifted Woodrow until her feet were off the linoleum, scrabbling madly for purchase.

Münster squeezed the woman's throat and shook her until her face purpled, her eyes bulged, and Simon's milkshake flew from her hand, splattering the wall with chocolate sludge. The moment she went limp, Münster tossed her aside.

But when he returned his attention to Simon, he encountered the leveled muzzle of Simon's small semiauto.

"*Stop right there!*"

Simon had used his best Marine voice, but his warning did not deter Münster nor did it slow his response. They both knew: Whoever shot first would live.

Münster jerked his gun toward Simon.

Simon did what he'd been trained to do.

He fired.

Three rounds. Direct hit. Center mass.

When Münster did not immediately fall and when his gun came to bear, Simon fired again.

Three additional rounds into the man's huge center mass.

The slide on Simon's gun locked open. His small concealed-carry weapon only held a single-stack magazine of five rounds. And one in the chamber.

Meaning he was out of ammo.

Lord, if this guy doesn't go down, I'm cooked.

Münster's eyes tracked to his own hand, and he watched, seemingly astounded, as his fingers lost their grip on his gun. The weapon tumbled to the floor. Slowly, he lifted his chin toward Simon.

"I will kill you . . . with my bare hands."

"No, you won't," Simon replied. "You are already dead. You just haven't figured it out yet."

Münster blinked in disbelief. Seconds later, he staggered and lurched backward. His back hit the wall, and he leaned his weight on it, motionless, for a long, charged moment . . . before a font of frothy blood gushed from his mouth. He slowly lifted a hand to his face, pulled it back and stared at the dripping stain. Then he slid to the floor and fell over sideways, the blood from his mouth pooling on the floor around his head.

Simon heard shouted orders from the hallway. He carefully placed his weapon on the foot of his bed just moments before hospital security guards burst into his room. He lifted both hands and tried to keep them up, but the adrenaline coursing through him, coupled with his concussion symptoms, were calling the shots, not him.

He swayed and was near to toppling off the bed when two nurses rushed to him and eased him back into his bed.

"Mr. Fletcher? Are you all right?" a disembodied voice asked.

"Not dead," was all he could reply.

―――――― ● ――――――

THE AFTERMATH WAS too much for Simon. Security guards and medical personnel cycled through his room. Overloud voices asked questions he could not quite understand and demanded answers he couldn't articulate. All of it overwhelmed Simon's frazzled sensibilities. Pushed him to the edge.

His head pounded, and every bone and muscle in his body shivered and ached from an incipient fever. He pulled in on himself. Squeezed his eyes shut. Checked out.

Lord, have I told you that I'm grateful to be alive?

He was cocooned elsewhere, unaware of how much time had passed, insulated from the goings on in the real world. He may have even slept . . . only waking when a commanding and familiar voice penetrated the dense fog swirling about him.

"You will do no such thing. Mr. Fletcher is a registered California security guard—the same as you. That handgun is licensed to him, and he holds a valid conceal carry permit. If you cannot see that Mr. Fletcher is the victim in this situation, you should resign your position here and now. The deceased is the same individual who put Mr. Fletcher in this hospital, and whose objective in coming to this facility was to kill Mr. Fletcher—a fact entirely obvious to anyone *with a brain*. It is also apparent—again, to anyone *with eyes in their head*—that Mr. Fletcher acted in self-defense and, had he been unarmed, would presently be *dead*. Besides which, who knows how much this terrible trauma has set back his recovery! So you can take your hospital regulations and stick them where the sun does not shine!"

Simon smiled to himself. *Ah, Finchy. You are truly a force of nature . . .* He heard the rumble of more voices, but could not understand words until she spoke again.

"Call Officer Jonah Phillips, SLTPD, to verify my statements. In the meantime, I ask you to clear this room of nonessential personnel so Mr. Fletcher can rest. No, you will not attempt to interview him at this time. You will wait until Officer Phillips or another officer from SLTPD arrives."

Yeah, Simon thought. *Phillips is gonna love this mess.*

A small, warm hand cossetted his. "You did well, Simon. The nurse will recover and has you to thank for her life."

Simon hadn't remembered Nurse Woodrow until Miss Finch mentioned her. *Glad she's okay. Thank you, Lord.*

Her warm hand held his for some time while he dozed. When she spoke again, he roused himself to listen.

"I am glad to see you, Officer Phillips, you and the crime scene techs."

"Well, I'm not glad to see this . . . mess. What do you know?"

"We know your deceased over there is Jürgen Münster, one of the attempted kidnappers of Sophie Nadeau. The one Simon fought off."

"Good grief; the guy's a freak of nature! I'm rather surprised Fletcher is still with us."

"He wouldn't be at this very moment if he hadn't been armed."

"Yeah, I get that, but this is California."

"Land of disarmed victims; home of the burgled and murdered."

"It's a hospital, Miss Finch, a restricted area. No weapons allowed."

"Then, in this instance, you should cite Münster, not Mr. Fletcher. Münster brought a weapon into the hospital to kill Fletcher. Fletcher was merely defending himself from such an attack."

"Sorry, but I probably can't help you if my commander sends me back to arrest Fletcher or the hospital decides to press charges and demand his arrest."

Phillips changed the subject. "No ID on the body, just your word for it that his name is Jürgen Münster."

"You will find him in the system. He has a sheet, but no current address."

"And you know this how?"

"Not germane to the topic at hand. What *is* important is that he is probably carrying car keys. Get the keys or key fob, find the car. Find the car, get a registration and owner and, hopefully, the person who ordered Sophie's abduction."

"I'll put my officers right on that."

Simon's aching head suffered more commotion when the ME and his assistant came on the scene to take possession of Münster's body. Finally, at long last, his room was empty except for himself and Miss Finch.

"This is certainly a fine kettle of fish, Fletcher," she murmured, fatigue evident in every syllable.

Simon's sense of humor attempted to assert itself. "Fish fry?"

She exhaled a shaky breath. "Do shut up. At present, I am just . . . grateful you are alive."

"Yeah. Me too."

CHAPTER 24

SIMON STIRRED AND woke slowly, fairly surprised but certain that he had, finally, turned a corner. When he turned his head, looking for Miss Finch, he realized his headache was gone, his thoughts were clear, and that while rotating his neck to find her, it no longer hurt as it had even twenty-four hours ago.

As for Miss Finch? Someone had lowered Simon's bed as far as it could go, and her chair was pushed up against it. Her upper body and face were supine, cushioned by her crossed arms as they rested upon his mattress near his feet. Simon took the opportunity to study her as she slept and was saddened to note the dark rings around her eyes and the deep furrows between her brows.

This case is taking a lot out of her. Maybe too much. And that blasted book she insists upon writing? Lord, please shake some sense into this woman.

The door to his room opened. Grayson entered quietly.

He drew near Simon's bed, glanced at Miss Finch's sleeping form, then back to Simon and whispered, "You're awake. How do you feel?"

"Loads better. Ready to blow this popsicle stand. What are you doing here this early?"

"Been here all night. Recent evidence would suggest that Sophie's not the only target around here."

"Ha ha—good observation. But if you're here, who's keeping an eye on Sophie?"

"Addie. Alberto and Dorian are sleeping; they come on shift shortly. But if you think you're ready to get out of here, I believe I can convince the doctor to file your release papers. Turns out the hospital doesn't want a repeat of last night's attack any more than we do. Hopefully, we can have you home within the hour."

"About time."

Grayson snarked. "Yeah, because you were *so* ready yesterday."

"Uh . . . I decline to respond."

"I suppose you should know, too, that the media are all over this story."

"Can't imagine why. Aren't hospitals known to be some of the most dangerous places to stay?"

"Because of germy infections maybe; they really aren't known for assassination attempts."

"Picky, picky."

"Anyway, the police are keeping the cameras and reporters out of the hospital, but the crowd out front is growing. We'll need to take you out the back."

Miss Finch sat up abruptly, one cheek bearing the impression of her sleeve's nubby fabric. "What did I miss?"

"A good night's sleep, apparently," Simon scolded her. "Why didn't you go home last night?"

"For the simple reason I needed to be *here*."

"And Skip—"

"Skipper spent the night in my trailer, taking care of Hugo, Pouncer, and Napoleon. Your questions are annoying; you must be feeling more like yourself."

"Gee thanks. Well, I *am* feeling better, and Grayson says the hospital wants to cut me loose."

"Thank the Lord!"

"Don't thank him just yet," Phillips said from the half-closed doorway. "May I come in?"

"What is this?" Grayson laughed, opening the door and gesturing him inside. "Did someone call a breakfast meeting? 'Cause I didn't get an invite."

"Nor will you," Phillips said evenly.

Grayson shrugged, but he didn't move. "Sure. I get it. You don't know me and trust has to be earned."

Simon studied the police officer as he came near. Didn't like what he saw in the man's expression. "Are you here to take me into custody? Because you have to know it was self-defense, right?"

"Custody? No. Nothing so simple . . . or feasible at this point."

Simon caught the dark undertone in Phillips' voice. "Why? What's happened?"

Phillips turned to Miss Finch. "You need coffee."

"My, the power to expound upon the obvious is strong in this one."

"Yeah, yeah; thank you, Master Yoda." Phillips jerked his chin at Grayson. "Take a walk, and grab her a cup, would you? I need to talk to these two alone."

Grayson nodded and left.

"Well?" Miss Finch demanded. "What is it?"

Phillips sighed. "Remember last evening when you suggested I have my officers grab Münster's key fob and search for his car?"

"Of course. Where did they find his ride?"

"They didn't."

"The man didn't mount a broom and fly here! How could they not find his car?"

"Oh, they found a key fob in Münster's pocket all right. On the other hand, strangely enough, they found no ID on him. Not a single, solitary scrap of evidence other than that key fob. But when I sent the pair of officers out to locate his ride, they didn't. Not in the hospital's parking lot or any lots nearby. Not parked anywhere along the surrounding streets."

"Are you saying it was already gone?"

"I am. In the same way Münster's fellow kidnapper had an extra key fob down on Emerald Bay Road, whomever accompanied Münster last evening drove off leaving his partner behind. Of course, being the thorough investigators they are, my officers studied the hospital's exterior video feeds and managed to catch a glimpse of Münster as the car he rode in dropped him off, then drove on and parked farther down the street, beyond what the hospital security cameras cover. The vehicle was a silver SUV. That's all we have. No plate. No other identifiable markings."

"Well, certainly the microchip in the key fob you found on Münster should provide *some* insight concerning the car Münster arrived in."

"Oh, no—that would be too simple, and that's where this tale gets better. Sooo much better."

Miss Finch held up her hand. "Stop. Turns out I do need that coffee you mentioned."

"Me too," Simon added.

Phillips blew out a long, exaggerated breath, then shuffled from the room. He returned juggling three steaming disposable cups and handed off two of them.

"Intercepted your security guy. He had these. Thoughtful of him to pick up three coffees."

"Indeed." Miss Finch downed her first gulp. "All right, now spill—the rest of your sorry tale, I mean."

"Well, buckle up, lady; it's gonna be a rough ride. When I checked into SLTPD around five o'clock this morning, my two investigating officers were already there waiting for me."

She sipped again. "Really? Are your officers in the habit of clocking in before sunrise?"

"No, but I shared your theories with them Thursday morning. Initially, they, too, thought your ideas farfetched. But after last night's attack, your conclusions seemed . . . less implausible. They got into work early and hit the ground running. And then?"

He hesitated.

Miss Finch huffed. "And then *what?* Do I need to drop a quarter for each additional minute?"

Phillips turned his eyes on Simon. "Is she always like this? Rude? Demanding? Sarcastic?"

"All that and a bag of chips."

Miss Finch bent a glare on Simon so glacial, it should have iced his coffee.

He just grinned.

As best he could.

When she turned the same glare on Phillips, the officer sighed again. "Fine. *Pressing on* to what happened overnight. Last evening my investigators checked into evidence Münster's key fob, his weapon, Fletcher's weapon, and the shell casings Fletcher's weapon expended. Not even an hour later, one Officer Doonesbury checked them *out*."

Miss Finch frowned. "Are we acquainted with Officer Doonesbury?"

"Let me save you the trouble. SLTPD does not have an Officer Doonesbury, Miss Finch, only a love-hate relationship with the satirical comic strip of the same name. Furthermore, as I began to sense an emerging theme—vanishing car and vanishing key fob, weapons, and shell casings—I called the ME's office."

"No . . ." Miss Finch hissed. "Tell me it isn't so."

"Can't accommodate you, I'm afraid. Seems an *Agent* Doonesbury, purportedly of the FBI, along with his partner, Agent Hedley, also FBI, appeared in the ME's office at the butt-crack of dawn. They presented their credentials and a court order allowing them to take possession of Jürgen Münster's body *immediately*, that is, *without delay*. They and the body had been gone exactly thirty-seven minutes when I called."

"And the night-shift ME let the body go, just like that?"

"This isn't LA, Miss Finch, and we don't have a night-shift ME. Our graveyard staff consists of one lowly forensic technician. He's trained to answer the phone and perform specified, mundane tasks during his shift, to include calling the ME in the instance of a suspicious death warranting his attention. From what this tech told us, the two 'agents' threatened him with legal action if he didn't follow the court order and release the body without delay."

"Did you call—"

"Of course, I called the feds! What do you take me for—no, don't answer that. I haven't heard back yet, but I'll go out on a limb here and predict they do not have an Agent Doonesbury or an Agent Hedley any more than we have an Officer Doonesbury."

Phillips ground his teeth. "I can't charge you with shooting Münster. I can't even charge you for possessing and discharging a weapon in a restricted area! And why is that? Because a) I cannot produce a body, b) I cannot produce a weapon, c) I cannot produce any shell casings—Nope, not done yet. Working up to my next point—and d), last of all, I cannot produce any of your rounds. See, as big as Münster was, not one of your rounds was through and through, meaning all your bullets were still inside his body when the ME took him. So where, exactly, is the crime?"

The three of them were silent, caught up in their own thoughts for so long that it took the grumbling of Simon's stomach to stir them. "Sorry. Haven't eaten much lately."

A frustrated Phillips stared at Simon.

"Uh, unbelievable?" Simon suggested, half-giddy with relief.

"Yeah? Well, if I didn't know for a fact that you were *and are* in no fit state to get out of that bed, I'd have you back at the station and in an interview room right now."

"But what about the nurse?" Simon insisted. "She was right over there when I shot Münster. She can confirm that I shot him!"

Phillips stared at Simon, askance. "Are you *trying* to get yourself arrested, Fletcher? My guys are already heading to her place to interview her, but I'd lay money that she never saw your gun and was already unconscious when you shot Münster . . . no doubt saving her life as well as your own."

"Blood," Miss Finch suddenly muttered. "The crime scene techs will have Münster's blood, yes?"

Phillips eyes lit. "That's right; he was bleeding from his mouth. The crime lab will have those samples if whoever is orchestrating this vanishing act hasn't already pilfered the lab too."

He pulled his phone and stepped away to make the call. Simon and Miss Finch stared at each other, listening in on Phillips' side of the conversation . . . which wasn't long or unexpected.

"Well, *of course* the lab work and samples have disappeared. Great. Just great!"

Fletcher and Miss Finch were silent, both considering the same set of facts: A person or persons, as yet unknown but cloaked in the murky penumbra surrounding this case, had ordered a hit on Simon. Why? Because as far as Münster knew, Simon was the only witness who could identify him as one of the two thugs who'd attempted to kidnap Sophie Nadeau?

Yet, when Münster failed to eliminate Simon, that same unknown person had acted immediately, expending resources and pure chutzpah to clean up the mess Münster left behind.

Rather confirms our theory that the architect behind the organ transplant machinery is amazingly well organized and staffed, Simon realized, *not to mention brutally without scruples.*

Whomever he is? That's the creep we're up against.

As though reading Simon's mind, Miss Finch whispered, "We cannot afford to underestimate our adversary again, Fletcher. The cost of our inattention or lack of foresight does not bear consideration."

AN HOUR LATER, an orderly wheeled Simon out the hospital entrance to Miss Finch's woody. Simon's chair was flanked by Grayson and Miss Finch. Miss Finch carried Simon's plastic bag of belongings and her purse stuffed with prescription meds.

While Miss Finch texted from behind her steering wheel, the orderly helped Simon into the passenger seat, fastened his seatbelt, then slid a pair of crutches into the woody's rear seat. He shut the back door and paused at Simon's open window.

"Crutches compliments of the hospital staff, with our thanks for saving Miss Woodrow, one of our favorite nurses."

"Tell the nice man thank you, Fletcher," Miss Finch said, as she put the woody in drive.

"Thank you, Fletcher," he growled.

The orderly laughed, grabbed the wheelchair, and headed back inside.

"Crutches. *Marvelous*," Simon muttered darkly as they pulled away from the hospital, Grayson close behind them.

Miss Finch sniffed. "Beats not being able to get around at all, you dodo. *I* should know."

"I thought dodos were extinct."

"Oh, they are, but they were a rather senseless species, you know. Rash. Impulsive. Hardheaded. The last of them went up against a Jurassic-era aberration twice his own size. Still, it was a glorious end, full of valor, honor, and self-sacrifice. We can all take comfort in that."

"And you can shut it right there, Finchy," Simon sputtered. "I *killed* that dinosaur, and this dodo is still very much alive."

She feigned surprise. "Goodness! Did you think I was referring to you?"

"What? You straight-out called me a dodo!"

She laughed under her breath. "Please do accept my apology. What I *did* mean to convey is that you, Simon Fletcher, are a beautiful, heroic, one-of-a-kind man. That said and seeing as how we cannot do without you . . . do please be more careful moving forward."

"Hmm." Simon didn't know how else to respond.

Who's the we in your "we cannot do without you," lady? Do you mean you cannot do without me? And just how can I possibly be "more careful" going forward, if I couldn't foresee either of my run-ins with "Herman Munster"?

Her voice softened. "Does it weigh on you, Fletcher?"

He knew what she meant. Couldn't avoid the question.

"I can't allow it to. Killing him was necessary."

"Your actions saved that nurse, Miss Woodrow."

"I suppose so."

"There is no 'suppose' about it."

They rode in silence the rest of the way, until she bypassed the turnoff to his cabin.

"Hey. Why aren't you taking me home?"

"I will, in due time. We must be quite careful to follow the doctor's orders, but I am compelled to make a short, very short, stop first."

She drove on; they rolled through Bright Star's gate, continued right, and drove past her own site. Not two car lengths past her driveway, however, she braked, put the woody into reverse, and backed down her drive.

The reason was immediately clear: Most, if not all, of Bright Star's residents were assembled and waiting for them. Centered in the small crowd, Becka and Melissa Gorman, assisted by Bruce Muller, held a large, colorful, and obviously handcrafted sign that read,

** Hail the Conquering Hero **
Welcome Home, Mr. Fletcher!

Skipper was the first to reach the woody. He yanked Simon's door open and stepped back, while those congregated in Miss Finch's site applauded and cheered.

"Surprise, Fletch!"

Simon was convinced his jaw had unhinged itself for the simple reason he couldn't retrieve the lower half of his mouth from where it had dropped into his lap . . . nor could he muster a sound.

Miss Finch scurried around the woody from the driver's side and took charge. "All right, all right. Very nice and much appreciated. Thank you, one and all."

When the applause thinned out and she had their attention, she addressed the gathering. "I assume Skipper has rehearsed the doctor's orders for Mr. Fletcher's recovery, yes?"

Wyatt shouted, "No activity other than moderate walking for six weeks. That means *no* lifting, digging, pulling, heaving, running, jogging, and no return to work until the doctor clears him."

Eli chimed in, "You forgot a big one, Wyatt. *No stress!*"

"Thank you, young gentlemen. Indeed, 'no stress' is essential while Mr. Fletcher heals from his concussion. Now, in order to abide by the doctor's orders and follow them to a 't,' have you a chair ready for Mr. Fletcher?"

The crowd parted, revealing Miss Finch's adult lawn chair. Beyond it were two folding tables, set end to end, loaded with food and beverages.

Sophie stood by the lawn chair, her hand on its back, studying Simon from afar, her expression serious. "This chair is for you, Mr. Fletcher. We made lunch for you too. I helped."

"Lovely, Sophie," Miss Finch answered. "If all of you would now be so kind as to give us a minute, Skipper and I will seat Mr. Fletcher. Then you may greet our guest of honor. *Furthermore—*"

She waited until she again had their undivided attention. "As you can imagine, Mr. Fletcher is in some pain. Please refrain, therefore, from touching him or engaging him in too much conversation. A quick 'welcome back' or a wish for a speedy recovery must suffice at this time. And absolutely *no* hugging!"

With the help of his crutches and with Skipper alongside and prepared to steady him, Simon made the short walk to the waiting chair and eased himself down into it. A line of well-wishers instantly queued up. Sticking to Miss Finch's admonitions, they avoided patting his shoulder, shaking his hand, or saying too much.

Lucas and Eva Nadeau, the clear evidence of worry written on their features, were first in line. "We have no way in the world to thank you, Fletcher," Lucas said. "You saved our baby girl . . . and we cannot ever pay you back."

"I don't expect payment, Lucas," Simon murmured. "I only want what you want: Sophie's safety and happiness." He glanced around. "She was just here. Where did she go? Is she all right?"

Eva and Lucas exchanged a look. "She's safe and well looked after, thanks to Miss Finch's friends, but . . ." Eva shook her head and stared at her feet. "She's very worried about you."

Lucas gave it to Simon straight. "She saw you when you arrived. I see now that we should have prepared her, should have told her . . . that you're not looking your best."

Simon felt an icy blade slide between his ribs and pierce him deep inside. "I scared her? She's afraid of me?"

Eva wrung her hands; Lucas answered firmly, "No, I would say she's more freaked out, in general, than scared of you, Fletcher. She was unconscious when you fought that man. She didn't know . . . what we know, how hard you fought for her. We should have prepared her to expect the extent of your injuries."

Simon sighed. "I guess I can understand."

"Please do not hold it against her, Mr. Fletcher," Eva asked.

"Never. Thank you for explaining it to me."

"No, it's we who are thankful. We owe you a great debt of gratitude."

The Nadeaus stepped back and Joe and Holly took their place.

"Fletcher, Holly and I are so very glad to see you," Joe said, holding out his hand, then jerking it back when Miss Finch, never far from Simon's side, cleared her throat. "Sorry 'bout that. Now, don't worry a bit about your job; your friends here have got you covered until you are healthy again and ready to return."

"Yes, we wish you a speedy recovery," Holly agreed, sliding her eyes away from the unnerving sight of Simon's battered face, and tugging on Joe's arm.

"Thanks, Joe; thanks, Holly," Simon murmured.

"We've been praying for you," the three Benowitz sisters whispered. "We appreciate you more than you know!" They made him smile when, as they withdrew, each of them blew him a coquettish kiss.

"Take all the time you need to heal up, Fletcher," Ray Kinzer told him, "Joe and the rest of us? We've got all your tasks handled. And, uh, by the way? Since Irene and I have taken over pool maintenance, we've developed a fresh appreciation for how clean you keep those pools."

Irene Kinzer nudged him. "And the other, Ray."

"I was getting to it—sheesh! I, um, apologize again for that time I fed our little granddaughter so much candy she upchucked in the kiddie pool."

Simon grinned through gritted teeth, staving off the strong urge to belly laugh. "Think nothing of it, Mr. Kinzer . . . but if you do it again, I'll ban you from the swim complex for life."

Ray stared in shock, those who were listening in laughed, and Irene Kinzer pulled her husband away.

"Glad to see you back safe and, er, well, *safe*, in any event, Fletcher," Mr. Gorman said. Mrs. Gorman added, "Now, don't fret about meals, Fletcher. We have you covered for the next week."

"Yes, indeed," Justine Bigalow at Mrs. Gorman's elbow supplied. "One of us will show up at your cabin, eight o'clock each morning, with a hot breakfast and an easy lunch for your midday meal. Dinner from another resident will arrive between 5:30 and 6:00 p.m."

"I'm already salivating!" Simon replied.

The line went on and on, Bright Star residents greeting him in similar fashion: Mr. and Mrs. Redwine, the Bhattacharya family, Wes and Polly Trujillo, Tom Petterman, and the new family, the Gillespies. Even James Crowley, last in line.

Crowley.

The singularly unsettling moment of the gathering occurred when Crowley leaned toward Simon and under his breath said, "Love the look, Fletcher. I'd have paid good money to see you get the stuffing beat out of you. No one deserves it more."

Without another word, the man turned on his heel. Simon stared after Crowley as the man picked up a plate and helped himself to the bounty laid out on the two tables.

No one else stood waiting to greet Simon, yet the one person he'd especially wanted to see had not approached him. Simon spied her, yards away, her young hands folded in front of her sundress, her expression grave.

A woman Simon did not recognize stood behind her but far enough off that she wasn't encroaching on Sophie's personal space.

Must be Addie, Simon realized, recalling that Alberto and the fourth member of their team, Dorian, were catching up on their sleep. Grayson wasn't that far from them either, but he hung back, taking in the whole scene, keeping tabs on who came and went.

"Hey, Sophie," Simon said softly. "Aren't you going to come say hi to me?"

She cast her eyes down to her sandals, sighed, and shook her head.

Simon studied the girl. "Is it 'cause I got beat with the ugly stick? Is that it?"

She wagged her head slowly back and forth one time.

Simon was at a loss. Finally, he said, "It's okay if you don't like me anymore. I'll . . . I'll understand."

He didn't understand, but he would never push himself on the timid child, even though her rejection pained him.

She lifted her chin. Tears streaked her cheeks. "I *do so* like you!"

"Then why . . ."

With a sob, she turned and ran off. Addie shot him a glance of commiseration, then loped up the drive, following Sophie.

Miss Finch appeared at Simon's elbow. "She's a sensitive child, Fletcher."

"Think I don't know that? I just . . ." Simon felt confused and bereft.

"Have you looked in a mirror lately?"

Simon slid his gaze toward her. "Not since you shamed that poor ER doc for putting one in front of me."

"And you call yourself a detective! Read the clues and figure it out, why don't you? You look like death warmed over, like you are really hurting, and it's all because you rescued her. She feels guilty, Simon Fletcher."

"Well, crud."

"See, I knew you were not obtuse, but you did have me worried there."

Simon's eyes watered without his consent. "Not funny. I need . . . I need to talk to her. Explain things."

She nodded. "Let me see what I can do."

She wandered off, Skipper brought Simon a TV tray, and Tom Petterman placed a plate piled high with food in front of Simon.

"Hope you like what I picked for you."

"Thanks, Tom." Simon *had* been salivating, hunger returning with a vengeance. But now that Sophie had run off, mistakenly shouldering responsibility for his pain and injuries, his appetite had flown away with her.

Skipper hovered. "Sophie . . . she's really broken up about how you look. We tried to tell her it wasn't her fault and all."

Reluctantly, Simon answered, "I know. Doesn't help that my face looks like . . ." He shrugged. "Haven't actually looked yet."

Skipper tittered. "Wyatt took one look at you and said you'd been mauled by a grizzly, but Eli said, no, your face got hit by a train. Bruce decided you could sign on with the circus."

"Really? That's the best you boys could come up with? I'm disappointed. You can do better than that! Truly, I expected more of you."

"Well, *I* said, Big Foot had found his long lost cousin."

Simon clutched his ribs, best he could, and gave way to painful chuckles. Skipper just grinned. And the food steaming on the plate in front of Simon suddenly appealed to him. He picked up his fork and stared with indecision at the variety of tempting foods before him.

"This is gonna be good."

———— • ————

SIMON WAS FULL. Replete. He was also starting to hurt and realized he needed his next pain pill.

Miss Finch has my meds. Hopefully, she's found Sophie and is talking to her, because I need something soon to cut this discomfort.

He shifted, growing more uncomfortable sitting in the lawn chair. After several minutes, he tried to lever himself up, but the strain on his ribs was too great. Finally, he waved Tom Petterman over.

"Tom, could I prevail upon you? Just hold your arm out so I can pull myself up."

"Sure, Fletcher."

When he was up, Tom handed him the nearby crutches. "Where are you off to?"

"Just Miss Finch's car. Need to find a more comfortable seat and stretch my legs on the way."

"Gotcha."

He was crutching his way to the woody, Petterman dogging his steps, when Miss Finch and Sophie appeared at the top of the driveway, Sophie's assigned guard, Addie, right behind them. Simon didn't stop—couldn't stop. He needed desperately to slide into the upholstered front seat of Miss Finch's woody.

Lord, I need my own bed and a long nap.

Simon sighed with relief as he eased into the woody. Petterman put the crutches in the back.

"Thanks, Mr. Petterman."

"Call me Tom. Hope you get well real soon, Fletcher."

Petterman had no sooner left than Miss Finch appeared.

"What's wrong?"

"Need my meds. Need to go home."

"Oh, dear! I am sorry—you are overdue. I will be right back."

She hustled off to fetch a glass of water, and Simon closed his eyes.

Tired. So tired.

A small hand touched his shoulder. Rested there. Simon exhaled and forced his weary eyes open.

"Hey, little pumpkin."

Sophie's brown eyes, even more reminiscent of Miss Finch's now that he knew of her Chinese mother, glistened in her scrunched-up face. "I'm really sorry, Mr. Fletcher."

"What for, Sophie?"

"For being mean to you."

"Were you mean to me?"

"I never told you thank you for saving me. I thought . . ."

"What did you think?"

She lost it. Sobbing, she blubbered, "It's my fault that man beat you up!"

Simon couldn't stand it. He twisted and put his arm around her, the agony well worth the reward.

"Sophie, Sophie, Sophie. Do you remember when Miss Finch was doing her card tricks down on the beach and she told that girl, Eldora, about the greatest love in the world? Do you remember what she said?"

She sobbed, "She said the biggest kind of love is when you give your life for someone else. She said that's what Jesus did for us."

"And do you remember the first day we rode bikes down on the bike path, you asked if I was a mean man?"

She shuddered. "Yeah. I'm really sorry!"

"Ah, but what did I tell you then?"

She sniffled and thought for a moment. "You said . . . you said you weren't a mean man anymore, that Jesus had made you a kind man."

"That's right. He put his love in my heart . . . the same love he showed us when he died for us."

Simon denied the pain of his arm around her; he refused to acknowledge it. "Listen, little Sophie. In the same way Jesus made me kind and in the same way Jesus loves us, I love you. That's why I could not let that bad man take you. Do you see? I don't care about how I look right now or how I feel. What I care about is *you*. I want you to be safe."

"Ohhh!"

"And you need to understand that what happened is not your fault—it was the bad man's fault, all of it. And one more thing? You should thank Jesus for keeping you safe. He made sure I got there at just the right time. He showed you his love too by helping me keep you safe."

"So it was really Jesus who saved me? Because he loves me?"

"Really and truly."

She lifted a tear-stained face to him. "And you care about me like Jesus does?"

"You'd better believe it, Sophie Nadeau."

"Thank you, Fletcher!"

She wrapped her arms around Simon's bruised neck and squeezed him tight. He patted her back gently. When she let go, Simon's vision spun like a top and his neck informed him it was wrecked.

"Go play now, little pumpkin, and stay close to Addie, okay?"

"I will!"

She scampered toward Addie, and the two of them walked up the drive.

Miss Finch appeared again, water and pills in her hands.

"Good talk?"

"The best."

"Pain pill?"

"Better make it a double."

When she started to tsk, his finger shot into the air.

"Do not test me, Finchy; I'm prepared to die on this hill."

She doled out the pills without another word.

CHAPTER 25

SIMON WOKE WITH a start, uncertain what day, or what time it was. *I'm home, in my own bed*, he realized. *It's Sunday morning. What woke me?*

There it was again. A timid knock on his cabin door.

"Coming," he called. "Please give me a minute or two."

He was incredibly stiff and sore and needed two minutes just to roll himself to the side of his bunk and get himself to a sitting position. What Simon noticed, however, is that the room didn't spin for more than a few seconds.

That's an improvement! And even better? I slept like a rock last night.

"Hang on; I'm coming," he called again.

"No hurry, Mr. Fletcher," a voice answered.

He grabbed shorts and t-shirt from the end of his bed and pulled them on, then took his crutches from where they leaned against the bedframe and, with much effort, levered himself to standing, then stared at the upper bunk.

Huh? Skipper's gone . . . and his bed is made? Did he actually get himself up and off to work on his own? And without disturbing me?

Wait. It's Sunday. Where is he?

He reached the door, opened it, and found trim retiree Justine Bigalow standing on the porch, a large sack in her hands. Something emanating from that bag smelled of warm, soothing deliciousness.

"Good morning, Mr. Fletcher. I have your breakfast and lunch things here. May I take them inside for you?"

"Right. I mean, great! Thank you."

"This is our way of thanking *you*, Mr. Fletcher. We are so very proud of you. You have no idea."

He exhaled. "Well, I'm sure grateful for these meals. I'm just getting my appetite back, and whatever you have in that bag smells pretty good."

"Ah! That would be my blueberry French toast breakfast bake."

Simon's mouth filled with water. "Uh, *yum . . .*"

She grinned. "Shall I set the pan on your table and fetch a plate for you?"

"Oh, yes. Please."

"And I'll put your lunch in the fridge—just sandwiches and a container of homemade soup you can reheat in your microwave."

"Sounds perfect."

While she set the table for him, Simon fumbled with making coffee. By the time he'd poured the carafe of water into the coffee maker, his ribs hurt and he was feeling weak.

"Please sit down now, Mr. Fletcher. You're looking a mite pale. I'll hang around until I can pour you a cup of coffee and bring it to you. Oh. And let me bring you a glass of water. Those are your prescriptions, I take it?" She pointed to the two pill bottles on the table.

"Yeah, thanks. Coming back from this is taking more out of me than I realized."

"I've heard that being a hero is hard work."

"If you say so," Simon laughed as he maneuvered himself into a chair at the table, relieved to be off his feet. He sniffed at the steam rising from the square pan in the center of the little table, and his stomach growled at the dueling scents of blueberries, vanilla, and cinnamon.

Before he knew it, Mrs. Bigalow had spooned an overlarge serving of the breakfast casserole onto his plate and placed a cup of coffee and a glass of water on the table.

"I'll be going now. You may expect Gretchen Muller to deliver your dinner between 5:30 and 6:00 this evening, enough for both you and Skipper." She ended on a cheery note, "*Bon appétit!*"

Simon shoveled a bite into his mouth and groaned with pleasure.

———————•———————

AN HOUR LATER, he'd finished breakfast, taken his meds, read three chapters in his Bible, prayed longer than he usually did, and emptied the coffee pot. He hobbled to the bathroom, then to his bed, which he made in clumsy fashion.

"Not even close to standards, Marine. Why, Skipper did better than this!"

Best I can do today, he told himself. *And now what?*

The day stretched out before him.

Long.

Stifling.

Boring.

Concerning in some manner?

"I can, at least, sit on the porch and get some fresh air. Maybe call Skipper and see what he's doing."

That teasing, "concerning in some manner" item came back around and nudged him.

"Huh." Simon, rather suddenly, wasn't at all convinced that a two-person protection detail was enough to keep Sophie safe.

It all comes down to need, he told himself, *to the person who needs Sophie's blood and how desperate they are to get it . . . because desperate people do desperate things . . . surprising, dangerous, diabolical things.*

Maybe he'd call Miss Finch and ask for the protection detail's cell numbers. Check in with them. He grabbed his phone and stepped out onto the porch. The first thing he noted was the absence of Skipper's bike.

He smiled. "Good on you, Skip. I applaud your improved work ethic—except it's Sunday—isn't it?"

Simon checked the date on his phone to confirm it, then glanced around. His smile widened. Someone had parked his maintenance truck just off the side of his cabin. Instantly, a list of things he could do from the comfort of his truck's bucket seat scrolled before his eyes.

"Doctor said to abstain from all physical exertion above a sedate walk. And no stress. Well, driving takes less energy than walking and getting out of my cabin will actually reduce my stress."

Right?

His idea had a few holes. *I don't dare show up at Miss Finch's site; she will pitch a royal fit. Call instead.*

He pressed her number and heard the phone ring.

"Good morning, Fletcher. Have you eaten?"

"Yes—and I've taken my pills," he hurried to add. "Even made the bed. Sorta. Merely pulled the covers up. All activity well within the scope of the doctor's orders. Say, you haven't seen Skipper, have you?"

"Oh, yes. He is with me. We are about to leave for church."

"Right, because it's Sunday. Maybe I—"

"No, you cannot come with us, and we really need to get moving if we are to be on time."

"*Fine.* Be that way." *You old crab.*

He rushed on to his subject of interest. "I was wondering, though, about security around the park perimeter."

He almost heard her sharp mind snap into focus.

"Why? Do you have concerns?"

"No, it's more that I was merely thinking a moment ago about how few Rh null individuals actually exist worldwide—that we know of, anyway—and I was recalling that many of them suffer from similar medical issues, such as hemolytic anemia. And then I thought about Sophie's botched kidnapping—thank the Lord!—and began to wonder if it wasn't more than a hair on the brazen side—not to mention how reckless it was of Münster to enter a hospital in order to take me out—"

"You were *merely* thinking? You forget that I know you, Fletcher. Your 'merely thinking' is like a dog worrying a bone. You obviously have too much time on your hands and are letting your thoughts wander too far afield."

She added, more to herself than to him, "I must stop on the way home from church and buy you a jigsaw puzzle and . . . and a sudoku book."

"I don't need a stinking jigsaw puzzle, BeeDee! I need reassurance!"

"But are you not suggesting that Münster's motive in his attempt to kill you at the hospital was not revenge but rather . . . something of a strategic move? Remove you from the equation as prelude to taking another crack at Sophie?"

"Exactly! He didn't know for certain how badly he'd damaged me, didn't know that I was in no shape to pose a problem the next time. So, yeah. It's the 'another crack at Sophie' bit I'm anxious about."

"Because . . ."

"Because if Sophie's blood is needed, it's needed desperately, and—"

"And desperate people do desperate things."

He had her full attention now.

"Exactly. I also, well, this morning I remembered something I'd read when I stumbled across golden blood while doing research on blood types."

"I'm listening."

"This 'mild hemolytic anemia' Sophie has? It can worsen on its own over time. Or if an Rh null patient contracts an infection, it can send that patient into what is called hemolytic crisis or massive hemolysis, which, in turn, causes . . . kidney failure."

Simon hadn't been able to bring himself to say those words aloud until now. Hearing them out in the open turned the wonderful blueberry French toast breakfast casserole in his gut to stone.

"You are putting organ harvest back on the table?"

"I'm not putting anything anywhere. I'm only saying what is *possible*. I woke up concerned, and as the morning wore on, that concern clarified. Should our killer's theoretical patient desperately need blood or a kidney, his minions will try for Sophie again, sooner, rather than later—and since people can donate one kidney and live healthy lives, once they had Sophie, they'd be able to-to-to take one of her kidneys and still keep her for blood transfusions!"

The horrid images he'd shunned and evaded all morning raised their ugly heads.

"Look, I'm sorry, but I need her security detail's cell numbers. I have to check in with them. Raise their alert status."

She went silent on him for a long moment. "You will not try to actively help them or interfere in their duties?" It was a question that sounded more like an order.

"If you hired them, I'm certain they know their stuff. Furthermore, I'm sticking to my doctor's orders. That said, every one of us needs to rehearse the stakes more often and stay frosty. We can't allow ourselves to become lax when it comes to Sophie's safety."

"I agree. I will text you the detail's numbers and include their shift assignments so you don't accidentally disturb any of them while they are trying to sleep."

"Got it. Thanks."

They hung up, and Simon worked his way down the porch and over to his truck, intent on removing as many of the anxieties pounding in his head as he possibly could. He hadn't, however, anticipated how merely getting himself *into* the truck would strain and fatigue him. He was sweating and shaking by the time he'd pushed his crutches over to the passenger side and managed to get himself into the truck and behind the wheel.

"I'll just rest here a minute. Cool down. Catch my breath."

He jerked awake fifteen minutes later and ran a hand over his face.

Lovely. I've had my morning nap. Check.

Let's roll.

He pulled out onto the gravel road and turned left, intent on checking the three cameras guarding the road up to Bright Star's gate. He drove slowly, blinking his eyes as he went, hoping they wouldn't go "buggy" on him again. He located the two cameras he'd mounted along the road and found them just as he'd placed them. When he stopped at the turnoff, he craned his neck to see the camera above the large Bright Star sign.

Ow. That hurts. Note to self: Don't do that . . .

Simon turned left on the dirt feeder road that ran by Bright Star and intentionally drove on the left side of the road, which put him closer to the fence. With his foot barely on the gas, he visually inspected the fence line bounding Joe and Holly's property. The fence line, dating back to Joe's grandfather, was made of heavy-gauge woven wire mesh with two-by-four-inch rectangular openings secured to faded green-and-white metal posts sunk deep in the earth.

He hit the north end of the Mitchell's property line without seeing anything amiss, so he found a place to turn around and drove back toward the graveled road leading to Bright Star. When he reached it, he kept going, driving the fence line in the opposite direction, studying it through his rolled-down passenger-side window, until he reached the south end of the Mitchells' land, finding nothing amiss.

He kept going, though, checking the fence of Bright Star's adjoining neighbor for several yards. Joe had inherited the thirty acres from his grandfather, and the fence had been up for many years. Over time, the six-foot high woven wire mesh had acquired spots of rust. A few sections also sagged here and there, but in the main, the fence was intact.

Regardless, his subconscious was now acting the part of a burr caught on his sock, touching, tickling, and itching a place in the back of Simon's mind he couldn't scratch.

He wasn't certain what he'd seen or where he'd seen it along the several hundred feet of Mitchell fence line, but he *may* have noted an ever-so-slight difference between two sections.

What was it? What had sent up that silent, subliminal alarm?

This is about Sophie. It's about her safety and her future. Whatever triggered me, I need to find it, inspect it, and figure out what it means—even if I have to drive this south part of the fence line a hundred times.

He was tiring, though. *Didn't think I'd be out this long. Should have brought water. My pain pills.*

From the far south end, he started again, looking out his own window, driving on the wrong side of the road so he'd be closer to the fence. He scrutinized each section until his eyes couldn't tell them apart, until his neck ached from having it turned to the left.

Simon reached Bright Star's graveled road. Nothing had *popped.*

"Maybe I'm going about this wrong. Maybe I need to be looking at the bigger picture."

He used the graveled road to make a "t" turn, raced back to the south end of the fence line, and turned around again. This time, instead of driving slowly on the wrong side of the road, he set off quickly on the right side, so that the fence flashed by, section after section, each section uniformly the same as the last . . . *there.*

He braked hard, skidding, and jarring himself in the process, and backed up. It took him a few seconds to again find what it was he'd seen, but once he'd spotted it, the difference stood out.

He grabbed his phone and dumped it into his shirt pocket, threw open his door, and eased himself down onto the road. He panted for a few seconds until the dizziness passed, then pulled his crutches across his seat and settled them under his arms.

He took his time hobbling around his truck to the offending section, eying it the entire time. Awkwardly, he scrabbled down the slight slope into the runoff channel, until he was close enough to reach a hand to a bit of wire that attached a section to its nearest post. His thumbnail scraped along the wire and came away with a fine powder, some sort of mottled, sprayed-on texture, quite close to the colors of older metal and rust. But underneath the scraping? The attaching wire was shiny and new. His eye identified similar short bits of wire down the section's edge.

Someone had cut the wire mesh from the post, then wired it back into place, yet his subconscious had somehow noticed the difference?

More like your Holy Spirit pointed it out to me, Lord. Just like I woke up this morning with that sneaking suspicion of something wrong running around in my head.

Simon pulled his phone from his pocket and dialed Grayson's number. After two rings, the man answered.

"Grayson, Simon Fletcher here. I'm on the road outside Bright Star. I've been checking our fence line. Someone cut a section of the fence here, then rewired it to the post. Made themselves a quick way onto Bright Star land they could come back to."

Grayson soaked up the info in an instant. "We'll move Sophie immediately. Are you carrying?"

Simon had never felt such a fool. "No."

"Then get out of there."

"Where will you take Sophie?"

"Bright Star's office, initially. Meet us there."

Simon had to resort to crawling up the slope to the road, dragging his crutches after him. He stood one crutch on the road and used it to pull himself up to his feet. His ribs screamed bloody murder under the strain, but he steadfastly ignored them. By the time he got himself behind the wheel of his truck, he was dizzy, shaking, and soaked through with sweat.

"Okay, so I admit that this might qualify as stress," he mumbled. He didn't want to contemplate what Miss Finch would have to say.

He put the truck in gear and let it find its way back to Bright Star.

The TAHOE MYSTERIES

CHAPTER 26

GRAYSON AND ADDIE stood on the office porch as Simon pulled up to the office. The two guards scanned the area around the office as they walked out to his truck. Simon managed to open his door but was too exhausted to get out.

"We have the Nadeaus inside," Grayson said, his head still on a swivel, his eyes sharp and alert. "I'll want you to show me where you found the breach in the fence line—good grief. You look like death warmed over, worse now than yesterday!"

Addie nodded her agreement.

"Thanks. Just the encouragement I needed."

"Are you even supposed to be driving?" Grayson demanded.

"Driving isn't an issue," Simon hissed. "Getting in and out of my truck and climbing up and down ditch banks to check suspicious-looking fence sections? Those might be problems."

"Need help getting inside?"

"What I need is to go home and go back to bed," Simon confessed.

"Too late," Addie said out of the side of her mouth.

In his rearview mirror, Simon recognized the approaching woody. He also realized it was traveling at a speed Miss Finch never drove on that road—lest any loose gravel damage her beloved woody's fresh paint job.

Uh, Miss Finch stopped at my cabin to let Skipper out, only to find both me and my truck gone?

"Help me!" Simon begged.

Grayson shook his head. "You, crazy person, are on your own."

The woody came alongside Simon's truck. Skipper's wide-eyed face stared at him through the passenger window, interposed between Simon and the woody's other occupant.

Otherwise, at this moment, Simon thought, *I would be suffering twin laser burns.*

"I'll . . . just be inside," Addie muttered, edging away.

"Good plan," Grayson answered. He gestured to Simon. "Speaking of plans, we need a plan to move the Nadeaus, and we need it now."

"Got it."

As Grayson and Addie turned tail and fled up the office steps, Skipper jumped from the woody to join them.

"Dead man walking," he mouthed to Simon as he followed Addie and Grayson.

"You see me walking?" Simon shot back. He wondered why Miss Finch was still seated in her car.

She's probably counting to ten.

Maybe fifty?

That's when he glanced in his sideview mirror and spotted a dust cloud rising from down the gravel road. A line of vehicles was approaching Bright Star, kicking up dirt and loose rock. As they drew closer, he identified the lead vehicle's distinctive profile: a news broadcast van. It wasn't the only van of its kind in the line, either.

Well, Grayson had tried to warn him. "*I suppose you should know, too, that the media are all over this story.*"

"Crud and double crud!" Simon whispered.

Miss Finch must have recognized the lead vehicle for what it was also, because she immediately whipped the woody into a U-turn, rolling down her window and shouting to Simon as she wheeled by him, "Follow me and park!"

She roared into the small parking lot behind the office. Simon followed suit and pulled into a slot, but Miss Finch did not. Instead, she backed the woody across the parking lot entrance, denying access to it, then raced around front and up the steps to the office.

Just as the line of cars and vans reached Bright Star's open gate, Simon heard the sound of that impressive structure sliding closed.

Whew. Well done, Finchy.

Seconds later, the office's infrequently used rear door unlocked and opened. Grayson and Skipper hustled out. Without a word, they hauled Simon and his crutches from his truck, through Holly's private office, and into the main office.

"Put him in that chair," Miss Finch ordered while glaring at Simon, "and tie him to it if he even *looks* like he is thinking of getting up."

Grayson and Skipper plunked Simon into the rolling chair Holly kept behind the counter. Skipper offered him a grimaced, "Sorry," before he stepped away to relock the rear door.

Simon took in the scene in a glance: The office blinds were pulled down, their slats shut tight. The terrified Nadeaus were huddled against the wall to his right, Sophie flanked by her parents, Wyatt and Eli in front of her. Addie and Grayson had interposed themselves between the family and the front door.

Holly peered through the blinds on the office's front door and stared as the line of vehicles disgorged their passengers. "What is it? Someone tell me what is happening!" she wailed.

Miss Finch answered her. "Mrs. Mitchell, the news media have caught the scent of a juicy story. They have learned, no doubt, of the attack on Fletcher while he was hospitalized. To make the situation even more salacious, they have likely been told that Fletcher shot and killed his attacker."

She took a breath. "Surely you know that the media will sensationalize their reporting, do you not? Furthermore, the probability is high that some reporter will dig and eventually uncover the reason behind Simon's hospitalization, how Simon quashed the attempted kidnapping of a child. And *that* information, when published, would turn the media spotlight squarely onto Sophie, putting her at even greater risk."

Holly, unusually subdued, nodded. "Well, what should we do?"

Simon interjected, "Miss Finch—"

She rounded on him. "Not. One. Word, *Mr.* Fletcher!"

Simon struggled to his feet. "No! You listen to me, you stubborn, hardheaded, controlling woman! These media people are not the only danger threatening Sophie at present. Not more than thirty minutes ago, I found a break in Bright Star's fence line near the far south end alongside the feeder road. Someone cut a section from the post and reattached it with new wire cleverly disguised to match the worn and rusted wire. I'm thinking those who are after Sophie entered Bright Star through the woods, followed the trails to the park's trailhead, reconnoitered the park's layout—including the Nadeaus' site—and intend to return in strength."

"Which is why we removed the Nadeaus from their site and brought them directly here, Miss Finch," Grayson supplied. "Fletcher called and told me about the break in the fence line."

"Then we must remove Sophie from Bright Star immediately."

"We agree."

"Yeah? And where do you plan to take Sophie that this bloodthirsty media mob won't follow?" Simon demanded. "Once they're onto a story, they won't leave or quit digging. You take Sophie out of here before they are gone, you may as well paint a target on her."

Miss Finch nodded slowly. "I take your point and am open to suggestions."

Simon exhaled. "For the moment, we must consider Bright Star under siege. We put the Nadeaus out of sight in Holly's office. Next, we address the media directly and then dismiss them. Once they are gone, we can consider how and where to move the Nadeaus to someplace safer."

"And just how do we 'address and dismiss' the media?"

"When I was a Marine investigator and involved in high-visibility cases, I often dealt with the media. The only way to get rid of them is to give them what they want. Give them a story that satisfies both their questions and their hunger for a scoop. A story they will rush to send in.

Several sets of footsteps sounded on the office porch followed by brisk knocking. Just as the doorknob began to turn, Grayson quick-stepped to the door and flipped the lock.

The audible *snap* of the deadbolt elicited a loud, "Hey! Hey, your sign says you're open! Let us in!" from the other side.

Grayson jerked his chin at Addie, who silently ushered the Nadeaus toward Holly's private office. As soon as Addie closed Holly's office door, Grayson, Holly, Skipper, and Miss Finch stared at Simon.

Simon blinked. "What?"

"You have media experience, Fletcher. Get out there and give them their story," Miss Finch murmured. "Take Holly with you. Holly, when Fletcher finishes spinning his tale, you will inform the media circus that Bright Star's *private* property begins at the turnoff from the feeder road and that they are to set neither wheel nor foot on Bright Star property again without your explicit permission."

Holly squared her shoulders. "I can certainly do that."

"I am aware," Miss Finch replied, her lips twitching.

The two women suddenly smirked at each other and snickered.

"Er, *wow*," Skipper muttered to Simon from behind his hand.

A wide-eyed Simon agreed. In fact, a line of dancing elephants clad in pink tutus wouldn't have surprised him more.

Skipper offered Simon his crutches and whispered, "Go get 'em, Fletch."

"Right."

He hobbled across to the door, Holly on his heels. Holly unlatched the door and opened it. Five individuals crowded the low porch; three others with cameras filmed from the road. The five reporters shouted at once.

Simon lifted a hand and, in his best Corps voice, thundered, "*Quiet please!*"

Into the astounded silence, he ordered, "Kindly step off the porch. I will make a statement, then entertain questions."

The reporters tripped over each other to get off the porch and secure the ideal position from which to ask for details, while their camera people jockeyed for the best camera angles.

When the small crowd settled, only feet below him, Simon, employing a dry, matter-of-fact tone, began. "My name is Simon Fletcher. I am Bright Star's Facility and Security Manager." He tipped his head toward Holly. "This is Holly Mitchell, co-owner of Bright Star with her husband, Joe Mitchell."

Simon then realized he didn't know where Joe was. *Lord, please don't let Joe show up in the middle of my spiel and throw off our plan. Thank you!*

He continued. "Today is Sunday, July 20. On Wednesday, July 16, I was escorting several Bright Star residents on a bike ride along the Pope-Baldwin

Bike Path. We had reached the end of the path where it meets Emerald Bay Road when two individuals in a black van stopped alongside the road and attempted to abduct some of the children riding with us."

Hands shot into the air; Simon ignored them. He was intentionally obscuring and blurring details of the attack, both to streamline his statement and to protect Miss Finch, Skipper, Sophie, and her brothers from further media harassment.

"I fought with one of the kidnappers before the two kidnappers fled the scene. Police and ambulances subsequently arrived, taking me to the hospital where my injuries were diagnosed as being mainly superficial. However, as a precaution in cases of suspected concussion, I was kept in the hospital for observation."

More hands wagged below Simon's face. He did not respond.

"Late in the afternoon of Friday, July 18, one of the kidnappers entered my hospital room carrying a firearm. I can only surmise that he meant to kill me so I could not identify him to the police. He was interrupted by the unexpected entrance of a nurse. He accosted the nurse and subsequently fled the hospital."

In the ME's hearse, he added silently.

"That ends my statement. Questions? Yes, you."

"Mr. Fletcher, you said the two purported kidnappers attempted to abduct, and I quote, 'some of the children riding with us,' as in more than one. However, a hospital emergency department staffer told us only one young girl was admitted when you were. Was she the kidnappers' objective? And why would she be?"

Simon scoffed. "Was she the kidnappers' objective? Really? Now I'm supposed to read kidnappers' minds? I have no idea what their objectives were. Move on, please. Next?"

"Mr. Fletcher, hospital employees who were down the hall from your room when you were attacked say shots were fired."

Simon nodded. "That is entirely possible. However, please remember that I was concussed at the time. Consequently, my memories of that afternoon are muddled."

Münster's attack was crystal clear in Simon's mind; only after Münster was dead but *still that afternoon*, when the nurses helped Simon to lie back down in his bed, did his memory fade to gray. Simon wasn't lying; he just wasn't about to provide the media with the spicy details they sought.

"But some of those employees say *you* fired those shots!"

Simon poured contempt into his reply. "Really? Don't you know guns are strictly prohibited in hospitals? And just how or even *why* would I happen to have a concealed firearm on my person, while stuck in bed with cracked ribs and head trauma?"

Lord, I'm not lying. I'm deliberately misleading the media, letting these reporters make their own assumptions. And next, I'll close with my biggest misdirection . . . all to protect Sophie.

"In conclusion, *human trafficking* is a horrid, unconscionable crime. Thus, in order to protect the safety and privacy of some of Bright Star residents who are *minors*, I will not identify those who were attacked—and you should be quite careful to follow my lead."

He shook his head as more questions were shouted at him. "That is all, except for a statement from Mrs. Mitchell. Holly?"

Holly managed to pull herself together and sound like her familiar, over-bearing self. "We have allowed your questions this one time. I must point out, however, that Bright Star's *private* property began at the turnoff from the feeder road, meaning you are presently standing on our premises without permission. Do not encroach upon Bright Star's property again without our explicit permission. Trespassers will be prosecuted."

"Thank you, Holly. And thank you all," Simon said to the media. "Please make an immediate U-turn, head on down the gravel road you drove in on, and vacate Bright Star property."

Simon nudged Holly, jerked his chin toward the office door, and he waited until she had crossed the threshold before he summoned the strength to get himself moving. He followed Holly inside, shut the door, then sagged against it, gasping.

The looks Grayson and Miss Finch bent on him were hardly sympathetic. Miss Finch said, "We should probably get you home. You are, no doubt, past due for your medication."

Simon scowled. "I'm in pain—so what? Do you hear me complaining? You and I, Miss Finch, are partners. You do your part; I do mine. Remember?"

"What I remember is the doctor telling you no activity beyond a moder-ate walk—to the bathroom and back, if memory serves—*which it does*. Your physician certainly did *not* authorize you to drive a truck!"

"According to Fletcher here, driving isn't an issue," Grayson drawled. "It's the 'getting in and out of my truck and climbing up and down ditch banks to check suspicious-looking fence sections' that might be problems."

Miss Finch set her jaw. "Mr. Fletcher said that, did he?"

But Simon had eaten his fill. "That's it. No more, *Finchy*. I can manage my own care going forward, thank you very much."

"Hmph."

"And a big ol' *hmph* right back atcha! I am *not* going back to my cabin until we have decided where best to send Sophie."

Miss Finch pursed her lips and studied Simon. "Grayson and Alberto have recommended a safe house in LA owned by Gibson Security Services. He and his team can escort the Nadeau family there tomorrow."

Simon nodded. "I will accompany them—as a passenger. I want to check it out and ensure the location is safe enough."

"*Oho!* And I am the stubborn, hardheaded, controlling one in this partnership, am I?"

"Without a doubt."

Grayson sniffed. "If you ask me, you two deserve each other."

Simon and Miss Finch rounded on him and issued the synchronized retort: "Nobody asked you!"

Grayson grinned. "Kinda just made my point."

CHAPTER 27

WHEN HOLLY LEFT the office to update Joe on the media frenzy, Grayson said, "Listen. We all agree that Bright Star's perimeter is entirely too porous, particularly now you've discovered that someone has cut through the fence line and mostly likely reconnoitered an approach to the Nadeaus' site. So, I had Alberto arrange for a couple of connecting rooms at Hampton Inn & Suites. The Nadeaus will be safer there overnight than here. We've also taken the room directly across from them. Meanwhile the home office is prepping the safe house."

Alberto added, "Those rooms are on a fourth floor, end of the hall, and have only two angles of attack—from the stairs leading up from the fire exit and from the elevator banks down the hall. We will set up watch in the corner alcove nearest the fire exit and inside the doorway across from the Nadeaus."

Grayson looked to Simon. "Since you are so spun up about our safe house in LA, do these overnight arrangements meet with your approval, Fletcher?"

"They sound reasonable enough," Simon acceded grudgingly. "However, as much as I don't want to add to our concerns, I probably need to."

Grayson eyed him. "Do tell."

"Thanks. First off, I haven't suffered a beatdown like I did at the hands of Münster in years. Well, I loathe inactivity, so you can imagine how my present restrictions are about to drive me up a wall. That said, those restrictions have given me time to think, time to ponder what all has happened in the last five days since those guys tried to take Sophie . . . and I believe I've stumbled upon something we've overlooked."

What Simon didn't say was that while in the hospital, drugged to the gills yet in wretched pain, the question of *how* Münster and his partner had been able to show up, all "johnny on the spot" the morning Miss Finch and the four kids were out riding their bikes, had haunted him.

Grayson snorted. "Can't wait."

"I suggest you give Fletcher the benefit of your attention," Miss Finch murmured. "As he alluded to, he spent a decade as a military investigator."

Grayson's and Alberto's brows rose in unison.

"Uh, I may have spoken in haste," Grayson muttered, afterward mouthing, "Jarhead."

Simon grinned. "No worries. We Marines are accustomed to mopping up after grunts and squids."

"Now, children," Miss Finch interrupted. "Play nice, please."

"But *Mom!* He started it!" Simon whined, snickering as he did so.

"Hey!" Grayson grumbled.

Simon turned serious. "Look, Grayson, we've been so harried and on the defensive since the two attacks, that we haven't taken the time to talk this thing all the way through and break it down."

"Nor do we have the time at this very moment," Grayson ground out through gritted teeth. "Cut to the chase, please."

"Sure thing, *pal.* The question that's been bugging me is this: How did those two thugs know Sophie would be riding her bike on the Pope-Baldwin Bike Path that morning? We went early, before most people are up, to avoid the heat and early-morning walkers. So how did Münster and his partner know we'd be there?"

Three sets of eyes narrowed as his question sank in.

"We did not make our plans until the afternoon before," Miss Finch added, jumping aboard Simon's train of thought.

"Exactly, and that leads me to believe that someone in close proximity overheard us making those plans."

Miss Finch's mouth turned down. "Someone at Bright Star? Again? Say it isn't so! Those people are our friends."

"Nonetheless, it would have to be someone in the park, wouldn't it?"

And not all of the residents are necessarily our friends, Simon thought, thinking of James Crowley.

"What about someone surveilling Bright Star?" Alberto suggested. "They could have just followed you down to the bike path."

"I considered that too, but we left Bright Star pretty early that morning, around 5:00 a.m."

Grayson spoke up. "Seems to me Alberto has it right. The guys who attacked you could have spent the night outside the park, watching and waiting, then simply followed you down to the bike path at a distance. Easy."

"Hold up," Simon said. "Think about Jürgen Münster and his buddy for a sec. I know trouble when I see it, and I can spot the kind of people who make the most trouble from a mile off. What I can state, categorically, is that Münster and his accomplice are specialists, big-money mercenaries with big, fat egos, *not* surveillance lackeys. Not only do I doubt our adversaries would put two high-dollar mercs on basic, boring, nighttime surveillance, I doubt Münster himself would have stood for it."

Grayson responded, "If we take your word for it, it means the lackeys standing surveillance would have needed to call the kidnapping duo at that early hour to let them know Sophie was on the move, which," he hesitated,

"I guess, implies, in turn, that the timing doesn't work. Bottom line: The kidnappers wouldn't have had enough time to reach the bike path and get set up."

Miss Finch said slowly, "I suppose I have to put a measure of credence into Fletcher's analysis. As much as I dislike his conclusion, it is more likely that our leak came from someone inside the park, someone who overheard us making our plans and made a call *the evening before* the attempted abduction."

She growled in her throat, "I shall sic my techs onto finding our leaker immediately."

"Thank you," Simon said, relieved to get his drug-crazed theories off his chest. Validation, however, remained to be seen.

"Then, given your theory, moving the Nadeaus to this hotel is the right move?" Grayson asked Simon pointedly.

"As quickly and quietly as possible so as not to attract attention inside the park. As far as my approval goes? When I've seen your setup at the hotel, I'll be satisfied."

"Gee, thanks," Alberto snarked.

"Good," Miss Finch sighed. "Now that our plans are settled, Fletcher, I shall drive you back to your cabin so you can take a nap or kick back in your recliner and read a book."

"Funny thing," Simon muttered, "I don't own a recliner. The sum total of my furnishings are a kitchen chair with a hard, unforgiving seat and an old-school, wood-framed bunkbed leftover from Joe's grandfather's horse camp. Neither are conducive to restful inactivity . . . unless I'm actually in bed asleep."

"I'll rent you a recliner. Have it delivered today."

Simon started to object when Addie opened Holly's office door and peered through it. "Okay for us to come out now?"

"Yeah," Grayson answered. He, Simon, Miss Finch, and Mr. and Mrs. Nadeau put their heads together, and Grayson updated the Nadeaus.

"Are you certain you can keep Sophie safe in that hotel?"

"Yes, but we intend for you to be there overnight only," Grayson answered. "We have a better location in mind, a safe house belonging to our employer. It's being prepped as we speak."

"For how long, though?" Lucas demanded. "And what will become of our RV and truck? The kids' bikes?"

Simon saw that Lucas was beginning to see his family's life and freedom being stripped away. Panic was setting in.

"Your site is paid for through Labor Day," Miss Finch supplied, her tone soothing. "We shall watch over and take good care of your belongings."

"But that said, we need to move now—quickly and quietly," Grayson said.

"What about our clothes and other necessities?"

Grayson glanced at his watch. "I can give you thirty minutes to pack what you need."

Lucas and Eva began herding their children toward the office door.

"Uh, Mr. and Mrs. Nadeau?" Simon asked. When the two turned to him, Simon whispered, "Your fifth wheel doesn't, by chance, have a recliner?"

"Why, yes," answered Mrs. Nadeau. "Why do you ask?"

Miss Finch saw where Simon's question was going. "Excellent idea, Fletcher. Mr. and Mrs. Nadeau, as you know, Fletcher's doctor has ordered him to stay off his feet while he recuperates from his concussion . . . although Fletcher himself has exhibited less than compliant regard for his doctor's orders. Of course, what I actually mean is that he has been *ignoring* his doctor's orders."

"Ha ha. Very funny, *Finchy*. What Miss Finch here forgets to mention is that my cabin has no living room to speak of, thus no living room furnishings, let alone a chair comfortable enough to sit in for hours on end. You, on the other hand, have a recliner. How would you like for me to, free of charge, house-sit for you while you are gone?"

Lucas appeared dubious. "I suppose that would be okay."

Grayson, lurking nearby, stepped into the conversation. "Look at it this way, Mr. Nadeau: You're leaving your RV, your truck, and even the kids' bikes. With Simon recuperating in your RV, turning on the lights in the evening but mostly staying out of sight himself, if anyone is keeping tabs on your site, they may continue to believe Sophie is still at Bright Star—which might serve as a diversion."

Miss Finch shook her head. "Perhaps, but I must tell you that Bright Star's gossip network is a robust microcosm. I would be amazed if the Nadeaus' absence remains under wraps until dinner time."

Sophie squirmed into the tight circle formed by the adults. "Daddy, please let Mr. Fletcher stay in our RV." She grabbed Simon's hand and held it protectively. "If it would help Mr. Fletcher to get better, we should do it. I wouldn't even be here if he hadn't saved me from those awful men."

Lucas Nadeau capitulated. "She's right on that count. Mr. Fletcher, you are more than welcome to our RV while we are gone. Come along with us to our site and I will acquaint you with our RV and its workings."

"I shall deliver him there shortly," Miss Finch said. "Please go ahead to your site, as normally as possible, and begin packing what you need." To Simon she added, "Mrs. Gorman is in charge of the meals committee. I will let her know you will be staying in the Nadeaus' RV."

Alberto spoke up. "Uh, if Bright Star's gossip line is as vigorous as you say it is, won't whomever is leaking info from within Bright Star know straight off that the Nadeaus are gone? Can you, instead, have the meals committee deliver Fletcher's meals to you?"

"Yes, I can do that . . . although, as I said, I doubt the Nadeaus' absence will go unremarked upon for long."

Simon recalled the blueberry French toast breakfast bake Justine Biga-low had piled on his plate that morning, and his mouth watered. "Wow. I haven't eaten since breakfast."

Miss Finch snorted. "And whose fault is that?"

———— ◆ ————

CLOSER TO FORTY than thirty minutes later, the Nadeaus and their essen-tial belongings were surreptitiously split between Grayson and Alberto's car and Addie and Dorian's car. Miss Finch and Simon would accompany the little convoy to the hotel in Miss Finch's woody.

Then Miss Finch called Skipper and asked him to gather Becka, Melissa, and Bruce and direct them down the Nadeaus' driveway to the firepit. After the children pledged to keep secret what he was about to tell them, Grayson revealed that the Nadeaus were leaving. The goodbyes between them and the Nadeau kids were hard on them all.

Finally, Simon called a halt, saying, "Skipper needs to get back to work, and we need to hit the road."

The two groups of kids reluctantly parted. Sophie, more teary-eyed about leaving Simon than she was about leaving her friends, pleaded with her par-ents to let her ride to the hotel with him in the woody. Understandably, Mr. and Mrs. Nadeau wanted to keep her close to them.

"It's not actually a bad idea, Mr. and Mrs. Nadeau," Grayson offered. "Our two cars can box in the woody, one vehicle in front, the other behind, provid-ing protection front and rear."

Half-heartedly, the Nadeaus agreed, and Sophie scooted into the woody's front seat to ride between Miss Finch and Simon. Minutes later, the little convoy departed Bright Star.

"I hate that I won't see you anymore, Mr. Fletcher," Sophie sniffled, leaning gently into Simon's side.

"We don't know that," Simon answered softly, gladly suffering the small discomfort her weight on his tender ribs caused him. "If we catch the bad people, you can come back to Bright Star for the rest of the summer."

"Really?"

"I should hope so! But may I tell you a little secret?"

She nodded, anxiously twining her fingers together.

"The people who belong to Jesus will always see each other again, no matter what. I belong to Jesus. Miss Finch belongs to Jesus too. One day, she and I will both arrive in heaven, and we will see each other there. How do we know that? Because Jesus said so. See, he died on the cross to forgive our sins, so that those who give their lives to him can also live with him forever.

"You can belong to Jesus too, Sophie. If you ask him to forgive your sins and choose him as your King and Savior, he said he would come and make his home inside of you. Then, no matter what happens today, tomorrow, even all the way to the end of our lives, we can be certain that we *will* see each other again."

She stared up at Simon. "Truly?"

"Truly, little pumpkin."

"Is that what Miss Finch meant when she did her card tricks?"

Simon was thrown for a moment, then remembered. "You mean when she said, *There is no greater love than to lay down one's life for one's friends*?"

"Yes. Is that what she meant, that Jesus died on that nasty cross for you and Miss Finch?"

"Jesus died for you too, Sophie."

When Sophie lapsed into her own thoughts, Miss Finch smiled at Simon over Sophie's head. Minutes later, their little convoy arrived at the hotel in South Lake Tahoe without incident.

———◆———

ALBERTO HAD ARRANGED for the reserved rooms' key cards to be ready and waiting at the counter. Without delay or issues, the Nadeaus moved into a two-bedroom suite on the top floor, and the Gibson Security team made the room across from them their command post.

"Satisfied?" Grayson asked Simon.

"Tell me about this safe house in LA and your security arrangements there."

"We're adding to the team when we arrive, so that three of us will be in the house at all times. Four bedrooms, three for the family, one for the team."

"Getting the Nadeaus to the house without being followed or tracked will be the tricky part."

"We know our business, Mr. Fletcher," Grayson said evenly. "Do you know yours?"

Simon snorted softly. "I do; however, I have more people up in my business at the moment than I can shake a stick at."

"I could say the same."

"Fair enough. I'll butt out now."

They made their goodbyes to the Nadeaus, and Miss Finch drove Simon to his cabin where she relegated him to a kitchen chair at the table, plopping under his nose the sandwiches Justine Bigalow had left in his refrigerator. She then followed his instructions on where to find a duffle and what to pack in it.

Miss Finch had never been inside his cabin. She took in the rustic, minimalistic space and made unhappy little sounds in her throat. "I had no idea how sterile an environment this place is."

"Well, I don't spend much time here, so I don't mind. When I *am* here, I have all I need—that is, when I'm not in need of a comfortable chair in which to stagnate—*oops*, I mean recuperate."

"Very funny. Well, this place is not much of a home."

"You mean you wouldn't want to live here with me?"

Simon had no idea those words, spoken half in jest, were lurking anywhere near his mouth. He was more surprised at Miss Finch's reaction.

She turned to him, her heavy-lidded, chocolate eyes sad. "Please do not jest on that subject, Simon."

"BeeDee, I am sorry! Can you forgive my big mouth?" When she nodded, Simon used the toe of his foot to push the other kitchen chair out from the table. "Good. I would like us to talk. Please?"

He figured she would balk and refuse; he certainly did not expect her to meekly take the seat across from him . . . and wait for him to speak.

Wow. Okay, Lord. Here goes.

"BeeDee, the other day at the hospital, I took a chance . . . and told you I cared for you. You said you knew I cared, but added, 'It is hard.' Why is it hard? Can you tell me? Have you . . . have you never had feelings for someone?"

She sighed and said nothing. Drummed her fingers on the table. Sighed again. "I suppose I should get this over with, if only to put a merciful end to your pipe dream."

"Please! I need to know. Who was he?" He frowned. "Did he hurt you?"

The idea of someone jilting Miss Finch, breaking her heart, spawned a sense of outrage in Simon.

"He did not hurt me. Not intentionally."

Simon's outrage melted away, leaving behind *dread* in its place.

"What happened?" he whispered.

"Do you . . . do you remember me telling you, Skipper, and his friends that I had learned to fly while I was in the Civil Air Patrol?"

A scene from that night flashed into Simon's mind.

"*After I'd been a senior CAP member for a year, one young instructor, a few years older than me, offered to teach me to fly . . .*"

Her voice had stuck on that sentence and, at the time, had faintly concerned him. Now his memory of that moment took on darker meaning.

"That young instructor, the one who taught you to fly?"

She nodded.

"How . . . how did he die, BeeDee?"

She shuddered. "He was flying patrol when a freak storm formed around him. We never learned the exact details of what happened, only that he crashed in the mountains. It took two days to find his plane. He had . . . he had just asked me to marry him the previous week."

Simon saw that she was far away in her thoughts, reliving her anguish, and his heart ached for her.

"It was decades ago now," she whispered. "I tell myself it shouldn't matter so much after all this time, but somehow it does."

Simon whispered back, "Dear BeeDee, I don't think the grief of losing someone you love has an expiration date."

"Then you understand?"

Simon stared at the tabletop, thinking, mustering what he hoped were the right words, before he looked up. "Of course, I understand—at least I hope I do. Since that wretched event, through all the time that has passed, it has been very difficult for you to care about someone else, to risk your heart again. Is that what you meant when you said, 'It is hard'?"

She nodded. "Yes. Thank you."

Simon thought another moment. "May I suggest something personal to you? As a fellow Christian, may I speak into your life what may be a difficult word for you to receive?"

She was slow to respond. When she did, she seemed resigned. "Very well, but after this, may we agree to put this subject to rest?"

"But not quite yet, please. Let's wait until we determine how this goes. See, what I wanted to share with you was that, in the Corps, we were taught to press *in* to what is difficult, press *in* to what is painful or fearful, because the only way *past* what seems insurmountable is *through it*."

She started to shake her head. He reached for one of her tiny hands then, and she allowed him to take it into his. He liked how it felt in his big paw. "I'm not saying you should act like a Marine, BeeDee; you and I don't share that culture or experience. But, when I became a serious believer in Christ, I started perceiving parallels between my Marine training and God's word. I found scripture passages that told me how the Lord wanted me to overcome the burdens of this hostile world."

Simon then quoted,

> *"In fact, this is love for God: to keep his commands.*
> *And his commands are not burdensome,*
> *for everyone born of God overcomes the world.*
> *This is the victory that has overcome the world,*
> *even our faith.*
> *Who is it that overcomes the world?*
> *Only the one who believes that Jesus is the Son of God."*

"1 John 5," Miss Finch murmured.

Simon smiled. "I love that you know God's word so well, and I admire how you so easily broke it down so Skipper and his friends could understand and receive it."

"Thank you," she said softly.

"One more relevant verse that Paul himself declared was his MO?" She nodded, and he recited,

> *"Not that I have already obtained all this,*
> *or have already arrived at my goal,*
> *but I **press on** to take hold of that*
> *for which Christ Jesus took hold of me.*
> *Brothers and sisters, I do not consider*
> *myself yet to have taken hold of it.*
> *But one thing I do:*
> ***Forgetting what is behind***
> ***and straining toward what is ahead,***
> ***I press on** toward the goal*
> *to win the prize for which God*
> *has called me heavenward in Christ Jesus."*

"Philippians 3:12-14," she murmured.

"Bullseye. I appreciate that Paul, even at that later stage of his life, was still pressing, still intent upon moving forward to accomplish God's plan for his life—but in order to do that, he had to make a choice, the choice to set aside what was behind him."

Simon took a deep breath. "See, if we do not press past our pain, how can we fully live our lives for Jesus? Put a different way, doesn't staying stuck in the pain of the past keep us from the future God has for us?"

"I take your point, Simon, and I receive your gentle nudge. I know I need to, with the Lord's help, continue to move forward, even at my age."

She shook her curls gently. "But the years between us, between you and me . . ."

Simon was astounded at this giant leap forward. He was shocked—but delighted—that she would call out the elephant in the room.

"Our age difference is just a number, BeeDee, and not all that huge. And look here: We are already the best of friends and brother and sister in Christ. If the Lord, who rules both our lives, is in this friendship, and if he leads us to make it something more? Fourteen years difference won't matter a whit."

His penetrating gaze met her cautious one. "I'm asking you to give us a chance, BeeDee."

CHAPTER 28

SIMON HAD BEEN near the end of his strength long before they arrived at Site 19. Getting up the steps and through the fifth wheel's doorway put him over the top. He collapsed, groaning, into the Nadeaus' recliner.

Ahhh.

The chair's upholstered lines cushioned him in all the right places, particularly the throbbing, aching pain across his lower back where Münster had pummeled his right kidney mercilessly. Without meaning to, he slipped into a much-needed doze.

"Simon."

He came awake with a start and glanced around.

How long have I been asleep? Who called me?

Sophie stood in the hallway that ran alongside the open, three-sided space lined with the children's bunkbeds, each bunk atop a set of built-in drawers. Simon instantly recognized the little pleated skirt and short-sleeved top she wore.

But it had not been Sophie's voice that roused him.

Simon jerked upright. "What in the world!"

She came closer. "Sophie left the contents of her dresser strewn upon her bunk when she packed to go. I only meant to fold her clothes and put them right, but when I saw these lying there . . . I realized she and I wear very nearly the same sizes."

"You . . . from a distance and wearing that outfit, you look remarkably like her."

Then her point about gutted him. "No! No way! You will *not* be bait for those people! *You will not!*"

She released that breathy *heh-heh-heh* that often tickled his funny bone —except it did not at this moment.

Not in the slightest.

"I said no!"

"Calm down, cowboy. I have no intention of dangling myself out there in Sophie's place. It could serve no purpose, really, but . . . but perhaps riding Sophie's bike around the park, say, with Skipper, Becka, Melissa, and Bruce surrounding me, might reinforce the illusion that Sophie is still here, make it last a few hours longer. Long enough to prompt our leaker to make a call and for my techs to identify the phone used to call our adversaries?"

"Nope. Don't like it. Not a bit."

She put her fists on her hips, which, when dressed as eight-year-old Sophie, was outright ludicrous.

"How badly do you think those Cretans would want the organs of a sixty-two-year-old woman, Simon Fletcher?"

"Well, I read that age isn't a barrier!"

"*Posh!* My only aim is that, should someone in Bright Star be feeding information to our adversaries, then that someone will contact them—and my tech guys will pick up on the call and identify him or her, even, possibly, the identity and location of the person called."

Simon finally made himself consider the idea. "You wouldn't leave the park? You wouldn't go into the woods?"

"I am many things, Simon Fletcher. Foolish, I pray, is not one of them."

Someone tapped on the RV's door.

Simon and Miss Finch stared at each other until Miss Finch called, "Who is it, please?"

"Miss Finch, it's Gretchen Muller. I have Mr. Fletcher's dinner."

Miss Finch winced. She opened the door. Simon couldn't see Gretchen Muller's expression, but he heard her gasp.

"You had better come in," Miss Finch murmured.

Bruce's aunt's stepped inside and nodded to Simon. Her expression still showed her shock. "I thought you were—" then, "What is this all about?"

"You thought I was Sophie. *Good.* If I were to ride around the park with the Gorman's granddaughters, it might make anyone watching, anyone who didn't know better, believe that the Nadeaus are still here."

"What! The Nadeaus are gone?"

"Yes, taken somewhere safe for little Sophie's sake. But how did you know to bring Mr. Fletcher's dinner *here?* We were hoping to keep the fact that the Nadeaus are gone quiet for a day or a few hours by not having meals delivered to him here."

"Well, just a bit ago, Mrs. Gorman told me Mr. Fletcher's meals were to be delivered directly to you. I was on my way to your site and had to pass the Nadeaus' site, of course, since the road runs only one way. But then I noticed your woody parked down the Nadeaus' driveway. Since I could not leave his meal unattended at your site, I stopped here. I figured Mr. Fletcher's dinner would be fine in your car until you took it to him."

She glanced toward Simon. "Is Mr. Fletcher staying here? Is that what is going on?"

"Yes. The Nadeaus are allowing Mr. Fletcher to use their RV while they are away. You see, his cabin does not have a comfortable chair for him to sit in while he recuperates."

"Okay, I get it. And how are you feeling, Mr. Fletcher?"

"Better than yesterday, thank you."

Which isn't saying much.

"Well, I hope you have an appetite. I put together a pan of lasagna and a side salad. Garlic bread too. Enough for the both of you," she added, sliding her eyes back to Miss Finch.

"Many thanks, but the second portion had best be for Skipper," Miss Finch replied. "He's working very hard to help Mr. Mitchell keep up. Of course the assistance of our Bright Star family is invaluable."

"Oh, it's more than that! My Frank is really enjoying himself," Gretchen laughed. "He's a small motor mechanic by trade—owned a thriving business until we sold it recently. Now, he's like a kid in a candy shop, Bright Star being the shop. So far, Frank has fine-tuned Joe's riding lawnmower, the log splitter, two washers, a dryer, and the AC in Bright Star's office."

"He's going to put me out of a job." Simon was only half joking.

"Oh, baloney. You'll be back to work in no time. By the way, Mr. Red-wine—Sam—is helping Frank, and Frank is mentoring him. Sam mentioned he needed to earn some cash on the side. Perhaps he hopes to learn enough to pick up some jobs here and there."

"Good for him," Miss Finch murmured, "but would you do us a great favor?"

"Certainly!"

"Will you promise not to tell anyone you saw us in the Nadeau's rig or mention my being dressed up like Sophie, in particular saying nothing to Mr. Muller or to Mr. Redwine? It is rather important that you do not."

Gretchen Muller looked momentarily taken aback. "I . . . yes, all right. I promise."

"Thank you. As I said, it is important."

Still looking uncertain, Gretchen said, "Of course. Well, Mr. Fletcher's dinner is in this shopping bag. Enjoy, Mr. Fletcher."

"Oh, I will, I guarantee. Thank you for your kindness. I appreciate it more than you know."

Miss Finch continued to stare at the door after Gretchen Muller departed, seemingly heedless of Simon's presence.

Simon frowned. "What is it?"

She broke from her trance-like state. "Oh, just a curious thought, one that perhaps bears further scrutiny."

"Would you tell me? I'd like to know."

She glanced at a clock on the RV's wall. "Poor Pouncer and Hugo! I have left them alone most of the day—and it is their dinner time. Perhaps later."

"Indulge me? I'll suffer Pouncer's wrath."

She murmured the under-her-breath *heh-heh-heh* he liked so much and said, "I may need to hold you to that. But, instead of telling you straight out, let me ask you a question that will, perhaps, illuminate my line of thought."

"Shoot."

"All right, then. Given the exclusive requirements of this park and the hefty price tag on each site, how many Bright Star residents would you assume require 'side jobs' to bolster their income?"

Simon stared at her. "Not a one. To say that our residents are well-heeled would be like pronouncing water *wet*."

"Precisely."

"Another individual for your techs to investigate?"

"As I said, the idea bears further scrutiny. Please excuse me while I wander home and feed my poor darlings and attempt to make amends to them. As I walk, I will make that call to my tech crew. They do so love the little challenges I send their way."

———— ✦ ————

LATER, MISS FINCH joined Simon and Skipper for dinner, Miss Finch bringing her own supper preparations to the Nadeaus' RV.

"Seems weird being in here without Mr. and Mrs. Nadeau," Skipper observed, digging into Gretchen's lasagna for seconds.

"Would you go in for something even weirder?" Miss Finch asked while she forked the last tiny bite from a small square of broiled salmon, then addressed a similarly sized square of baked squash.

Skipper eyed her. "Define your kind of 'even weirder.'"

"You shall see."

After dinner, she went down the hallway to the rear of the RV. Minutes later, she reappeared wearing one of Sophie's summer outfits: shorts and matching top. She had pulled her hair into two curly pigtails.

Skipper gaped in disbelief. "Holy cow! You look like Sophie!"

"Sacred bovines aside, that was my intent. But here's the truly weird part: Would you be willing to recruit Becka, Melissa, and Bruce to take a bike ride a couple of times around Bright Star's road with me?"

Simon watched as Skipper's brain processed the request and the possible reasoning behind it. He noted the exact moment Skipper hit upon that reasoning.

"Because you . . . you want people to think you're Sophie?"

"Yes."

"But . . ."

"Are you asking why?"

Skipper shook his head. "I can guess why, so please don't! I don't want anything bad to happen to you, Miss Finch, any more than I want something bad to happen to Sophie."

"As long as we stay on the road inside the park, I shall be fine. What we hope to gain from this little exercise is the identity of whomever has been passing information to those who wish to take Sophie."

Skipper, already shaken, teared up. "You mean someone *here?* You're saying one of our residents is a *snitch?*"

"Sadly, that is what we think. Will you go now to recruit Becka, Melissa, and Bruce and return here with them?"

"We really need you to do this, Skip," Simon added.

Skipper sighed. "All right. I will." He glanced again at Miss Finch and shook his head. "You're freaking me out, you know."

"For which I am quite sorry. But go now, Skipper. Please. But say nothing to your friends except that I would like them to bring themselves and their bicycles here to the Nadeaus' site. I will rehearse the plan to them when you are all assembled."

As soon as he left, Miss Finch again got on the phone. Simon listened to her talk to her tech team and could, for the most part, follow the flow of the conversation by listening to her end of it.

When she hung up, she said. "My team will monitor cell service in and around the park for the next three hours."

Skipper returned in twenty minutes, Bruce, Becka, and Melissa in tow. They entered the Nadeaus' fifth wheel and, one at a time, stopped, gaped, and stared.

"Miss Finch? Not Sophie?" an incredulous Bruce managed first.

"Yes, Sophie, in as far as we hoped you would think. Nonetheless, I ask that you keep quiet about my little charade, please. Furthermore, I ask for your help."

"Is this about catching the persons who tried to take Sophie?" Bruce asked.

"In roundabout fashion, it is."

"Well, you can count me in!"

"Us, too," Becka answered for herself and her sister.

"Then you must tell no one about our little experiment until we have achieved our desired outcome. Can you do that?"

"Lie?" Becka asked, gulping on her question.

"No, certainly not. I ask only that you do not speak of my impersonation for a brief time."

The kids nodded.

"For Sophie," Skipper said.

"For Sophie," came the echo from Bruce, Becka, and Melissa.

Minutes later, having explained exactly what she wanted of them, Miss Finch and her four helpers departed, Miss Finch riding Sophie's bike, wearing a whistle on a chain around her neck—at Simon's insistence. Simon had also insisted on Skipper helping him get down from the RV and hobble up to the top of the drive to keep tabs on them as they circled the park. He sat in a lawn chair off to the side and behind a bush where a passing car or walker wouldn't immediately observe him,

It's not as though I'm going to see much of their ride as they make each circuit around the park anyway, but I might hear a commotion if one breaks out or if BeeDee blows her whistle, and he heaved a disgruntled sigh, hating the knowledge that he'd be of absolutely no use should something go wrong.

Roughly ten minutes later, the five cyclists pedaled by. Bruce and Skipper rode in front with the three girls tightly bunched behind them. "Sophie" rode between Becka and Melissa, where she was less obvious to those who might watch as they rode by.

Simon stuck his head out from behind the bush and waggled his fingers at Miss Finch. She pointedly ignored him, intent on staying in character.

Another ten minutes later, the riders appeared a second time and turned into the Nadeaus' driveway. Simon levered himself up and, using the lawn chair as an awkward walker, made his way down the drive. Miss Finch had already gone inside to change out of Sophie's clothes. She reappeared shortly, and Simon realized he could breathe again.

"Well?" he asked.

"Now we wait."

CHAPTER 29

MONDAY, JULY 21

SIMON SLEPT THAT night in the Nadeaus' recliner and enjoyed the best sleep he'd had since his fight with Jürgen Münster. He was about to help himself to the Nadeaus' coffee and coffee maker when a knock sounded on the RV's door. He opened the door and ushered in Miss Finch, large sack in one hand, a covered cup of coffee in the other.

"Bless you, woman!" Simon exclaimed as he took the coffee from her, pulled off the lid, and inhaled deeply. *Inhaled?* He had to stop himself from sucking the coffee in through his nose.

"Hey, my ribs feel a whole lot better today. I can draw a full breath."

"That is wonderful news."

As Miss Finch laid out breakfast things, Simon sniffed with appreciation. "Smells spicy."

"Are you ready to eat?"

"Yup. I'm ravenous."

"Your appetite is also improving," she answered, smiling.

They sat at the RV's table, and Simon blessed the food. Then he lifted the cover from a baking dish and peered at a large serving of sliced sausages fried together with chunks of potatoes and diced onions. A smaller covered dish held four slices of toast made from fresh, home-baked, whole wheat bread slathered with butter.

"Yum! Who do I thank for today's bounty?"

"That would be the Gillespies, my new neighbors. Very nice folks. But better than this good breakfast, I have good news."

Simon was scooping food onto his plate as fast as he could. "I refuse to agree that your good news is better than this food, at least until I hear your news, because this food looks and smells like sweet triumph to me."

"O ye of little confidence! Very well, my news then: It was Sam Redwine who made a call last evening ten minutes after the children and I finished our ride."

Simon set his fork on the table and sighed. "Well, I'm sorry to hear it was him. Have your guys—and gals—identified who Redwine called?"

"No, but they did provide the location of the burner he called."

He scooted back his chair. "Let's go."

"No. *No.* **No.** We will not leave until after you have eaten, Moreover, you will not disobey the doctor's orders today. *Moderate* walking, Fletcher, and nothing more. Those are his strictures, and you promised to abide by them."

"Hmph."

Simon was just reaching for his fork when she added, "By the way, Mr. Grayson will be joining us when we go."

"What the devil does that mean, 'by the way, Mr. Grayson will be joining us?' He, his crew, and Sophie's family were supposed to have left the hotel early today. They should be on the road right now!"

"Ah, but given the information my tech team provided late last night, plans have changed. Now stop stalling and eat that lovely meal Mrs. Gillespie prepared for you—"

Simon retrieved his fork. "*Fine.*"

"—after which you should get cleaned up."

"Are you saying I stink?"

"No. I am saying that I would describe you as 'scruffy around the edges.' You need a shave and clean clothes, at the barest minimum, Fletcher." She tipped her head and studied him, "And perhaps a visit to your barber, should you care to keep your hair off your collar."

Simon ran a hand over his head. "I suppose I could use a trim, but not today. I'll wash, change, brush my teeth, and shave. Then we go."

"How did I know that would be your response."

"Because you know me, *Finchy* . . . and you care."

"Cheeky monkey," she growled back.

———————— ◆ ————————

GRAYSON ARRIVED THIRTY minutes later, and the three of them left Bright Star in his vehicle, heading west on Emerald Bay Road. Simon felt as if he'd won a battle when he was able to navigate the RV's steps on his own and join Miss Finch in Grayson's rear seat with much less discomfort.

"Sheesh. I'm healing at long last," he said, with relief. "Swelling is down some today, ribs are mending, bruises are fading."

Grayson glanced in the rearview mirror. "You're right. Instead of your head looking like a mutant eggplant, it now more closely resembles a plate of scrambled eggs gone bad. You know, green eggs, skip the ham?"

A snicker—instantly extinguished by the little hand she slapped over her mouth—leapt from Miss Finch's throat.

"Turncoat!" Simon snarled, "And you can knock that right off, Grayson."

"Yes, please do leave off provoking Mr. Fletcher, Grayson," Miss Finch remonstrated, and Simon was partially mollified.

Until she added, "at least until his concussion heals."

"I know where you live, lady," he muttered.

"Indeed. Have you met my watch kitty?"

Simon shuddered. "Burglars and assailants beware!"

They proceeded in silence, as Grayson's car climbed the steep road overlooking the stunning bay from which Emerald Bay Road got its name, then descended, and after catching glimpses of Rubicon Bay on their right, took the turnoff to a neighborhood on the left side of Emerald Bay Road. The houses of that neighborhood were built into the high hillsides more or less centered above the bay. Grayson wound his way up Scenic Drive, passing many homes, all facing the lake. The views of the lake from here, glimpsed as narrow slices between the homes, were stunning.

They passed a beautiful home sporting a realtor sign. This house, built into the hillside but not on the coveted "lake side" of the street, boasted four stories (if one were to count the garage built at ground level as its own floor) and was, thus, tall enough to also own a decent view of the lake from its third floor and fourth floor windows and verandas.

"Wow. Cannot imagine the prices on these homes," Simon muttered.

"This one, on the 'wrong' side of the street but still with a decent view from its upper floors? Think in the two-million-dollar range," Miss Finch murmured. "Think also of the many, *many* steps one must climb daily to enjoy such a view."

"No thanks. Just the idea of climbing three flights to reach my bedroom took the 'enjoy' part right out of it."

"I'm curious as to how you know the price of houses in this neighborhood," Grayson mused.

Miss Finch shrugged. "My propensity for accumulating trivia may someday be my downfall."

They took a right, then another right, and continued to meander until Miss Finch pointed out a home on their left that, sadly, did not have a view of the lake. Boasting only two floors, the property was still quite lovely: The lot was larger than most homes nearby, the house cossetted by pine trees, the landscaping gorgeous.

"Drive on farther, flip a U-turn, and park alongside the road where you are out of sight but can put eyes on the front door," Miss Finch directed Grayson as they motored slowly past.

"You mean me to stay with the car?" Grayson asked. "Is that wise?"

"No. I mean Fletcher to stay with the car. Did you count cameras as we passed?"

"Two in the front: one at the door, the other overlooking the garage, neither of which covers the sides of the house."

"Correct. When we get out, walk until you have passed the house, then turn back and make your way up the far side of the lot. Position yourself at the front corner of the house where you are out of camera range but can monitor my exchange with the person who answers the door. Before we split up,

I will call you on my phone so that you can listen in on the conversation. When I knock on the door, I will pretend to be responding to a barking dog complaint. You are to come to my aid should things go awry."

"You got it."

"Oh. And do give me your key fob. I will drive your car up the street and pick you up after I finish."

Simon cut in. "I would like—"

"What you would like is irrelevant, Fletcher. You will *stay put*."

Simon sighed. "I was merely going to ask that you include me in your phone call.

"Oh. Well, yes. I can do that."

"And am I allowed to roll the window down and use my binoculars, the better to see you with . . . *Nurse Ratched?*"

She had the good grace to blush. "Certainly. In fact, I will angle my body toward you so you can observe as well as hear my exchange with the house's resident."

"Peachy."

After Miss Finch made the call to connect with Grayson and Simon's phones, she and Grayson left the car. Grayson immediately walked ahead of Miss Finch and crossed in front of the house until he was beyond it.

Simon watched as Grayson doubled back and crept up the neighbor's side yard, taking care to stay out of range of the two cameras in front of the target house. Grayson ducked from the neighbor's to the corner of their house of interest, then signaled Miss Finch that he was in place.

Miss Finch had waited to move until Grayson had taken up his position. Now she glanced at Simon through the open window and muted her phone.

"I do apologize for overstepping, Fletcher."

He nodded and murmured, "Accepted. I'm praying for you, BeeDee."

"Thank you . . . Simon."

Aha! Progress, Simon smiled to himself.

She unmuted her phone. She held it in her left hand and glanced down at it occasionally as she marched up the house's sidewalk and steps and rang the bell. No one immediately answered.

Simon watched Miss Finch ring the bell a second time. Finally, a voice from inside called, "Coming."

Simon scowled over the distance between him and Miss Finch and tried not to worry for her. At least, by training his binoculars on the front door, he could easily make out the dark-skinned woman who answered it, her expression guarded.

That initial expression, however, flipped in an instant. Her eyes widened, and her mouth opened slightly. In an unsteady voice, she asked, "Y-yes?"

"Ah, yes, good morning," Miss Finch said, again pretending to read from her phone. "I am Astrid Wheeler of the Rubicon Tahoe Owners Association.

Are you the party who called in a complaint concerning a neighbor's dog barking throughout the night?"

Miss Finch looked up then, and Simon thought she *had* to have observed the woman's flustered state. That was when Simon noticed the woman's left hand, hanging down at her side. It was moving. Clenching and unclenching? He had to shift his position before he could better make it out.

Keeping her thumb tucked into her palm, the woman repeatedly opened and closed her fingers in what was the now widely recognized signal for help . . . particularly in human trafficking situations.

Miss Finch has to see that, right?

"No, that wasn't me," the woman answered, regaining her composure. "I think you must have the wrong house. Besides, I am not a member of the owners association. I am just leasing this house."

Simon's brows lifted as he listened. The woman's accent was Australian.

"I beg your pardon," Miss Finch replied. She appeared to study her phone again, then laughed. "Oh dear. I cannot believe I am on the wrong street. I do apologize for bothering you. Have a nice day."

Without another word, she turned and retraced her steps to the car. She got into the driver's seat, pulled away from the curb, and drove straight ahead. Two houses down, she stopped the car and got out. Grayson joined them, and Miss Finch climbed into the back with Simon.

"Did you see it?" she demanded of Simon and Grayson.

"I could hear the conversation but couldn't see the woman at all from where I was," Grayson said.

Simon replied, "The 'help' signal? Yeah, I saw it."

"So, she is not alone in the house and is being held against her will. We must call Officer Phillips and report this."

"Uh, I believe you missed the other important sign while you were pretending to study your phone," Simon said.

"Oh?"

"That lady was perfectly calm and cool when she answered the door, but her façade lasted about a second. The moment she laid eyes on you, she recognized you."

Miss Finch's heavy eyelids dropped to half-staff. "Did she now? But what does that tell us?"

"That either she or someone with her is connected to the attempted abduction?"

"Conceivably. In any event, we shall soon find out," Miss Finch promised.

———— ◆ ————

"SOON" LINGERED, THEN languished, until it lost all possibility of being "soon" and moved on to "quite a while," certainly a lot longer than Simon and Miss Finch were happy with. Eventually the three of them met up with

Phillips and his five-man SWAT team at a pull-off on Emerald Bay Road several miles south of the neighborhood and house in question.

Inside their command vehicle, two additional SWAT members, who functioned as support personnel, produced a set of plans for the house. Miss Finch—again—went through her brief encounter with the woman who answered the door.

"Front cameras at the door and over the garage, you say?"

"Yes."

"And this woman used the sign for help? You are completely certain?"

"Mr. Fletcher can verify."

"Yes, I saw it too," Simon assured Phillips, leaning against a table in the cramped van. He demonstrated the woman's hand signal. "I was watching the front door through my binoculars from Grayson's car. I also saw the woman's eyes go wide when she opened the door. She appeared shocked to see Miss Finch standing on her own porch."

Phillips pointed to two of his guys and detailed them to reconnoiter the target. They drove off in a nondescript car and returned twenty minutes later.

The senior of the pair reported, "All the windows in the house are closed and draped. Infrared shows four individuals inside, one of them slightly smaller, perhaps a juvenile or teen. The teen and one adult appear to be sitting next to each other in what the house plans has labeled the living room. Of the two remaining adults, one is in the living room with the adult and teen but a couple yards from them. The fourth individual seems to be seated in a room just off to the left of the front entry. Plans call this a library; we assume it is used as a home office and that this person is monitoring the security feeds."

The second reconnaissance officer reported, "The house also has two cameras in the back. By going up the side of the house, making a sharp turn and by sticking close to the walls, I stayed out of camera range, jimmied the garage's back door, and entered the garage. I slipped a flexible camera line under the door leading from the inside of the garage into the house. That door leads directly into the kitchen, which opens to the living room. I could see into the living room and can confirm that the three people there are the woman Miss Finch described, a teenaged girl, and a man I took for a guard."

"Armed?"

"He was standing in the living room, watching television, holding a plate of food." He smiled as he added, "Left his weapon on the kitchen island."

"Not very professional of him. Recommendation?"

The senior of the pair spoke again. "Carson sets up in front of the neighbors' with an angle to the office window; Crutchfield and Benson crawl across the front of the house to the front door. You, Georgio, and I enter the garage and wait. When Carson launches a flashbang through the office window, Crutchfield and Benson breach through the front door and we breach into the kitchen. We will take the unarmed guard; Crutchfield and Benson will take the stunned guard in the office."

"Good plan, Mackey."

"Finally," Simon growled. "Some action!"

When SWAT's tactical vehicle rolled, Grayson, Miss Finch, and Simon followed behind. The SWAT vehicle wound through the neighborhood and parked three houses *south* of the target, on the same side where Grayson had taken up position while Miss Finch rang the doorbell.

Phillips' team, in full protective gear, poured from their vehicle and formed up in two short lines. The leaders of both lines gripped ballistic shields.

In moments, they had left Grayson, Miss Finch, and Simon without eyes or ears on the team's movement. Simon, needing to move, got out and walked a few yards on stiff legs toward the SWAT vehicle and back. While he walked, he silently prayed for each man on the team and for the innocent parties in the house.

"What does it mean?" Miss Finch murmured.

"What does what mean?"

"That the woman at the door recognized me."

"Good question. Not sure I'm going to like the answer."

They walked together back to Grayson's car, then a ways beyond it. Simon was certain his body was healing, but he was already tiring, and it was getting hard for him to pick up his feet. Miss Finch must have realized he was flagging, because when the toe of his shoe caught on the uneven asphalt and he reached for her shoulder to steady himself, she anticipated his move.

"Thanks. Guess I should have brought my pain meds with me."

"Don't you mean you should be plopped in the Nadeaus' comfy recliner after breakfast, walking only to the bathroom and back?"

"Yeah. That too."

He didn't realize, until they'd walked on a few steps, that they had clasped hands.

He hadn't immediately realized it because it felt so natural. So right.

Well, well, well. Will you look at us . . . holding hands?

AFTERWARD, ACCORDING TO Phillips, SWAT's breach of the house could not have gone any smoother. The two men guarding the woman and her daughter had grown lax and were caught with their proverbial pants down.

Carson launched a stun grenade through the office window. Three members of the SWAT team entered the kitchen from the garage. Their target still stood across the living room, a plate of food in his hands, while he stared at the television, his weapon on the kitchen counter. At a shouted command from the breaching team, the guard jerked and dropped his plate.

The second guard, disoriented, blind, and coughing from the flashbang, but with his cell phone in his hand, stumbled to the office door. Morales was ready at the door when it began to open inward. He rammed his shield, with his body's weight behind it, into the door. The door slammed into the unprepared guard's face, knocking him temporarily unconscious.

With the action over, Phillips called Miss Finch, briefed her on the takedown, and invited her and Simon to view the results of his team's action. Grayson stayed with his car. Entering the house behind Miss Finch, Simon observed both guards disarmed, cuffed, and seated on the living room floor against a wall. The two hostages were still seated on the living room sofa,

Miss Finch had scarcely taken stock of the situation when the woman who had earlier answered Miss Finch's knock on the door exclaimed, "You! You saw my sign for help? You sent the police to rescue us?"

"Indeed, I did," she answered, moving toward the sofa. "I immediately called our friend, Officer Phillips here. By the way, I am BD Finch. This is my friend and associate, Simon Fletcher. You are?"

"Ebanee Barkinjee. This be my daughter. Ayla."

Simon studied the two women from across the room. Ebanee and Ayla were very dark-skinned, darker than most African Americans these days. Their features and body shapes, too, were distinctive—both women stocky, their facial features broad, their eyes deep-set and heavy-browed. Simon estimated that Ayla was around seventeen years old. He looked closer, and detected pale, sickly undertones beneath her nearly black skin. Then there was Ebanee's distinctive accent.

"You are Indigenous Australians?" Miss Finch asked.

"We are, although we be city people now and hail from Adelaide, South Australia."

With one ear on the conversation between Miss Finch and the Australian women, Simon's gaze shifted to the men in police custody . . . and got stuck there. He pulled his phone, keyed in a number, and let it ring. Just feet from him, one of the prisoners flinched. He tried to cover up his reaction. What he could not do was end the vibration of a confiscated phone on the kitchen island.

Simon lifted his chin to Miss Finch to catch her attention, then tipped his head toward the two cuffed men and their angry glares. He saw when she caught the phone's vibration . . . and the other salient info Simon had noted.

She glanced at Simon. "That phone received Redwine's call?"

He nodded.

Turning back to Ebanee and Ayla, she gestured to the prisoners, "These men. Do you know if they are Chinese nationals?"

Ebanee's mouth hardened. "Yeah, that they be. Too many of them messing about in our country to mistake them otherwise. We have been their prisoners three days now. Since Friday." Her expression softened when her gaze returned to Miss Finch. "We cannot thank you enough for rescuing us!"

"We are glad and grateful also. And can you tell us, did that one," she pointed at the man whose vibrating phone had gone to voicemail, "did this one receive a call last evening?"

"Yeah, then he immediately called someone else, a man he treats with great respect."

Miss Finch looked at Simon and pointed at the prisoner. "This one, no doubt, is a cutout, to maintain a degree of separation between Sam Redwine and their boss. Of course, a look at the cutout's phone should give us their boss's number. God willing, my team will be able to zero in on the boss's location."

Phillips, who understood little of Miss Finch and Simon's back and forth, asked, "Ms. Barkinjee, is it? Can you help us understand what this is all about? *Why* have those men been keeping you prisoner in your own home?"

Ebanee's expression froze, then shuttered. She did not answer.

"Perhaps Simon and I can help untangle this snarled tale and explain Ebanee's reticence," Miss Finch said quietly, shifting her attention to Ebanee's young daughter. "It begins with you, Ayla, does it not?"

Ayla's chin dropped to her chest. She remained as silent and closed off as her mother.

Phillips gestured his frustration. "Miss Finch? Since you appear to know what is going on here and I am, apparently, clueless, please continue."

"Thank you, Office Phillips. As I said, we must begin with Ayla. Ayla's blood type, I presume, is Rh Null, the same type as Sophie Nadeaus' blood. But unlike Sophie, Ayla's form of anemia is no longer well-controlled. Sadly, at this juncture in Ayla's young life, she now requires regular transfusions." She shifted her attention to Ebanee. "Am I correct so far?"

Ebanee shook her head minutely, not in the negative, but as an expression of painful resignation.

"I must also assume that you and your family are financially independent, Ebanee."

"Do *not* make assumptions about me or my family," Ebanee retorted, low in her throat.

"And yet you told me you are leasing this lovely house, I believe? I venture to say the month-to month is quite steep."

When all she got for her trouble was more silence, Miss Finch said, "Perhaps we could come at this from a different angle—but do please correct me, should I veer off in a wrong direction."

She studied Ayla's mother. "Ebanee, you have found it difficult to procure a regular supply of Rh null blood for Ayla, have you not? In your understandable desperation, I believe you reached out to a bulletin board on the dark web, a place where you were told that those who offered human organs and illicit medical procedures lurked and watched for messages.

"You posted your need, perhaps only admitting to the need for a regular supply of a rare blood type—not mentioning which type. You reached out, and someone reached back, an individual, you found out later, who resides somewhere near here in the lake area. Someone who promised to do his best to procure a regular supply of Rh null blood for a simple broker's fee."

Phillips looked skeptically from the two Chinese prisoners to Miss Finch. "What? These two?"

"No. Someone much brighter than either of these must be the 'brains' of this outfit. We're talking about an individual who arranged for the disappearances of Whatley, Morales, Xú, and young Allysson Sharma, was responsible for the attempted kidnappings of Cameron Easton and our little friend, and built a surgical transplant suite."

"Then who are these thugs?"

Miss Finch studied the angry, hard-edged expressions of the cuffed men. "Oh, I think these two gentlemen—and I use the term 'gentlemen' loosely—represent the competition."

The line between Phillips' brows deepened. "You're saying they horned in on our local organ purveyor's business?"

Miss Finch touched her nose, watching the two prisoners for their reactions. "Spot on, Officer Phillips. Not them personally, of course, but *their* bosses. The black-market organ business is extremely lucrative and well established, particularly in Asia and especially in China. In fact, although this knowledge is not widely reported, the specially formed China Tribunal in London has declared there is no doubt that the Chinese government itself conducts forced, state-sanctioned organ harvesting *on a massive scale.*"

She turned her eyes to Phillips. "The Chinese Communist Party draws upon political prisoners—dissenters, prisoners of conscience, 'cult' members such as those belonging to Falun Gong, or anyone whose beliefs contradict the Party—as their source of saleable organs."

She shifted her attention back to the cuffed men. "That said, however, I would venture to say that these two fine specimens of humanity work not for the Chinese government but for a branch or offshoot of Chinese organized crime."

Simon saw one of the men sneer at Miss Finch, and his thoughts dropped into a dark hole.

Chinese organized crime? In comparison, members of the Lucchese Crime Family were pussycats.

Oh, BeeDee! Now what have we stumbled into?

CHAPTER 30

MISS FINCH'S ATTENTION shifted back to Ebanee and her daughter. Ebanee's eyes were wide, staring in horror at Phillips' two prisoners.

"Ebanee," Miss Finch murmured, recapturing the woman's attention, "let us be perfectly frank, shall we?"

Ebanee, marginally dazed, slowly nodded.

"You come from money, yes? You can afford whatever Ayla's care costs?"

Ebanee again nodded. Reluctantly. "My family is, unlike most of our people, quite wealthy. My grandfather abandoned our traditions and adopted the ways of the white capitalists and prospered. He owned *his* grandfather's land, land rich in the kind of minerals corporations would pay millions to mine. Then he put the land in a trust for his children and their families. All my siblings and cousins share equally in the trust."

"I am curious. Did he sell the land or only lease the mineral rights?"

"He leased his land's mineral rights to a European company for a period of fifty years."

Simon could tell she wasn't comfortable with the source of her family's money.

Doesn't keep you from spending it, though, does it?

Miss Finch went on. "Ebanee, tell us what happened when you reached out on the dark web, hoping to buy golden blood. Who responded and how did that contact result in you being here?"

Ebanee's black eyes squeezed shut. "Don't know who the man is, but he and I spoke several times . . . at least I think it was a man. His voice was distorted."

Miss Finch interrupted. "Distorted, you say? In what way?"

"Garbled and a bit slow. This voice on the phone reached out to me in early April and said it would take time to locate a willing donor and for blood donations to begin, but he was confident he would succeed. Then he said that once a donor was found, he would broker the deal and arrange regular deliveries."

"But of course, he wanted significant cash up front?"

"Yeah, he did."

"And you paid him."

Ebanee swallowed and her hand fumbled for and found her daughter's hand. "Of course. We thought the transaction was equitable: Cash for blood, fee for the broker. Good deal all around."

"Walk us through your communication with the broker after that, please."

"Well, he promised to call every two weeks and keep us updated. Each time he called, he said he was still seeking the right match for us, someone who would agree to payment for regular donations.

"Finally, the third week in June, he called and said he had found Ayla's match and was close to closing on the deal. He told us to be ready to fly here the next time he called."

She exhaled slowly. "We needed for Ayla to receive her first two transfusions here, you see, to prove she and her donor were truly a match, but also because Ayla needs two units to start."

Ebanee's voice caught. "My girl isn't well. We were starting to get desperate, and yet the man did not call again until two weeks ago. He said the arrangements were proceeding nicely and we should come immediately. We had leased this house online months ago in preparation, but only arrived here eight days ago."

"Date please?"

Ebanee searched her phone again. "We flew into Reno July 12 and drove here the next day."

Simon ran a timeline of events in his head. *Today is July 21; Ebanee and Ayla arrived in Tahoe July 13. Münster and his pal made their failed attempt to take Sophie July 16.*

He broadened the timeline. *When our altruistic "purveyor"—let's call him Purv; yeah, that sounds about right—when he received his initial fee from Ebanee, he then sent his army of AI bots out into the world to snoop through private hospital, physician, and blood bank servers until they came across an Rh null donor and reported back to him. But then, because Sophie lived in Canada, our wily Purv had to devise a means of drawing her and her unsuspecting parents to Tahoe.*

That's when Purv devised the "you've won a brand-new RV" gambit.

Purv posed as some never-heard-of, prize-bestowing entity, and informed the Nadeaus that they had won a brand-new fifth wheel. Lucas and Eva were initially wary, which speaks well of them, but when the RV was dropped at their door, they were overjoyed—so overjoyed and certain of their good fortune, they purchased a new-to-them truck to haul their unanticipated blessing. Why? Because the fifth wheel also came with a free vacation at Lake Tahoe.

Simon's calculations hit an abrupt wall.

Wait. Why would Purv lay out half a million dollars for an RV? Wouldn't that expense devour his profits? Why didn't he send Münster and his pal to kidnap Sophie from her home in Canada? So much simpler . . . unless this guy is a complete novice to the game and hasn't honed his skills. Yes, a much better doctor than a career criminal. That would fit with the second profile Miss Finch and I cobbled together.

Note to self: Take a deeper look into this.

He returned to constructing his case against the guy behind Münster and his accomplice.

The vacation part of this farce meant securing a spot where the Nadeaus could park their rig for at least a couple of weeks. And Purv wouldn't much care **where** *around the lake area he parked the Nadeaus, would he? Any old RV park would do, and there are a number of them. Then, once the Nadeaus settled into their vacation and let down their guard, Purv's thugs would snatch Sophie.*

So why Bright Star? I mean, the timing had to have been impeccable in order to work.

Let's see . . . Terri Rickert and Marie Santini were arrested mid-June, and although it took Holly a week to have their rigs hauled off Bright Star property, had she updated Bright Star's website right away to announce that two sites were available through the end of the season at prorated prices?

Simon tapped out a text to Holly and sent it. Her response came back quickly.

Hmm. So, Holly did post that two sites had come available on Bright Star's website. But . . . but then there's the fact that Bright Star doesn't come cheap. Again, wouldn't the lease payment bite too deeply into Purv's profit margin?

So, why Bright Star, indeed? What did it offer Purv's scheme that other lake area RV parks did not?

When the answer hit Simon, the reason was so simple, it bled the air from his lungs.

. . . Summer bookings of any and every kind around the lake, but especially over the Fourth of July weekend, were like hotcakes sizzling on a perfectly heated griddle: They flipped fast and were snapped up just as quickly.

Put plainly, finding a spot to park an RV—*any RV*—even remotely close to Tahoe, once the season commenced *but particularly over the Fourth*, not to mention for more than two weeks, was nigh unto impossible. It had to have been the fly in Purv's ointment, the one detail he had not anticipated . . . until his frantic online searches—probably aided again by AI bots—turned up Bright Star's two vacancies.

Cue the deceptive letter ostensibly from the Nadeaus' "travel agent," providing them with the details of their free Lake Tahoe vacation.

Again, the outlay to deliver the Nadeaus to Bright Star seemed outrageously high to Simon. Too high not to outweigh the expected profit margin.

So, why didn't Purv skip all these convoluted maneuvers and expense and just abduct Sophie from her home in Canada?

His thoughts flipped back to the Nadeaus' RV, and he spoke without realizing he'd cut in on Miss Finch's interview with Ebanee Barkinjee.

"Phillips? Need you to run the Nadeaus' fifth wheel VIN through Quebec's motor vehicle division."

Miss Finch stared at Simon, as confused as Phillips was by Simon's off-topic demand.

Phillips said dubiously, "I suppose I can do that. What's the rush?"

"I believe it may help us confirm the identity of the person or persons who tricked Sophie's parents into bringing her to Tahoe."

"Someone tricked Sophie's *parents?*" Ebanee asked, dismay in her voice. "Whatever do you mean?"

"Ebanee," Miss Finch asked quietly, "what do you know about Sophie?"

"Why, she . . . she's the person whose blood is a match for Ayla, the person who made an agreement with our broker to provide regular units of blood for Ayla."

Miss Finch pursed her lips and considered how to proceed. "When I knocked on your door this morning, Ebanee, you seemed . . . disconcerted. Did you, somehow, recognize me?"

"Yes, because our broker sent us your picture. Yours and his." Ebanee pointed to Simon. "He said you were attempting to lure Sophie away from our arrangement, that you had offered Sophie more money than what we had initially agreed to pay. Why, our broker even told us he had to enter into a bidding war to keep Sophie from breaking her agreement with us!"

She rushed on hurriedly, "But I don't care. I don't hold it against you, certainly not after you saved us from these men!"

"My dear woman, I am very sorry to tell you this, but the idea of a bidding war is an outright lie, a ploy to make you offer to pay even more for the blood Ayla needs. Moreover, Sophie is not an adult able to enter into such an agreement on her own say-so. She is but an eight-year-old child! And we, Mr. Fletcher and I, have not been outbidding you for Sophie's blood. Rather, we have been *protecting* Sophie from the people who tried to kidnap and traffic her for her rare blood. It is how Mr. Fletcher received the bruises still evident on his face. And furthermore . . ."

Miss Finch hesitated, "And furthermore, I have reason to believe that the man who posed as an honest broker between you and Sophie is actually both a procurer and seller of human organs on the black market. When I say 'procurer,' it means we believe he is responsible for the abductions of at least four individuals . . . in order to harvest and sell their organs."

"No!" Ebanee moaned. "No, it cannot be!"

"I am so very sorry, but Officer Phillips can attest to the fact that two of the young men abducted from around the lake area have now been found, both with multiple organs surgically removed . . . removed as a transplant team would remove them. However, quite recently, as recently as Friday evening, I believe this man, this 'broker' as you refer to him, found himself no longer in charge of his own enterprise."

"What do you mean, he is no longer in charge? If he isn't, then who is?" Ebanee's voice sounded strangled.

Miss Finch pointed at Phillips' prisoners. "I think it likely that the Chinese criminal organization to which these two reprobates belong has hijacked your 'honest broker's' operation but has been using the so-called broker to continue feeding you lies—including those whoppers about a so-called bidding war. Moreover, not only does this criminal group plan to milk you for as much money as they can *and never* provide Ayla with the blood she needs, they likely intend to traffic Ayla as well . . . for as long as is feasible."

As Miss Finch's words sank in, Ayla caved. She fell into her mother's arms and began to shake and weep . . . then wail, and Ebanee soon joined her in doing the same.

Simon felt like he was witnessing a death . . . and the devastating grief that follows.

———⧫———

MISS FINCH'S PHONE vibrated. "It's Grayson." She excused herself to take the call in the office where the security camera feeds were on display. She had been in the office for less than thirty seconds when she ran back into the living room.

"Phillips! Grayson says we have a problem, and the house's front camera confirms it. I just caught two cars driving by slowly, scoping out this place. I used the camera's zoom function, and the faces I saw were Chinese." She pointed at the two prisoners. "One of them must have alerted their bosses."

The prisoner on the left couldn't hide the derisive grin that tugged at his mouth.

At the same moment, the radio on Phillips' vest warbled. He picked up, listened, then said to Miss Finch and Simon, "It's my support crew in the SWAT vehicle around the corner. They spotted the same cars and tell me we're about to have company."

Phillips shouted to his team, "Defensive positions! Prepare to return fire!"

He pointed at Simon. "Get these ladies out the back door, through the side gate, and into the neighbor's yard, quick as you can. If bullets fly, take cover pronto."

Simon gestured to Ebanee and Ayla. "Come on. Gotta go." He grabbed Miss Finch by the elbow. "That means you too, lady."

Behind them, he heard Phillips declare, "I have five crack shots with me in the house and two more around the corner in our command center. Those guys coming for us are about to find out they have bitten off more than they can chew."

The yard out back, built into the hillside, was much smaller than the front. Simon huffed as he rushed Miss Finch out the back and turned toward the gate between this yard and the next-door neighbor's, following Ebanee and Ayla.

They had only reached the gate when they heard the first shots. Seconds later, Ayla shrieked as a round flew between her and her mother.

"Hit the deck!" Simon shouted.

As they pressed themselves into the grass, a torrent of gunfire opened up. Glass shattered. Dust and debris filled the air. Chips of wood and plaster rained down around them.

Simon cared only about the little woman he'd thrown to the ground and covered with his own body . . . her and the selfish prayer he murmured over and over.

"Lord Jesus, please keep BeeDee safe!"

The TAHOE
MYSTERIES

CHAPTER 31

WHAT HAD STARTED as a fairly uncomplicated hostage rescue had, in a matter of minutes, morphed into a full-blown, gangland-style shootout that ended as abruptly as it started. Soon after, one of the SWAT team came out back to check up on Simon, Miss Finch, Ebanee, and Ayla.

"Everyone okay?"

"Yeah. Just covered in dust and grit," Simon answered.

"Us too. Uh, Phillips wants all of you back in the house—or what's left of it."

"Well, I need a shower," Miss Finch mumbled.

Ebanee shrugged. "And, obviously, we need somewhere else to stay."

"Let's see if we can get you and Ayla relocated to a hotel," Miss Finch suggested. "Then I need to get Mr. Fletcher home."

But to Simon and Miss Finch's surprise, Phillips refused to let them leave the scene.

"I'm not cutting you loose until I'm certain I fully comprehend what happened here today.

"We can come in tomorrow, any time, and flesh out the details," Miss Finch protested. "I really must get Mr. Fletcher back to some sense of normalcy. He *is* recovering from a severe concussion, you know."

"And you've milked that thing for all its worth," Phillips grumbled.

"Believe it or not, it has only been four days of him thoroughly ignoring his doctor's orders."

Phillips snorted a laugh.

"If we cannot leave, then let us help."

"Anything to stop your complaining," Phillips grumbled, "as long as you don't impede the official investigation.

"Well," Miss Finch asked, a bit distracted, "have you by chance confiscated all the shooters' phones?"

"All nine of them."

Indeed, nine body bags, containing the bodies of seven attackers and the two unlucky prisoners, handcuffed and caught in the furious crossfire, lay on the lawn of Ebanee and Ayla's rented home. Police roped off the street and the scene while an ambulance attended members of Phillip's team. Not one of the six had been shot, but three had suffered minor shrapnel wounds as the attackers poured indiscriminate automatic weapons fire into the house.

Basically, the SWAT team's Kevlar tactical gear, the team's two ballistic shields, and the kitchen's refrigerator, pulled down onto its side, had saved them from the fate of the two prisoners and allowed them to return fire when the attackers broke off firing and, thinking the house was safe to enter, left their cars and approached the house.

Ah, the house.

What remained of it would not be fit to be lived in without significant renovation, but the living room, wrecked as it was, became the investigation's command center. Someone had collected the attackers' cell phones, bagged and tagged them, and piled them on what remained of the kitchen's island.

Simon collapsed onto the sofa and rested his head on what remained of the sofa's back cushions. Ebanee and Ayla huddled together on the other end, physically unharmed, but silent in their shock.

Simon watched Miss Finch sidle up to Phillips. "You want answers? Give me a few minutes with those phones," she whispered. "Have one or two of your men watch over me while I look at them. They can ensure proper chain of custody. I feel confident those phones will yield some of the answers you seek."

"Fine. Crutchfield! Benson!"

Miss Finch used a relatively unscathed kitchen countertop to lay out the phones, each in its own evidence bag with writing on one side. She turned the bags over, and since the backs had no print on them, took a black pen from her handbag and, in the lower right corner of each bag, numbered them one through nine. Then she manipulated each phone in its bag so it faced the side with no print, leaving the phone's front side visible and without obstruction.

"What are you doing?" Crutchfield asked.

"Determining which phone belongs to which body. Officer Crutchfield? Officer Benson? Help me take these phones outside."

Simon heaved himself to his feet and followed her.

She led the officers to the line of body bags and unzipped the first. She took the phone whose bag was marked with a 1, held it up to ascertain whether it unlocked with a print or facial recognition, then attempted to open it with the face of the body in the unzipped bag. That initial body was the hardest to match; they tried a number of phones before his face unlocked the seventh. Miss Finch then scrawled the number "7" on the man's forehead, the number that matched the number on the phone's evidence bag.

Catching on, the three of them worked together and had matched six phones when a crime tech rushed up to them.

"Hey! What are you doing?"

"Phillips knows we're doing this. The phones are properly bagged and tagged; these officers are monitoring our actions to preserve proper chain of custody."

The tech wasn't okay with it. "But what's your objective?"

"My objective is to determine a common origination point among these phones before these men drove here and shot up the place."

"Oh. I can help with that."

"Perfect. Let's finish matching phones to bodies, then check each phone's map app. It is likely someone mapped the route here."

Twenty minutes later, they had two phones, both mapped from the same location to Ebanee's leased house. Miss Finch took photos of the coordinates with her own phone and rushed to Phillips' side.

"Want to put an end to this?" she asked. "I have a location. You can apprehend both the organ-harvesting mastermind and this Chinese gang boss."

"I might need a court order first. That would take time."

"Exigent circumstances! Lives at risk! If your team moves quickly, we might have a chance of saving Caesar Morales and Allysson Sharma."

"I need to call in my off-duty team."

"No you don't, boss. We got this," Crutchfield interjected.

"I get you and cannot fault your willingness, but we don't know what we might be facing, so I want every able-bodied SWAT officer pulled in. Besides, while you and Benson escaped injury and are fit to go, I don't know about the rest of the team. Go check on them while I call in our off-duty guys."

He made the call, then turned to Miss Finch. "Give me what you've got."

Miss Finch read off the GPS coordinates, and he fed them into his phone.

He studied the map that came up. "This location is just beyond far north Incline Village. Multimillion-dollar homes up there, and this one is on a particularly large, isolated lot."

"As Fletcher and I already told you, our killer needed a location where construction of a building large enough to house a surgical suite and all it entails would not be remarked upon, considering how much renovation the lake area sees annually."

"First things first. I'll send a recon party."

She huffed, clearly frustrated, then said quietly, "Please think a moment, Officer Phillips. If the men who died here less than forty minutes ago do not report in soon, what will their superior do? No idea? Well, let me tell you: He will 'up stakes' and flee Tahoe—but not before erasing every shred of evidence that might be used against him, including *people*. Including Caesar Morales and little Allysson Sharma. Innocent lives hang in the balance, Officer Phillips. You must go *now!*"

Simon from behind her spoke up. "Sorry to contradict you on one point, Miss Finch, but this gang boss is not likely to 'off' any organ donors still alive. Given their blood types, they are far too valuable a commodity. Instead, he will take them away with him, and, as Miss Finch said, if *you*, Phillips, don't get after them *now*, we will have missed our one shot at saving them—"

"And will have sentenced them to horrible, unthinkable deaths," Miss Finch finished for him.

Phillips swallowed hard and admitted to his agreement. "We cannot wait."

"No, sir, you cannot," Miss Finch murmured. "Indeed, *you must hurry*."

Phillips got on his radio and mustered his crew, pulling all but one of his men into the van now parked across the street. Minutes later, the van tore away from the scene, leaving the crime scene techs, the bodies, and Ebanee and Ayla in the care of the officer he'd left behind.

Simon breathed his relief. "He's going!"

"Not without us, he is not!" Miss Finch threw over her shoulder, halfway to Grayson's car where he had parked it in front of the neighbors' house. "Come, Simon! Hurry!"

Simon realized with a start, *What? If I don't hustle, she's going to leave me behind?*

He plucked up his flagging energy and hobbled after her, arriving at Grayson's car to the sound of the passenger front door slamming shut on Miss Finch's one-word command to Grayson, "Go!"

Simon yanked the back door open and threw himself inside, breathing hard, head pounding, ribs protesting.

"I like how precisely you're following your doctor's orders," Grayson said slyly, pulling away from the curb.

"Oh, stuff a sock in it! And while you're at it, stomp on that gas pedal, Grayson."

"Roger that." To Miss Finch, Grayson asked, "Where to, once I clear this neighborhood and hit Emerald Bay Road?"

"Left. Emerald Bay Road becomes West Lake Boulevard. Once you clear Tahoe City, it becomes North Lake Boulevard or California State Route 28 all the way into Incline Village where it becomes Tahoe Boulevard. At the roundabout you'll take a left onto 431. After that, I'll direct you."

Grayson drove, pushing the speed limit as they skirted the lake shore, ignoring the two-lane road's double yellow line to pass slower cars, knowing the SWAT van was ahead of them, doing the same thing, probably faster, with lights and siren.

Miss Finch studied the map surrounding the target location until she had a thorough grasp of it. "The property's driveway slants away from the road below it, and the driveway is about a quarter of a mile long. It looks to be the only way up to the house from the road. If Phillips gets there before the gang boss pulls out, he can block them in. The only means of escape at that point would be on foot."

For Simon, the drive was interminable and frustrating. Finally, he calmed and began to pray.

Lord God, I don't believe you led us into this investigation to fail. In fact, I believe you want Caesar Morales and little Allysson to be rescued. But before I pray over this situation and over Phillips and his team, I first want to thank you for what you have already done.

Lord, you saved Sophie from these wicked people, and I will never stop being grateful for your grace and mercy over that child. You know I love her, my God. Thank you for keeping her safe.

Father, you also saved Ebanee and Ayla from the hands of this Chinese gang. How I thank you for your great mercy over them! I also pray you make an opportunity for us, BeeDee and me, to tell them both how much you love them and share with them how you proved your love by sending your only Son to rescue them from sin and death.

Simon let his pounding head fall back on the seat's headrest. *Now, Almighty God, this is just me, just Simon, but I am going to pray boldly over this situation and ask you to move with power over Phillips and his team. Right now, I call upon you in Jesus' mighty name to place your hand upon the coming action and orchestrate it for your glory and honor. Phillips' men are weary, Lord, and a few are wounded, but they are eager to see justice done and innocent lives saved.*

*Therefore, I pray right now that you put your heavy hand upon what remains of this Chinese gang's presence here in our beautiful lake area. I'm asking that you prevent them from escaping, that they will be bottled up at this house BeeDee has identified as our original killer's home. I ask that you allow Phillips' team to apprehend or take down **all** those behind these monstrous crimes but preserve every innocent life.*

See, Lord? I said I would pray boldly, and it's a pretty big ask, right? But I ask these big things of you because I trust you. I trust your word, I trust your heart, and I trust your justice. And Lord? I pray this all in Jesus' mighty, powerful, and beautiful name. Amen.

They reached Crystal Bay, then the outskirts of Incline Village, and finally the roundabout that spit them out onto 431 or Mount Rose Highway. Immediately, the road widened considerably and climbed steadily upward, first northeast, then more directly north.

Around seven miles later, Miss Finch declared, "We're very close now!" Her voice betrayed her excitement.

"Yeah, and we've got company," Grayson muttered. He slowed and eased over onto the wide bike lane.

Simon heard it then, the insistent warble of multiple sirens. Four cruisers belonging to the Washoe County Sheriff's Department flew by them, lights flashing and sirens blaring. An ambulance followed directly behind.

"Good! Phillips has called out reinforcements," Miss Finch muttered. She reached for her phone, hit the number for Phillips' cell, and put it on speakerphone.

Simon was frankly amazed that Phillips actually picked up.

"Miss Finch?"

"Have you bottled them up?"

"Just missed the first vehicle, but t-boned the second as it was leaving the driveway. We have the driver and a passenger, both appearing to be Chinese nationals, in custody, and have dispatched two sheriff's cruisers to pursue the vehicle we missed."

"And Morales and Sharma?"

They could hear relief bubbling in Phillips' voice. "You were right. They were in the trunk of the second vehicle, being spirited away. But we have them, both alive."

"Hallelujah! Thank the Lord! What about the evidence? And the others left at the house?"

"We're heading up to the house now. Gotta go."

"Take the next left," Miss Finch directed Grayson.

Grayson turned and wound his way up that road. He didn't have to be told when the target's driveway came into view: A sheriff's cruiser, LED light bars flashing on its roof, was parked across it.

Miss Finch jumped from Grayson's car the moment it came to a complete stop. She jogged to the deputy standing behind his cruiser's open door.

"Miss BD Finch, Simon Fletcher, and our security guard. Officer Phillips is expecting us."

Simon was again amazed when the deputy nodded, got in his car, and backed it out of the way.

Miss Finch climbed back into Grayson's car, and he drove up the long drive where it ended at a circular turnaround in front of a large and imposing house. A sheriff's cruiser was parked where the drive emptied into the turnaround, but they saw no deputies. The SWAT van sat just past the front entrance, and the ambulance that had passed them earlier was parked behind the van. The ambulance had its rear doors wide open, and two individuals sat on the ambulance's rear step while paramedics examined them.

Grayson parked away from the official vehicles. "Don't see any LEOs out here. Everyone must be inside," he murmured.

Miss Finch didn't answer; she got out without a word and made a beeline for the ambulance. Simon hustled along behind her as quick as he could. He was panting when he reached the ambulance. Miss Finch was waiting for him to catch up.

She was smiling a great, wide smile that showed off all her small white teeth. She turned toward Simon, her smile a beacon of joy. He grinned back.

She addressed the paramedics. "May we have a moment, please?"

The two paramedics, a man and a woman, stepped aside.

Miss Finch then addressed herself to the young man and much younger girl seated on the ambulance's rear step.

"Mr. Morales? Miss Sharma?"

The young man, outwardly healthy in most respects, shook uncontrollably. He did not look up. Indeed, he seemed unable to respond.

Miss Finch's smile softened, became conciliatory. "Please do not be afraid, Mr. Morales. We know what you have suffered . . . and what they intended to do. You are among friends now. Those wicked people will never harm or threaten you again."

Simon had seen broken men in the military, those wounded by war in heart and mind. He saw the same in the man before him.

Caesar Morales, age 22, taken by surprise while mountain biking, had been kept prisoner for six weeks. During his captivity, he had likely overheard his captors discuss in unguarded, unsympathetic conversations, their barbaric plans for him. Had likely seen two of his fellow captives taken away, never to return.

The shattered young man began to moan, to rock forward and back. His moan became a great, shuddering wail, so desperate and wracked with pain, it made the hair on Simon's arms and the back of his neck prickle and stand straight up.

Simon had a sudden image of Sophie in his mind, how she, but for the grace of God, could have easily been sitting here with Caesar and Allysson. Into that image rolled a flood of compassion and an overflow of love. He couldn't stop what he did next. Despite his own pains, miniscule compared to Morales' agony, he did what was needed, what was necessary and life-saving.

He squatted before Morales and put both arms around the young man.

"You are all right, Caesar," he murmured. "And you will *be* all right. I want you to know how much Jesus loves you, how he led us to find you and help you get free, all because he loves you."

Morales caved within Simon's arms—and as weak as Simon was, he should have fallen backward. But someone put a knee in Simon's back and leaned forward, his added weight keeping Simon from falling backward. The knee at Simon's back stayed where it was while Morales gave way to the grief and fear and trauma within him, until the man was empty, and the paramedics intervened to get him on a gurney.

A hand reached out to Simon to help him stand. Simon grabbed onto it, for his legs were too weak and shaky for him to stand without help. Simon looked up as he was pulled to standing.

"Well done," Grayson whispered, tears standing in his eyes . . . eyes that were hungry.

Simon nodded. "To God be all the glory. When . . . when this is over, can we talk?"

Grayson slowly exhaled. "Yes."

Simon got his legs under him and looked around. Allysson Sharma stared fixedly at him. Miss Finch, from a foot away glanced at the girl, then back to Simon.

Allysson, whose family had described her as a shy twelve-year-old, swallowed, and lifted her arms to Simon. "Can you . . . please?"

Simon staggered, but moved toward Allysson and held out his arms. "This? You would like me to hug you?"

She didn't answer. She came off the ambulance's step and barreled into him, sobbing, wailing, clutching him, burrowing into him, and Simon thanked God in that moment for his broad shoulders and thick, muscled arms. He held her, pouring into her ears and her heart the same comforting words he'd poured into Caesar's. He let her weep until she exhausted herself.

He gently pulled back. "Allysson, I promise you that I am your friend. If you call me, I will answer. If you need to talk, I will listen. If you want me to pray with you, I will. Anytime. Anywhere."

She clutched him again. "Thank you. Thank you!"

Eventually, one of the paramedics said, "We'd like to get on the road with these two. I understand Allysson's parents are meeting us at the hospital and they are . . . anxious."

"Ready to go see your mom and dad?" Simon asked Allysson.

"Oh, yes! But I don't even know your name."

Miss Finch reached out her hand to Allysson. "This is my card, dear girl. I have written Simon's name and number on the back."

Allysson took the card with trembling fingers. "Thank you . . . Simon. Thank you both for finding us. They were going to—" Her throat seized up and she could not finish.

Miss Finch nodded. "We know what they planned to do; I thank the Lord for saving you from their evil intentions. As Simon said, they will never bother you again. Now, go to your mom and dad. They will be so happy to see you."

The paramedics took charge, and moments later, the ambulance rolled away, leaving the three of them in holy silence.

It was Grayson who finally broke their reverie. "We don't know what they've found inside."

Miss Finch exhaled. "Let's go find out."

THE INSIDE OF the house was eerily quiet, and the stone-paved foyer echoed with their footsteps. The foyer led to a living room of fantastic proportions with an unimpeded view of the mountainside spread out below. From there, without saying a word, the three of them wandered in different directions but not out of earshot from the others.

Simon found the dining room, then an enormous kitchen with a commercial gas range, a commercial refrigerator, a walk-in freezer, and two separate sink areas. His entire cabin could have fit into that kitchen.

"Simon, Grayson, come here, please."

Miss Finch stood in a doorway at the far end of the living room. She stepped aside to let them look inside.

It was a hospital room, softened by artful décor: flowing, colorful curtains, lovely wallpaper, a loveseat with decorative pillows, a corner net overflowing with stuffed animals . . . but the centerpiece of the room was a hospital bed in which lay a young man, perhaps near the same age as Caesar Morales.

Simon noted an IV tree and heart monitor on one side of the bed. An active ventilator and another machine, this one switched off, occupied space on the other side.

Simon walked over and looked closely at the patient. What he saw . . . or rather, what he intuited, was not favorable.

"Is he . . . ?" he asked Miss Finch, his voice low.

A woman's voice behind them caught them unaware; they whirled about, Grayson automatically reaching for his concealed semiauto.

"He is . . . brain dead, I am afraid," the woman answered quietly.

"Who are you, and where did you come from?" Grayson demanded.

"Dr. Helen Reilly. I came from there." She tipped her head, gesturing behind her. She was in her mid-forties or a perhaps little older, her hair an artful, multifaceted palette of reds that only wealth could maintain, her face and figure belying her age, aided, no doubt, by the best of treatments. And yet, her gesture was that of a woman who no longer cared.

Simon stared in the direction of her gesture. Something was "off" about that corner of the room. Then he saw it, the cracks so cleverly concealed in the wallpapered corner, that only with the door left marginally ajar, did the door's outline become noticeable.

"What is that?" he asked.

"The door that leads to one of two panic rooms I had built into our home when we came here," the woman murmured. "The second is upstairs, hidden within my bedroom's walk-in closet. Those . . . people knew nothing of these rooms, of course, so when I heard the shouted orders and screams an hour or two ago, I hid myself. I watched what they did on the camera system inside the room."

She looked away. "They shot the remainder of my staff. All of them. The surgical staff, my personal assistant, my gardener. Even my housekeeper. She had been with me fifteen years."

"The Chinese killed them?" Miss Finch asked.

"Yes."

"When did they arrive?"

"Two days ago. Saturday. I had security guards and other men, but . . ."

"By 'other men' you mean hired muscle like Jürgen Münster and his partner, the men who tried to kidnap Sophie?"

She nodded. "Münster and Gliese, both supposedly high-dollar experts in their field."

Simon's words were toneless. "Right. Münster and his pal—expert kidnappers. You also sent them to the hospital to kill me—so you could take another crack at Sophie Nadeau."

"No, I did not send them. Münster had an overinflated ego and a decidedly nasty habit of disobeying orders. Apparently you bruised his fragile ego, so he went after you on his own."

"Oh? And yet you managed to clean up after him quickly enough."

"I had to. When Gliese returned alone, saying Münster was either dead or captured, I had to move quickly to protect my . . . investment here. I paid dearly for other 'experts' Gliese recommended to clean up Münster's mess—his quite *expensive* mess."

Miss Finch continued softly. "But you say the Chinese rolled in the next day, Dr. Reilly? Saturday morning? Seems an unlikely coincidence."

The woman sighed. "I fear the 'others' I hired to clean up after Münster's debacle sold me out to the Chinese. *They* appeared Saturday morning out of nowhere, killed Gliese and my security team and took over everything. Everything! They wanted me to continue my . . . enterprise, at least in the near term, and required my team to do whatever was necessary to fulfill the transplant appointments already on the calendar."

She looked away, her voice extraordinarily calm, as though speaking of anything other than the cold-blooded murder of Caesar Morales and Allysson Sharma. "Then, this morning, something must have happened. Suddenly, their boss man started shouting frantic orders. I was here with Teddy when his people, including my assigned guard, started running around the house, doing whatever their boss demanded they do. It was when I heard shooting from the direction of the medical suite that I realized they were erasing their presence here and would be coming for me shortly. That was when I ducked into my panic room."

She laughed, the sound brittle and hard. "So, when they searched for me, they could not find me. They wasted a great deal of time hunting me until their boss insisted they leave before the police arrived."

"Speaking of the police and deputies, where might we find them?" Miss Finch asked softly.

"Across the backyard," the woman said. "In the medical wing, where those men . . ."

"Where the Chinese gathered and shot the remainder of your staff?"

"Yes. Everyone except my two remaining patients. They took them away with them."

Simon's mouth opened on an outraged retort, but Miss Finch gently elbowed him while pointing to the hospital bed.

"And who is this young man?"

"My son, Theodore. Teddy." She shrugged and stared unblinking at her son. "I have done . . . many things to give Teddy a second chance at life, but while his body accepted his new heart, and he showed every sign of improvement and recovery, he quite unexpectedly suffered a series of strokes. That was just two days before the Chinese arrived . . ."

"Is that," Miss Finch pointed to the inactive machine beside the bed, "an electroencephalogram machine?"

"Yes. The EEG proved what I already knew: Even though Teddy's new heart is still strong and beating well, his brain did not survive the strokes. He could no longer breathe on his own."

She shook her head, her words measured, objective, and dispassionate. "I would have disconnected him . . . but that awful man, their boss, would not allow me to. He thought to treat Teddy as a donor, like one of my patients."

"Wait. That's the second time you've referred to 'your patients,'" Simon growled. "Are you calling Caesar and Allysson *your patients?*"

She shrugged. "I am a doctor."

"*Really?* What happened to *first do no harm!*" Simon shouted.

She turned a cold eye on him, her dispassion falling from her like a sheet of ice slipping from a window. "I needed them. My *son* needed them. *Their* lives were common and mediocre, but Teddy was brilliant. *He deserved to live!*"

A red mist clouded Simon's eyes. "Tell that to the families of Donald Whatley and Haoyu Xú," he shouted louder, "because I'm certain they would tell you *their* sons deserved to live every bit as much as yours did, *you butcher!*"

"Ah, there you are." Jonas Phillips' calm, professional presence stood in the doorway, eyeing the doctor. "Been looking for you, Dr. Reilly."

"Have you?"

"Yes. Property records can be helpful police identification tools. Next time? Use a shell company."

"I will keep that in mind. Did any of the Chinese gang members escape?"

"Not a one. We stopped the second car before they exited your driveway, and the sheriff's department caught up with the first car and the deputies nabbed the gang's boss."

"I am pleased to hear that. Tell me about the fire in my medical suite? I was watching the video from my panic room, but the suite's camera feed went out before I could ascertain the fire's outcome."

"Looks like the Chinese intended to burn your 'medical suite' and the eleven bodies they shot and left there. They, however, hadn't reckoned on your automatic sprinkler system."

He shrugged and smiled. "Although we will certainly lose some of the evidence of your crimes due to smoke and water damage, I believe we can salvage enough to find you guilty of kidnapping, a couple of counts of first-degree murder, and a wide variety of other felonies."

Reilly's expression slackened in dumbfounded amazement, as if she had never considered the consequences of her actions, but Phillips' next words really threw her.

"So, it's really too bad for you that you built your house in *Nevada*, and not in California, Dr. Reilly. California, of course, enacted a moratorium on the death penalty in 2019. The State of Nevada, on the other hand, still holds to death by lethal injection—although a shortage of the execution drugs seems to be holding things up." He shrugged. "Perhaps they'll make an exception for you, because, after your execution, you too could donate your organs to deserving candidates."

Phillips stepped aside. "Crutchfield? Benson? Take dear Dr. Mengele into custody."

"My pleasure," Crutchfield muttered.

Helen Reilly seemed to waken from her daze. "Wait. One moment, if you please. I want . . . I need to say goodbye to Teddy. Please! I beg you!"

Phillips studied her. "I wonder . . . did Xú beg you for his life? Did Donald Whatley?"

His eyes shifted to Miss Finch, then the hospital bed. "What's with the patient there?"

Miss Finch cleared her throat. "The young man is Dr. Reilly's son, Teddy, the recipient, I believe, of Mr. Xú's heart. Sadly, Teddy suffered several strokes and is brain dead. I believe Dr. Reilly wishes to say goodbye and switch off the machines."

Crutchfield swelled with indignation. "You haven't seen her little house of horrors across the way, have you? She doesn't deserve any such special consideration."

Phillips frowned. "What do you think, Miss Finch?"

"Oh, I think Dr. Reilly deserves the full, unmitigated consequences of her heinous actions. That said, if you are asking my opinion concerning Dr. Reilly's request, I would say that an act of kindness in this moment might, with time and thought, result in repentance down the road. It is not about deserving such a kindness, of course, for surely she does not deserve it. Then again, I did not deserve the kindness of Christ either."

Phillips exhaled and, clearly conflicted, his hands went to his hips.

"Boss! You're not going to listen to her, are you?" Crutchfield expostulated. "You saw the restraints and the cells they kept those kids in, didn't you? Why does she get to say goodbye to her kid when the parents of those young men she killed did not?"

Helen Reilly frowned and blinked at Miss Finch. "Why are you advocating for me?"

"I am advocating for a single, simple act of kindness in the face of your unspeakably wretched acts."

"But he," Reilly pointed at Crutchfield, "is right. Even though I am begging to be allowed to say goodbye to my son, I don't deserve any favors."

"And that, right there, is the gospel of Jesus Christ in a nutshell," Miss Finch murmured. "He offers what we do not deserve, and *it is his kindness that leads us to repentance*, repentance being an old-fashioned word meaning an acknowledgement of and sorrow for our sins and a complete turning away from them."

The woman's frown deepened.

"Dr. Reilly, Jesus offers you a forgiveness that we, those who are privy to your barbarism and the pain you have caused, have been commanded to also give you in Jesus' name, even if you do not as yet acknowledge your guilt. Frankly, I do not *feel* like forgiving you. However, I choose to do so, and I hope you will think on Jesus and what he offers you in the days ahead . . . while you are tried and found guilty by a jury of your peers."

Crutchfield spoke up again. "Can't her kid's organs be used by those who need them? Seems to me that would be fitting."

The woman spoke up. "You cannot get permission from him . . . and I will not give it in his place."

"That's not fair!" Crutchfield roared. "Boss? Boss!"

Phillips, with a sour twist of his mouth, made up his mind. "Sadly, she's right. *We* have to follow the law. Benson, escort the doctor to that bed and let her say goodbye to her son. But make it snappy."

"Well, excuse me while I step outside and throw up," Crutchfield snarled.

Dr. Helen Reilly, with Benson's meaty hand wrapped firmly about her upper arm, went to her son's side, touched his cheek once, hesitated, then switched off the ventilator. The sudden silence in the room was short, displaced almost immediately by the heart monitor's alarms as the patient flatlined. Reilly, tears running down her face, turned the heart monitor off too.

As Benson pulled her away from the bed, Simon hung his head and confronted his own anger.

*Lord, this-this-this **creature**—this child of hell!—would have killed Cae-sar and Allysson without a flicker of remorse. Dear God, she would have killed Sophie, too . . . or worse. Not to mention that she hired Münster, a psychopath, regardless of whether or not she gave him the order to kill me.*

He stood there, wrestling with his grief and fury, long after everyone else had left the room. Everyone but Miss Finch. She said nothing, but she waited with him while he fought his battle.

Oh Jesus, Jesus! I confess that this is the hardest thing you have ever asked me to do.

Finally, he sighed and acquiesced. He set his will to make a choice that had nothing to do with the rage coursing through his blood, nothing at all to do with his emotions or his sense of right and wrong.

I will do what you ask of me, my God, regardless of how I feel.

*I will do it—I **can** do it—but I confess I can only do it because you did the same for me.*

The TAHOE MYSTERIES

CHAPTER 32

THURSDAY, JULY 22

OFFICER GEORGIO SHOWED Simon and Miss Finch into a South Lake Tahoe PD interview room. Moments later, Phillips and the station commander joined them. No one spoke for a moment while Phillips' boss took the measure of his guests.

"Miss Finch, Mr. Fletcher, I'm David Ulibarri, SLTPD station commander," he finally said. "Thank you both for coming in today. I'm hoping you can clarify a few details for us concerning this . . . unusual case."

He looked at his notes and frowned. "Although, it bears noting that this is not the first unusual case that has brought you to our attention."

Miss Finch cocked her head to one side. "Oh? Unusual cases that brought *us* to your attention? Do you perhaps mean the precise opposite, that we brought the unusual cases to *your* attention?"

Ulibarri's expression did not change. "I said what I said." He waited, looking from Miss Finch to Simon and back. "Well?"

"I apologize," Miss Finch murmured, her face heating, "but was there a question buried in that backhanded accusation?"

Ulibarri snorted. "So it's like that, is it?"

"Like what?" Simon intervened. "You asked us to come. Here we are. We're happy to help where we can."

"Fine. How did you know the lake area was home to a criminal organ-harvesting operation?"

"Pardon me," Miss Finch said, still hot under the collar, "but I had not, until just now, heard of the *non*criminal sort of organ-harvesting operation. Is that a relatively new trend?"

Simon's foot connected with the one dangling from Miss Finch's chair. *You promised you wouldn't cause trouble, lady.*

She did not react.

Ulibarri flushed. "My mistake. Please answer the question."

"I am a private detective licensed in both California and Nevada, Commander Ulibarri. I have cultivated some resources and admit to a few technological advantages, including one that, on a daily basis, feeds me online news articles selected according to the keywords and phrases I provide. The search terms turned up articles on three persons missing from around the lake area over a period of six weeks. Since the young men went missing from widely differing locations and jurisdictions around the lake, their disappearances went largely unnoticed by law enforcement and media alike."

"And that led you to an organ harvesting scheme how?"

"It was not their disappearances," Miss Finch said softly, "but rather the condition of Mr. Xú's body, the first of the three to disappear and the first to be found."

Ulibarri's eyes narrowed. "Although his death was ruled a homicide, the exact details of his autopsy were not released to the public . . . not until someone recently leaked those details to the media."

Miss Finch maintained a slightly quizzical air, as if waiting for him to say more.

"Have you nothing to say, Miss Finch?"

"Oh, dear. I was anticipating another question."

"Fine! Try this: How did the press find out the results of Mr. Xú's autopsy?"

"Well! You can hardly expect such lurid information to remain a secret for long, can you? Although, I do believe such information should be public knowledge."

"That is not an answer."

"Begging your pardon, but in response to your rude and unwarranted aggression, it is the only answer I shall make."

Ulibarri swiveled in his seat and glared at Phillips. "I thought you said she's been cooperative."

"She has been, sir. Very helpful."

"Indeed, I have been inclined to be cooperative and helpful," Miss Finch chimed in. "I have just now, however, reached the terminus of that helpful inclination."

Simon's neck cracked as he swung around to stare at her.

Ulibarri reddened. "You refuse to cooperate further?"

"Well done! You have grasped my meaning." Miss Finch smiled as if pleased with him.

As if, Simon snarked to himself.

Certainly, Ulibarri was not pleased with *her*. "That's it; I'm done. Phillips? You're up. If you cannot pry anything useful from either of them, cut them loose. We have too much on our plates right now as it is. What a waste of time!"

He stormed from the room, slamming the door on his way out.

Phillips' mouth twisted in chagrin. "Was it your intention to torpedo my relationship with my boss or is it merely a casualty of the clash between his boorish behavior and your winning personality?"

"The latter, Officer Phillips. I do, however, feel you owe me the courtesy of answering a few of *my* questions."

"*I* owe *you?*"

"Well, yes. Mr. Fletcher and I did put you onto this case to start with, and we have included you in its progress all along the way. I should think that our cooperation would guarantee *some* measure of reciprocity."

Phillips closed his notebook and sighed. "Fine. Whatever. Ask away."

"Tell us more about Dr. Reilly."

"Brilliant woman. Physician. Widowed twelve years ago. Only child, a son named Theodore. Wealthy in her own right . . . although she does appear to have tapped out her fortune over the past year."

"I must assume one tends to do so when building and equipping a state-of-the-art surgical suite on one's own property," Miss Finch murmured, "not to mention the ongoing expense of qualified staff willing to commit the unthinkable—said staff including specialized medical personnel, contract kidnappers and killers, and general, all-around, miscellaneous criminally skilled elements."

She sighed. "What else do you have?"

"What do you mean, what else? That's about it."

"I did request *more* about Dr. Reilly, Officer Phillips. You gave us nothing my tech team had not already provided."

"Well, excuse me!"

"You are excused. Moving on. Were you able to crack Dr. Reilly's computer system and extract a list of individuals who benefitted from the deaths of Mr. Xú and Mr. Whatley?"

"We seized the hard drives and other evidence found at Reilly's residence, of course. Predictably, the FBI has ordered us to surrender everything we have to them, and we will, possibly later today."

"Understood, but were you, by chance, able to crack the drives, perhaps come across future 'bookings' for organ transplants?"

Phillips pursed his lips and slow-walked his response. "I shouldn't tell you this, of course, and if you ever mention that I did, I'll deny it, but . . ."

"But what?" Simon demanded.

"Let's just say that late last night, we perused Dr. Reilly's schedule, and took special note of two surgical dates blocked out—both days quite long. The first date is this coming Thursday, day after tomorrow. The second date is next Friday. We have apprised the FBI of this info, and I have the sense they will be waiting for those organ recipients and those accompanying them at whichever Tahoe airport or airstrip they arrive."

An image of Caesar Morales and Allysson Sharma, saved from horrifying deaths, sitting on the ambulance's rear step rose in Simon's mind, and his breath whooshed out. "Such a close thing. So very, very close."

Miss Finch nodded. "Indeed. To God be the glory."

"Amen."

Miss Finch addressed Phillips again. "Now, about the Chinese villains you arrested. What is their status at present?"

Phillips barked a wry laugh. "I suppose I'd want to know that too if I were you, seeing as how, in unmistakable terms, their head honcho promised you an unsavory end—and a quite colorful one, I might add."

"Yes, their threats are concerning. They are where, at present?"

"The FBI Sacramento field office has taken over this case, and the 'villains,' as you labeled them, have been remanded, without bail, to federal lockup in California pending trial. Not," Phillips added, "that any one of their pals or associates couldn't or wouldn't do the job for them."

As an afterthought, he said, "I find it interesting that this branch of Chinese organized crime is the *second* gangland family you've ticked off in recent memory. Careful with these Chinese gangsters, or you'll make the Lucchese Family jealous."

He laughed again, then added more soberly, "You know that saying, 'the enemy of my enemy is my friend'? If these two criminal organizations ever decide to make nice with each other, I'd watch out."

"Your advice is noted," Miss Finch sniffed. "Now, about the Nadeaus' fifth wheel. Did you look up its VIN as Mr. Fletcher requested?"

"Tell me why it matters, and I will tell you what we found."

"Very well. Mr. Fletcher could not make sense of it, and when he explained his conundrum, I agreed. His problem was a practical one: How could the means of enticing the Nadeaus to Tahoe cost as much or more than what our pathological yet financially strapped Doctor Reilly would profit from selling Sophie's blood, even over time? Her ROI would have been nonexistent."

Phillips blinked once. Twice. "Wow. Did not . . . You're right. The Nadeaus' rig is a cool half mil on the showroom floor."

He nodded to himself. "Downright clever of Dr. Reilly."

"We might be inclined to agree with you—should you actually share what you have found."

"Right. Well, it's like this: The VIN on the Nadeaus' RV doesn't belong to their RV. Someone swapped its VIN with an nearly identical model, one a bit older and already paid off in full."

Simon frowned. "Wait. How does that work, exactly?"

"Like this: Dr. Reilly had one of her people purchase the Nadeaus' RV on a monthly payment basis—the lowest possible monthly payment they could manage—and her guy made two payments in advance. I doubt they intended to make further payments since the account was closed immediately after the first two payments were made."

Simon said, "But . . ."

"But, the VIN on the Nadeaus' rig actually belongs to a totally unencumbered RV?" Miss Finch suggested.

Phillips nodded. "Yup. No loan, no payments. Using that VIN, Dr. Reilly produced a phony bill of sale so they could register the RV in Lucas and Eva Nadeaus' names. The Nadeaus, in turn, purchased insurance, and with valid registration and insurance, had few difficulties bringing the RV across the border into the US."

"So some owner in Canada has a fully-paid-off RV sitting in his driveway, but according to their RV's VIN number, he owes the bank big time?"

"Looks that way, but now that we've opened that can of worms, the Canadian authorities are all over the situation. The bank, once informed, may send a repo man to Bright Star, let the Nadeaus know they've been hornswoggled, and haul that fifth wheel out from under them."

He shook his head. "Dastardly. Brilliant, yes, but wicked to the core."

Miss Finch thought for a moment. "Mr. Fletcher and I are still left wondering why Dr. Reilly didn't dispatch Münster and his partner to Canada and simply kidnap Sophie. Why the convoluted plot to lure Sophie's family here?"

Phillips shrugged. "Your guess is as good as mine."

Simon spoke up. "I've thought about it quite a bit and have come up with a couple of plausible explanations. The first is that Dr. Reilly, for all her coldblooded actions, is still pretty new and inexperienced at this 'being a criminal' thing.

"And then I thought, what if? What if she had sent Münster to kidnap Sophie in Canada? Both Canada and the US have Amber Alert systems, and Münster would have needed to transport Sophie around forty-six hundred miles from Laval to Lake Tahoe. That's maybe a week on the road with a kid—and with the police and the public at large hunting for Sophie. I mean, what if Sophie got sick? Say, her anemia worsened?"

Miss Finch nodded thoughtfully. "You may be on to something, Fletcher. Münster would have had to go through a US-Canada border checkpoint twice, and he has a record that would have flagged him as a person of interest. I cannot see him agreeing to that plan. He was too much of a pro to make that play."

Simon added, "Well, I think Reilly's determination to get Sophie despite the expense tells us something else."

Miss Finch's eyes narrowed. "Oh?"

"As much as I hate to think of this, when you told Ebanee and Ayla that the Chinese would likely use Ayla for her golden blood, then eventually use her for rare-blood organ donation? I began to think Reilly planned do the same to Sophie. Reilly was all about the money. Making a profit to recoup the expenses for her son's heart transplant . . . maybe planning to turn her little operation into a major endeavor."

Just putting his suspicions into words sent a shaft of pain into Simon's heart, and he grimaced. And then, he felt a very small hand come to rest on his and offer a gentle squeeze.

"She is all right, Simon. Safe."

"Thank you," he whispered.

Phillips hadn't noticed the exchange. "Well, whatever Dr. Reilly's rationale for choosing to lure the Nadeaus to Bright Star, and for what it's worth, I feel bad for this family. They can't seem to catch a break."

"Oh, I have a sense their fortunes are turning," Miss Finch murmured. She gathered her handbag and stood. Simon joined her.

"Wait. What does that mean, 'their fortunes are turning?'"

"I am sorry, Officer Phillips, but the Nadeau family deserves some semblance of privacy, do you not agree?"

———— ◦ ————

AS THEY LEFT the police station, Simon was still mentally sorting details and tying up more loose ends.

"Say, do we know how Sam Redwine got caught up in this mess and why he would rat us out?"

"Ah, that. Yes, I received a text from my tech team last evening. Those enterprising young people found that Sam enjoys the occasional low-stakes poker game. However, it appears he visited one of the Stateline casinos and was lured into a private game where he lost a substantial amount of money— all planned and executed by Dr. Reilly's 'hired muscle.'"

Simon nodded. "That explains why Redwine needed some side jobs."

"Moreover, it explains his perfidy—why, in response to my little masquerade as Sophie, he called and reported that she was still at Bright Star. Mr. Redwine did not want his wife to know the extent of his losses, and Dr. Reilly's thugs threatened to tell her if he did not keep them apprised of our dear Sophie's whereabouts."

"Had to have also been Sam Redwine who tipped them off about our early morning bike ride Wednesday, eight days back, the day Münster and pal tried to take Sophie?"

"Indubitably."

"Gotta say, that stings a little. No, a lot, actually. Do you think he also told Münster's boss where to find me when I was in the hospital and Münster tried to kill me?"

"Unknown, but we must certainly talk to Mr. Redwine soon. You can play the bad cop to my good cop."

Simon chuckled. "Riiight, except I think you play a more convincing bad cop than I ever could."

Then he turned inward. "*Huh!* I just thought of something. The evening Redwine called to report your 'bike-ride masquerade' as Sophie? The Chinese had already horned in on Dr. Reilly's operation, and Redwine's call was answered by the guards at Ebanee's house, right?"

Miss Finch, her eyes on the road, nodded.

Simon became very excited. "So . . . wow. Think it through, BeeDee. Everything that's happened in the last, what, twenty-four hours? Just that *one detail*, Redwine's call, cracked open our case. I mean, listen: If that gang boss hadn't decided to use the guards at Ebanee's as a cutout to protect himself—in other words, if he hadn't told the guards to answer Redwine's call, exactly as you theorized, by the way—and if your tech team hadn't been able to identify the location of the phone that received Redwine's call, and then if we hadn't called Phillips to bring SWAT to the house, and one of those guards hadn't managed to pop off a distress signal to the boss just as the SWAT team hit Ebanee's house, and if Mr. Boss Man hadn't sent reinforcements to rescue his henchmen—"

"For heaven's sake, Fletcher! Take a breath. Can't have you stroking out."

"Whatever. Pay attention here: If the boss hadn't sent a team to attack us and shoot it out with SWAT, then you would not have had the attackers' phones and been able to extract the mapping data from their phones' apps, meaning we may not have located Dr. Reilly's lair for days longer . . . most likely too late to save Caesar and Allysson. Do you see? Sam Redwine's call triggered it all."

Miss Finch's brows knit together. "Fletcher, you are absolutely right. That entire chain of events began with Sam Redwine's call."

"Yup. Hard to be mad at Sam now, right?"

"In fact, you have summed up the grace of God in operation over these last several days, Fletcher, and his ways are awesome. Some may say, 'the devil is in the details,' but for us who believe and who pray, it is *God*, by his Holy Spirit, who frustrates the plans of the wicked and leads us to victory."

"Right on. Say, speaking of the wicked, I feel a bit naked since losing my gun—or rather since SLTPD lost my gun, which is actually a blessing since, if they can't produce my gun, they also can't charge me with possessing and discharging a weapon within a restricted area."

She sniffed. "Hardly matters at the moment. The Ninth Circuit court upheld the preliminary injunctions on carry bans in hospital and medical facilities."

"What? It *isn't* illegal to carry in a hospital? And you're just telling me this now?"

"I only found out myself. It is a preliminary, thus *temporary*, injunction that may be withdrawn at a later date when the court rules on the case."

"Still need a replacement gun, and since they lost it, SLTPD should pay for it, right?"

Simon looked at the scenery as they passed by and shook his head slowly, amazed once more at the goodness of the Lord. They had left Emerald

Bay Road, the turnoff to Bright Star not far ahead when he realized Miss Finch had gone quiet.

"Hey, what are you thinking about?"

"What am I thinking? Oh, I am considering Phillips' warnings about the Lucchese Family and this offshoot of some second-rate Chinese organized crime gang and that tired, prosaic quote, 'the enemy of my enemy is my friend.' I am pondering how those two organizations might choose to aid each other to a common end . . . getting rid of me."

Simon rubbed his eyes. *Great. Now my headache is back. Lord, I trust you, but would you mind sharing how you intend to extricate BeeDee from this mess?*

"Say, I forgot to tell you that Skipper's dad called him yesterday. He told me all about it last evening. "

When he didn't get a response, Simon added, "Listen, we don't have to rush back to Bright Star, do we? It's not as though I need to report for work, right? Want to go back into town and have lunch? My treat."

But she seemed distracted and testy. "Thank you, no. I have a book to finalize or . . ."

Her words drifted away. A minute later, she was back. And she was in a hurry.

"Where can I drop you?"

"Uhhh. Not my cabin, but the Nadeaus are back in their RV. How about the rec hall? It has a decent cushy chair and a TV and I could lay my head back and take a nap. But could we stop at my cabin first so I can pick up the lunch the Benowitz sisters dropped by this morning? I'm starving, and there's nothing to eat in the rec hall. Oh, and I might need some help navigating the steps up onto the island when we get there."

"Do make it quick, please; I have calls to make."

"What calls? You just said you needed to work on your book."

She didn't answer, and Simon could tell she'd 'checked out,' once again deep in thought.

No doubt hatching some new sort of trouble, Simon thought.

For surely trouble followed Miss Finch like sharks followed chum in the water.

What is going on inside that cute but devious little head of yours, BeeDee Finch? And don't think for a minute that you can box me out. Whether you like it or not, and whatever you're scheming, I'll be right there with you.

Partners all the way.

POSTSCRIPT

FRIDAY, JULY 25

LATE THAT EVENING, Miss Finch, with Simon beside her in the passenger seat of her woody and Lucas, Eva, and Sophie Nadeau in the rear seat, drove west toward a hotel in Tahoe City.

"Are you absolutely certain this is safe?" Lucas asked for the third time.

"Yes, indeed. Grayson and Alberto are already there. They have scoped out the hotel and have declared that our little gathering will be quite safe for all involved. And do remember, please, that you are not obligated in any manner."

"You say so," Eva whispered, "but Lucas and I have something of a deficit when it comes to trust these days." She sniffed. "Please do not get me wrong: I am grateful beyond belief that our family is safe and intact and that those who wished to take Sophie will never bother us again, but . . ."

"But the loss of both your RV and your remaining stay at Bright Star will sting considerably," Miss Finch answered. "Of course, we do not fault you for grieving those losses."

"Thank you for understanding! Since we cannot afford the outrageous payments on the RV, I suppose a week more at Bright Star must suffice for our little dream vacation before we return to Quebec and surrender our lovely fifth wheel to the bank there. It was nice of the bank's management, since we were as wronged as they were, to grant us that option."

They pulled up to the hotel and got out. Grayson met them. Regardless, Lucas and Eva held Sophie's hands as if they would never let go.

"You okay, Sophie?" Simon asked.

"Yes, but my hands feel awful squished."

The adults laughed, and the Nadeaus lessened their grip. A hair.

Ebanee and Ayla waited for them inside their hotel suite. The greetings were stiff and uncomfortable for both families, but eventually, Miss Finch coaxed the parties into seats around the suite's dining table.

"I have a juice box for you, if you'd like one," Ayla said to Sophie.

The two girls, one a healthy eight years of age, the other seventeen and sallow complexioned, studied each other.

"Yes, please," Sophie said at last.

"I can grab it," Alberto announced. "That way no one needs to get up."

He also brought glasses of ice for everyone and a pitcher of water, to go along with Sophie's juice box.

With Sophie sipping on apple-cranberry juice and studying the box, Miss Finch said quietly, "Ebanee, I believe you and Ayla said you have a proposition for Lucas, Eva, and Sophie?"

"Yes," Ebanee said, her voice barely above a whisper, "and we promise that we will, in no way, pressure you. We just . . . rather, we *hope* you will find our proposal amenable."

Lucas and Eva could scarcely meet Ebanee and Ayla's eyes. Everyone in the room, perhaps excepting Sophie, understood that if the Nadeaus rejected the Barkinjees' proposal, it meant Ayla's certain decline and eventual death.

Ebanee clasped her hands on the table top. "Before we start, we wish you to know that our family is fortunate to be well off. What we offer here today, we can afford."

She cleared her throat. "To begin, we wish you to know that our proposal has three parts. In the first part, we propose to fund Sophie's college savings account over the next ten years, adding the amount of twenty thousand Canadian dollars to it each year. She will be eighteen at that point and will be able to draw on the account semiannually during her university years. Whatever remains in the account when she turns twenty-five will be hers."

The astonishment on Lucas and Eva's faces drew a smile from Simon.

Lord, this could be a very good thing all around . . . but only if Sophie is willing. Not coerced or pressured.

Ebanee swallowed to clear her throat. "Secondly, we propose a schedule of one unit of fresh frozen glycerolized blood every eight to twelve weeks depending upon Sophie's health and her doctor's advice and starting, initially, with two units rather soon, before we go home. Thereafter, we will hire a courier, someone trained to transport preserved blood and who will pick up and deliver each unit to us. For each delivered unit, including the first two, we will deposit twenty thousand dollars in the account of your choosing."

Eva blanched and muttered, "Mon Dieu!"

Lucas, just as stunned, blurted, "But such money would be very difficult to-to explain, yes? The legalities! The taxes! Also Canada is not very friendly to people who receive regular cash gifts. Our government is quite suspicious of money laundering, and there are certain laws . . ."

"Our lawyers are versed in the legalities, Mr. Nadeau. In order to comply with the laws of both Australia and Canada, they recommend that you form a business, a corporation, as the proper means to receive and declare the income derived from our exchange and also to pay the taxes on it."

Things became quiet until Miss Finch said softly, "And the third part?"

"Yes, the third part. We will pay off the loan on your RV. It will be yours, paid in full."

"You would not," Ayla quickly added, "need to leave Bright Star sooner than you had planned."

Eva and Lucas seemed thunderstruck. Finally, Lucas shook his head. "I will agree to nothing our daughter does not wish to do. It must be Sophie's decision."

Ebanee, calm and stoic, nodded. "Of course."

Hearing her name, Sophie looked up from her juice box. "What is the blood for?"

Ebanee and Ayla averted their eyes and waited for Lucas or Eva to answer.

When they shrugged and said nothing, Ayla lifted her gaze to Sophie's and said, "It is for me, Sophie. You and I have the same kind of blood, very rare. And like you, I also have a problem called anemia, only my anemia is getting worse, and now I need transfusions. Our blood is so rare, however, that not many people in the whole world have it."

"Your anemia is worse than mine? Is it very bad?"

Simon watched Ayla attempt to soften her response. In the end, she was gentle but blunt.

"I need your blood so my anemia does not kill me."

"You will die if you cannot have my blood?"

Ayla couldn't look at Sophie. She nodded, just once.

Sophie stared at Ayla for a long time, and Simon had a sudden, jarring impression, the sense that Sophie had been engrossed in the colorful characters on her juice box and hadn't listened all that well to the preceding adult conversation. Had not, in fact, paid attention until Ayla spoke directly to her.

But she was paying attention now . . . and was deep in thought.

Finally Sophie whispered, "Ayla, I will give you my blood. You don't have to pay for it. I want to give it to you."

Ayla's mouth opened and closed, and Ebanee leaned toward Sophie.

"But it is only fair that we pay you, Sophie. It will help your parents now and pay for college later."

Sophie thought a moment. "Well, I would like to help Mama and Papa. And I know Wyatt and Eli will want to go to college." She slowly turned to her parents. "May I say goodbye to my brothers and to my friends at Bright Star first?"

The silence was so profound that Simon could hear the anxious thundering of his heart. He was the first to react.

"Sophie . . . what do you mean by 'say goodbye?'"

She blinked in surprise. "Because I'm going to give Ayla my blood, like Jesus did for me. You know? Like what Miss Finch talked about, when Jesus said, 'no greater love for your friends' in the Bible?"

All the air left Simon's lungs. Lucas started to say something. Miss Finch placed her hand on his arm and gently shushed him. "One moment, if you please."

Simon finally squeezed the words from his tight, airless throat. "Ah, I think I see."

Oh, dear God!

It took all his self-control not to break down. To squeeze out, "But Ayla won't need *all* of your blood, little pumpkin. Just a small amount every two or three months. And if you do give her some of your blood, why, your body will just make more for you. You would not run out of your own blood."

"Oh, that's good!" Sophie said, relieved and smiling. "I really wanted to stay longer at Bright Star. And I do want to belong to Jesus like you and Miss Finch do, so I can see you again someday. Can we do that part now?"

Simon felt the presence of the Holy Spirit descend so powerfully that his entire body felt weighted. Pressed. It was all he could do not to slide from his seat onto the floor and lie there in a puddle of worship.

"Are . . . are you saying you would like to make Jesus your Lord and Savior right now?"

"Yes, please. I don't always treat my brothers nice. I would like Jesus to forgive me. Oh. And I don't like that man who beat you up. I even wanted a bear to eat him."

She looked down, pink with embarrassment. "I really *did* want that bear to eat him. Will Jesus forgive me for that too?"

Simon glanced at Lucas and Eva. They were sobbing in each other's arms. Ebanee cradled her face in her hands, and Ayla rocked back and forth, weeping unabashedly.

Softly, Simon said, "Everyone? Sophie says she would like to ask Jesus to forgive her sins and proclaim him as her Lord and Savior. If anyone else would like to join her, feel free to pray with us."

Several others in that room responded, and Simon and Miss Finch were witnesses, not to death, but to the birth of new lives . . . and the overwhelming *joy* that follows after.

It was glorious.

The End

The TAHOE MYSTERIES

will return
October 2026!

ABOUT THE AUTHOR

VIKKI KESTELL'S passion for people and their stories is evident in her readers' affection for her characters and unusual plotlines. Two often-repeated sentiments are, "I feel like I know these people," and, "I'm right there, in the book, experiencing what the characters experience."

Vikki holds a PhD in organizational learning and instructional technologies. She left a career of twenty-plus years in government, academia, and corporate life to pursue writing full time. "Writing is the best job ever," she admits, "and the most demanding."

Vikki and her husband, Conrad Smith, make their home in Albuquerque, New Mexico.

To keep abreast of new book releases, sign up for Vikki's newsletter on her website, **http://www.vikkikestell.com**, find her on Facebook at **http://www.facebook.com/Vikki.Kestell**, or follow her on BookBub, **https://www.bookbub.com/authors/vikki-kestell**.

www.ingramcontent.com/pod-product-compliance
Lightning Source LLC
Chambersburg PA
CBHW070447030726
47503CB00004B/933